Hunger

all te best,

S L Rosewarne

S L Rosewarne

x

First published in 2025
Print ISBN 978-1-0683704-0-3

Also by S L Rosewarne

The Rescue

Lainy's Tale

Chapter One

11 June 2021

Laura

'Come on, Jess, we're going to be late,' muttered Laura, staring at her phone, willing a text from her daughter. She sat on the double bed, picked absently at her cuticles, hoping Chris wouldn't notice the time and start shouting.

Ping!

C U in 5. J x

A brief message and only one kiss, Laura thought, her spirits sinking: so Jess was in one of *those* moods.

In her twenties, Laura regretted not having gone to university or having a career, but becoming a mother had swept those doubts away. Despite the anxieties and sleepless nights, motherhood fulfilled her, and Jess grew into a funny, carefree individual. Laura had a purpose, and was exceptionally proud of the girl she and Chris had brought into this world.

But recently, Jess's moods had flipped: one minute she was her giggly self; the next a grizzling teenage monster, and

Laura never knew who would surface. Although other mothers complained that their daughters behaved the same way, Laura kept feeling it was her fault, that she'd gone wrong and should be doing more. At the same time, she didn't want her entire identity to be bound up in motherhood.

The door slammed. 'Mum? Dad? I'm ready. Are we going?'

Thank God she was back, and sounding cheerful. Laura grabbed her phone and was at the top of the stairs when she heard Chris's bellow.

'What the hell have you done?'

Laura's stomach plummeted. What had happened? She hurried down, saw Jess standing in the hall, her chin tilted defiantly upwards, never a good sign. She wore her new cargo pants and a cropped top that her father would hate, showing something glinting from her belly button. A stud? Chris would go nuts. But worse, her lovely long, wavy fair hair was bright green and looked like it'd been attacked with shears. Was she trying to emulate Billie Eilish? If so, it had gone horribly wrong. Laura was part horrified, part wanted to laugh, but realised how mortified Jess must be.

Jess shrugged, wouldn't meet her parents' eyes. 'Well, we're going to the Billie Eilish gig. Everyone's got hair like hers.'

'I haven't. And you're not going out like that.'

'Dad, I'm thirteen now, I'm not a baby.'

Like father like daughter, Laura thought, noting the identical chins jutting out. But shouting at Jess wouldn't help. Laura couldn't help feeling sorry for her, remembering a time when she'd also savaged her hair at a similar age. Not only had she felt humiliated, but she'd had to live with the results for months until it grew out. Laura took a deep breath. 'Look, we've got to leave now or we'll miss the gig.'

'She can't go to a gig looking like a… a…'

'There's no point wasting all that ticket money just because of Jess's hair.' It was a terrible mess, and Laura wondered if Jess would ask her to fix it, or if she'd wear a beanie for the next few months. However, Laura was determined that the birthday weekend would be salvaged. She turned to Jess. 'Where's your rucksack? Come on, let's go.'

Fifteen minutes later they were on their way, Jess sitting in the back plugged into her phone while Chris shot his daughter frosty looks in the rear-view mirror.

Laura looked out of the window at the countryside whizzing by, relieved the crisis had passed. But she had to do something to stop them sulking.

She turned to Chris. 'I'm guessing Kate cut Jess's hair, and as those two always do things together, I'd like to see what *Kate* looks like.' Laura smiled. 'Perhaps she's pink. Or yellow?' She nudged Chris gently. 'Come on, darling, it's not that bad. It'll wash out. And her hair will grow.'

Chris glanced at her and a slow smile appeared. 'You're right. As ever.' He patted her thigh.

Phew, Laura thought. She'd been looking forward to this evening for ages: Jess was already wearing her new cargo pants, and Laura would change into the new green dress she'd made; everything else she owned was too tight and she wanted to look good to go out. Chris was wearing his usual chinos and a white T-shirt, a recent addition to his wardrobe that did little to hide his belly.

'I'm so glad you were able to take the whole weekend off, darling,' Laura said. 'I know you're really busy but…'

'My daughter only becomes a teenager once. I wouldn't

miss her birthday weekend for anything,' Chris said. 'Even if it does mean going to some godforsaken gig.' At last he smiled at Jess. 'But tomorrow we're doing a photography workshop.'

Jess's face was a picture of trying to appear cool while being delighted. 'Yeah? Mum, too?'

'No.' Chris glanced at Laura. 'Mum's got the morning off.'

'So what's the workshop about?' Laura said. She hated being excluded, but had accepted photography sessions as dad and daughter time.

'The mechanics of photography. I want Jess to understand when to use different lenses, the internal workings of the camera and developing film.'

'That sounds quite advanced,' Laura said, noting her daughter's frown, the flare of determination in her eyes.

'No, it's cool, Mum.'

'If she's going to be a good photographer, the sooner she understands the basics, the better. 'I'm only treating her as I would a boy of the same age,' he said. 'She's a bright girl; she should use her brain. Now, where on earth do we park for this wretched gig?'

That evening, as they walked back to their B&B, Jess's eyes were huge. She had temporarily forgotten the hair disaster.

'She's so cool,' she breathed. 'Imagine singing like that for over two hours – in front of all those people.' She hugged her mother. 'Thanks, Mum, that's the best present ever.'

Laura closed her eyes, absorbing the hug. If Jess was happy, she was too. 'I'm glad you enjoyed it, darling,' she said. 'She's very impressive on stage.' In fact, while she enjoyed the music, she felt as if all her senses had been assaulted on a grand scale. The singer was a great performer, but why was everything so deafeningly loud and over the top visually? Still, she was glad Chris had come with them; it meant a lot to Jess, and Laura had enjoyed people watching.

'Well, I've got earache,' said Chris. 'Shame the pubs are shut. I could do with a drink.'

'Oh, Dad, stop grumbling. Didn't you think she was amazing? She's a real feminist,' Jess said. 'We've been discussing women's rights in history, and that's so important.'

'Very important,' said Chris, his face softening as he looked at his daughter. 'I trust you'll use your right to vote, when the time comes.'

'Course I will, Dad.' Jess rolled her eyes. 'As if I wouldn't.'

Laura felt such happiness when they had family conversations like this: all her doubts vanished. And it was lovely to see Chris relaxed for once, even if he did keep disappearing to make calls. He definitely worked too hard: his hair had turned grey, and he had bags under his eyes. But she felt lucky: he was a good father and worked hard to look after them.

The next morning, while Chris and Jess went to the photography workshop, Laura headed off to an indoor market to look for fabric. She loved making clothes for other people, and enjoyed choosing colours that matched the person's character.

Jess was the main splash of colour in her life: confident brush strokes in primrose yellow with splashes of daffodils

5

with bright orange stamens. Pure joy and hope. Although nowadays Jess only wanted to wear muted greys or creams, like her friends. Chris was dark brown with hints of grey, like his salt and pepper hair. Solid, kind and dependable; a good father, a good provider.

When it came to herself, Laura was worried that she had become a watery pale blue. Lacking in substance, fuelled by doubts that had been held at bay while Jess was young. Wasn't age supposed to bring wisdom? At forty-two, Laura felt just as insecure as she had at eighteen, and now she wasn't needed as much, these insecurities swarmed around her like gnats.

Her dream had always been to have a workshop where she could sew and design clothes. Last year, she was sick of trying to work at the kitchen table, where she was continually interrupted and had to clear everything away before Jess and Chris came home. But she couldn't tell Chris. She could just imagine his look of incomprehension and he'd dismiss the idea, asking if she needed more housekeeping money.

Still, she kept this idea as a kind of lifeline. Otherwise, thinking about what it would be like when Jess grew up and moved out made her feel panicky. A blank fog would envelop her, and she felt a tightening in her chest.

Sometimes she allowed herself to think of the life she and Ben had imagined, when they were eighteen. They'd shared such great thoughts and ideas. They'd laughed a lot (and had great sex), she remembered. Their ideas had been big and bold like abstract paintings, with vibrant colours and blobs of thick paint. Knowing him, they would have laughed and cried over their mistakes, but rather than painting over them, they would have moved on to another canvas.

Laura was eighteen when her father died suddenly and Ben had been abroad, waiting for her to join him. Seeing how fragile she and her mother were, neighbour Chris stepped in and took charge. Both women were everlastingly grateful, but that was over twenty years ago, and since getting together with Chris, Laura felt she'd led a watercolour life in pastels. While she knew she was much luckier than most, her brush strokes were too tentative. Wouldn't it be nice to redesign herself as an oil painting, to wear orange and red and purple? But what would it take to do that?

Last autumn, just as she was despairing, she saw an advertisement for space in a cooperative gallery in Newlyn. Visiting, she realised it would be perfect: not only did it give her an ideal outlet for selling her clothes but the rent was cheap and she could fit her hours around school.

Soon she became known in Newlyn for her designs, for repairs of old favourite clothes, her use of material like curtains which could be made into a boiler suit or a cloak. But choosing fabrics was like being let loose in a sweet shop: a delight to her senses.

When she arrived at the market, she was cheered by the array of cloth in all colours and textures. She examined the rolls carefully, rubbing the textiles between her fingers to see how they would sew, imagining them as shorts, a skirt or trousers, moving from one fabric to another with delight.

'I'd like some material to make a pair of dungarees,' she told the stall owner. Laura's mother, Merryn, had commissioned a pair. 'I need something that's sturdy, colourful, and washes well.'

When Laura finally left, clutching her purchases, her fingers twitched with excitement. I can't wait to get home and start sewing, she thought, humming as she walked along.

Back at the B&B, Jess was buzzing. 'The tutor was called James and he was so cool. He taught us how to really look at what would make a good picture,' she said, eyes sparkling. 'You know, the composition.'

Chris ruffled Jess's hair. 'You've got a good eye for a photograph, Jessie,' he said, and the look he gave her was so full of pride that Laura forgave him for pushing Jess too hard. After all, he only wanted the best for her, didn't he?

Walking back that evening, having explored the city and eaten a delicious dinner, Jess gave a huge yawn and Chris put one arm around his daughter, the other around Laura. She looked at Jess and saw a flash of the child she knew so well fast becoming an adult. Don't hurry to grow up, she thought. Enjoy being young.

'Lovely to have the whole weekend with you, Dad,' Jess mumbled.

'Yes, it's been wonderful to have time together as a family. We should have more breaks like this.' Laura couldn't remember the last time they'd been away together. Even if he had spent a lot of time this weekend texting.

Chris smiled. 'I hope it's been a birthday to remember.'

Lying in bed that night, Laura relived the weekend, while beside her, Chris snored gently. He might not be perfect, she thought, he'd never had much of a sense of humour, he worked much too hard, drank too much and had an annoying way of chewing, but their relationship was steady. It had never been passionate, but whose was after over twenty years together? (And look where passion got me, she thought, remembering Ben.) At least he didn't look at other women, and he'd do anything for her and Jess.

Laura snuggled up against him. I will never forget this weekend, she thought, and I'm grateful for every moment.

After Jess's birthday weekend, life went on as normal. Laura took her to the hairdresser who made the most of the botched hair job, and Jess filled the house with her friends, laughing and shrieking, before disappearing upstairs with their phones.

Laura loved the different seasons in Newlyn. Autumn was full of dog walks with crunchy leaves, and the trees changing colour from green to rust, turmeric, ochre and burgundy. Vibrant strong colours that inspired Laura's designs. At Christmas there were school plays and fundraising events, parties at each other's houses, panto in the village hall, and Laura's crafts community put on open evenings with mulled cider and mince pies.

Spring meant primroses, snowdrops and crocuses, swallows and cuckoos, and in the summer she loved the long evenings when she and Jess would take a picnic tea to the beach, go swimming with Eddie their dog. Her best friend, Anna, often joined them, and Laura loved the sense of truly belonging. This is my home, she thought. I'm so lucky to have such good friends, a wonderful family and a great community. And the best dog in the world, of course.

Chapter Two

13 July 2021

Laura

Late afternoon, Laura was finishing a pair of dungarees. It was one of those days when rain fell in monsoon bursts, making the house seem dark at noon, and even Eddie wasn't keen to go out for a walk. Laura hummed as she worked, enjoying the peace and time to herself: she loved her space in the gallery, but it wasn't big enough to design clothes and sew, so she kept the sewing machine at home.

Now she had an outlet for her work, she felt much less stressed over Jess's teenage angst. The birthday weekend had been such a success that she was thinking of other weekends they could have together, or even just her and Jess if Chris was working.

When her phone rang she jumped, stabbing the tip of her finger with a pin. Sucking the emerging bead of blood, she grabbed her phone and saw it was Chris.

'Are you at home? I need to talk to you.' He sounded breathless, agitated. Not like himself at all.

'What is it? Are you OK?'

'What time's Jess back?'

'Not for a bit. She's got photography.'

'Right. I'll be there in ten'. And he rang off.

Laura put down the phone. Chris hated those stock phrases like 'see you in ten', so what was going on? Why wasn't he in the office at ten to five? Had something happened to him? He sounded... weird.

When he came in, fifteen minutes later, he looked reassuringly like himself. Tall, dark, stocky (he had never been slim but had started putting on weight in his forties and now, at fifty, he'd developed a significant paunch). Dark jacket, white T-shirt (the T-shirts were a new idea) and dark chinos.

Eddie rushed to the door, barking his greeting which, as usual, Chris ignored. Undaunted, Eddie danced around him for a while then returned to lie beside Laura.

She stroked Eddie and looked up at Chris. 'What's up? You sounded really strange.'

Chris stood in the doorway, opened his mouth. He shut it and pushed one hand through his salt and pepper hair. 'I'm not sure how to say this.'

Laura's smile froze as she had a sense of impending doom, like a train whistling into a long, dark tunnel. 'What?'

'I-I've met someone else.'

Laura stared at him blankly.

'We're in love.'

'You're *what?*' Her world tilted, and she felt seasick.

Chris looked like a little boy being told off by his mother. 'I'm sorry,' he said, addressing the dark-blue carpet. 'I didn't mean it to happen.'

'What do you mean?' She felt stunned; he wasn't making sense.

'I met her at a business meeting. She's called Kayla. She's great. You'll love her.'

'I doubt that,' Laura said grimly. As his words began to sink in, she felt as if he was jabbing her guts with a red-hot poker. 'Where did you meet her?'

'At an away day.' He looked up, gave a brief smile. 'She was offering free yoga sessions. That's what she does; teaches yoga.'

Laura stared at him, a horrible realisation growing. 'But we haven't had any of those gatherings since before Covid.'

Chris was silent, staring at his hands as if they contained vital information.

'This has been going on all this time?'

'Well, no. We couldn't see each other in lockdown. Obviously.' He sounded pained.

'You bastard,' Laura could feel a hot rage rising inside her. 'You absolute bastard.'

Chris examined his nails intently. 'We never meant for this to happen.'

Laura felt like hitting him. 'So you ruin a perfectly good relationship for the sake of a fuck.'

'It's not like that.' He sounded hurt.

'It bloody is like that.' Laura took a deep breath, unsure whether to cry or scream, or both. But as much as she wanted to kill him, she didn't want Jess to be taken into care while her mother was jailed for murder. She forced herself to try and think straight.

'So what does this mean?' This conversation seemed to be happening on another planet, in a different universe. Perhaps if she pinched herself, everything would go back to normal. Surely this wasn't really happening?

Chris stood, looking sorry for himself. 'We couldn't help

it,' he muttered. 'The feelings were just – too much. Too overwhelming.'

Laura looked at him in astonishment. Disbelief. Gathering rage. A growing realisation that the biggest cliché of all was happening to her. Right now. She stood up, trying to still her shaking legs. 'You'd better get out of here,' she said, trying to keep her voice steady. Pretend he hadn't just thrown a grenade at her. She took a deep breath, prepared to lob a grenade back. 'But before you go, you can tell Jess exactly what you're doing and why.'

Chris looked as if the grenade had hit him in the stomach. 'I can't do that,' he whispered. 'Please, Laura. Not that.'

'How did you plan on telling her?' Anger gave Laura strength. Her legs felt steadier now. 'You bastard. It's one thing doing this to me, but how could you do this to Jess? She adores you. This will fucking break her.'

Chris looked at her in astonishment: Laura never swore.

In fact, the F word easily rolled off her tongue. Laura liked the illusion of power it gave her. And glancing at the clock on the wall, she realised that any moment now…

Sure enough, the front door opened, and she heard Jess's voice. 'Hi, Dad! I saw your car outside. You're home early. Where are you?'

Laura cleared her throat. 'In here, darling.'

'Eddie! Hello, bit wet for your walk.' Jess came along the hallway, prepared to launch herself at Chris for a hug but stopped at the doorway. 'What's going on?'

Laura took a deep breath. 'Your dad's got something to tell you.' She looked pointedly at Chris, enjoying his look of sheer terror. Not the great Casanova now.

'What is it, Dad? Are you OK?'

'Yes, I…' he looked at Laura beseechingly.

She crossed her arms, enjoying his discomfort. Wriggle your way out of this one, she thought.

'Jess, darling. I'm afraid, well, it's good news, but ...' He cleared his throat. 'Thing is, I've met a wonderful woman called Kayla.'

Jess was looking at him as if he was mad. 'So?'

'And we – I – well, we're going to live together.'

'Live together? What do you mean?' Jess stepped forward, confusion written all over her face.

'Well, I'll be living with Kayla.'

Jess stared at him, disbelief visible on her face, like a thunderstorm. 'You mean... you're *leaving* us?'

'Well, yes. No. I mean, I'll always be your dad, and I'll always love you, but from now on I will... yes, I won't be living here.'

Laura wanted to kick him in the nuts. Stupid fucking bastard. She now knew why it was called seeing red. She thought she might explode, she was so furious, and it was agonising to see Jess's hurt and confusion. How could he do this to her? She was about to tell Chris to fuck off when Jess took a deep breath, stepping back as if Chris was contaminated.

'I don't believe it,' Jess said, her voice wobbling, and she sounded just like a little girl again. The little girl who'd been teased at school until Laura told her how to stand up for herself.

Now Laura would have to do the same thing, only this time it wasn't because of bitchy girls but Jess's beloved father, whom she'd put on the biggest pedestal of all. Now he was tumbling off like an out-of-date statue, and the pain and anguish on her daughter's face was excruciating.

'Come here, darling.' Laura held her arms out and Jess rushed into them, while Laura held her tight, breathed in the citrus smell of her shampoo, the faint smell of sweat and classrooms and the outdoor smell of her. She held her as tight as she could, as if to ward off the pain that would soon flatten them. At their feet, Eddie whimpered softly. Laura stroked Jess's back as she had done when she was a baby and looked up at Chris. 'Get out,' she hissed. 'Pack your bags and fuck off.'

Chapter Three

Laura

The days following Chris's departure seemed so unreal and required so much effort, Laura felt she was wading through a quagmire. The life that she'd thought so strong, so steady and reliable, had collapsed in rubble around her.

'I can't believe it,' said her best friend, Anna, who turned up one evening with a bottle of red wine. She bent to stroke Eddie who wagged his tail so hard his entire body wriggled. 'We're right off men, except you, of course, Eddie.'

'It's such a bloody cliché,' said Laura, giving Anna a big hug. 'I could kill him.'

'If you don't, I will,' replied Anna. 'But right now, we both need a glass of wine.' She poured two generous glasses of Shiraz and sat opposite Laura at the kitchen table.

There was silence, except for the ticking of the clock on the wall and the steady rumble of the washing machine. The fridge was covered in photos of Jess over the ages, together with a list of her after-school activities. The wall had markings of her height at various ages. Eddie's battered bed lay in one corner, and a range of kicked-off boots lay in scattered ones and twos by the door.

Looking round her, Anna was silent for a moment, then said, 'What are you going to do, Laura-Lou?'

She sighed and took a sip of wine. 'I don't know. Chris wants to buy a house with lover girl, but I don't earn nearly enough to pay the bills here.' She gave a wonky smile. 'Have to sell my body, I guess, but what's the going rate for a forty-two-year-old with a saggy stomach and drooping boobs?'

'Oh, I think you'd make a killing!' Anna looked at Laura. 'Why did you never marry? I often wondered. I mean, you'd been together long enough.'

Laura shrugged. 'I'm not sure. It didn't seem necessary.'

'Even when you had Jess?'

'No. I mean, lots of our friends aren't married. It seemed a bit old-fashioned.'

Anna snorted. 'Not when it comes down to supporting you and paying the bills it doesn't.'

'No. But you don't think about that, do you?' Laura's stomach lurched as the enormity of everything hit home. She'd known things were bad, but not this bad. 'I was checking online and legally, he doesn't have to give me anything.' Her voice wobbled.

Anna sighed. 'Is your name on the deeds of this place?'

'I can't even remember it was so long ago; before Jess was born. Chris took care of all the finances.' She looked up defiantly. 'I know that sounds pathetic but he always did. You know, when Dad died, Chris looked after everything. It was a relief not to have to deal with the money side of things.' She bit her lip. 'And now, of course, I'm going to have to learn pretty quickly.' She looked up.

'Do they do Adult Ed courses in Home Finances, do you think?'

Anna smiled faintly. 'It's not that hard, Laura, you were always OK at maths at school.' She paused. 'When are you seeing him? I mean, you need to work out what to do, don't you?'

Laura nodded. 'Yes. I've asked him to meet me this weekend. Looking online, it seems he has to pay child maintenance, based on his earnings, but that's not much.' She groaned. 'I'm still reeling, to be honest.'

'I bet.'

'It's the last thing I would ever expect him to do. And I can't understand how he could do this to Jess. He adores her.'

Anna snorted. 'If he loved her that much, he should have kept his cock in his trousers.' She squeezed Laura's hand. 'Sorry, Laura. I'm just so bloody mad, I really am. But it's so unlikely. I mean, Chris – he's not exactly sex on legs, is he?'

Laura smiled faintly. 'Certainly not.'

'Unlike Ben…?'

Laura blushed. 'Oh, that was at school, Anna. Over twenty years ago!'

'I know, but he was very sexy.'

'Well, I thought so then.' Laura shrugged. 'He's probably got middle-aged spread now.'

'Has lost his hair…'

'And most definitely isn't sexy,' added Laura. 'Anyway.' She stared at her glass of wine. 'I'm going to see the CAB. I need to know what my options are. If I might be entitled to any other benefits.'

'What about Jess? How's she coping?'

'Badly. You know, she worshipped Chris. Bless her, she

looks like she's stumbling round in the dark. She spends most of the time at Kate's at the moment, or superglued to her phone. I'm going to pick her up later.'

'Poor darling. Well, do tell her to message me any time, won't you? And let me know if there's anything I can do.'

'I will. You're her favourite godmother.' Laura smiled. 'Actually, perhaps you could take her out while I see Chris on Saturday? That would be a great help.'

'Of course.' Anna looked round the familiar kitchen, at Eddie snoozing in his basket, the bunch of wildflowers in a jar on the table, the sewing machine in the corner of the room. 'I do hope you don't have to move. I can't imagine you living anywhere else.'

'Nor can I.' Laura bit her lip. 'I feel as if a tornado's driven through my life. God knows what it's going to be like in the aftermath.'

The following weekend, Laura's mother, Merryn, was due to come and stay.

'What was Gran like when you were my age?' Jess leaned against the kitchen worktop, listlessly chewing the ends of her green hair. For once she wasn't looking at her phone.

Laura felt her daughter's eyes on her, watching her thread the sewing machine. It was such a treat having the old Jess back, if only for a moment.

'Were all your friends envious of having such a cool mum?'

'She wasn't cool then.' Laura smiled, trying to cheer them both up. 'You know we lived in a small village called St Budy? Well, she used to be really quiet and wore jeans and blue sweatshirts and pearl earrings.'

'Gran? No way,' said Jess, wide-eyed. 'Everyone said they'd like red dungarees like Gran's and I love her dangly earrings, and her pottery's famous now.' She looked at her mother. 'Why was she so different then?'

'You know that my dad, your granddad, died when I was eighteen?'

'Yeah. So sad.'

'It was hard for me, but much much harder for Gran. She missed him so much she sort of...' How to describe her mother's rapid retreat, her quiet breakdown?

'Disappeared inside herself?'

Laura nodded, proud of her daughter's quick understanding. 'Exactly. But then one day she started coming back to life again and she decided to sell our family home and move away. She bought the cottage she lives in now, and got a job working in a café, then she joined a philosophy group, a book group, a walking group, cookery classes, a choir. She was incredible!'

'Wow. What about the pottery?'

'That started at an evening class; the tutor saw she was really talented so he helped her get exhibitions and soon people started hearing about her work, and buying it, and now she's making a name for herself.'

Jess grinned. 'And when did she stop wearing blue?'

Laura laughed. 'It's hard to say. One day I noticed she was wearing bright green boots. Those big dangly earrings were a present from a friend, and she found the dungarees in a charity shop. It was a gradual transition.'

'She's so confident, I can't imagine her being afraid, or unhappy.' Jess sighed. 'I'm glad she's not sad any more.' She grinned. 'Do you reckon she's got a boyfriend?'

Laura looked up. She and her best friend, Anna, often wondered about Merryn's private life. 'Not that I know of, darling,' she said. 'Though knowing Gran, anything's possible.'

Laura loved her mother, but this newer, confident version sometimes made her feel that she'd been exchanged for a stranger. Albeit a highly capable, empathetic one.

Before Chris left, he and Jess always spent Saturday mornings taking pictures with his new camera, leaving Laura and Merryn at home with Eddie. Now Jess sat, weeping quietly in the kitchen as she cleaned his camera, which no one else was allowed to touch.

'Very expensive bit of kit, that camera,' said Merryn when Jess had disappeared upstairs with her phone. They hadn't talked about Chris yet – that would wait until Jess had gone to bed.

'It was his 50th birthday present to himself. I don't know how much it cost but he spent ages researching it online and he wanted to encourage Jess, too.' Laura sighed. 'I hope he doesn't stop taking her out. She lives for those photography trips.'

'And she's talented?'

'Yes, she's got a really good eye. She doesn't understand the technicalities of how a camera works, but I think, while phones have such brilliant cameras, does she really need to?'

'I suppose if she's going to become a professional it would help, but that's a long way off,' said Merryn. 'I'm glad she's found something she likes and is good at.' She smiled. 'Like your sewing, darling. How are my dungarees coming on?'

Laura pulled them out. 'What do you think?'

'Marvellous! Can't wait to wear them.' She looked up as Jess came down the stairs, red-eyed and blotchy faced. 'Ah,

Jess, I've got something for you, darling.' She handed over a wrapped gift.

Jess blew her nose, temporarily diverted from her misery. 'Thanks, Gran,' she said, frowning uncertainly as she unwrapped the package to find a book.

'It's a diary – journal – whatever you call them nowadays,' Merryn said, clearly noticing the lack of response. 'I know you wanted a camera, but writing is a skill that is rapidly being lost. Anyway, teenagers always go through an angst-ridden stage; you can write it out in private.'

'I don't get angsty.'

Merryn kissed the top of her head. 'I'm delighted to hear it. But you can write anything in a diary.'

'Like what?'

'Confidential things,' said Merryn shortly. 'I wrote about being bullied at school.'

'You, bullied?' cried Jess. 'You're much too brave.'

Merryn laughed. 'I wasn't then, darling. I started keeping a diary again after your grandfather died. I also had a section for poetry, and another for planning things.'

'Oh, so it doesn't have to be thoughts,' Jess said. 'I could make photography notes?'

'Absolutely.'

Diary of Jessica Kate Hocking

8 Tehidy Street, Newlyn, Cornwall, UK, The Universe

15 July 2021

Dad left two days ago. He's gone to live with this Kayla but he rang last night to say he was sorry. Sorry! He's just blown up our family and he was talking like he'd just gone off for a few days. I can't believe Dad would do such a thing. I'm not even angry, which is pathetic. I just feel gutted and can't stop crying.

I keep thinking he's going to walk through the door and tell Eddie off for jumping up. Even though he wasn't at home much, you could feel him here. Now, there's a huge sort of blank and I miss him so much I can hardly breathe. If he got back in time he'd help me with my homework. He was good at explaining maths and stuff. He gave the best hugs. And he always made me feel special. Now I feel shit.

He's going to pick me up on Saturday and we're going to have brunch. What about our photography sessions? I was too gobsmacked to ask. Does Kayla take pictures? I hope not cos I want that special time with Dad. She's coming along afterwards which will be gross.

Mum looks like a zombie. She cries most of the night. I crawled into her bed and joined her last night, cos hearing your mum cry is just the pits. But who's going to look after me?

Gran's come to stay. She's calm and comforting and I feel I can say anything to her, but Mum's all over the place. I feel I've fallen over a cliff, down and down like Alice in Wonderland, and I'm shit scared of what's at the bottom.

Chapter Four

Laura

That Saturday, Laura laid her clothes out on the bed. Cleanish pale blue shirt, jeans and sandals. God, I look just like my mother did, she thought in horror. All that blue. Why didn't I realise? I can't wear these clothes. But everything else is too tight.

'Jess? Are you ready?' Laura pulled a brush through her hair, added an angry swipe of lipstick (which she never usually wore) and hurried downstairs. 'OK, I'll drop you at Anna's, then I'll ring as soon as we've finished and Dad can collect you and have some brunch.'

'Will Kayla be there?' Jess's voice wobbled slightly. She clutched her phone like a lifeline, and kept glancing down at it like a nervous twitch.

'I think so. But you have to meet her sometime.' Laura gave her a hug. 'It'll be fine, darling.' She gave what she hoped was an encouraging smile. Think positive. Don't say anything derogatory about the fucking cow who'd stolen her partner. Not to Jess, anyway.

'OK. Cán I take Eddie?'

They both looked at their scruffy terrier who sat watching them, his head on one side. His right eye peeped out from a blob of black hair on an otherwise white background, and he sported a brown patch on his back which was frequently covered in fox poo. Despite his smelly proclivities, he basked in their adoration which was duly returned.

Laura had been going to take Eddie for moral support but one look at her daughter indicated that she needed him more. 'Of course.'

'Oh, cool.' Jess brightened. 'Come on, Ed. Let's get your lead.'

Twenty minutes later, having dropped Jess and Eddie at Anna's, Laura drove into Penzance, finally found a parking space and took a deep breath. The café where she'd arranged to meet Chris was at the end of the street. You can do this, she thought. It's only Chris. Although Chris had morphed into a betraying stranger.

'He has to support you and he has to support Jess. He's the one who fucked up,' Merryn had said. 'Fight for money.'

Laura's mother, like her, used swearing only for emergencies. 'I certainly will, Mum.'

'He's been your partner for the last sixteen years, and Jess's father for thirteen of those. You brought her up, not him, so he bloody owes you both.'

With her mother's fury added to her own, Laura had felt sure of herself. Now she was full of doubts; how come she was having to fight the man who'd been her rock all these years? When had he stopped loving her? (When had she stopped loving him…?) It didn't make sense.

Stop being so feeble, she told herself, and lifted her chin (like Jess, she thought wryly), strode down the street, pushing open the door of the café. Chris was sitting at a table near the window glued to his phone, as ever. Had he actually been working any of those times, or had he been messaging bloody Kayla?

He looked up as the door opened and rose, smiling nervously as Laura approached the table. 'Hi,' he said (he never said hi). He got up and leaned forward, about to kiss her, then realised that was the wrong thing to do and shrank back. 'Er, what will you have?'

'My usual,' Laura said shortly. After sixteen years surely he could remember what she drank?

'Right.' Chris got up and went to the counter to order. His trousers were new. Denim jeans rather than the chinos he usually favoured. So was the pale blue T-shirt which emphasised his paunch (what was he *thinking?*). And he was wearing trainers! He hated trainers, had worn deck shoes for the last twenty years. Laura seized gleefully on these details, storing up ammunition. Strength. Courage. She bit her lip, took a deep breath as he returned to the table.

'So.'

Chris sat down, crossed those long legs that had wrapped round hers in bed for so many years. How long had they been wrapping round bloody Kayla's? When did they first have sex? What did she *see* in him?

'I'm sorry about this, Laura, but I wanted to reassure you that I will do what I can to make sure you and Jess are looked after.'

His words sounded alien; had he been talking to a solicitor? Still, Laura felt the air rush out of her lungs. At least they wouldn't be destitute. 'Good,' she said, doubting he'd catch the irony. 'But what do you mean, exactly? Will we stay in the house? Because I can't afford the mortgage and bills. Not on my own.'

Chris looked down at his coffee, stirred it thoughtfully. 'No, well, the thing is, Kayla and I want to buy somewhere together. With a spare bedroom, so Jess can treat it as her own.'

Over my dead body, thought Laura, but Chris was still speaking.

'...and a garden, of course. For the dog.'

He's no longer Eddie, thought Laura. He's been demoted to The Dog. Though Chris had never liked Eddie anyway. Too much fur shedding, poo and inconvenience. I should have realised: anyone who doesn't like dogs isn't to be trusted. 'Does Kayla like dogs?'

'No, but Jess does,' Chris said. 'In fact, Kayla's allergic to animals, so Eddie would have to stay in the garden.'

'He can't sleep outside,' Laura cried. 'He's never done that. What are you thinking?'

Chris's nose twitched; a sure sign of stress. 'No, well, we'll sort that out when the time comes.'

Laura felt hot with rage. Jess was devoted to Eddie, who slept on her bed every night. Keeping Eddie outside was patently not going to work but they'd soon realise that, she thought viciously. 'So what about the house?'

Chris looked up and she saw a tic in his jaw. Like most people, he hated confrontation, but Chris avoided it at all costs. This was really hurting, Laura thought. Good. Serve him bloody right. She waited.

'Well, as I said, we'll have to sell it.'

'I'm entitled to half,' she said. 'It's worth £350,000,' she added. 'I've looked online.'

'Right.' Chris stared fixedly at the white laminate tabletop. 'Well, unfortunately your name isn't on the deeds, so you're not legally entitled to anything. I mean, you haven't been earning all the time we've lived there.'

'No, because you wanted me to stay at home and look after Jess.'

Chris re-crossed his legs. 'Well, I appreciate I'm the one who is necessitating the sale of the property, so I'm prepared to give you £10,000.'

'Ten grand?' Laura stared at him, a red mist rising in front of her eyes. 'Out of £350,000? I brought up our daughter and significantly contributed to the upkeep of the house. What value do you put on that? Think of how much a nanny would have cost. And a housekeeper. So I'm entitled to at least half of what the house sells for, and that's letting you off lightly.'

'You chose to bring up Jess,' he said sulkily.

'I didn't choose, Chris. You wanted me to give up work. And it made sense because childcare was so expensive.' She stared at him, anger giving her strength. 'You utter bastard. What could I buy with ten grand? No, I'm entitled to half.'

Chris licked his lips nervously. 'I'll pay you £300 a month.'

'OK, but I'm still entitled to half the sale of the house.' Tears were stinging her eyes but she was determined not to cry. Not in front of him. 'Chris, I don't have a job. How on earth are we going to rent anywhere for £300 a month? And what about the bills?'

Chris finally looked at her and there was a blankness in his eyes that she'd never seen before. 'You don't understand about finances.'

'I don't understand because you never included me,'

she shouted. 'You dished out housekeeping and pocket money when Jess needed anything, but I had to beg for that.'

'You don't understand – I'm having to run two households now.'

'That's entirely *your* fault.'

Chris took a deep breath. 'OK, we'll come to an arrangement over money when we sell the house. But I'll pay you £300 a month for now. I'm prepared to be generous.'

'*Generous*?'

At that moment the waitress came over with Laura's coffee, placed it on the table with a sing-song voice. 'Cappuccino for you. Sugar's on the side table. Anything else?'

Laura couldn't speak, she was so furious. Chris shook his head and the waitress disappeared with a toss of her ponytail. Laura watched her go, and grim reality began to sink in. 'I am entitled to half the proceeds of the house,' she repeated, glaring at him.

He sighed. 'We'll sort that out when it's sold.'

'I've taken legal advice,' Laura said. 'Half. Mine.'

Chris paled. 'Legal advice?'

Laura wasn't going to say it was from CAB. 'Yep. And Jess is entitled to maintenance.'

'I've offered you £300 a month.'

'Chris, that wouldn't keep Jess in food for the month let alone clothes and shoes, bills, school outings; you know how much everything costs.'

Chris looked down at his hands. 'I'll do my best, but times are hard now,' he said. 'We're all struggling with the cost of living increases.'

'Bullshit.' Laura was getting to like swearing. 'Jess is

entitled to twelve per cent of your weekly income in maintenance.'

'Yes. Well... I'll instruct the estate agents and put the house on the market next week,' Chris said. 'Apparently there'll be a lot of interest, so it could sell quickly.'

'It's a lovely house, of course people will like it,' Laura said bitterly.

'The agency will be in touch about viewings,' Chris said. 'And I'll come and get my things in the week, if that's OK?'

'I'd rather you came in the daytime, when we're not there,' Laura said. Everything was happening far too fast and her burst of anger seemed to have evaporated. But it could be months before the house sold, and they couldn't live on fresh air. What about benefits? Back to the CAB, she thought dismally. 'What about Jess? You are going to see her today, aren't you?'

'Yes. Of course. Kayla's coming here in a minute, then we'll collect Jess and have some brunch. In her favourite place. 'He smiled, as if he should be congratulated for being so thoughtful.

Laura was about to use the F word again when the door opened and Chris got up. 'Here she is,' he said proudly.

Laura watched as a young woman approached. She was about the same height as Jess, five foot nine at a guess, and looked to be in her late twenties. Possibly early thirties. So to add to the clichés, fifty-year-old Chris was fucking someone young enough to be his daughter.

She wore the same amount of foundation as Donald Trump, her eyes framed by extravagant eyelashes like furry caterpillars, and dark red lipstick. Her hair was ironed flat, carefully highlighted as far as Laura could tell. Worse still, she looked like a model: long legs encased in ripped jeans with expensive holes near the knees and she wore a camisole top with a shirt artfully tied round her narrow waist. On her feet were trainers, of course. Bright white ones, with black laces.

Christ, what does she see in Chris, Laura wondered. Does she think he's rich? It can't be the sex, surely. Chris had never been an exciting lover... but was that my fault? Am I just boring in bed? Laura remembered her first experience of sex, age sixteen. With Ben, and it had been very far from boring. It had been fun and funny and exciting and... Laura could feel herself colouring and tried not to think of Kayla and Chris on the job.

'Hi, babe.' She greeted Chris with a kiss on each cheek and turned to Laura. 'And you must be Laura? Hi, I'm Kayla. I've heard so much about you.' Her voice rose at the end of each sentence as she held out a hand with frosty manicured nails.

Babe, thought Laura. She calls him *babe?* She ignored the outstretched hand. 'Funny, he hasn't said anything about you.' She tried not to think about her middle-aged self, with middle-aged spread, faded jeans and a home-made shirt. Some lipstick, but she'd never worn much make-up, apart from the odd bit of mascara. Scuffed sandals. God, no wonder Chris had looked somewhere else. But why didn't he say I looked so drab? So like your mother, whispered a voice.

'What will you have, Kayla? Your usual?'

She smiled and sat down. 'Please. Skinny, though, don't forget!'

Chris bobbed a smile and went to the counter to place the skinny order. Laura watched the familiar way he slid his hand into his pocket to reach for his debit card. How many times had he done that? And how many times had he used it to pay for bloody Kayla? She avoided looking at her until

Chris came back. He sat down and the uneasy silence stretched.

'Well, I think we've gone through everything,' Chris said in a faux hearty voice. 'I'd like us all to be friends, and of course for Jess to think of our place – when we get it – as her home, too.'

Laura stared at him. Did he have *any* idea of what he'd done? Blown apart sixteen years of a relationship, left his only child, effectively made them homeless, and then expected everyone to be chummy?

'Sure,' Kayla said, taking one of Chris's hands. 'Jess is welcome any time. I'm sure we'll be great friends.'

Not if I have anything to do with it, thought Laura.

'I can't wait to meet her,' continued Kayla with a smile. 'She sounds like a great girl. I'm an only child so she can be like my little sister!'

Oh God, let me die, thought Laura. Can this get any worse?

'Kayla set up her own yoga studio,' Chris said proudly. 'She used to work for an investment banker in London, didn't you, darling?'

Kayla nodded and Laura stared, fascinated by those caterpillar eyelashes. Would they fall off into her skinny coffee?

'Yes, but while the money was good, it was such long hours and I started thinking, what for?' Kayla flashed a smile at Chris. 'I wanted more meaning out of life, you know? So several years ago I went on a yoga retreat, and realised that the pursuit of money and power is ruining our souls. As well as destroying the earth, you know? So I decided to radically change my life.'

'By fucking someone else's partner?'

Kayla looked down at the table. 'That came later.'

33

Laura nearly choked; Kayla obviously didn't appreciate irony: so *that* was what they had in common.

'Four years ago I decided to train as a yoga teacher and come down to Cornwall, open a yoga studio and sell eco-friendly clothing. And be near my aunty,' she added.

Chris smiled at her, seemingly oblivious to the silent death threats being issued by his former partner. 'She's doing ever so well. Aren't you, babe?'

Kayla smiled at him and nodded. 'Not bad.'

Despite herself, Laura was curious. 'I understand you met at an away day.'

Kayla nodded and fluttered those eyelashes at Chris. 'Yes, at a corporate team-building event one weekend,' she said. 'One of the hotels in Newquay. I was providing yoga sessions in the afternoon, you know?'

Laura dimly recalled a weekend when Chris was away on some corporate do. But he'd often worked at weekends. However, this time he'd been getting to know her successor in the bar over a downward dog? For God's sake. Cliché after cliché. She stood up, unable to bear any more. 'Chris, I told Jess you'd pick her up from Anna's. OK?'

'Of course. Can't wait to see her.' Chris's smile seemed genuine at the thought of his daughter.

'In that case, I'll tell her you'll pick her up in half an hour. And have some lunch.'

Chris nodded. 'Great.'

Laura grabbed her bag and prepared to flee. 'Oh, and you'll have to go somewhere dog friendly. She's got Eddie with her.' And she turned and left as fast as she could.

Diary of Jessica Kate Hocking

30 July 2021

OMG. Dad's girlfriend, Kayla, is like someone on Love Island. Or a model. She says it's important to look good as she runs a yoga studio. I thought beauty was supposed to be on the inside? Mum's never bothered much about what she looks like, but you can tell Kayla spends ages on her appearance.

She also stocks eco-friendly yoga wear, leotards, leggings and stuff, so I guess she has to look good to be able to model them.

It was so weird meeting her. I couldn't imagine her and Dad together, but they were holding hands and stuff which was so gross. I wanted to thump her and say get your hands off my dad, you cow. But I decided to ignore her.

We had brunch and Dad had poached eggs with spinach and he hates spinach. But he didn't say anything so I didn't either.

Dad said they'd be selling our house cos he and Kayla want to buy somewhere together with a bedroom for me but when I asked where Mum and I will live, he went a bit quiet and said somewhere a bit smaller, I expect. He obviously didn't want to talk about it.

35

Kayla said she could help me with make-up and style and she has lots of old clothes from when she worked in London and said I could try some on, see what I like cos I'm tall like her. Which made me feel so confused. I don't want a sister, and she certainly isn't my mum.

I asked Dad if we'd still do photography on Saturdays and he said of course, when he's free. And I'm not sure if that means he's going to be busy with Kayla or what. But Saturday mornings has always been our time together.

And just as I was about to ask, Kayla started sneezing cos apparently she's allergic to dogs. How could anyone be allergic to Eddie? I told her that he always sleeps on my bed and she went a bit pale and we left soon after that. Thank God. I hate her.

Chapter Five

August 2021

Laura

Every Thursday evening for as long as they'd been old enough to drink legally in a pub, Laura and Anna had met at the Miner's Arms on the seaward side of the harbour; an old, dark inn not usually frequented by tourists as no food was served, apart from the odd ham roll and packets of crisps.

The girls knew all the other locals there who'd kept an eye on them when they first started drinking, just in case they had too much cider and needed walking home.

Now, when Laura walked through the front door, into the public bar that still felt as if it should reek of smoke as it had in days gone by, she saw Anna already at the bar. She tapped her on the shoulder and gave her friend a hug. 'Good to see you.'

'And you.' Anna pulled back and examined Laura critically. 'How's it going? You look terrible.'

'Thanks.' She tried to smile. 'Not surprising. I can't sleep and I feel dizzy, my mind's going round so much, like one of those robots with spinning heads.'

'Poor love, I can well imagine. But how did it go with Chris?' Anna led the way back to a small table by the sultry fire. 'Tell me all.'

They sat down and Laura took a grateful sip of red wine, told Anna the outcome of the meeting. 'So I'll just have to make sure he does pay me my share of the house, but that could be months away, and right now I haven't got enough money to rent anywhere.' She blew her nose loudly. 'I mean, I'm applying for all kinds of jobs, but I haven't worked in an office since before Jess was born.' She sighed. 'I have zilch confidence, which doesn't help.'

Anna looked at her, hesitated.

'What is it?'

'Well, I never thought Chris did much for your confidence,' Anna said carefully. 'I mean, he was the one who said you should give up work when Jess was born, and he was always the breadwinner, and he always – well, he always seemed to be in charge.'

Laura looked at her in slowly dawning horror. 'My God,' she said. 'You're so right. Why didn't you tell me? I've been such a wimp, all this time.'

'You haven't,' Anna said quickly. 'You were happy bringing up Jess – and making a brilliant job of it – but otherwise, you did seem to… diminish a bit over the years.' She gave Laura a hug. 'Don't look so panicked. It happens.'

Laura stared at her and the silence grew. Then she said, 'Well, in that case he's done me a favour by being a cheating bastard.'

'Absolutely. Just make sure you get what you deserve financially. What about the gallery?'

'I've had to give it up.'

'What? But I thought the rent was peanuts?'

'It is, but I can't afford peanuts now.'

'Shit,' Anna muttered. 'That place was so good for selling your stuff – and you loved it, didn't you?'

Laura nodded. 'But I've got to cut out any unnecessary expenditure. I'm waiting to claim Universal Credit, but that takes ages to set up, and it's paid in arrears so it's all a fucking pain.'

'Any more interviews?'

'A few, but no luck so far. I'm not exactly proficient in technology. I mean, I can send WhatsApp messages but not much else.'

'Same here,' said Anna.

'No but you're a specialist nurse. You don't need to do databases and stuff.'

'No, true. But I'm sure something will come up.' Anna smiled. 'So tell me, what was Kayla wearing? I feel like a real bitching session.'

Laura smiled wanly. 'First of all, I must tell you about Chris's new wardrobe.'

Anna groaned. 'No!'

'Yes! Skinny jeans instead of those old chinos he always wore, pale blue T-shirt and – get this – white trainers!'

Anna burst out laughing. 'What I wouldn't give to see that! Does he realise he looks like a real prick?'

'Well, he is. It's clearly all Kayla's work. She was dressed like someone straight out of a magazine; you know, freshly ironed hair, ripped jeans, strappy little top emphasising her tiny waist – and dazzlingly white trainers of course.'

'Those two must look such idiots. I mean, honestly. He'll be wearing baseball caps next!' Anna sipped her wine. 'What does she do?'

'She's got a yoga studio in Porthleven, apparently, sells

eco-friendly yoga kit and spends a huge amount of time on social media, according to Jess. She also said that Kayla's put Chris on a diet so he's eating salads and spinach and he hates all that rabbit food, as he calls it.' She gave a half-hearted smile. 'And he's given up the booze and is going to the gym.'

'Bloody hell. I give it six months,' said Anna. 'If that. Then he'll come crawling to you. But don't take him back. Promise me? You're worth so much more than that.'

'Don't worry, I wouldn't trust that bastard with anything now.' Laura gave a smile that didn't quite reach her eyes. 'But what about you? How was the date on Tuesday night?'

Anna shrugged. 'Well, at first I thought he was OK. He was polite and good-looking. But once he started talking – oh my God – he went on and on about the work he'd done in Africa, what a hero he was. He didn't stop. It was torture!' She made such a face that Laura laughed. 'So in the end I had to fake an urgent appointment. I was just about to text you, when my brother sent a message, and you know my phone gives a loud ping, so I said that my elderly mother was really poorly and I had to go and look after her.'

Laura smiled. 'The mother who died three years ago?'

'That one.' Anna grinned. 'So I downed my drink, grabbed my coat and got out of there quicker than you could blink. That was a close shave. How could anyone want to spend time with someone who just bangs on about themselves all the time? He didn't ask anything about me – not one single thing!'

'You had a lucky escape there.' Laura stretched her legs out. 'What's the matter with all these men? Can't they see what a prize you are? I mean, look at you. Intelligent, attractive, great sense of humour, love dogs, great godmother to Jess. You could always be an Anne Hathaway double if you get sick of nursing.'

Anna smiled. 'Thanks. I'll bear that in mind. But I'm enjoying work so I've decided I'm going to focus on that.'

'Good idea, and I'm so glad work's going well. How much longer will you be working in A&E?'

'Only a few more weeks. It's so fast paced, you have to have very quick reactions, and I love it.' She grinned. 'Turns out I'm good at it, too.'

'I bet you are. They're very lucky to have you. Who needs men, anyway?'

'Exactly. But what about Jess. How's she coping?'

Laura shrugged. 'She's devastated, poor darling. Particularly as we're going to have to move. She spends most of the time at Kate's, or glued to her phone.'

'There must be somewhere you can rent in Newlyn?'

Laura shook her head. 'The cheapest two-bedroom cottage is way more than I can afford. I'm looking near Helston at the moment, maybe Redruth, which is cheaper. Also, of course, we've got Eddie, and lots of landlords don't allow dogs.'

'How about St Budy? You'd be nearer me, and property's a lot cheaper there.'

Laura made a face. 'I know. But it feels like going backwards: back to where I spent the first twenty years of my life. I couldn't wait to get away. Though I appreciate I can't afford to be picky.'

'I'll put an ad on the staff accommodation site at work,' Anna said. 'There's got to be somewhere near here. Leave it with me.'

'Thanks so much.'

The two women sat in silence, contemplating the future.

'Does that mean Jess will have to move schools?'

Laura sighed. 'I really hope not. But I can't afford to run a car, so we'll be reliant on school buses.'

Anna leaned over, squeezed Laura's hand as she had done when they met in the school playground, many years ago. 'It'll work out. Don't worry. This is the start of the new you.'

Laura tried to smile but felt a rush of tears threatening and a now-familiar blockage in her throat prevented her from speaking. She returned the squeeze, grateful to have such a good friend on her side.

Diary of Jessica Kate Hocking

18 August 2021

Dear Dad,

I decided to write to you even though I won't send it cos I don't feel I can talk to you like I used to. Partly cos Kayla's there, partly cos you've changed so much since you moved out, you don't feel like my dad any more. And now we're broke and it's all your fault.

Mum keeps going off to interviews wearing a horrible shiny black suit and tacky black shoes from the charity shop. Neither fit properly and she hobbles back, looking even worse cos they always turn her down.

She's got huge bags under her eyes and she's too thin and it makes her look ancient. Mind you, I've lost weight and I feel better for it. I'd love to have cheekbones like Margot Robbie. I know I've got the wrong shaped face – it's too round – but apparently if you chew gum it gives you a good jawline so I'm doing that.

I keep hoping things'll get better. That I'll wake up and find it's all been a bad dream. But so far all that happens is that I wake up and it gets worse. And worse. And worse.

43

I HATE YOU DAD. Why did you have to LEAVE US? Why can't you come back?
Jess

Chapter Six

Laura

Laura stood in the kitchen, rubbing her forehead, trying to ease the headache that lodged behind her eyes. Where the hell were they going to live?

'Mum?'

She looked up, saw Jess leaning against the doorway. She used to be such a happy girl, Laura thought. So full of life and bounce. Now she looked drained. At least her hair had grown considerably, though the green dye had faded to a jaundiced lacklustre yellow.

'Yes, darling?'

'What are you doing?'

'Thinking. Let's get a drink. Tea? Chocolate?'

'Tea, thanks.'

Laura got up, went to the kitchen and filled the kettle, waited while it boiled, glad to have something to do with her hands.

'Mum, you're fiddling.'

Laura tried to smile. 'Sorry. Thing is, darling, I can't find anywhere to live in Newlyn. We're going to have to move.'

'From Newlyn?' Jess looked up from her phone, horrified. 'But we can't. What about my friends? School? Photography? Your sewing? We can't move.'

Laura poured water on the teabags, gave them a half-hearted swirl. 'I'm afraid we're going to have to, darling. I want to stay here as much as you do, but it's just not possible. I've tried everything I can think of.'

'But we can't leave here!' Jess's face scrunched up, turning pink. 'I won't move, I won't. My life is here. So's yours,' she added.

Laura sighed. 'We can't afford to rent anywhere here. I've tried, Jess, really I have, but there's nothing.'

'This is all Dad's fault,' Jess spat.

Laura added milk to the drinks. She'd ranted and raged long into every night, but it didn't get her anywhere. Jess was her priority and, of course, she felt betrayed and abandoned. She pulled Jess close, gave her a hug. 'I know it's really hard,' she said, her voice muffled against Jess's hair. 'But don't forget that he loves you more than anything.'

'That's crap.' Jess raised a blotchy face to her mother's. 'If he loves me that much, why did he do this? He knows how much we love this house, our life here, school, our friends. Why ruin all that, Mum?'

Laura sighed. 'I don't know, darling. But you'll still see him, have your photography mornings.'

Jess pulled away, started texting furiously. Then she looked up. 'Was it something I did, do you think?'

'No, darling, definitely not. He may have got sick of me, but never you.'

Jess hesitated. 'Dad said I could have his camera.' She

took a deep breath. 'I know it's worth a lot of money but would that pay for us to rent somewhere?'

Laura bit her lip to stop herself crying. The camera would pay for a rental deposit, but it was worth everything to Jess. Darling girl. 'Of course we won't sell it.'

'Thanks, Mum.' She smiled, relief shining in her eyes. 'I don't know how to work it yet, but Dad said he can't do photography every week, he's too busy.' Her eyes welled with tears.

Fucking bastard, thought Laura. 'Don't they teach you at school? Better to learn from someone qualified.'

'But what if we have to move?' Her voice quivered. 'Can I stay at the same school? That's where all my friends are. I can't leave.'

Laura handed Jess her mug of tea. 'I know, darling. You've got some lovely friends and you're doing so well at school, and I'll do everything I can to make sure you stay there.' Though she was beginning to think it was increasingly unlikely. 'We used to dunk digestives, didn't we?' She tried to sound cheerful. 'Want a biscuit?'

'No, I don't,' cried Jess, and twisting away from her mother, she thudded upstairs on noisy footsteps before slamming her bedroom door.

Laura's spirits crashed. I'm her mother, and I'm supposed to look after her, keep her safe, she thought. It's like being out in a storm with no shelter, and no waterproofs, when the rain and wind is lashing down from all directions. What can I do to make sure Jess is happy?

Diary of Jessica Kate Hocking

26 August 2021

Dad,

I was so pissed off that you couldn't meet up last weekend. Saturdays aren't the same without our photography sessions. Even though it did mean I could spend time with Kate and I so need my friends right now.

The only place Mum can afford is in St Budy, where you both grew up. Anna found it through someone at the hospital. The cottage is dark and cold and there's only a tiny back yard for Eddie; no garden. We've still got the car but only until we move and then Mum's got to sell it. It's all happening so fast it freaks me out. I keep thinking this is a nightmare and I'm going to wake up but when I do it's still a nightmare and it's all your fault.

But the worst bit is that I'll have to move school. Is this why you didn't want to meet? Mum said the school bus from St Budy doesn't go to Newlyn and she can't find anyone to give me a lift.

I thought you might come with us to see the school in Helston but you can't even be bothered to do that. It's huge compared to here. I'm not used to big classes. What if I'm bullied, like Gran? Mum took me to the hairdresser but my hair still looks crap and term starts next week and I'm panicking. I keep hoping something will happen to stop me going. But what?

And what about my photography? What's the matter with you? You're supposed to look after me but you don't seem to care.

Tummy still in knots but got used to it now. Thank God I've got Eddie, cos no one else seems to care.

Chapter Seven

1 September 2021

Laura

So much for a new start, Laura thought, looking round the house she loved so much. She remembered arriving here with Chris, thirteen years ago, full of excitement at their new home. Just as well I didn't know how this would end, she thought viciously. On cue her phone rang: it was Chris. 'Hello?'

'Oh hi,' he said. He never said hi till he met Kayla.

'I'm glad you rang,' Laura said briskly. 'I still haven't received any maintenance.'

'But I paid you the ten grand. Did you not get it?'

'Yes, I did. And I see you've set up a standing order for three hundred a month. But that doesn't begin to cover Jess's school expenses, and she needs new shoes and new uniform, and there will be after-school activities too. We've been through all this.' Laura was fuming. It was one thing Chris depriving her of things, but to deprive Jess was unthinkable.

There was a long silence, then Chris said, 'How much does she need?'

'Maintenance due is twelve per cent of your weekly income, as you well know,' Laura said. 'If you don't set up a standing order, I will have to see my solicitor.'

'Your solicitor? But that's John Richards.'

'Not any more it's not,' Laura said. 'So I'd be grateful if you could sort that out immediately, and in answer to your previous question, from now on I will send you the bills for Jess's school activities and you can settle them.' She was on a roll.

Chris cleared his throat. 'It's difficult, Laura. I'm trying to support two families.'

A red film crossed Laura's vision and she thought she might explode. 'And whose fault is *that*?'

Chris gave a long sigh. 'All right,' he said. 'I don't want to go through legal channels. That costs too much. Send me the bills and I'll get maintenance sorted.'

'I'd like confirmation of a standing order as soon as you've set that up with the bank.'

Silence. 'You never used to be like this, Laura. You've become hard. It's not attractive.'

Laura nearly exploded. 'And why do you think that is, Chris?' Before he came back with another ridiculous answer, she said, 'If I don't hear from you later today, I'll contact my solicitor. And when the house has sold, I'm due half of that too.' She ended the call. God, I feel better, she thought. I just hope he pays up. And soon.

As if sensing upheaval, Eddie got up from his basket and trotted over to her. He jumped on her lap and licked her face slowly, thoroughly. Laura held him tightly while he patiently licked her tears away. 'Thank God I've got you, Ed,' she whispered and kissed his rough coat.

As he jumped off her lap, Laura stood up slowly, gave Eddie a few treats, and went to the basin and splashed cold water on her face. She felt fractionally better now that she'd had the last word with Chris: he'd die rather than pay a solicitor. Glancing at her watch, she realised Anna would be here soon.

Laura looked around the house that had seen the birth of Jess and had housed every step of her growing up. Saw the arrival of darling Eddie, who was such a constant source of comfort. The house was stripped of all their belongings now, apart from the fixtures and fittings the buyers wanted. Everything else had been sold apart from the few things that would fit into the horrible tiny cottage.

'Are you OK, Laura?'

She looked round to see Anna in the doorway, jangling her keys.

'Yes, just… you know. Feeling a bit wobbly. Couldn't keep a partner, can't make my daughter happy, and now I have to move back to bloody St Budy. Even Mum's moved on, and I'm going backwards.' She shrugged. 'Stuck in reverse, you know?'

'Just shove it in first gear and off we go.' Anna hugged her. 'You know none of this is your fault. And it's a new chapter, which is good. Come on, we'd best get going. Where's Jess?'

'I thought she was with you.'

'Nope. Is she upstairs?'

Together they climbed the familiar stairs, automatically avoiding the one second from the top that creaked. The door to Jess's room was shut, but they could hear muffled sobs. They looked at each other and Laura gave a huge sigh. 'Oh God,' she said. 'I would do anything to stop this happening. Bastard.'

'I know you would. And I know she might call you names right now, but she knows it's not your fault.' Anne squeezed her hand. 'Shall I talk to her?'

Laura bit her lip. 'That might be best. I'll go and wait in the car with Eddie.'

She headed outside, got into the car where Eddie gave her an ecstatic welcome, despite having only been left for five minutes, and she let him jump on her lap. He was such a lovely scruffy dog, so affectionate and understanding. He didn't even complain when her salty tears rolled onto his back. He turned round, looked at her with those molten dark eyes and gently licked her face. That was the final straw for Laura, who broke down, holding Eddie's warm little body to hers. 'Oh, Ed,' she cried. 'What are we going to do? I'm so glad we've got you.'

Eddie licked her face, unperturbed, then started barking. Laura looked up to see Anna and Jess walking out of the house. Quickly Laura blew her nose, gave Eddie a stroke and put him onto the back seat. She wiped her eyes and got out of the car, hugged Jess and looked at Anna. 'All OK? I've got to drop the keys off with the estate agent, then we can go.'

Anna looked at Jess. 'Want to come with me? Or ride with your mum?'

'I'll come with you, please.' Jess looked at her mum with reddened, swollen eyes. 'That OK, Mum? We can follow you, can't we?'

'Course you can,' said Laura, summoning a smile. She walked up the path and locked the door. She didn't dare look behind as she walked to the car. Another chapter beginning, she told herself. Things always happen for a reason. What a trite, meaningless thing to say.

· · ·

By five that afternoon, Laura, Anna and Jess sat round the small kitchen table nursing mugs of coffee.

'I think this place will be really cosy once we get some knick-knacks up,' said Laura.

'You're so good at making places homely, Laura.' Anna grinned. 'There's a new charity shop at the bottom of the row of shops round the corner, so we can check them out.'

'And the Co-op has yellow sticker bargains after five o'clock. I checked the other day.'

'Even better.'

'I thought we could take Eddie for a walk along the harbour, and there's a short cut to the coastal footpath.'

'Good idea. We can get fish and chips on the way back – my treat.' Anna gave Laura a fierce look. 'I insist. And Jess, look, the sun's coming out. It's perfect for taking pictures.'

Jess nodded and got up. 'Thanks, Anna.' She stretched and yawned. 'I feel as if today's gone on forever.' Looking down, she jabbed at her phone. 'But there's no signal here,' she wailed. 'I can't message Kate.' It sounded like the last straw, and Laura knew how she felt.

'We've got to do it now,' cried Jess, her voice rising in anguish. 'I can't *not* message her.'

'Sorry, darling, we can't do anything about it right now. But we'll sort it out later.' Laura stood up, gathered the mugs. 'There's probably a signal by the harbour. We all need a walk: it'll clear our heads, and poor Eddie needs to go out. It'll be fun to explore, and I love fish and chips.' She busied herself at the sink while Jess headed up the tiny stairs to her bedroom.

'It'll be OK, Laura-Lou,' said Anna. 'Honest it will. I know it's all shit now, but it'll settle down, Jess will be fine at the new school and, you know, good to start again and all that.'

Laura pinned a smile firmly in place. 'Of course,' she said determinedly. 'We've got through the worst. It can only get better now.'

Chapter Eight

23 September 2021

Laura

As the weeks went by, Laura kept thinking that the pain of rejection would ease. But it was still so raw, so visceral, as if an animal had savaged her guts. She felt such shame, that she'd obviously been so lacking as a partner, that she'd been thrown over for a girl almost young enough to be her daughter. Worse still, that their own daughter was suffering so much as a result. How could Chris have done this?

Anna was right; he had stripped much of her confidence, had rendered her too timid to see what was going on. But still she missed him, and hated herself for being so weak. Perhaps it wasn't him she missed, but the companionship of living with another person whom she could talk to about Jess.

But now bills had to be paid, and after endless fruitless job interviews, ranging from factory work to stuffing envelopes, bar work and waitressing, Laura wondered if she would ever get a job. She was either too old or too young and any previous experience seemed to be of no use.

'What about care work?' said the girl at the Job Centre. She had long fingernails painted bright green and a stud in the side of her nose.

She spoke nasally, as if she had adenoid problems or a cold, perhaps. How does she blow her nose? Laura wondered. She'd always secretly wanted a nose stud, but Chris would have been appalled at the idea. Why didn't I just do it, she thought?

'I'll try anything, but remember I don't have a car,' said Laura for the umpteenth time.

'That's no good then.' The girl sighed heavily and scrolled down the list of jobs. 'Oh, this has just come in. Art gallery on the outskirts of Helston. Can you get there?'

'I can walk there, yes.' Laura struggled to summon up enthusiasm.

'OK. You need to be able to do admin duties, blah blah, yes, OK.' She picked up the phone and made an appointment for thirty minutes' time, then handed Laura a card with the address and details on. 'There,' she said. 'You should be able to do *that*. It's easy.' As if Laura was a complete imbecile.

Laura was nervous but, she reasoned, it was unlikely she would actually get the job, so why worry? She tugged down the hem of her black skirt, realising she should have polished her court shoes, but it was too late.

She walked to save the bus fare, her shoes pinching as she went. How did people walk in these stupid heels? She passed a chippie, and her stomach rumbled as the smell of frying floated out. She could almost taste the chips: bitingly hot with a tang of salt and vinegar, fluffy inside. Those lovely crunchy bits left at the bottom.

The Dorian Gallery was in a busy road on the outskirts of the town, alongside an estate agent, a gift shop, a charity shop and a newsagent. Laura stood outside, noted the white paint peeling in places. The art in the window consisted of seascapes, a landscape and some colourful abstracts. She ran her fingers through her hair (should have washed it), pushed the door open, and a man looked up from a desk at the back of the room.

'Laura Hocking?

'Yes.' She tugged her skirt down again, wishing she'd worn something else.

'Andrew Wilson. I'm the manager.' As he walked towards her, Laura noticed green eyes, a large nose and a scar above one eyebrow. Smaller than Chris; about five ten? He smiled and shook her hand in a firm warm clasp. 'Pleased you could come so quickly.' He turned. 'The current exhibition is mostly abstracts painted by a local artist, and the second room...' he indicated the other room with one arm, 'has more traditional paintings, some pottery, jewellery, local crafts, that kind of thing.'

Laura looked at the dark geometric paintings, peered at the watercolour seascapes, noticed some drab-looking pottery bowls and a tree of earrings. There was a faint smell of damp. It could do with cheering up, she thought, with a flicker of interest. Some more interesting pieces of artwork. Perhaps she could sell her clothes here?

'Come into the office and we can have a chat.'

Laura followed Andrew down a narrow corridor into a small office that contained two desks and chairs, and two elderly looking computers. Posters of past exhibitions adorned walls that had once been white, along with an empty cork noticeboard and a stack of paintings leaning against one wall.

'Bit of a mess, I'm afraid; it needs sorting out,' he said. His voice was deep, easy to listen to. A disarming smile made Laura warm to him. 'The last manager left in rather a hurry so I'm standing in until they find a permanent replacement, which could take a while.' He looked at her appraisingly. 'I need someone who can take over the day-to-day organisation. There was a system according to the previous owner, and she's left a contacts book, so that part shouldn't be too difficult. What experience do you have? The Job Centre didn't say much.'

Laura swallowed, wondered how much to lie. She'd been rehearsing what to say on the walk over. 'I've got plenty of office experience, and I used to sell my home-made designs in a cooperative gallery in Newlyn,' she said.

'Perfect! So you know how these places work.' It was a statement rather than a question. 'I take it you can do general admin on the computer?'

'Of course,' Laura said, mentally crossing her fingers. 'Though I'd need to learn how the previous owner did things.'

'A bookkeeper comes in a few times a week. I'm sure she could show you the ropes.' Andrew paused. 'I'm going to be out a lot so I need someone who can hold the fort. Organise exhibitions, private views, that sort of thing. Can you do that?'

'I think this sort of business is about networking,' Laura said. (Where had that come from?) 'I'm local, so I've got a lot of contacts. And I'm a mother so I'm used to networking and multi-tasking.' And I desperately need this job, she thought. This would be so much better than care work or working in the chicken factory.

Andrew looked at her appraisingly. 'How many children?'

'Just one. She's thirteen.'

'Ah, terrible teens, eh?' He grinned.

She smiled. 'Yes.'

'Good. Well.' He named a salary considerably more than care work. 'If that's acceptable, can you start on Monday?'

Laura stared at him. 'Monday?' she repeated. The salary seemed huge, even if it was only slightly over the minimum wage. 'Next Monday?' A slow smile spread over her face. 'Yes!'

'Excellent. Let's have a trial period of a month, see how you get on.'

'Fine.' Then Laura realised the drawback. 'There's one thing...'

Andrew raised his eyebrows. 'Yes?'

It was perhaps cheeky to ask, but she had no option. 'Would it be all right to bring my dog?' She watched his face closely, but he betrayed nothing. 'He's ever so well behaved, he could sit in his bed in the corner.' She saw Andrew hesitate. 'You see, I can't leave him all day...' and she didn't want to admit she couldn't afford a dog sitter.

'I don't see the problem. As long as he behaves himself.'

'He will. Thank you so much.' Laura was going to explain but stopped, afraid he'd see how desperate she was.

'No problem.' He held out his hand. 'I'll see you on Monday. Nine thirty.'

'Thank you so much. I really look forward to working here.' Laura tried to sound professional rather than graspingly needy, and left the gallery, feeling as if she was floating.

Fuck you, Chris, she thought, and rang Anna with trembling fingers. 'Guess what?'

'What?'

'I've actually got a job, Anna!'

'That's brilliant! What is it? Where is it? What's the pay? Where are you? Shall I pick you up and we can give Eddie a walk? Tell me all about it then.'

An hour later, they were walking along the beach while Eddie bounded ahead, shaking a long strand of seaweed. There was an eerie stillness and the flat greyness of the sea merged with the horizon, so it looked as if boats were suspended in the sky. As they walked, pinpricks of rain punctured the surface of the mirrored grey water while seagulls soared overhead, and Laura filled Anna in.

'It sounds interesting, and what's the pay like? Better than minimum wage, I hope.'

Laura nodded. 'Well, not much, but I'm not exactly in a position to negotiate. I'm just so happy to have work.'

'And it could be interesting, by the sound of it.'

'Exactly. You know how I loved History of Art at school.' Laura smiled. 'So this really is a new chapter!'

'It certainly is.' Anna gave her a hug. 'You'll need some work outfits; we'll have a look on Vinted. My treat.'

'Thanks, Anna, that would be great.' Laura whistled to Eddie, who was trying, unsuccessfully, to outrun a lurcher. 'This job will cover the rent and most of the bills, which is the main thing. And maybe I can continue making clothes in the evenings and weekends at home. Or sell them there.'

'Hang on,' replied Anna. 'Get your head round the job first. Listen, why not come over for tea? I can drop you back later.'

Laura was going to insist that Anna came to them, but she didn't have enough food for three, and it would be lovely to get away from that poky cottage.

'That would be brilliant. What shall I bring?'

'Just yourselves.'

And so a few hours later, Laura sat in Anna's kitchen while she prepared a spaghetti sauce. 'Sure I can't do anything? I feel very idle sitting here.'

'You can open that bottle of wine.' Anna peered round the corner of the kitchen, keeping an eye on Jess, who was in the living room with the TV on. 'Is she OK?'

Laura glanced over. 'There's no wifi signal at the cottage yet, so she's suffering from acute phone deprivation, which is why she's glued to it now.'

Anna chuckled. 'Poor love. I do understand it's difficult; they rely on their phones for everything, don't they?'

Laura groaned. 'It's how she keeps in touch with friends, so if she can't get on social media and chat to Kate on FaceTime, it's like she's been cut off from the world. And she doesn't know anyone locally yet.' She sighed. 'You know she's having trouble settling into school?'

'Yes.' Anna fried onions, chopped up some garlic and threw that into the pan with a satisfying sizzle. 'She's had so much to deal with, poor lamb.' She accepted the glass of wine Laura held out. 'Thanks, but remember you went through the same sort of thing at about her age.'

'It wasn't as bad. We didn't have to move house, or school.' Laura shrugged. 'Plus, I was five years older. And I had Ben – or rather, Chris.' She put her wine down and screwed up her nose. 'And we didn't have to worry about money. That's the biggie. Never again will I take it for granted.' She sighed. 'Poor Jess, she's lost everything. I'd like to take Chris's nuts and stick them in a coffee grinder.'

'I'd love to see that.' Anna grinned. 'Given all that Jess has gone through, she's doing amazingly.' She gave the pan a quick stir, releasing the pungent scent of caramelising onions and garlic. 'Does she say much?'

'Not really. I'm hoping the school thing will settle down.'

'I'm sure she'll be fine.' Anna put some water on to boil and pulled out a packet of pasta. 'Hungry?'

'Anything I haven't cooked will be wonderful.'

'I'll make lots; you both need feeding up. Here.' She passed Laura a lump of cheese. 'Can you grate that?'

'Sure. How's work going?'

'It's going well. Hard work but good,' said Anna. 'And I've got a date on Saturday!'

Laura looked up. 'Who? Where did you meet him?'

'He's called Dave and he's another doctor, met him in the canteen at work. He's thirty-seven, not bad looking and lives in Penzance.'

'Sounds good.' Laura mentally crossed her fingers that this guy wouldn't be another hapless bastard. 'I want all the details on Sunday morning.'

'You bet. Though knowing my luck, you'll probably get the details on Saturday night.' She poked her head round the door, called to Jess, 'Tea's ready, chick.'

Jess got up slowly, made her way through to the kitchen. She looked pale, Laura thought, and had been unusually quiet. 'You OK, darling?'

Jess gave a wan smile, sat down at the table as Anna began to dish up. 'Not too much for me, thanks, Anna. Not very hungry.'

'Can't have you fading away as well as your mum,' said Anna cheerfully. 'It's that veggie pasta sauce you like. Here, and have some cheese.' She passed it over. 'So tell me, have you made any friends yet? What's school like?'

Jess stared at her plate in silence; slowly picked up her

fork as if it were a lead weight. 'It's much bigger than Newlyn,' she said quietly. 'There's a girl called Emma who isn't bad. She's not like Kate, but at least she's someone to talk to.' There was a quiet desperation to her words that brought a huge lump to Laura's throat. She so needed to protect her girl, wanted everyone to realise what an amazing person she was.

Anna sipped her wine, exchanged a quick glance with Laura. 'I swapped schools when I was your age, and it took a bit of getting used to, so I know how you feel.'

'Yeah?' Jess looked up, hope flickering in her eyes. 'How long did it take you?'

'Oh, not long. Few weeks,' said Anna. 'I think you need to find your tribe, you know? People with common interests. What about photography? Can you still study that?'

'Yes, there's a huge lab with dark rooms and stuff – I haven't used them yet, but I'll be able to later on.' For the first time there was a glimmer of enthusiasm in her voice.

'Fab,' said Anna cheerily. 'By the way, there's a photography exhibition opening this weekend at the Guildhall in Helston. Fancy going?'

'Yeah, OK.' Jess ate a few mouthfuls of pasta, but slowly, not bolting it as she usually did.

'In that case, let's go on Sunday,' said Anna. 'We'll meet Mum for coffee afterwards, OK?'

'OK.' Jess pushed her plate to one side. 'I've got a stomach ache. Do you mind if I get down?'

Anna looked at Laura, who nodded. 'OK, love.'

When they heard the noise of the TV again, Anna whispered to Laura, 'Is she OK? She's usually got an appetite like a horse.'

'Neither of us have felt like eating much recently. I feel

so awful that she's having to go through all of this. But I think we've both lost weight with all this worry.'

Anna looked as if she was about to say something, then smiled quickly. 'I'm sure that's it. Teenage hormones and all that. She'll be fine, I'm sure.'

Diary of Jessica Kate Hocking

30 September 2021

Dad,

Finally got wifi sorted – it's taken all month, so I haven't been able to FaceTime Kate or anyone and it's been really shit.

Though I hate you most of the time, I still want to see you on Saturday. Will you make it this time? Please? Why don't you want to see me?

I hate school: all those huge, long corridors with so many people milling around, shouting, and the classes are massive. It smells funny, too – a mix of sweat, cleaning fluid and I think it might be weed. You should see the older pupils behind the science lab vaping and exchanging stuff. It's shit.

I keep getting lost, trying to remember where all the classrooms are; it's like a maze. The subjects I used to be good at like art and games aren't important here. It's like they all speak a different language. Maths is awful so is chemistry and physics – I can't understand any of it.

Kate's got new friends now and I don't know who she's talking about. This girl Emma talked to me at school today, which is more than the others do. Now we've got wifi again I can spend all night on my phone. Hours go by when I'm on TikTok and Instagram, but it's a way of connecting with people.

I so miss you, Dad. Saturday mornings aren't enough. I miss hearing the thud of your shoes as you walk down the street. You made me feel safe, but now it's like you're a different person and I don't feel safe at all.

You haven't been inside the cottage but it's dark and cold even though it's not winter yet. Mum shouts at me for leaving the lights on so I sit in the dark. My bedroom is so narrow that when I get out of bed I bash into the opposite wall. There's a damp patch of mould by the window which spreads when it rains and smells like bad breath.

Sometimes I get so angry I get scared so I run. I have to use up this energy somehow. I run somewhere quiet and shout at you, Dad, for leaving us. I shout at Mum for making us live in this horrible cold house, and I shout cos she's always worried about money and I shout cos I haven't got any friends and I don't know what to do and it's ALL YOUR FAULT.

I've decided to get fit. Kayla was banging on about diet and fitness, and I thought, perhaps you left because Mum and I are unfit? Maybe if I lose weight and start looking cool, you'll come back? I wonder if she thinks the same thing, cos she's said she wants to get fit too.

When I get home from school, Eddie and I run along the footpath to Loe Bar and back along the beach if the tide's out. Mum comes too sometimes, but she's much slower than me. Thank God for Eddie – he's my bestie so I can rely on him. And getting fit makes me feel I'm doing something.

When the anger wears off, I feel gutted. I really miss your hugs – when you put your arms around me, I felt everything would be all right. Mum's hugs are good but they aren't the same.

At last she's got a job but she has to wear make-up every day and look smart which is so weird; I've only ever seen her in jeans. I used to be able to tell her anything but now it's like there's this big wall between us. She still looks pale and miserable but at least she doesn't cry so much now.

I cry at night into my pillow, so she can't hear. On the way back from school. In the toilets. Behind the bike sheds. When I'm running. I've got good at crying so quietly, no one can hear.

Fuck you, Dad.

Chapter Nine

November 2021

Jess

'How's work, Mum?'

She looked up and smiled, which was a relief. Neither of us had talked much, let alone smiled since Dad left. 'It's good, darling. Thanks for asking. It's interesting, because I get to meet the artists, and I used to go to school with Deb, the part-time bookkeeper. She's good company, and always asking me to go to the pub.'

I looked up from texting Kate. 'You should go.'

Mum shrugged. 'Once a week with Anna's my limit. But that's fine.'

She hesitated and I could see she wanted to Have a Talk so I shoved my phone into my back pocket and said, 'I'm going out with Eddie.'

'Oh, shall I come?'

I could see Mum getting up, but I didn't want company. 'Not today, Mum. Another time, OK?' I grabbed Eddie's lead, called him and headed out of the door, fast.

I couldn't say how much I hated school. What was the point? There was nothing Mum could do; we couldn't move back to Newlyn.

I could almost feel her watching as Eddie and I ran down the street. We turned left at the bottom of the hill; the tide was out so we could run along the beach. Then we climbed up the hill, along the coastal footpath and finally ended up at Loe Bar. I loved the feeling of running, leaving behind all my horrible thoughts about not having friends at school, having the worst hair in the world, really struggling in classes. About Dad fucking up our lives. Everything, really.

But when I ran, my head cleared and I forgot everything. I just concentrated on my breathing and listened to my trainers thudding on the ground, Eddie's happy panting as he ran alongside me. We had a breather at Loe before turning round to run back. I was training to run to Penrose. The round trip is about seven miles, ten if I go to Helston and back.

Later, Mum cooked pasta, again, because it's cheap. 'But I'm trying to get fit and lose weight,' I said. After all, Kayla had said I could do with losing a few pounds. 'I'm training, Mum. I need stir fries and stuff, not macaroni cheese.'

'Jess, I told you – no phones at mealtimes,' she said, in her pissed off voice.

Reluctantly I put it away. She doesn't realise that we use our phones all the time.

'Thank you,' she said. 'Anyway, if you're running you need protein and carbohydrates. Even I know that. And you don't need to lose weight.'

'You have,' I said. Why should I put my phone away when we're eating? No one else does. 'It makes your face look thin and old.' I then wished I hadn't said that, because her face went white. 'Anyway, I get plenty of carbs at school.'

I could see by Mum's face that she didn't believe me. 'Well, I need to eat better, so it's about time we overhauled our diet. What do you think?'

'Yeah, sounds good. Raw food and seeds are superfoods, you know.'

Her face fell. 'Oh, right. Well, we'll start tomorrow.' Mum smiled. 'Still going to Photography Club? I haven't heard you mention it recently.'

'That's Thursdays,' I said, glad we were off the topic of food. 'We're using wide-angled lenses next week for a new project. And we're going to Truro museum to look at the history of the camera and stuff.'

'That sounds great, darling.' Mum leaned forward as if to give me a hug but I ducked, and her face fell. Again.

I felt bad so I said, 'Are you making any more clothes, Mum? I haven't seen you doing any for ages.'

She shrugged. 'I mean to, but by the time I get home I'm so knackered and the light's not good here now the days are getting shorter. Maybe it'll be better in the summer.' She looked up. 'Why? Is there anything you'd like?'

'No, I just wondered. You always looked happy when you were sewing.' I got up. 'Got to do my homework,' I said, and headed upstairs, which was a good way of shutting her up.

In fact, I wanted to look at Instagram. There are loads of videos of people trying to get fit and talk about nutrition and stuff, and it makes me feel I belong. There's a lot about self-harm, which scares me – I wouldn't do that, but I need people who understand what it's like not to fit in.

. . .

On Tuesday, I was getting an apple from the canteen when a voice behind me said, 'Hi, Jess, mind if I sit with you?'

Emma's in my form and she has bouncy dark curls, a wide smile and dimples. The sort of person that makes you feel better.

'OK,' I said, though I didn't really want to sit with anyone as I didn't want to eat my packed lunch. Still, we found a table and sat down. Emma got out her packed lunch: chicken and tomato sarnies, crisps and a yogurt. Mine was a cheese and tomato sarnie but that had far many carbs, an apple and a yogurt.

As she ate, Emma talked about her younger brother, who was a pain, about her father who loved astronomy, and how she liked looking at stars with him. It didn't sound very cool at first but as she talked, it sounded great. 'You can come over if you like,' she said. 'Dad always loves someone new to talk to.'

First of all I thought, no way, but Emma smiled and I found myself saying, 'Thanks, that'd be cool.'

'Why not come over after school tomorrow? Have tea with us and we can have a look through Dad's new telescope.'

I was torn. Part of me was desperate to have a friend, however pathetic that sounded, but the downside was trying to eat healthily and get fit, which had become super important, and I didn't know what kind of food Emma's family would eat. The prospect of having a friend won, and I'm so glad I said yes, because Emma's family is *so* cool. Her mum is a journalist and likes to hear what we both think of politics, euthanasia, women's rights, all that stuff. Her dad likes hiding away with his telescope in his study in the attic. He's got a lovely twinkly smile and said, 'You're welcome any time, Jess,' and I could feel myself going red, but in a good way.

I left there feeling that life was looking up. At last, I'd got a real friend!

On Saturday Dad picked me up outside the cottage. I think he was embarrassed about where we lived, but as Mum doesn't have a car anymore, he had to collect me. I noticed his tummy was a bit smaller but he was still wearing a T-shirt, pale blue this time, and denim jeans that so didn't suit him. He has big thighs and jeans just make them look bigger. White trainers looked cool on Kayla but on Dad they just looked stupid. It's embarrassing when your dad looks so try-hard.

He leaned over and kissed me and he didn't smell like he used to. Different shower gel and shampoo. This one smelt of fake apples which was just weird.

'We don't have too long, I'm afraid, as we've got to go and see Kayla's aunt in Bodmin,' he said. 'But I thought we could have half an hour's photography before we meet her.'

'I thought we were having the whole morning.' The words blurted out before I could stop them and he looked really awkward. I'd been determined not to show him how shit I felt.

'Sorry, Jessie,' he said and ruffled my hair which I hated. 'Needs must. I'd much rather spend the morning with you but it's Kayla's family and that's important.'

'I'm family – am I not important?'

He sighed and drove off. There were a few moments silence while I kicked myself. Why had I said that?

Finally he said: 'It's difficult for me, trying to please everyone all of the time.'

I felt so angry I very nearly told him to take me home. He was being so bloody selfish. Me and Mum were his family, not bloody Kayla. But I took a big breath and decided to be quiet. Keep it all inside.

After a few moments, as we turned onto the main road, he said, 'I thought we'd go to Godolphin. The house is 17th century and was owned by an old Cornish family called the Schofields until several years ago when it was bought by the National Trust who have spent a lot of money doing it up. It's got a beautiful pillared portico which runs along the front of the house.' Dad works for a construction company so I'm guessing he had a hand in this deal, but he can sound like an estate agent sometimes. 'And there's a café. Kayla said she'd meet us there later.'

'OK.' I shrugged. As I couldn't do anything, I decided I'd make the most of it. The house sounded cool, at least. We parked and walked through some woods and I was just thinking Eddie would love the trees – he sniffs everything – when we came to a clearing and a hut where Dad showed his National Trust card (he'd always had one through work) and we walked along to a long, low building that looked like a cowshed.

'These used to be the farm buildings, this one's the café, and further on are some barns with really old wagons. Come on, let's have a look.' He sounded all keen and enthusiastic, like my proper dad, and I forgot about being pissed off at him as we hurried along to the barns.

'I think these were the stables, or milking parlours,' Dad said. 'See the wooden partitions and the gulleys in the floor? And look at these wagons; these are original.'

The wagons were huge and made of wood, with tiny dots of woodworm, but they were impressive and although there wasn't much light in the stables, I started taking pictures, my mind fizzing with ideas. It was cold inside, but you could just imagine the horses or cows in there years ago.

When I'd finished, Dad said, 'Now, let's look at the facade of the house.' And we walked along a bit until we came to a long, low frontage with loads of pillars. 'This must have been the original drive,' said Dad, pointing to a gravelled drive opposite with a circular turning point and at the far end, a big iron gate.

I was more intrigued by the portico pillars, which were great to photograph. Then I spotted a huge old wooden door, which was open. 'Look, Dad, can we go in?'

'Yes, let's.' Dad smiled and looked like his normal self, so I took more pictures of the door, then headed through it into a courtyard that led to another door leading into a garden. 'It's like a fairy tale,' I said. 'I can't believe we've never been here before.'

Dad laughed. 'We have, but you were very young so you wouldn't remember. Now, take some more pictures then we'd better head back to meet Kayla.'

My heart sank, but the courtyard was amazing; I was imagining what it was like in the olden days, when they wore long dresses and the stables would have been full of horses, and carriages coming up the drive, like in *Bridgerton*, and I wished I could hop back in time for a while.

Reluctantly we went to the café, which was an old piggery according to the lady outside. Kayla was waiting, wearing her usual tight top, skinny jeans and dazzlingly white trainers. Her make-up looked so perfect, I wondered how long she spent on her face. She smiled and waved, looking a bit self-conscious, and all of a sudden I knew how she felt. Awkward. Embarrassed. But that feeling went quickly as she kissed Dad like she owned him and said to me, 'Hi, Jess. How are you doing? You're looking good. Lost some weight?'

I nodded, pleased that she'd noticed. 'Yes, I've been running every day. With Eddie.' She looked puzzled, so I added, 'You met our dog. He loves running; he's really good company.'

'Oh, yeah,' she said, her smile sliding off her face a bit.

'So I feel fitter.'

'Yeah, well you will if you're running, like, every day,' she said. 'You're welcome to come to a yoga session whenever you like. On me,' she added. 'I can kit you out with the right gear and a mat and everything.'

The thought of going to a yoga class with a group of sweaty women in bulgy leotards made me want to throw up, so I said, 'Thanks, but I have to fit in homework and everything…'

She nodded. 'Well, keep at it. You're looking good!'

Then Dad came back with our drinks and said, 'You're looking very slim, Jess.'

He'd noticed! 'Yes.' I wasn't going to tell him about my new eating regime. Cutting out carbs mostly. It's important to eat pure food: it makes you feel good about yourself, so everyone says on Instagram.

'How's school?' Dad said. 'Getting on better?'

I could tell he was expecting me to say yes, I'd settled in fine, and I felt so angry; it was his fault I was miserable. 'No. I hate it,' I said. And once I'd started, I couldn't stop. 'I used to like school. I met my friends there. I used to like learning. School was where I could find out about myself. Now I just get lost there.'

Dad frowned. 'What do you mean? Surely someone can show you where the classrooms are?'

I felt like hitting him. 'I don't mean *that*. Of course I can find out where they are.' I sighed, wondering how on earth to get through to him. 'I mean, I've kind of lost my confidence.' What I meant was, I'd lost the old me and couldn't find the new one, but I knew he wouldn't get that.

'I'm sure it's just a matter of time,' Dad said, squirming in his seat. 'How about photography?'

I looked down. 'Photography's the only thing I do like.'

'You can use my camera; it's the best.'

'Thanks, Dad. But I wouldn't dare take it to school, it'd be nicked or damaged.'

Dad looked horrified; he has no idea about school, honestly. 'Where is it?'

'I keep it in a box under my bed and I take it out and clean it in the evenings.' I looked down at my bitten nails. 'I love it.'

'What do you like about it?' Kayla sounded puzzled.

'I love feeling its smooth rounded edges,' I said. 'It's chunky and heavy and solid and sturdy.' She looked like I was talking Japanese. 'It's just practical; it doesn't have any emotions and it's powerful and valuable.' What I didn't say was that I don't feel any of those things, so it's a lifeline, which I so need.

Dad laughed uncomfortably. I don't think he had a clue what I was talking about either. 'When you were little you used to take the lens cap off my old camera and look inside. You thought there was another world in there, with little people who made photographs.' He turned to Kayla. 'She used to turn it upside down, looking in every corner to see if they'd come out!'

Kayla smiled but I could see she didn't get what we were talking about. I was glad.

'I used to wonder how to unlock all those hidden secrets,' I said. 'But photography's so complicated – all those

F stops and different apertures and stuff don't make any sense. But our tutor said don't worry, just go and take pictures and learn the process that way.'

Dad nodded. 'Yes, that's good advice. You've got a good eye for composition, Jess.'

I felt a warm glow when he said that. Whenever I take a picture I'm happy with, it gives me a real thrill. I look at it and think, did I really take that? And I almost feel good about myself. But Dad wouldn't get that.

It struck me that my camera is my escape; a way of expressing myself. 'I'd love to be a professional photographer one day,' I said. 'You and Mum would be proud of me then.'

Dad's face went red and he looked at his coffee, drained it and said gruffly, 'I'm always proud of you, darling.' Then he added, 'I know Mum is too. And Kayla.'

I could feel my face going pink. Dad never said things like that. 'I've been thinking, photography is about seeing life through a different lens, from different angles, isn't it?'

He nodded. 'Yes, that's it.'

'So isn't that what life's about?'

'Yes, I suppose it is,' he said slowly. 'You're a clever girl, Jess.'

No one said anything, then Kayla leaned forward. 'I've been thinking about your keep-fit regime,' she said. I think she felt a bit left out. 'I know you're running and that's a great way of getting fit, but it's good to share your experiences, you know? It helps you keep motivated. Who do you follow on socials?'

'Well, I don't really,' I said. My Instagram and TikTok feeds were full of diet stuff, but I wasn't going to tell her that.

'Right. In that case, I can help.' Kayla leaned forward

and she had a slightly sweet smell. 'This is what I do. I post carousels and videos of my yoga classes, you know? That's a good way of attracting customers, but also spreads the yoga vibe.'

She showed me a few videos of her in weird yoga positions. I'll stick to running, I thought.

'And diet and nutrition tips. Look, here's a video I did of a good vegan stir fry recipe. I also do post-workout snack ideas and weight loss tips. Great healthy eating ideas to help people smash their fitness goals.'

'OK,' I said, leaning over. I wasn't keen on posting recipes but I liked tips for losing weight.

'You could also call your community to action with a fitness challenge. This could be – oh, a thirty-day push-up challenge or star jumps, whatever you like. But share *everything*.'

'OK.' I sneaked a look at Dad who was looking utterly lost.

'And I do behind the scenes content to show folks what my studio is like and I also love sharing fitness and inspirational quotes – they're really important.'

'Right.' Though that didn't apply to me.

'And lastly, workout playlists – they're such fun and help keep your momentum up. I'll send some over to you.'

'Thanks, Kayla.' I still didn't like her, but she was trying hard.

'But to start us off, we must have a selfie, you know?'

She edged closer and stuck the phone in front of us while she pouted at the camera. I hated selfies, but needs must. I forced a smile and her sweet smell was more noticeable. Cloying, not like shampoo. Weird.

'Come on, babe. Have a selfie with your girls!' She beckoned to Dad who put his hand in front of his face. Too late, she'd already taken the picture and there was a ping as she sent it to our phones. 'There!' She laughed – a shrill sound – and I felt a bit sick.

I don't think Dad liked it either, as he said, 'Now if you two have quite finished, we're going to have to drop Jess back and head off or we'll be late.' He turned to me. 'Sorry we haven't got time for lunch, but Kayla's very fussy about what she eats.' He smiled at her as if she was a goddess. 'No pasties or sandwiches for her.'

Kayla shuddered. 'Oh no, think of all that processed crap in your system. Got to eat organic as much as possible.' She bent to peck my cheek. 'Glad you're looking after yourself, Jess. Good food is so important, particularly when you're a teenager. It'll help your skin, too. Make sure you don't get acne.'

'I hope not,' I said, horrified. I hadn't thought of that teenage delight in store.

Kayla gave that shrill laugh again as we walked back to the car. 'Tell you what, Jess. If you keep on with this ace fitness regime, you'll look like a different person. We can do a makeover if you like?'

'Maybe,' I said. Because I was sick of the Jess I knew. Perhaps a total makeover would be the answer? But no way with Kayla.

Chapter Ten

December 2021

Laura

Laura looked forward to her weekly phone calls with her mother. She'd changed so much over the past few years that Laura felt she could say almost anything without worrying what Merryn might think.

'Good news, the house sale is going through so I'll get my share soon. It won't be enough to buy anywhere, but at least I can pay the rent and bills for a while.'

'That's wonderful news,' said Merryn. 'I know you don't like that cottage much, so can you move?'

'No, I'm tied into a lease for twelve months and it'd be too disruptive,' Laura said.

There was a pause then Merryn said, 'Dogs have the right idea. Eddie's happy, despite everything, isn't he?'

Laura looked at Eddie, lying on his back, legs apart, eyeing her to see when she would give him a belly rub. She smiled and knelt down to oblige him. 'You're right. But I find it very hard to think like that at the moment. I always thought Chris was so dependable, so solid. So good for me. That was why we got together. So what went wrong?'

'People want different things, darling. Life is all about change, isn't it? You know that saying, we can't alter what happens, but we can alter the way we react to it.'

'I hate those sayings. It makes me want to thump someone. But yes, you're right,' Laura said. She swung between absolute fury and a burning desire to understand, but now she wondered if she'd just dug up painful old memories for her mother. 'Sorry, Mum. Here I am moaning about Chris when you must have been about the same age as me when Dad died.'

'Yes, you were eighteen, so I was thirty nine,' Merryn said. 'And it was a very different situation, darling. Death is final but it's clear cut. When your father died, I had a bank of love stored up from him. That has kept me going, and made me feel worthwhile. Loveable. But with break-ups, the feelings are much more convoluted. There's betrayal, jealousy, anger, abandonment, worthlessness, insecurity – a whole Pandora's box of emotions to pick from. That's much harder, I think.'

'You're right,' Laura said slowly. 'I'd find it very hard to trust anyone again.'

'In the short term, I think that's a good thing,' Merryn said. 'Means you won't make mistakes. But when you're ready, I'm sure the right relationship will present itself.'

'Maybe, but that's a long way off.'

'Your confidence will come back, darling,' said her mother. 'Give it time.'

At least the job was giving her confidence, Laura thought the next day, as she chatted with an artist on the phone, arranged a time for him to come in and discuss an exhibition for the summer. She added to a spreadsheet, made another note in her office calendar, grateful for her earlier admin training at the construction company. For the first time since stopping her clothing business, Laura felt pride in what she was doing. She liked the artists and, judging from the emails and cards she received, they liked her.

I look taller, she thought, staring at herself in the toilet mirror at work. Or perhaps I'm standing more upright. The face that stared back was thinner, warier, but she liked to think she was gradually getting stronger. She needed to be, to keep an eye on Jess, who had become increasingly remote and was constantly on her phone.

'That's teenagers for you,' said Deb cheerfully. 'My daughter didn't talk to me for years. It was quite a relief.'

Laura said nothing, painfully aware of Deb's daughter and husband at home. A proper family. It seemed years since she'd had a partner to share her life with, and a smiling, happy daughter.

If Laura didn't think about it too much, she could cope. But one day at work she looked out of the window and saw a couple walking hand in hand. A frail winter sun shone on the woman's blonde hair as the man looked down, stroking her face tenderly.

Laura felt as if someone had punched her in the stomach. Would anyone want her again? How long was it since Chris had held her, she wondered? How many days, weeks, months, had she slept on her own? She could usually ignore these feelings during the day, but at nights she was haunted by the ghost of Chris's arms around her.

She bit her lip and made herself concentrate on work. She had an idea for dressing the window; it needed a colourful theme now it was winter. A new artist had been in touch whose delicate botanical paintings would be perfect.

She'd mention it to Andrew, though he spent most of his time on the phone when he was in the gallery, which wasn't often. In fact, Deb had said the other day, 'You're almost running this place, Laura. We don't need Andrew!'

And for the first time in ages, Laura felt valued. It was a sensation that she'd almost forgotten and it warmed her like the first day of spring.

Diary of Jessica Kate Hocking

23 February 2022

Dad,

I'm even more determined to get fitter and thinner. I run every day, my clothes are a bit looser and I feel great.

I've taken Kayla's advice and I'm now following some fitness people who post about exercise and what they eat. There are so many different weight loss hashtags, I can't believe it.

I might not have many friends at school, but I've now got nearly 2,000 followers on Instagram. I post about my runs, what good foods I've eaten, how many steps I've walked, how many calories I've used up, and sometimes I do videos of Eddie – he's so cuddly and funny they always go down well. I get a real buzz when people like my posts; it spurs me on to do more.

I put my journal, where I write all this, underneath my mattress where I'm pretty sure Mum won't find it. I thought of taking it to school but I can't bear to think of anyone reading it. I'd never live it down. So it's staying here. Though occasionally I wonder what Mum would make of it if she found it? But she won't.

* * *

That afternoon, I put on my running shoes and flexed my feet. 'Ready, Mum?'

'Coming!' Mum appeared from her bedroom, wearing an old T-shirt, leggings and her ancient trainers. Not exactly cool running gear, but I knew she can't afford that.

'Your hair looks good in that ponytail,' she said. 'Suits you.'

'Keeps my hair out of my face when I'm working out. Shall we go?'

We headed downstairs, I clipped on Eddie's lead and we jogged down the street. I ran faster, so Mum couldn't ask about school. We used to talk a lot, but I didn't feel like it nowadays. What would we say? I still hated school, but at least I had Emma now.

When we reached the harbour, I turned right and we ran along the road, onto the coastal footpath, where we could pick up more speed. Eddie scampered beside us off his lead.

'Well done, darling, you're getting so fast,' Mum panted.

How was I to get fit with her slowing me down? 'I'll go on ahead, Mum, OK? Want to see if I can improve my PB.'

'OK. Wait for me at the end.'

It was a relief to let rip, feel the strength in my legs. It was the only time I felt good about myself, when I was running. My mind stilled and everything I worried about disappeared.

I broke my personal best getting to Loe Bar, and stood with Eddie on the sand, looking at the deceptively calm sea in front of us. In fact, there were rip tides and a deep shelf: a big board warned against swimming there, as people had drowned.

Eventually, Mum appeared, pink-faced, panting and sweating. She looked a sight but I was proud of her for trying.

'Well done, Mum,' I said, when she eventually joined us.

'You're so fit, darling,' she gasped when she had enough breath. We walked back the first bit, while she cooled down. 'Running makes me starving, don't you find?' she said. 'Shall we have spag bol tonight?'

'Can we have the bolognese with salad instead of pasta? I want to get fit.'

'Good idea, darling,' Mum said. 'I could do with getting fit, too. I've been eating too many biscuits.' She laughed. 'Deb is always bringing them into work. She's a shocker. But pasta is OK, isn't it?'

I frowned, thinking of the video Kayla sent me, going on about the evils of carbs and fats together. 'Stir fry would be better. What we put in our bodies is really important, Mum.'

Mum looked as if I'd whacked her in the face. 'Did Kayla say that?'

'Well, she knows all about nutrition. We are what we eat, you know.'

Mum wrinkled her nose. I could see she was getting ready to have a go about Kayla and I didn't want to hear. Not that I liked Kayla, but I didn't like being caught in the middle. So I said, 'I'm going to run back, OK? See you at home.' And I took off before she could say anything.

Later, after we'd had our showers, I heard Mum's phone ring. Only Gran, Anna and Dad ever rang, so I wondered which it was. Mum always put the phone on speaker as the reception was lousy in the cottage, so I soon found out. It was Dad.

'Laura, just checking that Jess is all right for Saturday.'

'Why don't you ask her?'

'Well, I will, but I thought I'd check in with you first.'

'You know how much she loves seeing you.'

'Good,' he said and cleared his throat. 'Kayla and I were wondering if Jess would like to come and stay for the weekend? We're still sorting out the new house, but she can choose things for her room. Kayla's looking forward to seeing her, too.'

Mum was quiet for a moment, then she said, 'You need to talk to Jess. It can't be easy for her, with Kayla in the picture.' Her voice wobbled.

'No need to be jealous of Kayla,' said Dad, sounding a bit smug. 'Just because she's younger and fitter than you are. She takes a lot of care with her appearance. She could probably give you some tips.'

'About nicking other people's partners?'

Dad was silent. Mum could always think quicker than him.

'While you're on, what's happening about maintenance? You said you'd set up a standing order but you missed this month's payment.'

'Oh, right. Well, I... I've got a lot on my plate.'

'I'm surprised it doesn't give you indigestion,' said Mum grimly. 'I need that payment tomorrow, so let me know when you've sent it, please.'

Dad grunted.

'And Jess has several school trips coming up and I can't afford to pay for them, so it's down to you. I'll send the details.' She waited a beat, then said, 'Don't let her down again, Chris.' And she ended the call.

And I felt like cheering, cos though I still hated Dad as

much as I loved him, it was ace having someone like Mum on my side. She wouldn't let him get away with anything if she could help it.

Diary of Jessica Kate Hocking

15 April 2022

Oh Dad,

I'm still struggling with photography techniques but am getting a bit better. Every time I hold the camera I sort of feel as if I'm connected to you. The old you that was properly my dad, not the idiot you've turned into.

There's a guy called Nick at Photography Club who's quiet but has a nice smile and he sat next to me yesterday. He looks a bit of a geek but he doesn't seem to care what people think about him. Wish I was like that.

Emma and I sit together in English and maths – she doesn't like maths, either. She's quiet but has a great sense of humour and this really infectious laugh. She's cool. I think she might be gay cos she keeps looking at one of the prefects like she wants to eat her. But she hasn't said anything so I haven't either.

Even though I hate you, I still miss you, but getting fit makes me feel better. I've got nearly 3,000 followers on Instagram now. I also spend ages on TikTok posting and commenting on stuff which makes my head hurt, though I tell Mum I'm doing homework. But a fitness company have noticed my videos and asked if I'd like some free leggings to wear when I'm doing my workouts – how cool is that?

Everyone at school identifies themselves somehow. In Newlyn I was part of my tribe so it didn't matter, but I don't know who I am anymore. Joining the keep fit lot gives me an identity and sense of achievement I don't get at school. I can focus on getting fit and losing weight, rather than worrying about everything that's gone wrong and wondering if it's my fault.

Chapter Eleven

23 May 2022

Jess

Dad's been gone nearly a whole year now.

'I thought we'd go to your favourite café for brunch,' he said on Saturday morning.

I shrugged. 'They don't have much organic food there.' That's what everyone's saying you should eat now: no processed food, everything pure.

He chuckled. 'You're sounding just like Kayla. Talking of which, have you noticed how much weight I've lost?'

I looked at him. His tummy had nearly gone, but his face looked saggy. It made him look old, but I couldn't say that. 'Yeah, cool, Dad.'

'And you're looking super slim and fit,' he said.

I glowed. It felt so good whenever anyone said that. Also, I sort of hung on to the fact that if I got fit like Kayla, he might come back.

'So what's happening at school?'

'Emma asked me for another sleepover last week.' Dad

looked blank. 'My friend at school.' I went after teatime so I could have a healthy tea at home. 'I like Emma's dad, we talk about photography, and her mum's really clever too. They've got loads of books about the sky cos her dad's into astronomy and stuff.'

'Good,' muttered Dad as we went left at the roundabout. 'Glad you're making friends.'

She's my only friend but I didn't like to admit that. Though there was Nick. Was he a friend? Sort of, but I only saw him at photography – he's the year above.

'The other day Emma said she wanted to tell me something, and she said about being gay which, of course, I'd already guessed.' Dad went pink. 'She looked part relieved and part scared when I said I'd guessed. She'd been so worried about telling her parents, but when she told her dad he was really supportive.' I paused. 'How would you be if I told you I was gay?'

The car swerved. 'Are you?'

I hid my smile. 'No. But if I was, would you support me?'

'Well, yes…' Which I could see meant, 'I don't know!'

I felt like sticking the knife in. 'Mum said of course she would, that she just wants me to be happy.'

'Well, yes….' Dad's face was crimson.

'Emma's in love with Sarah Millington; she's the head prefect, but she's not sure if Sarah's into girls. Sarah's gorgeous with long dark hair and big eyes and she had a boyfriend last term. Emma was going on about kissing Sarah and how she can't sleep for thinking about it.' And I had to stop there cos Dad was beetroot and I was getting embarrassed too. Mostly cos I was thinking about being kissed. Not that that's likely to happen. Who'd want to kiss me? But if I thought about Dad kissing Kayla I wanted to throw up.

What I didn't say was that I really missed Kate and all my old friends and the things we used to do together.

'You're not... being bullied, are you?' Dad said.

Where to begin? I looked down at the floor where I saw an empty crisp packet. So much for Dad's diet. He didn't have my willpower.

Bullies. There's this clique of girls at school; Sally Watkins is the leader and they make sarky comments as I go by so I hide in the toilets. But there's no way I could tell Dad that. He and Mum would go nuts and storm into Miss B's office and make sure Sally and her friends were given a bollocking and my life would be even worse than it is now. So I said, 'No, it's OK.'

I could hear the sniggers behind my back, but I was fitter than any of them, and I wouldn't let them see I cared. I wouldn't let them see that I was scared and sad and missed Dad so much it hurt.

16 June 2022

'What do you mean, you can't come? It's my birthday!' I was so upset, I could hardly speak. I mean, I know I'm fourteen now, but birthdays still matter whatever age you are.

'I'm so sorry, darling but I've got to have dinner with a client in Barnstaple so I'll have to stay overnight. But I promise I'll make it up to you on Saturday. I'll see if we can have the whole morning. I'm sure Kayla won't mind.'

I couldn't bear it. I could feel a whole cloudbank of tears welling up, so I rang off and thought of all the special birthdays we'd had with Dad when I was growing up, and that last lovely weekend in Plymouth when I thought everything was great. I cried till I was exhausted and couldn't feel anything anymore.

When I told Mum that Dad couldn't make it, her face went pink then white and I thought she was going to say something about Dad, but she gave me a hug and said, 'Well, how about taking Eddie for a walk. We can take the bus and have a picnic?'

I'd already said I didn't want a party (cos that involved eating crap food) so she said, 'Or how about that film on Netflix you were talking about? We can watch that.'

And I could see she was trying really hard and she was also pissed off with Dad so I blew my nose and told her that Emma had invited me over. She looked sad, which made me feel rubbish, so we took Ed for a walk and I went over to Emma's, but I said to Mum I'd see the film with her tomorrow and I tried not to think about Dad not being here and how having a birthday without a cake or your dad is possibly one of the most horrible things ever. Not that I could have eaten the cake. All those carbs are rubbish.

Chapter Twelve

Laura

Laura was glad to escape from the claustrophobic cottage and walk Eddie the half hour into work. The journey took them past the harbour, which was empty today as the fishing boats left at first light.

When Deb arrived at work, Eddie greeted her joyously. 'Morning, glories!' Deb said, sailing into the gallery like a small, stout superpower. 'Guess what?' she added in a breathy undertone.

Laura smiled, grateful for Deb's consistently good spirits. 'What?'

'A new auction house is opening up at the end of this week. Could be useful when it comes to buying work.'

'So where's it going to be?'

'That old industrial unit on the way out of town.'

'Oh, I know it. Bit run-down, but plenty of storage area. And lots of parking. Good place.' Laura looked at Deb's expectant face. 'Hang on, there's something you're not telling me.'

'Don't you want to know who's setting it up?'

'I'm sure you're going to tell me.' Laura smiled.

'Well, it's called Pedlar Auctions.'

'Pedlar as in… you mean, BEN Pedlar?'

'Yeah, the one you were joined at the hip with at school.' Deb grinned.

'Wow.' Laura's head span with a kaleidoscope of memories.

'I always thought you two would stay together.'

'No, it… it didn't work out.' Laura thought back to when she'd last seen Ben, the summer after A levels. When her dad died. 'What's he doing back here?'

Deb shrugged. 'Sick of London. Needs a change of scene.'

'Really?'

'According to Roger in the pub the other night, yes. To both.' She paused. 'So what do you reckon?'

'I haven't seen him for… must be twenty-six years. Wonder what he looks like now?' Laura thought back to their last meeting when they'd argued, not long after her father's funeral. Ben had stormed out and she'd been heartbroken.

'Probably overweight, divorced and balding. Twenty-six years is a long time.' Deb turned and walked towards the kitchen. 'Kettle's boiling, want a cuppa?'

'Please,' Laura said. Eddie came over, rubbing his cold wet nose against her hand as she pulled his ears. He uttered soft groans of delight while she stepped back in time.

Ben Pedlar. Who would have thought it? 'Blimey, Ed,' she muttered, remembering the funny, friendly, surfing boyfriend of her schooldays. 'What do you think about that, then?' Eddie looked at her with his head on one side and she could have sworn he winked.

Chapter Thirteen

20 September 2022

Jess

The holidays seemed to grind on forever. In Newlyn they never seemed long enough, but it's different here. Emma and I FaceTimed a lot, but she went away for three weeks so I gave myself fitness goals: I improved my running personal best three times, and gave myself points for losing weight. Mum kept saying, 'Well done, darling. You're smashing this, I'm so proud of you!' which made me feel better. But I really missed seeing my old friends, and it's not the same with Kate anymore. I swam a lot, ran with Eddie a lot and did lots of online classes, saw Dad and Kayla a bit. Not very cool.

But at least I've lost weight and several people at school said how well I look; I'm brown, too, and I know we've got to be careful of the sun, but having a tan does make me feel better.

On the first day back, my head of year, Miss Beaumont, said, 'You've lost weight, Jess. Are you OK?'

I love it when people say that; I get a real buzz. I smiled and said, 'I'm fine, thanks, Miss Beaumont. Just getting fit.'

But she must have rung Mum because she quizzed me when I got home so I had to calm her down. I hate it when she fusses. I mean, I'm fourteen now. I know what I'm doing.

Chapter Fourteen

October 2022

Laura

Autumn had been mild so far but tonight felt colder as Laura and Eddie walked along the darkened streets. She pulled her scarf tighter around her neck as they neared the harbour, listening to the reassuring shush of the waves at low tide. Ben had given her the Cornish tartan scarf, all those years ago. It was slightly scratchy against her chin, but kept her warm in the worst of the wind and rain. She'd found it in a drawer when she moved house and taken to wearing it again, which seemed prescient now she knew Ben was coming home to Cornwall.

She was glad to be out of the cramped, dark cottage. Even when Jess wasn't there, it was as if her unhappiness had seeped into the very walls. Laura had begun devising ways of murdering Chris, a habit that had grown over the past few months and involved varying forms of torture. Today she toyed with pulling out his fingernails, one by one. It wasn't very inventive, but it would do for the moment.

Her thoughts turned to Anna, and she wondered how she was getting on with her latest boyfriend. Anna should bring anyone she wasn't sure about to the Miners' Arms, Laura thought with a wry smile. Betherington would soon sort them out.

The Reverend Brian Betherington was not only to be found taking services at the church next door, but was the proud owner of the Miners' Arms, like his father and grandfather before him. The Rev, as he was known, was small and round, renowned for his expressive caterpillar eyebrows, his caustic wit, and his ability to take a sudden and long-lasting dislike to any customer for no apparent reason.

'How's it going?' Laura asked as Anna took a sip of red wine.

'I'm fine. More to the point, how are you? And Jess?'

Laura frowned. 'I've had Jess's head of year on the phone, concerned that she's lost weight. I hadn't even noticed, but now I look at her and think, how did I not see that?'

'Well, you don't notice when you see someone every day.'

'I suppose not. Miss Beaumont said they'd keep an eye on her at school and asked what she was like at home.'

'Is she eating OK? I'd noticed that she'd lost weight, but just thought she looked very fit.'

'She's very fussy about what she eats, and that changes from week to week; I can't keep up. One minute she's into stir fries, the next she acts like I'm trying to poison her with them. She's so angry with me all the time, I think she hates me. Really, she drives me nuts.'

'She's fourteen; teenagers are aways stroppy. And

anyway, if she's angry that's good; it means she feels safe with you, and knows she's loved.'

Laura nodded. 'I guess. But anyway, what's happening with you?'

'Work's good but I'm trying to let Dad's place. I've got bookings for Christmas and New Year, which will help with the finances.' Anna paused. 'Sorry, I feel bad having that extra income when I know how tight things are with you.'

'Don't be silly. I'm really pleased your dad left you his cottage. You'll get good money letting it for Christmas and New Year, I would think?'

'Yes. People are prepared to pay crazy money in the holidays, which will be a help as I haven't got many bookings for the spring.' She paused. 'I wondered if Jess might want to help with changeovers. I'll pay above the going rate.'

'I'm sure she will,' said Laura. 'It'll get her off her phone.'

'I'm working over half term so if she was able to help, that would be brilliant.'

'Thanks so much, Anna. What news on the dating front?'

'I'm fed up with online dating. I'm going to stick to my career instead.' Anna looked at Laura rolling her eyes. 'I know I keep saying that, but I mean it this time.'

Laura smiled. 'Good.'

Anna stared at her. 'Is there something you're not telling me?'

Laura sipped her drink. 'The other night, I was going to collect Jess from Emma's when I walked along Frobisher Street; you know, the one with all the nice Victorian houses, and saw someone arriving home with a young boy – his son, I assumed.'

'And?'

'It was dark, and obviously I don't know what he looks like these days, but...'

'It wasn't Ben?'

Laura nodded. 'I think so.'

'Oh. My. God.' Anna paused. 'After all this time, do you want to see him?'

'I'm not sure. Part of me wants to know why he walked out on me. On the other hand, it was a long time ago.'

'Everyone at school thought you were so solid. You did everything together, and you had such plans. What happened? I can't remember the details.'

Laura sipped her wine thoughtfully. 'Ben and I were going to travel to India, but when Dad got cancer, we agreed Ben would go alone and I would join him when Dad had recovered from surgery. Unfortunately, Ben was really ill out there, couldn't contact me so he didn't know Dad died, and didn't make it back till the day of the funeral.' She sniffed. 'Meanwhile dependable Chris from down the street came to our rescue.'

Anna snorted. 'I know he helped you then, but...' She sighed. 'But what about Ben? How come he's here?'

'He's setting up an auction house outside Helston. And it looks like he's living in Frobisher Street with a lovely wife and a gorgeous son.' Laura stared at the fire, listened to the crackle and fizz. 'I wish I'd never met bloody Chris. But then I suppose I wouldn't have had Jess.'

'No, and she's worth it all,' Anna said.

Laura smiled faintly. 'Of course. I keep thinking of all the things that used to annoy me about Chris. The way he chewed. His paunch. The way he cleared his throat before speaking.' She lowered her voice. 'He was never much of a kisser, to be honest. And the sex wasn't anything to write home about, either.'

Anna laughed. 'Well, good luck to Kayla in that case. You're well rid of him.'

'Did I tell you he was wearing a baseball cap the last time I saw him? And he's on a vegetarian diet with no alcohol!'

Anna snorted. 'Oh I'd love to see that. Wonder what they're having for Christmas? Vegetarian bake?' She hooted with laughter. 'Talking of which, are you still going to your mum for Christmas?'

'I think so. What are you up to? Going to your brother's?'

'Yes. Which is always fun.' She smiled. 'How do you feel about Christmas?'

'Well, Mum always puts a brave face on things, but I know she still misses Dad; you know Christmas was his thing. But a change of scene will be welcome and maybe Jess will be a bit more relaxed at Mum's; they always get on well.'

The following Thursday, there was a pre-Christmas Antiques, Art and Collectors auction on in Helston that Laura thought would be useful to attend. She'd worked through the catalogue, marked a couple of interesting paintings, and Andrew wanted her to scout out any potential customers. She wondered idly if Ben would be there.

Matthew Trevaylor Auctions was a ten-minute walk from the gallery. Laura and Eddie walked in, following signs down a narrow corridor to the auction office. 'Is it OK for

Eddie to come in?' she asked a buxom lady who knew both her and Eddie well.

'Of course, love, you go and have a good look around,' she said, taking Eddie's lead. 'Who's a lovely boy then? Would you like a biscuit?'

Eddie trotted into the office without a second glance, tail wagging. Laura smiled and headed down another corridor, into an overcrowded room where every available inch of flooring had been covered with dressers, wardrobes, tables and chairs, old maps, china and glass collections. Paintings hung on the walls, crammed close to each other, next to a collection of maps. Every item had a lot number stuck onto it, to trace it to the catalogue.

The paintings she was interested in were propped up against a back wall. The modern landscape wasn't exciting but was in good condition and would probably sell easily. The still life was older, the artist had a good eye for colour, and the frame was good. She stood back to get a better view, and there, studying a Victorian dresser, was Ben.

She froze, her heart thumping slightly. Should she say anything? No, if he saw her, he could make the first move. She moved into the next room, examining a watercolour here, a portrait there. Where was Ben now? A 1920s dress caught her eye. It wasn't her size but it was beautifully made. Bending to admire an exquisite piece of laced ribbon at the hem, she heard a voice say, 'Laura?'

She whipped round. 'Ben!' He was taller than she remembered; at six foot she had to look up to see him, noted the same dark brown hair, wavy where it met his collar. The long nose with a bump in the middle from when he'd broken it during a rugby match.

Laura had, in the past, often imagined this moment, but

now she couldn't think what to say. 'Hello. How are you?' She sounded like someone at a garden party.

'I'm OK.' Ben gave her an awkward peck on the cheek, then shifted from one foot to the other, staring past her right shoulder, as if she was too painful to look at. 'How are you?'

'OK, thanks.'

This Ben was still slim but looked fitter, stronger, wearing a dark-blue trench coat. There were wrinkles around his eyes and mouth: laughter lines, worry, or just age? He had dark patches under his eyes: lack of sleep?

He glanced down at her. 'I heard you were working at a gallery nearby. I was talking to Roger Williams in the pub.'

'Oh, Deb's husband. Yes, I work with her at the Dorian Gallery.'

'You always liked History of Art, I think.'

Laura smiled. 'Fancy you remembering that.'

Ben grinned and his eyes twinkled. 'I'll never forget hours spent in various galleries on that very hot trip to London. You were so excited, whereas the rest of us just wanted to bunk off and eat ice cream!'

Laura laughed. 'I do remember. Standing at Penzance station early in the morning and it was unseasonably hot.'

There was silence while Laura wondered what Ben had been doing in the interim. 'You're living here now?'

He nodded. 'Yes. I worked in France for a long while, then moved to London, married, had a son, got divorced and now I'm back here.'

Laura nodded, surprised at his candour.

'How about you?' he asked. 'Any kids?'

'One daughter,' Laura said. 'She's fourteen.' If he'd been talking to Deb's husband, he would know she was separated. Or would he? 'I'm not with Jess's dad anymore,' she added. The first time she'd said it. Not such an admission of failure.

'I'm sorry,' he said, and he sounded it.

'How old is your son?'

'Jake's ten.' Ben's smile said just how much he loved him. 'Does Jess look like you?'

Laura glanced up into those conker-coloured eyes. 'No,' she said. 'Jess takes after her father; she's taller than me already.' She flushed, as if Chris were hiding around the corner. She cleared her throat. 'I hear you're setting up an auction house nearby.'

'I am.' He smiled and she remembered the boy she used to play hide-and-seek with, laughing and eager. The one who turned into her best friend, and her first lover. 'It's a lot of hard work, and capital, but it's what I really want to do.'

'That's brilliant, well done. How long have you been back?'

At that moment one of the valuers arrived and tapped Ben on the shoulder. 'Ben! Good to see you! Wanted a quick chat. You got a moment?'

'Of course.' Ben turned to Laura. 'Excuse me,' he said. 'Maybe see you later?'

Laura watched as Ben turned away, deep in discussion with the other man. She was glad to be alone for a moment, and decided to get a cup of tea from the staff cubbyhole that doubled as a café.

She sipped her tea, talked to an artist they'd exhibited, and tried to concentrate. It was so strange to witness a grown-up version of Ben. She'd looked for him online but clearly he wasn't on social media, or if he was, under a different name. She saw him now, on the other side of the room, shaking hands with a well-dressed woman in a fake fur coat. He was bidding for a Chinese vase, then an

111

unusual Dutch painting. An accomplished expert in his field, by the look of it, confident in his work. So different to the young man she'd spent most of her time with as a teenager.

At 12.30 Laura collected a smug-looking Eddie. 'He's been ever so good,' said the lady in the office. 'Will you bring him back after lunch? We'd love to have him.'

'No, I must go back to work. But thanks very much,' Laura replied. Eddie stared at her with such an air of innocence that she knew he'd eaten his body weight in biscuits. She had to laugh. 'Come on, mate, let's get some exercise.'

They walked off, Eddie bouncing in sugary excitement, his tail rotating so fast it looked like he was about to take off. The park stretched out in front of them: a long expanse of green, punctuated by muddy patches from the recent rain.

Laura could feel her cheese and pickle sandwiches getting squashed in her pocket so she pulled them out and sat on a wooden bench, under some dripping pine trees. She ate the sandwiches hurriedly, remembered when food used to be something to enjoy, rather than just being fuel.

Eddie pounced on his ball and scampered to the other side of the park, chasing a jogger. He then ran up to a man, dropping the ball at his feet. Eddie barked till the man picked it up, threw it a good distance while Eddie hurtled after it, jumped into the air with a pirouette and caught the ball neatly. He dashed back to the thrower, dropping the ball at his feet again. Laura smiled and walked towards them, realising too late that it was Ben.

He gave a powerful toss of the ball which bounced high and landed in some bushes. Glancing towards Laura, Ben gave a cautious smile. 'Hope you don't mind.' He nodded towards Eddie.

'Not at all. He'll play with the ball for hours, and you can throw further than I can.' They both watched as Eddie rooted in some shrubs before running back towards them, ball in his mouth. Laura was interested to see where he'd drop it; sure enough, at Ben's feet.

Ben picked it up, threw it back towards the auction house. 'I miss having a dog,' he said.

'You had one?' Laura turned towards him. 'When?'

'When I was in France. I did write and tell you.'

'You wrote?'

'Yes. Didn't you get my letter?'

'No. I thought you didn't care – you just went off, and…'

'How could you think that?' He looked agonised. 'I spent weeks writing that letter.'

Laura stared at him. If she'd received it, she wouldn't have started seeing Chris. But there was no point wondering *what if…* She sighed inwardly. 'You were saying about your dog.' Eddie ran back, nudging her hand with his cold, wet nose.

'He was a scruffy little fellow.' Ben's voice lightened. 'Just turned up one day and moved in. I called him Bruce.'

'After Springsteen?'

Ben smiled and his dark eyes brightened, transforming his face. 'Yes. He was a brilliant dog, such fun and good company. When I had to come back to England, I felt terrible leaving him, but he was too old to start a new life in London. An elderly couple said they'd love to have him and he seemed happy there.' Ben sounded wistful and patted Eddie. 'I still dream about him though.'

Laura imagined a younger Ben with Bruce who

probably followed him everywhere; one man and his dog. A life she knew nothing about. 'I've got to get back to work.' She didn't know what to say, was unsure how she felt, and turned away quickly. 'Thanks for exercising Eddie.' She clipped Eddie's lead on and hurried off, head buzzing. Why had he written a letter? Why hadn't he rung? Had he been going to apologise?

A sudden shower soaked Laura's hair but she ignored it. She glanced at Eddie, dancing on the lead before her. How different life might have been if she and Ben had stayed together. They might have settled in France or Italy. Greece or Portugal.

She might have had Ben's children. A boy with dark curly hair and his cheeky grin. A daughter, with his ability to make her laugh. One of each, as she'd secretly wanted. But then she wouldn't have had Jess.

Chapter Fifteen

December 2022

Laura

Laura chopped vegetables while listening to Radio Four but that was too depressing, so she switched to Spotify, singing loudly, if out of tune, and danced round the kitchen watched by a bemused Eddie. Finally she put the dish in the oven, set the timer and started thinking about a new artist she'd met with very promising work.

Laura looked up, saw Jess in the doorway. She looked even taller. And thinner. 'Hello, love. How was today? Did you get your English results?'

Jess shrugged. 'Yeah, did OK. Passed, anyway, just.' She looked up from her phone at the remains of the cauliflower on the counter. 'What's *that*?'

'A new cauliflower recipe.' Laura started clearing away, waiting for the inevitable excuses.

'I'm not eating cheese. It's not vegan.' She sounded shrill, defensive.

'Vegan? Since when are you vegan?'

'I told you last week, Mum. You never listen. It's terrible to eat animals, particularly after they've suffered a horrible life and are then slaughtered in the most awful way imaginable.'

Laura agreed, but she was getting fed up of her daughter's eating fads. 'But you can eat cauliflower. With lentils.'

'Lentils?'

'Yes. New recipe,' she said brightly. 'No animals harmed in the making of this meal. It'll be ready in fifteen minutes.'

'What else is in it? I'm not eating carbs.'

Laura suppressed a scream, took a deep breath. 'No carbs,' she said, mentally crossing her fingers behind her back. Breadcrumbs didn't count. 'But you need to eat some carbs, Jess.'

'I don't. They're really bad for you. I was watching a video last night and—'

'OK.' Laura didn't have the energy for another fight about food. 'Can you lay the table, please?'

Jess gave a huge sigh, but got out knives and forks, put them on the battered table. 'Mum, when are we going to Gran's?'

'Christmas Eve,' said Laura, glad of a change of topic. 'She's driving down the day before to pick us up. She said she'd give us the return train fare after Christmas, which is very kind of her.'

'Yeah. How long are we staying?'

Laura crossed over and dared risk a fleeting cuddle. Jess didn't respond but at least she didn't push her away. 'I thought we'd see how we feel when we're there. It'll be nice to have a change of scene, won't it? Is there something you want to be back for?'

'New Year's Eve. Emma's invited me to a party.'

'We'll definitely be back for then. And do you still want to do that cleaning for Anna?'

'Yeah. It'll help towards my Paris fund. It's the first school trip for ages after Covid.'

'When is it?'

'Not for ages yet. A few weeks after exams.'

'Something to look forward to, then,' said Laura brightly. 'When do you have to give the deposit?'

'End of January.'

'Right.' Laura thought quickly, wondering how on earth she could pay the deposit. Universal Credit was all very well but it was paid in arrears, and things were very tight this month. Well, that was another one for Chris. She smiled. 'Don't worry, we'll sort it.'

As usual, Laura was awake well before dawn on Christmas Eve but lay under her duvet on the lumpy sofa for as long as she could. The early hours seemed to be prime time for worrying about Jess, about money − about everything. Her mother was in Laura's bedroom, Jess was never up early, and the walls were so thin, Laura knew that any movement in the cottage would disturb their sleep.

Laura thought about what had to be done. Walk Eddie, pack, take presents. Clear the fridge. It would be lovely to be away for a few days. A ping from her phone made her look down, see it was from Anna.

Have a great time away and relax! Hugs to you and Jess − how's she doing? xxx

Laura's spirits faltered. *Not brilliantly. I just wish she was happy. Like she used to be xxx*

It's difficult, isn't it? It'll take time for her to find her feet. But you've done so well at the gallery – you've become a different person since Chris left. Well done you! xxx

Laura smiled. Anna always knew how to cheer her up. *Thanks, I do love my job, I've got the best friend in the world, best dog in the world – I just wish Jess was less picky over food. But you're right. It will take time. Enjoy your Christmas, too, and give your brother my love. See you NYE if not before xxx*

And to you and my favourite goddaughter! You're doing a fabulous job looking after her! It's not your fault SC left – you're much better off without him anyway xxx

Laura frowned. *SC?*

Shitty Chris xxx

Laura laughed. *Love it – and I agree. Have a lovely Noel, travel safely. Gotta get up now xxx*

Pushing aside the duvet, Laura pulled back the curtains. Outside the skies were grey and raindrops splattered noisily against the window, while gusts in the street blew litter in crazy cartwheels. Laura went into the kitchen and made tea. She needed to pack and walk Eddie next. And she could do with the others waking up soon.

Laura left a note to say where she was going and let herself out into the grey damp streets, glad of her one pair of waterproof boots, a present from Chris several Christmases ago. At the time they'd seemed extravagant but had proved invaluable since then.

Laura walked along, Eddie bounding ahead, and as they reached the fields, the clouds parted and the sky turned the palest blue, while a faltering sun broke through. The ground smelt beautifully fresh and clean, and Laura's spirits rose while Eddie tore off chasing a squirrel. A blackbird's clear song celebrated the morning, while in the distance she could hear the rumble of passing cars.

She greeted other regular dog walkers, wishing them

happy Christmas; she always knew the dogs' names but not their owners' and, looking ahead, wondered where Eddie was. Chasing rabbits or squirrels, no doubt, near the old mine up on the right.

'Eddie!' she called loudly, but got no response. 'Damn,' she muttered, climbing up the narrow track on to old mining land; so different from the coastal footpath, where the sea was such a vast, ever-moving presence. Inland was more like the old Cornwall, and on days like this, sometimes she felt you could almost hear the old mines working, see the bal maidens and children toiling above ground, while the men worked several miles below the surface.

Laura called Eddie again: her mother wanted to leave mid-morning and it was already nine thirty. She followed her usual route, looking out for the telltale flash of black and white ahead.

Laura walked on, trying to quell a rumbling disquiet then, to her relief, she saw him. He was covered in mud, and ran towards her, panting happily. 'Oh thanks, Ed,' she muttered. To clean him up before the drive, she threw his ball into the long wet grass. He tore after it, tail whirring like a propeller. But the ball bounced on a rock, was caught by the wind and disappeared into rubble near the disused mine, and Eddie followed.

'Shit,' she muttered, running towards him as he disappeared around the back of the shaft. 'Eddie!' she called. 'For flip's sake.'

There was silence, and Laura hurried towards the mineshaft. It was fenced off but there was a jagged hole in the wire where Eddie must have crawled through. 'Eddie!' she called again, but there was no reply. 'EDDIE!' She rattled the wires. Where was he?

Frantically she looked back, searching for anyone who

might help. Other dog walkers, runners; where were they all? Everyone seemed to have disappeared. Why hadn't she brought her phone? At last she spotted two cyclists, a man and a boy, pedalling towards her, and she waved and shouted.

The man speeded up as he saw her, then as he got near, he dropped his bike on the ground and ran towards her.

'Do you need help?' he yelled.

'No, not me – my dog!' Laura cried. 'He's gone down the mineshaft.' She pointed. 'Down there!'

The man peered down into the shaft. 'I can't see him,' he said, his face shadowed under a cycle helmet. 'Can you hear him?'

'No.' Laura's voice wobbled. 'And I'm really worried about him.' His voice sounded vaguely familiar but she couldn't think who it might be.

'We'll need ladders and ropes,' he said. 'I've got some in my car but it'll take a while to get them. I'll ring the coastguard.'

Laura was frantic, thinking of poor Eddie, lost underground. She felt sick, wished she could do something.

The man pulled out his phone, rang and gave directions. 'They'll be here as soon as they can,' he said. 'They're in the area, so they shouldn't be long.' He called over to the boy, 'Are you OK?'

The boy arrived on his bike and took his helmet off. 'What's happening, Dad?'

Looking at the lad, Laura realised with a shock that Ben's eyes stared out from the frightened face. This was the child she'd seen jumping out of Ben's van. 'Oh,' she said, as Ben took his helmet off. 'I didn't recognise you.'

'This is my son, Jake,' he said. 'Jake, this is Laura. An

old friend of mine. Her dog's gone down the mineshaft, so we've called for help, but I'm sure he'll be fine.'

He sounded calm and determined and Laura took a deep breath, hoped he was right.

'How did he get there? Can we go down and rescue him?' Jake said.

'He was chasing his ball,' said Laura, feeling her teeth beginning to chatter. 'I think he must have slipped and fallen.'

'It happens a lot,' said Ben swiftly. 'But no, we can't go down and rescue him, Jake. We need special equipment and the coastguards have all the ropes and ladders and things. They'll be here in a minute.'

'Why are you shaking?' Jake looked at Laura curiously. 'Are you cold?'

Laura realised that she was freezing and terrified. But to her relief in the distance she saw a coastguard 4x4 rattling towards them, and as soon as it got near, four coastguards jumped out. Laura ran towards them, thanking them, explaining what had happened, her words tumbling over each other.

'That's fine, love, no worries. Happens all the time,' said one, and Laura felt her panic begin to dissipate. She watched them cut the wire mesh surrounding the mine and lower several lines down inside. One of the men went down, while the rest stayed above ground, calling instructions. Laura held her breath. Where was Eddie? She pictured him lying in the dark, maybe hurt. He could be...

'What's your dog called?' asked one of the coastguards.

'Eddie.' Laura was shaking, hoping, hoping for a sign.

'Do you think he's OK?' Jake's clear voice echoed her thoughts.

'I hope so,' Laura said, tears stinging her eyes.

Then a muffled shout from the mine.

'He's found your dog,' called one of the men, leaning over.

Laura felt as if she'd had an electric shock. 'Is he all right?'

'He's a bit shaken, poor lad, and scared.'

'I bet he is,' said Ben swiftly. 'I would be too.'

'Is he… is he going to be OK?' Laura could hardly breathe all of a sudden. She noticed Ben talking to one of the coastguards, then he came over carrying a blanket. 'Here,' he said. 'Have this.' He draped the blanket around her shoulders.

'Thanks,' she said, aiming for a smile but tears burnt her eyes.

'OK, we'll bring them up,' called the coastguard at the top of the shaft.

Laura pulled the blanket around her and they all watched. Progress seemed agonisingly slow and Laura strained for any noise from Eddie.

'He's very quiet,' said Jake. 'What's the matter?'

'Dogs don't usually make a noise when they're lost or hurt,' the man said. 'We think they should, because that's what we'd do.' He smiled. 'That's dogs for you, eh?'

Laura nodded, grateful for his concern, and pulled the blanket tighter around her. She glanced at Ben and Jake next to her, looking anxiously down the mine, and was so grateful that they were here with her. She felt strength in solidarity.

At last, after what seemed like forever, the coastguard came up holding Eddie.

'Eddie!' Laura ran towards them. The man held Eddie closely, and she reached for him, took him gently in her arms. He gave a whimper, then licked her cheek. 'Oh, Eddie,' she said, tears pouring down her face. 'Oh, Ed, I'm so pleased you're OK.'

'His hind leg looks a bit sore,' said the man who'd brought him up. 'He might have sprained it; maybe take him to the vet to be checked over?'

'I can take you,' said Ben. 'My car's at the big car park by the fairground.'

Laura looked at him, eyes swimming with tears. 'Thanks,' she said, then thought of the cost. Would this be covered by insurance? She hoped so, for there was no way she could afford to pay vet fees right now. And it was Christmas Eve – the prices would be sky high. 'But is it necessary?'

Ben looked at her quizzically. 'We don't have to go, but I think it would be a good idea. Pop him on the ground and let's see how his leg is.'

Laura gently lowered Eddie down and he limped forwards for a wee. Sure enough, his back leg did look injured.

'Might need an X-ray,' said the coastguard.

Oh no, thought Laura. Please let that be covered by insurance.

'Tell you what,' Ben said. 'Jake and I will cycle back to get the car and get back here as soon as we can. We'll pick you up in about fifteen minutes. OK?'

Laura nodded, afraid to speak in case she cried again.

Ben smiled, pressed her shoulder briefly. 'It'll be OK,' he said, and calling to Jake, they cycled off at high speed.

Laura watched them go, then realised she had to let her mum and Jess know where she was. Why had she left her phone behind, today of all days?

She picked up Eddie and made her way slowly back to

the fork where Ben had said he'd pick her up. She was impressed by how calm he was in a crisis. How he seemed to know just the right thing to do. Chris, she reflected, would have been hopeless. And that thought gave her a small measure of satisfaction.

Chapter Sixteen

Boxing Day 2022

Laura

'So how long does he have to rest for?' Jess leaned over Eddie, who lay in his basket, basking in the attention.

'Several weeks of very short walks, just to have a wee and a poo, then back to bed,' said Laura firmly. 'No runs for a while, darling. And he needs fifteen-minute ice packs on his poorly leg; that's why I've moved his bed into Gran's living room, so we can shut the door and he can't wander out.'

'Poor Ed,' crooned Jess. 'I'll stay with him.'

'Thanks, darling.'

Laura headed off, grateful to have an hour to herself to clear her head. Life was difficult enough without adding an injured dog and vet bills into it all. She climbed over a stile and walked over the fields next to Merryn's house, enjoying the stretches of green fields, a few naked winter trees, old farm buildings in the distance, and blackbirds singing in the trees around her.

Gradually her thoughts slowed as she thought how lucky she'd been recently. It was such good timing that Ben and Jake had appeared when she needed help. And dear Mum had insisted on paying the vet bill. She walked to the top of the nearest hill, realised she rarely had time just to walk and think, though walking seemed odd without Eddie pottering beside her. Nevertheless it was soothing to do the familiar loop she normally did with him, and gradually her mind emptied.

Her head felt clearer and lighter as she passed a few dog walkers, and before long she was back at her mother's house. The light was on in Jess's bedroom but Laura decided to leave her: she might need a breather, too.

At the bottom of the garden, her mother's studio shed looked warm and welcoming so Laura walked down the garden and knocked on the door, pushed it open.

Merryn wore a jumble of colours that instantly cheered Laura: a scarlet jumper, orange dungarees and green boots with red laces. On another person the colours might have clashed, but Merryn had the personality to carry off the outfit.

Laura never ceased being surprised at how much her mother had changed since she moved to Wadebridge. She's such an inspiration, Laura thought. She's always up for trying new things, ditching those that don't work. The day after she moved in, she'd gone into every shop in Wadebridge asking for work and took the first job she was offered, cooking in a vegetarian café.

The friendship with that café owner influenced her strong feminist thinking, which she now discussed animatedly with Jess. The Middle Eastern Cookery classes led to an interest in Arabic, which in turn influenced her pottery. It was wonderful to see her mother so revitalised.

She looked up as Laura came in. 'How are you, darling?'

'OK.' Laura leaned forwards to look at her mother's drawings. 'What are these?'

'I haven't had a chance to tell you. I've got a new commission from a guy in Cardiff. He wants me to go there and make some pieces for him.'

'That's great.'

'Yes. It's not what I usually do, but I like the idea of exploring Cardiff.' She nodded to a small chest in the corner. 'Cuppa? I think there are some biscuits there though they may have gone stale.'

'I'm not interrupting?' Her mother hated to be disturbed while she was working.

'No, I was thinking,' she replied. 'Let's have some tea.'

'I'll make it, Mum.' While Laura waited for the kettle to boil, her gaze travelled round the large, dusty room, packed with shelves of ceramic pots, bowls and plates of all shapes and sizes. Even among the jumble of haphazard work, Laura could see that her mother's work had turned a corner. No wonder she was getting commissions far and wide.

A kiln and sacks of clay occupied one corner of the floor, as well as a battered, dented wooden table and an armchair that looked as if someone had lived in it. The earthy smell of clay permeated the room, as well as a faint smell of tobacco.

Laura looked up as the door opened and Jess walked in.

'Come and have some ginger tea,' said Merryn in the tone of voice that wouldn't countenance a no. Jess came in and accepted a mug of tea from Laura, who made another one for herself.

'Thought we'd have leftovers and salad tonight,' Merryn said.

Laura glanced at Jess who paled. 'I'm not hungry. We had a big lunch.'

'Soup isn't much, Jess,' Laura said, then wished she hadn't. Jess's chin jutted out, ready for another fight about food.

'We'll have leftovers and salad,' Merryn repeated in a voice that brooked no argument. She turned to Jess. 'Talked to your dad today?'

Jess shook her head. 'He rang yesterday.' She looked at her grandmother. 'Christmas still feels all wrong without him.'

Laura wondered if Merryn still felt like that about Laura's father: it was difficult to tell. But Jess sounded like a little girl again, thought Laura, and wished she could give Jess a hug, but knew she wouldn't like it.

However, her mother could and did. 'I know, darling. Sometimes life is really unfair, isn't it?' Without waiting for an answer, she continued, 'I don't know if you've got time, but I could do with a hand to clear my studio.'

Jess looked up from her phone and Laura noticed a spark of interest in her eyes. 'OK,' she said.

Phew, thought Laura. She knew Jess spent most of her time on her phone, either on FaceTime or… what did she look at? Health and fitness stuff presumably.

'I need to get rid of some of the old bowls – look at this lot here,' Merryn said.

Jess giggled. 'They're a bit wonky, aren't they? But these ones here look completely different. And I love the gold round the rim. They're cool, Gran!'

Merryn smiled. 'I will take that as the ultimate compliment, darling. Thank you very much.'

30 December 2022

Despite the much-needed break at Merryn's, Laura was glad to return to work. Have a sense of normality. It gave her something else to focus on, other than Jess's increasingly picky attitude towards food which was driving her mad, but it was a worry: Jess was obviously unhappy.

At the gallery, having checked the floor for crumbs, Eddie followed Laura around, then, with a contented sigh, settled in his bed near her desk. Thank God for Eddie, she thought, who was still hobbling, but seemed to be coping well with his injured leg. Or was he just relieved to have a break from Jess's endless runs?

Laura was finalising arrangements for the opening of the new exhibition, so she spent the morning ploughing through emails, though she couldn't concentrate properly. Jess was at home, but she was sure she wouldn't eat, and next week Laura had to take Eddie back to the vet for a check-up. Her phone buzzed in her pocket with an incoming text from Jess. *Need to ask a favour, Mum, will ring in a min XX*

She probably wants to stay over at Emma's on Saturday, Laura thought. Well, that's OK as long as her mum doesn't mind, but will she eat anything? As her phone rang, without looking at the caller, Laura answered it. 'What do you want, darling?'

There was a pause, then a man's voice said, 'Laura?'

She didn't need to look at her phone to see who it was. Heat burned her cheeks. 'Oh, Ben, I'm so sorry. I thought you were my daughter.'

He chuckled, a sound that took her right back. Sitting on his single bed in his parents' home, listening to music, surrounded by books, pretending to do homework. Talking, laughing, kissing – and the rest.

'How's Eddie?''

Hurriedly she banished the thought of snogging Ben. 'Oh, he's much better, thanks. Enjoying all the attention.'

He laughed. 'I'm so glad. I wondered if you and Jess – and Eddie – would like to meet for a walk sometime?'

'Well, I'd like to,' she said, glad he couldn't see her pink cheeks. 'Though I don't know if Eddie's up for a long walk yet, and I don't know if Jess will come.'

'I'm sure she'd rather be with her friends, but when's good for you?'

'I'm not working on Monday.'

'Great. Come over and have lunch then. I live on a boat and Jake's with me; we can walk afterwards. And if Jess would like to come, she's very welcome.'

'Thanks,' said Laura. This grown-up Ben was very thoughtful and considerate about her teenage daughter. 'Can I bring something?'

'No. There's plenty, thanks. Now, I'll give you directions. Do you know the wharf along from the school?'

'Yes.'

'My boat's down there. It's an old white fibre glass 35 footer. Called *Threnody*. Third boat moored up on the left.'

'Thanks. OK, see you then.'

Ben chuckled. 'Look forward to it.'

'Me too.' Laura felt her spirits lift a little as she got up and went to the kitchen to make tea. It'll do me good to have some adult company, she thought, with a smile.

Chapter Seventeen

2 January 2023

Laura

Patches of blue sky were visible in between puffy grey clouds, and the wind was from the south west, so it was milder: there was definitely a feeling of hope in the air, Laura thought, as she walked along the harbour, admiring the waves smashing against the pier. In the park, she exchanged greetings with other walkers. The grass looked greener, the mud less brown, and Eddie's leg was definitely improving. Even so, she'd left him at home with Jess and Emma.

Walking past the river, the terrier Moll came bounding up to her with her owner, Suki. She waved and as she drew closer, Suki called, 'Where's Eddie?'

'He sprained his hind leg.'

'Oh, I'm so sorry. But he's OK?'

'Yes, he's just on short walks till it heals.' But someone expressing concern brought tears to her eyes. Eddie might be getting better, but Jess certainly wasn't right.

'Oh, that's a relief.' Suki looked at Laura closely. 'Are you OK?'

Laura nodded, but the tears that she'd held back for so long trickled down her face.

To her astonishment, Suki stepped forward and wrapped her arms around Laura. At first, she resisted, just like Jess, she thought dimly, then relaxed into the woman's strong embrace.

Her coat was thick and smelt reassuringly of woodsmoke, and Laura sobbed for a few minutes before pulling back, horrified. 'I'm so sorry,' she said. 'It's just, we had a terrible fright with Eddie, and Christmas wasn't easy and...'

'You poor thing.' Suki dug in her pocket and pulled out a tissue. 'It's clean, just been scrunched in my pocket. If there's anything I can do...'

Laura gave a watery smile and blew. 'Thanks,' she gulped. 'That's so kind.' She bent down and stroked Moll, at a loss for words.

'My pleasure,' Suki said. 'Any time you want a chat, or a walk, just message me. I don't live far away.' She handed over a business card.

'Thank you.' Laura tucked the card into her pocket. 'I'd love to. But I've got to...'

'Don't worry, so have we! Hope to see you soon!' Suki gave a cheery wave, turned round and walked off in the opposite direction.

Laura went on her way, slightly bemused. She'd been feeling so cheerful, then suddenly she was bawling her eyes out over a near-stranger. Laura hurried along. How could she go and have lunch with Ben of all people, without blubbing even more? She wiped her eyes and continued walking, concentrated on taking deep breaths.

Soon she came to what she presumed was Ben's boat. At least, it was white and looked huge to her – was that fibre glass? It looked impressive, anyway, and she wondered what it would be like to live aboard. She checked the name; yes, *Threnody*. What a lovely name, whatever it meant.

The boat was moored up in a small wharf next to a similar sized dark-blue vessel. Two much longer barges, painted red, yellow and orange, occupied the remaining space.

Looking into the dark water, Laura noticed the reflections of the For Sale signs on the walls of the warehouses that stretched along the riverbank. Pigeons cooed as they flew out from cracks in the brickwork to settle in neighbouring trees; Eddie would love chasing them.

Under her feet, the mud of the riverbank path gave way to cracked tarmac as she approached the boats, and she noticed that a gangplank had been laid onto the shore from Ben's boat. Laura felt her sorrow subside, washed away by the tranquillity of this place, as if the world had passed it by.

She wiped her wet face, was about to walk up the gangplank, but hesitated, called, 'Helloooo?'

A black tousled head appeared instantly. 'You're here! Come aboard!' Jake came down to meet her and held out a hand to help her up the gangplank. 'Did you see the fireworks on New Year's Eve? They were amazing!'

'No. I was out with a friend in the pub.' Two swans swam by, long necks craning forward, while a mallard landed on the water with a clumsy splash.

'One of the fireworks got so near Dad thought it might set the boat on fire!'

Reaching the top of the gangplank safely, Laura had

time to observe Jake properly; a ten-year-old, Ben had said, with black curly hair and Ben's dark brown eyes.

She followed Jake down some steps and found herself in a large crowded cabin. A pine table in the middle of the boat was piled with food: a plate of sliced ham, another with different cheeses, a wooden bowl full of chopped up French bread, a slab of butter, a plate of mince pies, a small Christmas pudding, satsumas in a tottering pile.

Ben was sitting at a chart table and got up, smiling. 'Glad to see you, Laura.' They pecked each other's cheeks and she smelt his outdoor smell mixed with aftershave.

'Happy New Year.' She handed over a carrier bag with a bottle of wine and some mince pies. 'Not very original, but I didn't know what else to bring.' Ben was wearing jeans and a black jumper with a hole in one elbow. She looked over, tried to see what he'd been doing at the table, but it was covered in maps.

'Great, I love mince pies,' cried Jake delightedly. 'Though I'm not supposed to be eating them. Laura was out at a New Year's Eve party, Dad!'

Laura blushed. 'No, just the pub. I gather you had trouble with fireworks?'

Ben laughed. 'Well, it was the flares I was concerned about. Now, how about a Buck's Fizz?' He made his way towards a tiny galley, got out a bottle of fizz and some orange juice.

'Great, thanks.' Laura accepted a glass, looking around at her surroundings. Long seats either side of the cabin reminded her of being in a caravan and she wondered if they turned into beds.

'Good, we can eat now. Here,' Jake said to Laura. 'This is how you do it,' and he carefully piled a plate with a bit of everything before handing it to Laura. 'Yours,' he said gravely, then proceeded to start again with a plate that he handed to his father.

'Thanks, Jake, this looks delicious.' Laura looked around for somewhere to sit, and Jake pointed to the bunk next to him.

Laura sat, enjoying the prospect of a relaxed meal with no mention of 'pure' foods and no tantrums about carbohydrates. She took a surreptitious look at her host. Ben looked tired, but he'd probably been late on New Year's Eve, too. They clinked glasses as Jake piled another plate high, then removed some of the bread.

'Have you made any New Year's resolutions, Jake?'

Jake nodded, mouth full of ham. He swallowed. 'I want to learn to paddleboard,' he said. 'What about you?'

'I…' Laura stopped. Her resolution was to make Jess happy, but she couldn't say that. 'Nothing much,' she added. 'What about you, Ben?'

Ben shook his head. 'I haven't had time but I intend to look forward, not back.'

Laura smiled. 'Is this boat part of the new start then?'

'Yes. When I set up my own business I didn't have enough money to buy a house, so a boat was a cheaper option.'

'How long have you lived here?'

'Nine months now,' said Ben. 'I love it, actually, there's a real sense of freedom. The feeling that you can just sail away.'

'It's tidal here, presumably?'

Ben nodded. 'Yes, but I can only get out on high spring tides so that gives me a window of about four days every two weeks. Jake can't wait to get out on the water when it's a bit warmer, can you?'

Jake nodded. 'Yes. I love it when we go really fast and

heel over!' He selected a large piece of cheese. 'And also, I don't have to have a shower every day like I do at Mum's.'

Ben laughed. 'That of course is a big draw. The boat is a bit short on human comforts, but the pub down the way lets me use their shower, washing machine and tumble dryer, which is a bonus. Trying to dry clothes on a boat is a nightmare.'

Laura glanced around her, at the portholes that let in plenty of light. At the books, tucked neatly in a shelf beside one of the bunks. *Sell Up and Sail* next to a biography of Ellen MacArthur and a battered copy of *Moby Dick*. 'Are you planning a sailing adventure?' she asked.

'I'd love to travel more, but I need to put down some roots for a bit,' Ben said, glancing at Jake.

'You don't have to do that for me, Dad. I told you I could give up school and go sailing round the world with you. I'd learn so much more that way, and you can still do homework by email. There's this family...'

Ben laughed. 'We'd need a bigger boat to do that, Jake. Also, I have a business to run.' He looked at Laura. 'Have you done much sailing?'

She shook her head. 'No. We did a week's course when Jess was about ten, but not since then. I did enjoy it though.' She smiled. 'So how did you get into auctions? Last time I saw you, you were going to work in a vineyard.'

Ben put his plate down, sat back on his bunk. 'Yes. I started off picking grapes in France and then helped selling cases of wine.'

'What about your friend; the one you went out there to meet?'

Ben smiled. 'Ian. You have a good memory. Ian met this French girl and they bought a derelict house that they're still doing up. I go over there regularly for working holidays.'

'And I went last year,' said Jake. 'It was cool. They had the hugest spiders you've ever seen!'

'You should see the spiders in my cottage – they're the size of tennis balls.'

'Really?' Jake's eyes were huge.

Laura laughed and nodded. 'Sorry, Ben, you were saying?'

Ben smiled. 'Yes, I was interested in fine wine so I got a job working for a French auction house.' He paused. 'I was sent to London to look after their customers this end. Then I met Kathy, got married, bought a house and qualified as an auctioneer.'

'They were great auctions,' Jake said. 'There was one with loads of stuffed animals. Birds and ferrets and pheasants and foxes.'

'I thought he'd like the antique toys, or the stamp collections,' said Ben, grinning.

'There was a roadkill badger,' Jake continued. 'You could see the join in its stomach.'

Laura suppressed a smile. 'So why set up a business here? Why not in London?'

'I moved down here with Mum,' Jake said. 'So he had to follow us so he could still see me.'

'Thanks to my ventriloquist here,' said Ben. 'That's the gist of it. When Kathy and I split up, we sold the house in London and Kathy got half and I needed to put my money into the business.'

'Well done you. Do you know many people down here now, other than family?'

Ben smiled. 'Well, you know my family; they're spread all over the place. I've got a lot of contacts, but that's not always enough to make a business work.'

'I can help with some here if you like, and the London scene will impress the locals with money.'

'That would be great, thank you.' Ben smiled. 'I know I'm taking a big risk financially, but I've always wanted to set up on my own.'

'Good for you. What about staff?'

'I've got someone starting part time next week to answer the phone and do the books. I'm keeping it all to a bare minimum at the moment. But the start-up costs are far lower here than in London so once I'm established I can get investment for something more central.' Ben stood and had to bend slightly to avoid hitting his head; the cabin height was tall enough for Laura, who was well below Ben's six foot. 'What do you think? More buck's fizz or coffee?'

'Coffee thanks.' So Ben was planning on sticking around for a bit. And he was thinking ahead, was ambitious. Good for him.

Laura got up to help clear plates while Ben put the kettle on. She felt at home on this boat, reassured by the comforting clunk of cutlery on china, by the slow throaty whistle of the kettle on the gas hob. Laura watched Ben's deft movements: you had to be neat on a boat, she realised, because there was no room for untidiness. As Ben washed and she dried, Jake put things away and she saw that crockery was stored in a cupboard under the sink. Other cupboards held plates, bowls, dried supplies, while a cooling area under the cooker was used for milk and butter.

'I'll give you the guided tour,' Ben said, leading the way to a small door on the left. 'This is the bathroom, or heads.' The room was tiny but light thanks to a large porthole opposite the door. It contained a basin and toilet with a shower pipe next to the sink. There were several shelves of toothpaste, toothbrushes and razors, with brackets to stop things falling out, and it smelled of disinfectant.

'Next door is the guest cabin,' said Ben, showing her a built-in double bunk covered in sail bags, coiled lengths of rope and life jackets.

They returned to the main cabin and as they sat with their coffee, there was a momentary silence except for water slapping gently against the hull. It was reassuring, peaceful.

'So what's your role at the gallery?'Ben asked.

'I'm assistant to the manager,' said Laura. 'But he's not there much so I contact the artists and organise most of the exhibitions. I'm enjoying it.' She paused. 'It's so long since I worked in an office, it's helped my confidence a lot.'

'And what about your friend Anna? Do you still see her?'

Laura smiled. 'I saw her on New Year's Eve. She's a nurse and done so well.'

'Good for her. And is she in a relationship?'

Laura shook her head. 'No, she hasn't had much luck with men. I can't think why – she's clever, funny, attractive…'

'Have a choccie,' said Jake, thrusting a box of assorted chocolates in front of Laura. 'My favourite's that one.' He pointed to a rectangular sweet in the centre of the box. 'Though I'm supposed to be on a diet.'

'I'll have something else, then,' said Laura, suppressing a grin. She unwrapped the blue twisty metallic paper, watched how the light caught the blue, like a stained-glass window. She savoured the bitter outer shell of the chocolate, then came to the sudden sweetness of the toffee inside, which she tempered with a sip of coffee, freshly made from grounds.

'I'm sad that your partner left and I hope your dog gets better soon.'

'Jake!' Ben nearly spilt his coffee.

'What? You and Mum split up. It's sad.' Jake's curls bobbed animatedly.

'I'm sad too, Jake. But I don't want to be sad all the time.'

Jake started fidgeting, his legs swinging. 'Can we go out soon?'

'Course we can.' Ben looked at Laura thoughtfully. 'Do you still want to go for a walk?'

'Yes, I'd like to,' said Laura. 'Shame Eddie couldn't come – he'd love this boat. And a walk.'

'Bring him another time,' said Ben. 'We'll finish our coffee and go. Where do you suggest, Laura?'

Laura had already given this some thought. 'If we go along the footpath by the river, then we can turn off into the woods and end up by the creek café, if it's open.'

Half an hour later, Laura, Ben and Jake were walking through the woods. Twigs snapped underfoot, but pine trees kept out most of the southerly wind that sighed in the uppermost branches. She caught a sharp movement out of the corner of one eye as a squirrel darted up a tree trunk, while in the distance she heard the faint coo of a pigeon, hoo-hoooo-hoo, and a blackbird sang.

'Eddie loves it here, especially if we come early. I think he picks up all the night-time smells of rats and squirrels,' said Laura, while Jake scampered ahead.

'I bet. I do hope he's better soon.'

'Thanks. And for all you did on the day. I dread to think what would have happened if you hadn't come along.'

'Well, it all turned out fine.' Ben cleared this throat. 'I'm sorry we parted on such bad terms.' Laura opened her mouth to speak, but Ben continued, 'I'm so sorry, Laura. I was jealous of Chris, which was stupid and infantile. I behaved like a real idiot.'

Laura bit her lip. Memories of those days crashed in on her from all directions. 'I was eighteen, Ben. Mum was falling apart. I had to organise the funeral, tell everyone Dad had died, close bank accounts, change all the bills around...' She paused. 'But Chris helped a lot. I don't know what I would have done without him. He was there, Ben.'

'And I wasn't. I know that. When I finally got back for the funeral, I knew I'd blown it.'

'You didn't blow it. It was just – how it worked out.' Laura remembered crying herself to sleep every night for months, missing Ben so much. No way would she tell him that.

'So what happened with Chris?' Ben's voice was gentle.

'He got a job in a contracting company and was promoted, so we moved to Newlyn, had a lovely house overlooking the sea in a great community. Jess grew up there – we were very happy,' she added. Or at least, she thought they had been. But Chris evidently hadn't. 'Chris expected a lot from me, from Jess, most of all from himself. And then – the old cliché – he told me he'd met someone else. Someone much younger, and he wanted to buy a house with her. Which meant selling the family home, and as we weren't married, I wasn't entitled to anything, which is why we're living in a poky freezing cottage, and poor Jess is miserable.' Laura looked ahead to where Jake was joyfully running ahead, kicking leaves up.

'I'm so sorry, Laura.'

She couldn't bear to look at him. Strode on, hands in her pockets. 'I had to rent the cheapest cottage I could find, which was back in bloody St Budy, miles away from Jess's school. I finally got a job in the art gallery and got on with life. But it's Jess I feel so sorry for. She's had to leave all her friends, her school, everything that she loved.' She checked him to see what impact this had. 'She feels abandoned by her father, by her friends, by everyone who matters to her. It's destroyed her confidence and I don't know how to help her.'

Ben moved closer. 'Am I allowed to give you a hug?'

She nodded, unable to speak, and turned and rested her face against his shoulder while he pressed her close and she remembered exactly what it was like to be in his arms: the warmth of his body, the smell of salt and wood, his breath on her face. The sense of safety.

'I'm so sorry, Laura,' he said. 'Christmas must have been hard. And then you had vet bills on top of all that.'

He sounded so kind, so understanding, that Laura nearly burst into tears, but that would only have made matters worse. 'Dear Mum came to the rescue over the vet,' she said. 'She's been amazing and I'm so grateful.'

She drew away from him and started to walk on. She had to keep moving. 'Christmas was a nightmare. I don't have much money, and it's hard doing everything on your own.' She stopped, horrified. That sounded so self-pitying.

Ben caught up with her. 'Life is bloody hard sometimes, isn't it?' he said. 'I don't know if I can help, but I am one of your oldest friends. Just let me know.'

'Thank you, that's so kind.' Laura didn't dare say more or she knew she'd cry.

'I haven't got any money either,' he said quietly. 'Kathy got half the house money, I pay maintenance for Jake and I've taken out a big loan for the business. I have to make a success just to cover the interest. I daren't think about what happens if I don't make it.'

'And I thought I had problems. I'm so sorry, here I have

been moaning on,' Laura said. They walked on a few more paces. 'What went wrong with Kathy? Do you mind me asking?'

Ben shook his head. 'I should have seen it coming. I was working stupid hours and Kathy got fed up, met someone else. But it was still such a shock. Now I have to think of Jake; he's had enough upheavals.'

'Of course.' Laura smiled. 'You two seem to get on very well.'

'We do. I'm very lucky. He's quite grown-up for his age: I suppose that comes from being an only child.'

'Yes, Jess is an only child, too, and we get on well. At least,' Laura paused, 'we used to. We don't seem to now.'

'She's a teenager, Laura,' Ben said with a grin. 'I still remember at that age feeling my parents couldn't possibly understand anything because they were so *old*.' He grinned. 'I have that treat in store. Now, do you mind if we go to the café there? I promised Jake an ice cream. He's allowed a few treats on his diet, and he's been so good recently.'

'Of course.' Laura smiled, enjoying being with people who thought food was something to be enjoyed, not tortured over. 'I might have one myself.'

'In that case, we all will,' Ben said. 'Ice creams on me.'

Chapter Eighteen

March 2023

Laura

Laura sat frozen at her desk. The trailer for *Woman's Hour* carried on playing on the BBC app but she wasn't listening anymore: she was thinking about Jess.

Eddie, who was lying at her feet, shifted position and jolted her from her thoughts. She clicked on the app, rewound it so she could listen again.

'With a reported rise in teenage girls suffering from orthorexia, we talk to an eating disorder specialist about when healthy living goes too far…'

'Orthorexia,' Laura muttered. She turned off the app and typed the unfamiliar word into Google. The first result was from an eating disorder charity. Laura scanned the information, her blood running cold as she recognised her daughter in every word.

"Orthorexia refers to an unhealthy obsession with eating 'pure' food. Food considered 'pure' or 'impure' can vary from one person to another. But not everyone who tries to eat healthily or diet is suffering from orthorexia. Like other eating disorders, the eating behaviour involved – 'healthy', 'pure' or 'clean' eating in this case – is used to cope with negative thoughts and feelings, or to try to feel in control. Someone using food in this way might feel extremely anxious or guilty if they eat food they feel is unhealthy.

This can cause physical problems, because beliefs about what is healthy may lead to them cutting out essential nutrients or whole food groups. All eating disorders are serious mental illnesses, and should be treated as quickly as possible to give the sufferer the best chance of fully recovering."

Laura felt sick. There was no doubt that Jess had been restricting her food for months now, and exercising a lot. But it had never occurred to Laura that it might be due to trying to cope with negative feelings, or to feel in control. She felt a wave of guilt: it was so obvious now she thought about it, and the more Laura read, the more it fitted with Jess's increasingly vehement attitude towards food.

Why did I not realise? Laura thought. I'm her mother, for God's sake! Realising she wasn't going to get any work done, she decided to take an early lunch and spent her break researching orthorexia, reading advice on parenting and eating disorder forums, and trying to understand what other parents did and how they coped. And whether their children got better.

The more she read, the more her spirits plummeted. Despair wrapped round her like a damp, cold duvet with the awareness that Jess was indeed in the grip of an eating disorder. Most people advocated counselling, but that only worked if the person realised they had a problem and wanted to get help. What could she do?

Laura wanted to understand what Jess was going through. Surely then she could help her and all this would stop? I'll talk to her more about her diet, make her see where she's going wrong, she thought. She rang several helplines, casting for advice, and via the forums she messaged several parents in a similar situation asking if they had any ideas. We'll get through this, she thought. I'll do anything to help Jess.

Laura checked her phone as she left the gallery to take Eddie out and saw with a lurch of worry that she had two messages from the school. How had she missed them? Hurriedly she played them; both from the head of year.

Heart thumping, Laura dialled the number, heard the familiar tones of Miss Beaumont. 'Ah, Ms Hocking. Thank you for ringing back. I know we've spoken about Jess before, but we're still concerned about her: she looks thinner and seems to be tired all the time.'

The impact of what Laura had just discovered threatened to swamp her. Did Miss Beaumont know about orthorexia? 'I'm glad you've noticed it too – I wondered if it was all in my head. I'm so worried about her. Is there anything you can do? She's so picky at home. Mealtimes are becoming a nightmare.' Laura felt a lump rise in her throat and tears stinging her eyes. 'She's had so much to deal with, you know, with her father leaving, and moving house, moving school. It's been very hard for her.'

'I know. I do appreciate life has been extremely difficult for you both, and it's bound to affect Jess. I'm wondering if she would benefit from seeing a counsellor. We have a trauma informed practitioner in school who Jess might like to speak to.'

Laura blinked. 'What's that?'

'Our practitioner is an emotionally available adult who is here during school time. She's very good at discussing difficult topics like family break-ups, which are sadly very common.'

'Right.' Laura bit her lip. 'I had no idea this help was available. That's… good. If Jess will agree to it, of course. She might be quite… resistant to the idea.'

'I was going to suggest that you come in and we talk to Jess together. Also we could look at getting Jess to see the school nurse to keep an eye on her weight.'

Good luck with that, thought Laura. 'Certainly. Though she gets very defensive if I try and talk about food or her weight.' She paused. 'I've just been reading about orthorexia. Have you heard about that?'

'I have, but I'm not sure exactly what it is.'

Laura frowned. 'Well, it fits in with Jess's very rigid ideas of what she will and increasingly won't eat. To be honest, it sounds like a precursor to anorexia.'

'Let's hope it's not that,' said Miss Beaumont. 'I'll speak to the staff because I do think we need to keep a close eye on Jess at school, and I'm sure you do at home.'

'I do,' said Laura. 'But Jess is extremely stubborn about food. Still, I'll talk to her when she gets home.' Though she and Jess had had countless conversations about her diet, which got them nowhere. Jess decided what she would eat, that meal, that day, or week, and she would not change her mind.

'We've had other students like Jess, so I do appreciate the problem, Ms Hocking. None of this is your fault. Being a teenager is a tricky time.'

The voice was so kind and sympathetic, suddenly Laura wanted to bawl her eyes out, to tell this woman just how hard she was trying, how difficult it all was. 'Thank you.' She gulped. 'I'm very grateful. Jess does need help and I don't know what to do.'

'Don't worry. I'm sure once Jess has had a few sessions with our counsellor, that will help a lot.'

'Thanks. That's very kind.' Laura bit her lip hard to try and stop herself crying. And once she'd put the phone down, she thought what a relief it was that someone else had noticed Jess wasn't right. Jess hadn't been herself since they moved to St Budy. Should Laura have contacted the school earlier for help? It was much easier with hindsight. But at least there was help available if Jess was prepared to take it. And if not, she would follow up those other forums and websites.

The panicky fog inside Laura's head cleared for a moment: she had a plan.

Diary of Jessica Kate Hocking

23 April 2023

Dad,

Mum's on at me about my diet all the time now and we keep arguing. I wish she'd leave me alone. What I eat is my business but she won't let up. I mean, I'm nearly 15. I'm old enough to decide WHAT to eat, FFS!

The teachers keep reminding us that this time next year we'll be taking our GCSEs, which is just added pressure. It's difficult enough trying to concentrate in class though I don't know why. My form tutor keeps asking if I'm OK: she rang Mum and we had to go and talk to Miss B together.

Miss B went on about how hard it must be with Dad having left, and moving house and school and blah blah and would I like to see a special counsellor. I didn't like the idea, but Miss B has a way of putting things so it's impossible to say no. So I agreed to talk to this Mel who comes in once a week. Can't see how that's going to help, but if it gets Miss B off my back that's something. Then she said I wasn't eating enough and I should see the school nurse or my GP to get weighed weekly. NO!!! And she got rather huffy but said I must eat more, and they'll keep an eye on me, make sure I am. Shit.

I've worked so hard on my fitness and diet, I'm not going to let them ruin it. Mind you, I'm good at getting rid of food, so I'm sure I can outwit them. I've found a new influencer on TikTok who is SO skinny and she's always posting health tips, so I'll reach out to her for ideas.

I caught Emma looking at Susie, one of the prefects, the other day and she was just – gone. I wonder what it's like kissing a girl? I mean, I don't want to try it, but I wonder what it's like to fancy girls? Mind you, there aren't any boys at school I fancy either.

I have the hurtles, I call them. It's when I run and run and run and can't stop. Sometimes when I'm running with Eddie I feel really strong, but other times I feel like that girl in the film The Red Shoes *who can't stop dancing and that freaks me out.*

There's this other girl I follow and we take pics of the scales as we lose more weight and tell each other how amazing we look which makes me feel better.

If I concentrate hard enough I can stop feeling hungry. Hunger is greed, and I want my body to be hard and lean. To run fast, like those Greek gods with winged feet. Obvs I don't have winged feet, but I am getting fit and lean, and can even outrun Eddie sometimes.

I seem to be rubbish at everything else, but running and getting thin are what I do best. I'm hungry most of the time but I lie awake at night feeling my hip bones jutting out and the place where my stomach used to be is now a nice hollow. That makes it all worthwhile.

Chapter Nineteen

Jess

'Hi Dad.' I hadn't seen him for a while but when I got in the car on Saturday, Dad looked at me like I'd done something awful.

'Jess, what have you done? You look terrible.'

He looked really angry and I felt tears, hot and angry, sting my eyes. 'Nothing,' I said.

'You're too thin, Jess. Haven't you been eating?'

'Of course I have,' I said hotly. Why couldn't people leave me alone? We sat in a solid silence while he drove into Penzance, which took twenty-eight minutes. I counted them on the car clock while the tension got bigger and heavier and I wanted to get out of the car and run. But where would I go?

'Did you go to Gran's last weekend?' he said finally in a strained voice.

'Yeah,' I said, relieved that we were talking, and not about me. 'It was a relief to be away from the cottage.' I saw

151

him flinch at that and I was glad. 'Gran drove down to get us.'

What I didn't say was that she doesn't fuss about food like Mum does, and I heard her saying 'don't worry, leave Jess alone'. Good for Gran.

I also didn't tell him that I hardly sleep now and I can't get warm. All I can think about is food; it haunts me, but I can't eat. Too terrified, in case I start eating and can't stop. Part of me, the weak part, just wants to eat and eat and I'm so ashamed of that person. I spend a lot of time looking at certain Instagram accounts. They help keep me focused, and we compare how much weight we've lost, how to cope with hunger, that sort of thing.

Of course I couldn't tell Dad any of that, and during the rest of the visit I didn't know what to say. We had a drink (I had peppermint tea) and he dropped me home and I was really sad cos I miss him so much but I don't know how to say that, and I hate what he's done to us, but I was just glad to get home and away from him cos he made me feel worse.

On Tuesday, when I got to photography, I looked around for Nick, but he wasn't there. He's often late. But Ryan Williams came over. He's the year above, tall with fair hair and bright blue eyes you could drown in. He's really fit.

We've been doing black-and-white photography and had to split into twos and Ryan usually pairs up with Megan or Rosie and me with Nick. They were there, but Nick still hadn't arrived, and Ryan sat down next to me. 'OK?'

I couldn't move. Me? I looked round, but he *was* talking to me.

We had to go and take pictures of buildings and it was

so weird, working with Ryan, I couldn't think straight. We had to decide which buildings to photograph, from which angle, and why they would make a good picture. I don't usually know why, I just do it. So it was quite cool to think about why it would work.

'But I don't see why you'd take a picture from this angle,' Ryan kept saying.

'You see the way the light comes in? This angle shows up the roof, with all those twirly bits on it and the pigeons, and the right side is in shadow, but the left is in bright light,' I said. When he saw the picture, he went all quiet and I thought oh no.

But he said, 'You're good, aren't you? I never knew.'

I went all pink and flustered and then we had to go back and explain to the others what we'd done and why. I felt a bit better then cos of what Ryan had said. And I really enjoyed it, and the others listened to what I said as if it was important, rather than just ignoring me cos I'm minging and ugly.

Nick didn't turn up for club and I wondered why. Ryan and I were the last to leave class and he walked with me to the science block. We stopped outside and he looked at me and I wondered what he was going say, cos he usually looks kind of scary, but then he smiled, and he looked *so* fit. He's got incredibly sexy eyes and a crooked nose (he's always getting into fights) and very long eyelashes. My tummy did a sort of swoop and all I could think of was of hugging him. Well, and kissing him. And guess what? He leaned forward and kissed me properly. Tongues! He tasted of cigarettes and chocolate and it was a bit weird, and my legs went all shaky. Then he stopped, looked at me with a lopsided grin and said, 'How about meeting tomorrow after school? We can play pool.'

I said, 'OK,' though I don't know anyone else who plays pool, and I have no idea how to play.

But it was almost like he knew, cos he winked and said, 'I'll teach you.'

And then he went. I have no idea what was said in biology, or what we were supposed to do for homework. All I knew was that Ryan Williams kissed me. And he wants to meet up tomorrow. I'm guessing that isn't a proper date if we're going to play pool, but even so.

He wants to see me. ME!!!

I went round to Emma's after school again the next day. It's a relief cos Mum's always nagging me so it's good to get away from her. Emma knew about Mel the counsellor cos I had time out of lessons to go and see her. So she asked what Mel was like.

'I like her – she's friendly and nothing seems to faze her. I didn't think I'd be able to tell her about Dad leaving but I did, a bit. She's easy to talk to and said that she's there whenever I want to chat about stuff.'

'That's cool,' said Em, and I waited to see if she'd ask me about my weight. But she didn't, which was a relief. 'Does she know about Sally Watkins?'

I shook my head. We both know that if I said anything to Mel or Miss B, and Sally and her lot found out that I'd told, our lives would be even worse than they are now. Em reached over and squeezed my hand. I squeezed back cos having a friend like Emma is so special.

'How's Ryan?'

She's the only person I've told. I smiled. 'Ryan is cool.' I hesitated.'But I'm kind of scared of him cos he's *so* cool and I can't think what he sees in me.'

Emma laughed. 'Why wouldn't he want to go out with you? You're funny and clever, and you're really fit. He must think it's really cool you're his girlfriend.'

And when she said that, my face went hot again and tears rushed into my eyes and I couldn't speak.

'Does Nick know you're seeing Ryan?'

I frowned. 'Dunno. Why?'

Emma shrugged. 'I thought you two might go out. You and Nick look good together.'

'No way!' I paused. 'You mean, Ryan and I don't?'

'No. Just that… never mind.' And she smiled.

The other day, Jake Simmons was shouting about me being vile and ugly, but Ryan just glared at them and laughed. He said, really loudly, 'She might be skinny, but I like my girls thin. Can't stand fat girls. And no way is she ugly, but perhaps you're too stupid to see that.'

Chapter Twenty

June 2023

Laura

'Darling, please, will you just eat that piece of toast?'

'No. It's my birthday and I don't want any breakfast. Just leave it will you? I'm going to miss the bus.'

'Jess.' Laura faced her, wondering how on earth to persuade her to eat. 'You can't go to school on an empty stomach. You must eat something. If it's not toast, have some cereal.'

Jess gave a huge sigh. 'Oh all *right*. I'll have cereal. Just go, Mum, or you'll be late for work.'

'I've got twenty minutes before I need to leave. Now, do you want to pour it or shall I?'

'I will.' Jess snatched a bowl, pouring a tiny amount of muesli in the bottom. She added a dribble of milk and stared at it, as if it contained cyanide. Very slowly she ate a mouthful. Laura busied herself making their packed lunches, surreptitiously watching Jess out of the corner of her eye.

'How are you getting on with the nurse?'

Jess hesitated, which usually meant she was about to lie. 'Fine.'

'What does she do?' Laura knew that she was supposed to weigh Jess and encourage her to eat more. But she wanted to hear what Jess had to say.

'Just tells me to eat more. Blah blah, same every week.'

'Can you talk to her?'

Jess looked up. 'What about?'

'About why you don't want to eat.'

'Leave it, Mum.' Jess whisked her bowl off the table, scraping a few bits in the waste bin. She grabbed her rucksack and shouted 'bye' before hurrying out of the door.

Laura watched as Jess slowed at the end of the street and turned right, a desultory lone figure, now walking slowly by the harbour. Laura sighed. Oh well, at least she'd had a bit of cereal to start the day. Or had she? Laura flipped the lid of the waste bin and saw that Jess had tipped all of the muesli away.

Laura felt like crying. Is this all my fault? Or is it Chris's? God damn him to hell. She grabbed her phone and rang him.

'Chris? I know you're probably at work, but it's about Jess.'

'What is it?' He sounded worried.

'I don't know what to do. She just won't eat.'

'I told you last time we went out she wouldn't eat, either, but she said she'd had a bacon sarnie.'

'As if.' Laura sighed. 'She hasn't eaten bacon for about a year now. I wish she'd just eat a decent meal.'

'What do we do?' Chris sounded forlorn. 'I mean, I know the school are keeping a look out, and she's seeing this trauma counsellor and the nurse, but none of that seems to help, does it?'

'No. I've tried to discuss her diet, but she won't talk about it. I've rung an eating disorder charity and I've talked to other parents in similar situations, and spent hours reading forums.'

'And?'

'I think she needs to see a counsellor who specialises in eating disorders.'

'Are you sure?'

'Well, nothing else is working.'

'OK,' Chris said. 'What would that cost?'

'For God's sake, Chris. You make everything about money,' Laura cried. Though of course it was – and Chris would have to pay.

'How much would it cost? Can you find someone?'

'Why is it always down to me?' Laura said. Then she realised that Chris wouldn't have a clue how to go about finding the right therapist. 'It's not that simple,' she added. 'She needs to be referred by her GP. But first of all Jess has to acknowledge that she's got a problem, then she needs to want to do something about it.'

'We just tell her,' Chris said. 'No point in beating about the bush.'

'Like you did last time? That went well.'

Silence. That hit home, Laura thought. 'Listen, we need to ring the school together and see if Jess will agree to see her GP, and if she says yes, the doctor can refer her. That's a start.'

Chris exhaled loudly. 'OK. Whatever you say. Let me know when's good for a conference call with the school.'

'OK.'

As Laura rang off, she sighed so loudly that Eddie looked up, came over and nudged her leg with his nose.

'Thanks, darling Ed,' Laura said. 'What would we do without you?'

She got ready for work, realised Jess had gone without her packed lunch (which she suspected she wouldn't eat anyway) and tried not to think of what lay ahead. An abyss with a deteriorating daughter.

Chapter Twenty-One

Jess

I was so sick of living inside my head, so desperate to talk to someone, and so glad to see Emma, I blurted out, 'I think Ryan's dumped me.'

'What? You've only just started going out,' Emma said as we walked towards the science block. 'What happened?'

'Olivia Taylor's got her eye on him. Whenever I'm with Ryan she appears.'

'She's rubbish.' Emma snorted. 'Flicking her hair and pulling her skirt up so it shows her pants. Her shirt's always stretched tight over her boobs and I don't know how she undoes so many buttons and doesn't get detention.'

I shrugged, wishing I had her confidence. 'She's so popular.'

'If there's a boy that Olivia's after and someone else has got in there first, she moves in. She doesn't seem to think that the boys make any decisions.' She picked up an empty can of Coke and put it in the bin. Emma was like that: she cared about rubbish and the environment.

'Yeah,' I said. 'But last week when Olivia flashed her tits at Ryan, he smiled and said to me, "Come on, Jess." And you should have seen Olivia's face!' I giggled at the memory. 'It almost made up for how vile she's been ever since. All her friends snigger when I go past, but not when Ryan's there.'

'So what went wrong with Ryan?'

I shrugged. 'We did stuff together at photography, but yesterday I heard Olivia's friend, Ashley, asking him why he wanted to hang around with me and he said it was cos I was clever. He said it in a jokey way so I don't know whether he meant it, or if it was just an excuse.'

'I'm sure it's not an excuse,' Emma said. 'Boys just aren't good at giving compliments.' She paused. 'So why do you think he's dumped you?'

'Ruby said he got off with Lily last night.' I gulped, could feel my face getting hot and my eyes getting wet. What had I done wrong? 'I guess that's us over.'

'I'm sure it's not,' Emma said. 'Ruby's always winding people up — don't take any notice of her.' She smiled. 'You still like photography?'

I nodded. 'Yeah.' Nick was there, but I didn't talk to him. I mean, we never meet outside photography. 'They're mostly older and friendlier than the people in our year. Apart from you, everyone still treats me as if I'm from another planet. But the tutor, Mr Thompson, never talks down to me and gives us really sick projects.'

'That's cool.'

I looked up, unsure whether to tell her. 'The other day he said how good my work was. I didn't believe him at first, but he said "I mean it, Jess. You are very talented. It's a joy to teach someone like you." And I felt as if I was floating on clouds after that. Me, talented!'

Emma laughed. 'But you are, Jess. Your pictures are amazing. What are you doing at the moment?'

I groaned. 'Trying to write an essay on The Age of the Image, starting with the beginning of the Box Brownie and how anyone could buy one cos they were cheap, so people took photos of their friends, like, for the first time.'

'That sounds cool. Much better than what we're doing in biology.'

'The research and stuff is really cool.' What I didn't say was that my brain felt stretched and exhausted and I couldn't focus. I was cold all the time. It was like a constant battle going on in my head; trying to concentrate on schoolwork and making sure I was only eating pure food, when I could have murdered a plate of chips, or a burger.

I wasn't sure when this voice had come into my head, but it was there all the time now, telling me what not to eat (most things), how much exercise to do (loads), and then, when I'd done my homework, instead of chilling in front of the TV, the voice was on at me to do more star jumps and press-ups, post videos and stuff on TikTok and Instagram for my followers. It was like a full-time job and I was shattered and wanted to resign. But I couldn't. I was scared what would happen if I didn't obey the rules.

'How's your mum?'

I shrugged. 'In a grump.' She was always nagging me to eat. 'She's made an appointment for me to see the GP next week.' I'd begged and pleaded not to go, but I saw a side to Mum that I hadn't seen before. Determined. Non-negotiable. I couldn't get out of this one.

I didn't say what the GP appointment was about, and

Emma didn't ask. The silence stretched, full of things I wasn't saying.

Emma got up. 'Must go, got biology and I'm late. Don't worry, Jess. I bet Ryan asks you out again soon. He's crazy about you.'

I watched her as she shot off down the corridor. I was late for French, too, but I didn't care. In fact, it was hard to care about anything very much.

I took a deep breath. I must try harder, I thought. Every time I lost another kilo I felt amazing. But recently I felt like I was running a marathon and just when I thought I could see the end, someone moved the finishing line.

Chapter Twenty-Two

September 2023

Laura

Laura sat in their GP surgery, a stony-faced Jess beside her. So far she'd not spoken, but she had consented to be weighed. They didn't have scales at home, there'd never been any need, so Laura was shocked at how low Jess's weight was.

Blood tests were taken, and the GP asked both Jess and Laura many questions about Jess's eating and how long she'd been like this. Laura told her about Chris leaving, moving house, new school, Covid, everything she could think of. Still Jess didn't speak.

Finally the GP took off her reading glasses and rubbed her eyes. She looks as exhausted as I feel, Laura thought.

'I can see you've been through a lot, Jessica. Sometimes we can feel that life is spiralling out of control, and a way of managing this can be to restrict food. In your case, I suspect this is what's happened, and as a result, it seems that you're suffering from anorexia nervosa,' the GP said. 'You're very underweight for your height so I'd like to weigh you once a week from now on.'

Jess refused to look at the doctor, while her words resounded round Laura's head. Anorexia? What about orthorexia? Though she'd always suspected orthorexia was merely a door into full-blown anorexia. All those hours she'd spent looking up forums online, asking advice from other mothers whose daughters wouldn't eat. She'd persuaded herself that Jess was getting fit, was just being extra careful about what she ate. Why did I fool myself, she thought angrily. Why didn't I see what was happening, and stop it?

Laura's stomach fluttered with disbelief, then panic. What on earth should she do now? Did Jess really have this horrifying disease? Of course she has, said a voice at the back of her head. But why? What had Laura done wrong? Had this disease been lurking in the wings, ready to pounce? Or was it all bloody Chris's fault?

Laura bit her lip. Yes, Chris was partly to blame, but I should have noticed more, she thought. How could I have let her lose so much weight? But then again, how could I have stopped her? Jess had been impossible over food for a long time.

She tuned back in, to the GP saying what Jess should be eating. She was handing over a diet sheet. Good luck with that, thought Laura. There's no way Jess is going to eat three meals a day, let alone snacks.

'Can I have a word?' Laura said. 'Jess, go and sit in the waiting room, darling.'

To her surprise Jess nodded and crept out of the room, shoulders hunched, like an old woman.

With Jess out of the room, panic surged within Laura, engulfing her. 'What do I do?' She could feel tears welling up, stinging her eyes. 'She just refuses to eat. It's impossible.'

'I do appreciate how difficult it must be. Jess definitely needs help, so I'm going to refer her to CAMHS. Child and Adolescent Mental Health Services.'

A spark of hope. 'When could they see her? What could they do?'

'There is a waiting list, I'm afraid. As you know, the NHS is struggling, but we'll do what we can. Have you tried the eating disorder charities? BEAT and such like?'

'Yes, but at the time I didn't think she had anorexia,' Laura said.

The GP passed her the box of tissues. 'I know this is a very scary diagnosis, but at least if we've caught it early, there's a good chance Jess will make a swift recovery. She's fifteen, which is a common age for eating disorders. We'll see what help we can get her.'

Laura blew her nose then got up. 'Thank you.' She left the room, clutching at the small straws offered by this exhausted-looking woman. Anorexia. Such an ugly word, so full of hideous images that she tried to blot from her overstretched mind.

Jess and I used to be so close, she thought. I felt that with kindness and humour and love we could get through anything together. How wrong I was.

Jess insisted on going back to school; she didn't want to stay at home, so Laura rang Chris.

'How did it go?'

'The GP's diagnosed her with anorexia.'

There was a pause, while the word roared louder in

Laura's head. It echoed, like a sinister knowing cackle, and she wished Chris would say something.

'Are they sure? I thought you said it was orthorexia.'

'Well, I thought it could be, but she's lost a lot more weight since then.'

Silence. 'Don't they need to do blood tests or scans or something?'

'They did blood tests, then she was weighed and she's well below what she should be. She's been referred to Child and Adolescent Mental Health Services. Though there's a long waiting list, apparently.'

'Anorexia. I mean, that's serious,' Chris said, almost to himself. 'Surely she's not... I mean, why?'

Laura felt a flash of anger. 'I seem to remember Kayla started Jess on getting fit, losing weight, posting online campaigns. I follow Jess on social media and she spends hours posting what she's eaten, what exercise she's done, how many calories she's burned up.'

'You can't blame Kayla,' Chris said. 'How was she to know Jess would take this to such extremes?'

He was right, but Laura wondered when he might take some accountability himself. 'You do realise that this all started when you left?' she said.

'But I... I'd never do anything to hurt Jess.'

'For God's sake, Chris!' Laura longed to unleash all the hurt and fury and misery he'd inflicted on them. But she stopped herself. The blame game wasn't going to help anyone, least of all Jess. 'I feel as badly about this as you do, Chris, but the important thing is that Jess gets the help she needs.'

'I agree. I thought you were going to find a specialist counsellor?' He sounded conciliatory now.

Laura sighed. Couldn't he take any responsibility for all

this? Once again, it was up to her. He seemed to think that a therapist would appear from the heavens, wave a magic wand and Jess would be fine. 'It's not that easy, Chris, as we've discussed before. But I'll let you know as soon as I find the right person.' And when I find one, she told herself as she terminated the call, you are so going to pay for it.

That evening Laura and Jess sat in the kitchen staring at a mostly uneaten macaroni cheese. Laura felt like she'd wandered into a maze and couldn't find the way out. How could she help Jess when she didn't want to be helped? She'd lose her daughter if she couldn't make her see sense. But she couldn't fall apart: she had to keep strong for Jess.

The knock at the door startled them both, but she jumped up, was so relieved to see Anna standing in the doorway.

'Sorry for dropping in like this, but I was passing and…' She proffered a bottle of wine. 'Thought this might come in handy.'

Laura hugged her tight. 'You're always welcome.' She tried to summon a smile. 'But especially welcome with wine.'

Anna came in, went to give Jess a kiss. 'So how was it, chick?'

Laura waited for Jess to speak. When she did, her voice was small and tight.

'She says I've got anorexia.' From Jess's dismissive tone of voice, it appeared she didn't believe the GP.

Laura and Anna exchanged glances. Anna sat down beside Jess, took the glass of wine Laura gave her. 'So how do you feel about that?'

Jess shrugged. 'I dunno. What does it mean? I've lost weight, that's all.'

When Jess finally looked at Anna, Laura could see a spark of defiance in her daughter's eyes. Almost of pride. Then it vanished and her eyes clouded over, tears sprang up.

'Anorexia is a serious illness, love,' Anna said gently.

Jess looked down at her bony fingers. 'I dunno,' she said. 'Nothing makes sense.' She stood up. 'I've got to do my homework. Bye, Anna.' And with that she left the room.

The atmosphere lifted slightly when she'd gone, and the two women stared at each other. 'Fuck,' said Anna. 'Just fuck.'

Laura nodded. 'That just about sums it up.' She felt her face go hot and gulped. 'It turns out Jess's friend Emma has been to see her head of year, as well as several of the teachers. They're all so worried about her.'

'It's good that they're concerned,' said Anna. 'Is she still seeing the school nurse?'

'Yes, but apparently Jess refuses to be weighed. Though she did agree to it at the surgery today, and I was horrified by how much she's lost.' Laura paused. Hot tears were running down her face and she brushed them away. 'But at least they're going to refer her to CAMHS. I suppose that's something, but the GP did warn that there'd be a long wait.' She fumbled for a tissue and blew her nose? 'What do we do in the meantime? Just wait for Jess to get thinner?' The thought of it was too much, and Laura let loose the bank of tears that she'd stopped for so long.

Anna got up, sat beside Laura and held her while she sobbed, patting her on the back. She didn't speak, and Laura was grateful, realising how much she needed to let go of all the pain she'd been storing up. Eventually she stopped, blew her nose and gave a big sigh.

'That's better,' said Anna. 'You've been so strong for so long, you need to let it all out, Laura. You know I'm your lifebelt whenever you need it.'

Laura managed a watery smile. 'Thanks. I feel like I'm drowning right now. You know how grateful I am. I just… I'm trying to keep positive but it all seems bloody hopeless.'

Anna nodded. 'The NHS is very stretched at the moment, and there's a huge rise in eating disorders since Covid. But that doesn't mean you won't get help for Jess. She hasn't been ill for long, so there's a good chance she will recover.'

'Only if she'll accept help, and she won't at the moment.' Laura sighed. 'I've been spending ages online trying to work out how to get her counselling. But where do you start? Who's best? And it's all so expensive. How would I get Jess to see a counsellor? She gets so stroppy if I try and urge her to eat, or make a remark about her weight. I can't do or say anything right.'

'I know,' Anna said. 'Jess needs to understand that she's ill, and she then needs to be prepared to accept help. Until then, we just have to hang on, keep strong. I'll see if I can find any recommendations for eating disorder specialists.'

'That would be great, thanks. Sorry you've had to listen to me moaning.'

'It's not moaning, Laura. You need support and I'm more than happy to provide that. That's what friends are for.'

Laura sighed, exhausted now that she'd had a good howl. 'I'd thought that Jess and I had such a good relationship. But this is like living with that Edvard Munch painting; you know, *The Scream*? I feel like I've walked into someone else's nightmare and can't get out.'

'Oh, Laura. I am so, so sorry. It really is a brutal

disease.' She reached over, squeezed Laura's hand. 'I've got to go in a minute, but do you want to meet up tomorrow?'

'That'd be good. Jess has photography and then she's going to Emma's so I said I'd pick her up at eight thirty.'

'You're on. Seven in the pub?'

'Definitely. And Anna, thanks. You're one in a million.'

Anna grinned. 'Just remember. Everything might feel like crap now, but your hair looks good.' And with a wave, she left the house, leaving Laura with the lasting impression of her smile.

Chapter Twenty-Three

Laura

Having unloaded onto Anna, Laura's head felt a little clearer. It was such a relief to share the fear and pain with someone who understood and cared.

Since then, Laura had read as much as she could online about anorexia and none of it was uplifting. "Around 46% of anorexia patients fully recover, 27% improve considerably and 23% suffer chronically. Anorexia has the highest mortality rate of any psychiatric disorder."

A mental health charity offered a helpline and a number to find psychologists and therapists who specialised in eating disorders in the area, as well as local support groups. Laura had rung several and been given details of some therapists, but they were all so expensive and how could she know who would be any good? Jess would probably hate them and refuse to talk, and it would all be a horrible waste of money *and* she'd be no better.

Laura rubbed her temples, where a headache was brewing, and continued her search online. She pored over forums, reading what other mums had done, and talked to someone from the BEAT eating disorder charity. Advice varied, but none of it was encouraging, seemingly down to the fact that it could take a long time for anorexics to admit they needed help, and a dearth in support for eating disorders.

By the end of the day, Laura felt brain fuddled and utterly despondent and was glad of the walk home to clear her head.

As they rounded the corner, she saw a familiar figure walking ahead of them towards the pub. She called out and he turned round, his face breaking into a smile as he saw them.

'Laura! Good to see you. And Eddie – glad to see you're better, mate.' Ben bent and stroked Eddie then straightened. 'Out for a constitutional?'

Laura smiled. 'Yes. My head's buzzing and I needed to get out. Jess is staying late at school tonight so I thought some fresh air might help.'

'What's up? If you don't mind me asking.'

'No.' Laura wondered how he'd take the news. They'd always got on so well; she felt he'd be a good person to tell. Only one way to find out. 'Jess has been diagnosed with anorexia. I've known she hasn't been right for ages but I guess I was in denial. As was her father.' She sighed. 'And Jess. She doesn't seem to want to get better, or even admit there's anything wrong.'

Ben glanced at her and they walked on in silence, while Laura thought she'd blown it. Then he said, 'I'm so sorry, Laura. And I do understand a bit of what you're going through. My ex-wife's sister had anorexia and getting her to admit she needed help was hard.'

Laura fell into step beside him, glad they were talking easily again. He felt like the old Ben who she knew she could trust. 'What happened? I mean, is she OK?'

'She is now; she saw a really good therapist. I can get the details if you like.'

Laura looked at him, filled with a sudden sense of hope. Of possibility. 'Yes please. What was the therapist's name?'

'I can't remember, but I'll ask Kathy.'

'That would be amazing.' Laura felt as if someone had suddenly handed her an Olympic Gold medal. 'What happened? Was she very ill?'

'She was pretty ill at her worst; it was terrifying to see, so I sympathise. But the therapist really helped her.'

'Was that NHS or private?'

'Private. But she got help with the fees. I'll find out and let you know.'

'Thanks so much.' Laura felt as if she'd been in a washing machine on fast spin, with all her problems spinning around her. She'd come to the end of the cycle, and someone had pulled open the door and shaken her out. 'Wow,' she said, as it dawned on her. 'The idea that someone might be able to help Jess … it's the best news ever.'

As the timer went off, Laura took the broccoli dish out of the oven and caught Jess's expression. She was eyeing the dish as if it were a bomb about to go off at any minute. The two of them sat down, Laura placed a small amount on a plate for Jess and handed it over.

'It's too much, Mum.'

Laura eyed the pitifully tiny portion. 'You need to eat something. How are you going to be able to clean with no energy?'

Jess stared at the food as if it contained poison. She put a miniscule amount on her fork, glared at it, then finally swallowed. She pushed the rest of the food around her plate. Laura ate a few mouthfuls while trying not to look at her daughter's bony hand clutching the fork. They ate in silence, or rather, Laura ate a few mouthfuls that stuck in her throat, while Jess pushed the food around her plate. The clock on the wall ticked, ominously.

At last Laura could stand it no longer. 'Come on, Jess. Just a few mouthfuls?'

'You want to make me fat.'

'I don't; I just want to see you well. Be warm. Have some energy.'

'You don't. And I'm perfectly all right. Just leave me alone, you're always nagging.' Jess's voice rose to a shriek.

'I don't want to nag, but please will you eat something?'

'No!' Jess flung her fork down. 'It's horrible food anyway. It'll make me bloated and fat. Fat, Mum, FAT.' She got up and pushed her plate along the table. It fell off the other side and tinkled onto the floor, shards of white china and broccoli littering the floor. Jess glared at her mother. 'I will not eat that crap. So LEAVE ME ALONE!'

Laura glanced round to make sure Eddie didn't get near any splinters of china. She stood up, heart thudding. 'Jess, please…'

'I'm going over to Emma's.' She pushed past Laura and ran out of the door.

Laura was shaking as she shooed Eddie away, got a dustpan and brush and started picking up the bits of china and left over food. She wrapped it all in newspaper, dumped it in the bin and washed the floor, wishing that the monster who had taken over her daughter would be abducted by aliens.

She slumped into a chair, thought of Ben's sister-in-law, and the therapist. But how could anyone help Jess, given the state she was in?

Diary of Jessica Kate Hocking

15 November 2023

Dad,

I'm working so hard now, for my mocks. I'm so behind it's scary and such hard work. But Emma insists I go out with her sometimes. Tomorrow she's going to a party and says I must go with her: a girl she's keen on has also been invited, so she's all excited. I don't drink alcohol: it makes me feel really weird and it's full of calories, and I'm terrified I might stuff my face afterwards. But Ryan might be there so I might have a vodka... He and Lily are definitely not seeing each other, E says. I thought he liked me, so why is he ignoring me? What have I done wrong?

Everywhere I look, there's pressure. Teachers are going on about exams all the time, and Mum's always going on about food, plus I have to do all my exercises every day and post on my socials, and I can't think straight.

I need to lose more weight: that's the only thing that makes me feel better. I'm so tired, though, and can't sleep: food tortures me all the time. *If I carry on fighting, perhaps I can shut down the hunger. Weak, weak, must fight it.*

My tummy feels so empty sometimes I wonder if it will touch my back, though I know it can't really. Eating makes me feel dirty, but being empty is a really good, pure feeling and I feel clean inside. When I think of all that food I used to eat, I feel sick. How revolting. Being fat must be the worst thing ever and I will never, ever be fat. I'd rather die.

On good days, when I've lost weight, I feel like I'm part of a kind of elite club; I post on my socials and my followers like my posts and I feel great. But some people post really crazy stuff (before it gets deleted) and that scares me.

I feel so guilty whenever I eat anything now, I wish I could do without food altogether. Some days I feel so helpless, and I get so tired when I've done all my exercises after tea, that I go upstairs and cry. I could never admit that online.

I wish I could tell someone how I really feel, but no one would understand.

27 November 2023

Dad,

You seemed so angry when we met on Saturday, but I can't help what's happened. Like, why did you leave us in the first place? Don't you see this is all your fault?

My hands and feet are always freezing and my hair's falling out in handfuls. I didn't think Mum had noticed till she said how lovely and glossy my hair used to be, and now it's all lank and dull. Thanks, Mum. Make me feel better, won't you?

Tried really hard to eat tea but all I can think of is how fat it will make me. I have a huge lump in my throat now so it really hurts to swallow.

Is this how life will be? I can see Mum getting upset and hate myself even more for what I'm doing to her, but what else can I do? I so wish you were still here, Dad.

Ryan shouted across the canteen that Lily is minging and ugly and that's such a shitty thing to say, I almost didn't want to see him.

At least we're going to see Gran for Xmas. Can't be worse than being here.

I hate this life but don't know what to do. Both school and Mum keep going on about getting help but I'm scared of this thing gnawing away inside me. Can't sleep. I'm so frightened of eating anything now, I might blow up. Feel pathetic and disgusting. And FAT FAT FAT. Hate myself so much. Can't concentrate at school. Hate everything.

I sometimes wonder if it'd help if Mum read this. She might understand how I feel and that would be almost a relief. But if I don't understand, how the hell could she?

Chapter Twenty-Four

Laura

A buzz alerted Laura to a text. To her surprise it was Ben. *Got details of therapist for Jess. Could meet this eve? 7pm in Blue Anchor? xx*

Laura smiled. Hearing from Ben made her feel better, and she was so grateful they could have a good solid friendship after a rocky ending all those years ago.

Later, as she walked to meet Ben, Laura felt comforted by Eddie's soft snorts as he trotted beside her, stopping to sniff a lamp post or street corner. She'd always enjoyed seeing the way light spilled out from other people's houses, lighting up the unseen. She noticed a seagull eyeing the contents of a dustbin and wished she'd worn a scarf: it felt colder tonight.

The Blue Anchor loomed up out of the foggy evening: a 13th century pub where beer had been brewed on the premises for hundreds of years. The same battered sign creaked in the wind, the blue paint on the windowsills had always been chipped and weatherbeaten, but inside was like a dark, comforting womb. There were several small bars where locals supped beer, exchanged banter and treated everyone as friends. Especially dogs.

Inside it smelt of woodsmoke and yeasty beer. Laura peered into the first bar, where she and Ben sometimes drank when they were teenagers. It had been a great place to discuss the meaning of life over pints of cider. She noticed a young lad in a corner, knees tucked up under his chin as he read his book, undisturbed and sipping a pint. She felt eighteen again as she moved across the dark room, checking each cubbyhole.

Then she saw Ben, sitting at a corner table by the log fire, a pint on the table in front of him. He smiled as she walked over, trying to still her sudden nerves.

'Laura, lovely to see you. What can I get you?'

'Half of cider, please.'

Laura took off her gloves and coat while Ben went to get her drink. He seemed taller than she remembered, his long denim-clad legs seemed to go on forever, and his shoulders looked comfortingly broad and strong under his navy fishing sweater. He exchanged a laugh with the man behind the bar and reappeared with her drink and a couple of packets of crisps. 'Don't know about you, but I haven't had time to eat this evening.'

'Thanks,' Laura said, who'd been planning on cheese on toast when she got in.

'How's Jess?'

Laura sipped her cider. 'Well, she's…' She struggled to find anything positive. 'She's not at all well.'

'I remember what it was like when Evie, my sister-in-law, was ill. It's awful seeing someone you're fond of go downhill so fast. It takes over, doesn't it?' Ben pushed a piece of paper over the table. 'Here are the contact details of Evie's therapist. She works at an NHS practice and a private one, apparently.'

'Thanks so much.' Laura pulled out her own file in which she had printed off relevant sites concerning NHS help for adolescents with eating disorders in Cornwall. 'Anna found out that a new mental health clinic is opening in Truro. I don't want to get my hopes up, but it would be amazing if Jess could get in there.'

'Wouldn't it? Is she on the referral list?'

'Not yet. We've been to see the GP several times but Jess has to agree to get help, and so far she hasn't.'

'Fingers crossed that she changes her mind. That was the difficult bit with Evie. Kathy and her mum spent hours talking about ways to make her realise she needed help.' He paused. 'I remember how exhausting it all was. You must be shattered.'

His kind consideration was almost too much. Laura was always bone shatteringly depleted but tried not to acknowledge it, in case it got the better of her. 'I am a bit.' She smiled. 'So what happened with Evie?'

Ben stretched his long legs out towards the fire. 'Apparently she was fine till she was about fourteen. Then she got in with a group of girls who were always talking about who'd lost how much weight, how many meals they'd skipped. Kathy was at university so she didn't realise what was happening till she came back for the holidays.'

'How long was Evie ill?'

'Several years.'

'And did she… I mean, how bad was she?'

Ben reached for his pint. 'I'll never forget seeing these huge dark eyes in a white face over a black baggy jumper. But I didn't realise just how ill she was because she always wore loads of layers to disguise how thin she was.' He looked up. 'Does this sound familiar?'

Laura nodded as similar images of Jess flooded her mind.

'She was just… skeletal, and if she reached for something, you'd see this awful twig-like wrist poking out from a big woolly sleeve…' His voice tailed off as he looked at Laura. 'Sorry, is this a bit close to the mark?'

'Yes, but it's a relief to talk to someone who knows what it's like and doesn't try to pretend it's OK.' She paused. 'Did Evie get help from her GP?'

'She refused at first. Kathy said mealtimes were like a war zone, when Evie was either shouting and refusing to eat, or watching every forkful everyone put into their mouths like a starving dog. That went on for several years, and we were all worried sick.'

Laura shuddered. 'I know the feeling. So what made her want to get better?'

Ben opened a packet of crisps, pushed them towards Laura. 'Help yourself.' He took a few and crunched them thoughtfully. 'She fainted at school. She was taken to her GP who said she'd have to go to hospital. Evie begged and pleaded for a bit more time, and eventually agreed to see a counsellor, who said she'd have to put on some weight. That was preferable to going into hospital where, of course, she would have to eat.'

'And the counsellor helped?' Laura could hear the desperate hope leaking through her voice.

'Not immediately. She saw this woman for several months before there was any breakthrough.'

'So what happened?'

'Well, two things. Firstly, they discovered that Evie was autistic and apparently anorexia is more common among people on the autistic spectrum. Then she met another anorexic called Becky, and they became really close and they helped each other.'

'I'm glad Evie found such a good friend.' Was Jess on the autistic spectrum? Surely she would have realised by now?

'It seems really difficult to get through to anorexics; it's as if the disease takes over their minds as well as their bodies.'

Laura nodded. 'They can't see how dangerously ill they are.'

'Exactly. But Evie said she trusted this therapist and she also trusted Becky. Trust was really important for Evie, and I think both these women made her feel valued for the first time. So she had something to live for.'

Laura nodded. 'That makes sense. Jess has made good friends with a girl called Emma. There's a noticeable difference in her. I mean, she's still not eating but she seems a bit better in herself.'

'That's a good start.'

Laura bit her lip. 'Trouble is, she's still losing weight, I'm sure.' She glanced round the pub, saw a couple in a nearby booth eating steaks. It seemed another lifetime since she and Chris had eaten in a pub.

'Didn't her GP think Jess was too thin?' Ben pushed his fringe back in a gesture Laura remembered of old.

'Yes, but apparently she isn't thin enough.' Laura shook her head. 'It's crazy: her life needs to be in danger before she's hospitalised. And until they open the unit in Truro, there aren't any provisions for teenagers with eating disorders in Cornwall. The nearest unit is in Exeter, which is a three-hour train ride from here.'

Ben took a swallow of beer. 'It's shocking, isn't it? I

really hope Jess will agree to see this counsellor, and that she can get an appointment soon.'

'She's going to stay with my mum next weekend. They're very close, so I'm hoping Mum might be able to make her realise how much she needs help.'

'I always liked your mum. How is she nowadays?'

Laura smiled. 'She moved to north Cornwall about six years ago and reinvented herself. She bought a cottage near St Mabyn, discovered a passion for pottery, and now sells her work online. She's joined a book club, a philosophy group, goes to the quiz nights in the pub every Wednesday and now she's dating someone called Michael.'

'What a role model!' Ben laughed. 'And possibly just the right person to speak to Jess. I've always thought of your mum as being very loving and understanding.'

Ben's eyes crinkled up when he smiled and Laura noticed his laughter lines. 'You're right, she is all those things, but she can be prickly, very independent and bolshie.'

'Bit like someone else I know.' Ben's eyes twinkled. But before Laura could reply, he added, 'I'd like to see her pottery. Has she got a website?'

'Yes, just look up Merryn Hocking.'

Ben grinned. 'I will. You must be very proud of her.'

Laura smiled, pleased that her mother had achieved so much, and glad that Ben recognised it straight away. 'Yes, I am. Considering she didn't start working as a potter till she was in her late fifties, she's learned so much, and done so well. Her moving to north Cornwall was good for both of us. She stopped being so dependent on me and we appreciate each other much more now. She's been incredibly understanding and supportive about Jess.'

'Good. Let's hope they can work something out this weekend.'

Laura nodded and sipped her cider. 'How's it going at work?'

'Good thanks. I'm having an open night and first day of viewing the week after next, for my first sale. That's antiques, fine art and jewellery, though there'll be a general sale on the first day, too.'

'Sounds a good idea to get the punters in. Like a private view?'

'Exactly. It's amazing what some people will do for a free glass of wine!'

'Yes, I found that out at the gallery.' She gestured towards his glass. 'Another pint?'

'A half, thanks very much. It's Doom.' Ben handed her his glass.

Laura glanced around the pub as she waited at the bar, greeted a few locals, and was glad that Ben had suggested meeting here. A man she knew was teaching his dog to jump for dog biscuits. A group of elderly men sat by the window in earnest discussion then burst into peals of laughter.

The drinks arrived and Laura took them to the table. 'So how did you get into auctions? Something to do with the wine business I think you said?'

Ben settled back in his chair. 'Yes. I went to join Ian picking grapes in France. It was backbreaking but we drank lots of cheap wine. It tasted vile but we were past caring.' He smiled. 'It was fun though, and helped my French a lot. More importantly it took my mind off you.'

Laura stared at him. Had he really been as unhappy as she had? She looked down, unsure what to say.

'After a while the father of the family who owned the

vineyard asked if I'd like to learn more about wine,' Ben continued. 'So he taught me about the business, then later he taught me about fine wine and that led to meeting a friend of theirs who was in the auction business. And it went from there.'

'So if I ever find an old bottle of French wine I know who to ask?' Laura smiled and turned away from the fire; she could feel her face burning.

Ben grinned. 'Absolutely. Not just French wine, either. But you know I love history and antiques, so it all sort of melded together. I found a career that I love, so I'm very lucky.' He paused. 'Have you been to France?'

Laura nodded. 'We went camping a few times, down in the south. There was a pool and a bar and plenty of children for Jess to play with.'

'I think I told you my mate Ian and his girlfriend bought this house in North West France – Pays de la Loire – which was a real wreck. They've done amazing things with it and I go over whenever I can to help them.'

'Good for you,' Laura said. 'So, are you pleased with how your first auction is going? I suppose there's a lot to do.'

'Yes, we're really busy and I could do with more help, but I can't afford to pay anyone else. Tanya's very efficient, but she's got a young family so she has to be home to collect the kids from school.' He glanced at his watch. 'I should be getting back soon. I've got more to do tonight.'

'I could help,' said Laura. 'If you've got any leaflets, I could distribute some around town.'

'That would be great, thanks, Laura.' Ben smiled slowly. 'I know how time consuming it is looking after someone who's so unwell.'

'Be nice to think about something else,' Laura said. 'I

could share posts on social media, put up a poster in our window, if that would help.'

'That would be fantastic. We've got some good pieces so I'm hoping we'll at least break even.'

Laura drained her cider. 'It must be difficult when you see really lovely stuff then have to sell it.' She paused. 'I've always loved old things – imagining who owned them and why and when they were bought. Everything's got a story, hasn't it?'

Ben nodded. 'Yes, that's what I love about my job. It's very sensory, too: the musty smell of old books, the dustiness of old furniture. Sometimes you get a faint whiff of someone's perfume in a wardrobe, or find a shopping list in a book and I love all that; it makes the things so personal. And I enjoy meeting the sellers and hearing their stories. Sometimes you can get a good price for something that might not look valuable but means a huge amount emotionally.'

'That must be very powerful.'

'Yes, and no two days are ever the same. I'm dealing not only with someone's history but when a piece goes on to have another life, with a different owner, that's its future as well. It's fascinating seeing what comes in, how precious it is to some people, whereas others couldn't care less. Some people accord such love and care to their relatives' belongings, I always reassure them that we'll make sure they go to a good home. Which we can't always do, but I want to do the best I can for them.' He stopped, as if embarrassed, and cleared his throat. 'But you must know all about that from selling paintings.'

Laura nodded. 'Yes, it's great when you find a home for a piece of work you really like.'

A pause, then Ben looked at her. 'Well, I'd better be off.' He seemed reluctant to go.

'I'll definitely come to the sale.'

'And the viewings, I hope,' said Ben, getting up. 'I'm doing a mass leaflet drop and emailing everyone as I need a good turnout.' He put his jacket on. 'Can I give you a lift home?'

'No it's OK, thanks. Eddie and I will enjoy the walk home.' She stood up. 'Thanks so much for the information about Evie's counsellor.'

'Not at all, glad to help.' At that moment his phone pinged. He looked down. 'Damn, I'd better go.' He was brisk and businesslike all of a sudden. 'Bye, Laura. Best of luck. Excuse me, I must dash.' And he disappeared out of the door.

Laura and Eddie walked home under street lights casting pools of warm light, listening to the clinking halyards from moored boats in the harbour. Watching Eddie bolt a discarded bit of pasty, Laura smiled. Who would have believed that so many years on, Ben would reappear as a good mate just when she needed one, and also come up with a possible counsellor for Jess? Here, at last, was hope. If only Jess would agree.

Chapter Twenty-Five

December 2023

Jess

Got a message from Ryan first thing. *How about a game of pool? Just you and me. R XX*

I was sitting in maths and could feel myself blushing, even though no one else could see. I should have waited, but I typed back *OK. XX* and spent the rest of the day feeling sick and excited. Was this a date? Did that mean he still liked me? I know lots of boys use girls for their bodies; well, that's what Emma said. They lead you on and if your body isn't perfect, they drop you. I couldn't bear that, but I don't have a perfect body, so what would I do?

This evening was the last photography class before Christmas, and Nick slid into the seat beside me. I panicked in case Ryan came in cos sometimes he sits next to me. OMG what to do? But Nick smiled and there's something about him that makes me feel so much better about… everything really.

I smiled back and then Mr T came in so we had to shut up.

'This evening we'll concentrate on the use of a subject in the foreground to help composition,' he said.

Instantly I thought of an ad on TV. A heaped table of food with a smiling family in the background. You can't get away from food, it's everywhere and it haunts me at night when I can't sleep.

'That Christmas ad with the huge turkey,' I whispered to Nick.

He nodded. 'With all the trimmings. You get that at home?'

I shook my head. 'Well, we used to when Dad was with us. Not now.'

Nick stared out of the window thoughtfully. 'Neither Dad nor I are into cooking so we don't bother much.'

'That's why you're so skinny,' I said with a blast of envy. Imagine not having to eat.

'I'm always hungry,' he said. 'A real home-cooked roast would be ace.'

I wanted to say he could have my food any day, but I realised I was lucky to have a mum who cooked, even if I couldn't eat it. 'What happened to your mum?'

Nick drew his attention back from the window. 'She died two years ago. Cancer,' he said shortly.

I stared at him. Poor thing; I couldn't imagine life without Mum. No wonder he always looked so scruffy. 'What does your dad do?'

'He's a paramedic,' he said. 'He works shifts so I've learned to look after myself.' And the way he said it meant he didn't want anyone feeling sorry for him. I felt bad then, and wished I could invite him round for a meal. Before all this, I would have done. But I couldn't now.

'What do you do in the holidays?' I said.

'Go out with my camera. I like walking,' he said. 'I wish we had a dog but we're both out all day so it wouldn't be fair.'

'We've got one.' I pulled out my phone and showed him a picture of Eddie. 'He's lovely. We go walking a lot.' Should I ask Nick if he wanted to join us? It'd be really cool if he did. But he'd probably say no.

Nick laughed. 'He's great. Well, if ever you want company on a walk, let me know. I can give you my number.'

I looked at him and smiled. A big smile that I could feel stretching across my face. 'That'd be really cool,' I said.

Chapter Twenty-Six

Laura

'Laura?' Anna's voice echoed down the phone, into the dark room. 'Laura? Are you OK?'

'Yeah, I'm fine.' Laura's head was racing, she felt panicky, on the verge of tears.

'No you're not. What is it?'

Laura gulped, tried not to cry. 'It's these endless battles with Jess over food. It's wearing me down. She won't talk to me and screams at me if I try and encourage her to eat. She even shouted at Chris and Kayla last weekend, apparently. Chris was horrified.'

'Good. Serves him right.'

'The other evening I took some clothes into Jess's room when she was changing after school, and you wouldn't believe the abuse that followed. I mean, I'm no prude, as you know, but even I was shocked, and I'm used to her outbursts.'

'Oh Laura, I'm so sorry.'

Laura shut her eyes, as if to blank out the image of her skeletal daughter. 'I only saw her from behind, but I could literally count every vertebrae. And her ribs… I don't know how she keeps going.' She shook her head. 'But the good news is that I've got details of a therapist who helped Ben's sister-in-law when she was anorexic, so I've just got to try and get Jess to agree to see her.' Talking about it lifted her spirits – she *would* find a way.

'That's great news. I know it's difficult to find the right person. What about the school?'

'They're keeping a close eye on her which is good. They've said whenever she gets too tired or overwhelmed – which apparently she does, though of course she doesn't tell me – she can go into a support building and see their counsellor, Mel, who Jess likes.'

'I'm glad they're on the case. And I've got some promising news. You know that new clinic for teenagers suffering from mental health problems is opening at the hospital? Well, they've asked me to help oversee recruiting staff and also to work with the teenagers. You know I did that stint at the place in London and really enjoyed it.'

'That's brilliant news, Anna! I'm so proud of you.'

'Thanks. But what I was thinking is, why not ask your GP for a referral?'

Laura saw a glimmer of hope. 'Good idea, Anna. Thanks. Though I don't think Jess would agree to go.'

'If you saw your GP without Jess, and Jess is on the referral list for CAMHS, I would have thought she could refer her to the clinic.'

'Great, I'll try that,' Laura said. 'I'll try anything.' She smiled faintly. 'Though I promise not to sell my body.'

'Thank God for that!' Anna chuckled. 'You're making headway, well done. So when's Merryn coming?'

'She's driving down on Friday, staying overnight and taking us up there on Christmas Eve. Jess and Mum usually get on well, but Jess is so volatile at the moment, it's like walking a bloody tightrope.' She sighed. 'Sorry, I keep whinging.'

'Not at all. You must be exhausted. Can I help at all?'

'No thanks. It's just lovely hearing that work's going so well for you. You really deserve it.'

'Thanks, Laura. So you saw Ben? Are things OK there?'

'Yes, we met for a drink and had a good friendly chat. It felt… easy. No complications. Just what I need.'

'That's great news. What's he up to?'

'He's set up an auction house, lives on a boat, is divorced and looks after his son part time.' There was a comfortable silence while Laura considered Ben's situation.

'He was so in love with you,' Anna said gently.

Laura snorted. 'If he was so in love, why did he rush off so I never heard from him again?'

'Because he thought you were with Chris.' Anna laughed. 'You were so stubborn, you two. But how do you feel about him now?'

'We're different people.'

'Nothing to stop you being friends, is there?'

'No.' She smiled. 'No, not at all. I hope we can. We always got on so well.'

'Good – let's hope he feels the same way. We all need friends, and male friends are always a bonus.' Anna paused. 'Well, I'd better go. But we'll meet when you get back from Merryn's – come for supper?'

'I'd love to. Thanks, Anna. Have a good evening.' Laura

glanced over at Eddie, snoring in his basket. It was more than two years since she'd lived with Chris; a life that belonged to another woman altogether. (Good luck, Kayla, she thought viciously.) She wasn't sure who she was anymore. But, Ben or no Ben, she did know that she would find it very difficult to trust anyone, ever again.

Chapter Twenty-Seven

23 December 2023

Jess

'Dad's picking me up early, OK?'

Mum looked at me.' Are you OK about that?'

'Course. It's Saturday. Why shouldn't he pick me up?'

Laura shook her head. 'No reason, darling. What are you doing, do you know? Photography?'

I shrugged. 'I hope so. But he said something about having to go to Bodmin after to see Kayla's family or something. So I don't suppose we'll be long.' I didn't want to see Mum's disappointment, so I looked down at the floor, kicked a bit of lino with my Doc Martens. 'I don't know why we can't have Saturdays together like we used to.'

'I know.' Mum sighed. 'I wish you could, too. I'm so sorry, darling.'

She moved towards me like she wanted a hug but I pulled back quickly. I don't like anyone to touch me, to know how much weight I've lost. That's private. 'Oh, there he is. See you later, Mum,' and I hurried out of the house, clutching my rucksack.

When I got in the car Dad gave me a kiss. 'You OK, Jessie?'

It was ages since he'd called me that, and I felt tears sting my eyes. Why did I feel so weepy all the time? 'Yeah, fine.'

I could feel him looking at me, like he knew I wasn't OK, but was too worried to ask more. The silence lay thick and heavy between us. I could feel it growing and growing, and wanted to prick it like a balloon. Tension went straight to my stomach.

'Since when have you worn make-up?' he said.

I could feel myself going red. 'Everyone wears it,' I said. 'It's only concealer, bronzer and stuff – to look natural.' That's what I'd heard other girls saying anyway.

There was a long pause, then Dad said, 'Well, we've got to go and see Kayla's aunt later, so I thought we could give you our presents and have some brunch at that café we used to go to. I've booked a table for 11am, OK?'

He sounded too loud, too false, like booking a table at what had once been my favourite café, years ago, would smooth out all his cock-ups. Falling in love with another woman. Breaking up the family home. Ruining everything.

And now I had to cope with another bloody meal. Usually on Saturdays, we took pictures which kept me sane. It was nothing to do with food. I could feel a tight band stretching over my forehead. It would slither down my throat like slime and swirl around in my stomach, stopping any food going down. But what could I say?

I watched Dad as he drove, his hands broad on the steering wheel. He reached over and patted my knee, like he did when I was little. 'You're going to Merryn's for Christmas?'

'Yes. She's coming down tomorrow.' I wasn't going to ask what he was doing. I watched as he pulled into the street where the café was. He found a parking space straight away, which meant more time in the café.

'We're going to Kayla's aunt's, then on to see her brother. Busy time!'

I wanted to say, he should have stayed with us, but he was out of the car and walking down the street. 'Kayla's doing some last-minute shopping, then she'll meet us here. I've got strict instructions about what she wants to eat!' Dad looked at me and made a face. I used to laugh but my face felt frozen. Everything was building up inside me like a tidal wave, threatening to drown me. And yet I knew I couldn't tell Dad. He'd think I was bonkers. Everyone else was just so chilled about Christmas, with all the food, and sitting around for days just eating and drinking. How could they?

I bit my lip, something I used to tell Mum off for doing. Was it catching? Perhaps if I bit extra hard, it would stop me thinking about all those meals and snacks and – ow – I bit rather hard and felt the metallic taste of blood in my mouth.

'Here we are,' said Dad, holding open the café door. 'In we go.'

I felt like someone on death row, whereas he looked so pleased with himself, telling the waitress that he'd booked a table for three at 11 o'clock. She showed us to the table and put big cardboard menus in front of us. I tried not to look at mine, but Dad was busy pretending nothing was the matter.

'Right then, Jessie, what will you have? You always loved eggs Benedict. How about that?'

I froze. The thought of all those calories: muffins,

hollandaise sauce... I glanced at the menu, saw with a fascinated horror that each dish had the calories next to it. Eggs Benedict had... *how many?* Everything was just piled with calories. What the hell could I have? Or rather, not have. Fresh fruit salad. That was the least damaging.

'I've already had a sarnie,' I said. 'I'm not hungry.'

Dad's face fell. 'I thought we could have brunch, like we always used to,' he said.

I glared at him. 'Things aren't anything like they used to be.' *And we know whose fault that is*, went unsaid.

He shifted in his seat, glanced at his watch. 'I've just got time to have a full English before Kayla gets here.' He smiled at me and winked. 'Sure you won't change your mind, Jess? Be nice to eat together again.'

I shook my head, gave what I hoped was a convincing smile. 'No, I'm fine, Dad, but you go ahead.'

He got up looking like a naughty boy, hurried to the counter and gave his order. Then he came back with a latte for himself and a peppermint tea for me.

'How's the diet going, Dad?' I couldn't resist saying.

He looked a bit sheepish. 'I've always eaten meat, so I don't think it does any harm to have it occasionally. Does it?' He didn't seem to require an answer, cos he leaned forward and said, 'She's great, Kayla, but she's a bit obsessive about what we eat. It's got to be organic, vegan, though actually she did agree to have some salmon the other day. But she's very strict. Quite right of course. Got to maintain her looks and her body image.'

I raised my eyebrows. That was obviously Kayla speaking. Dad would never use words like 'maintain looks' and 'body image'. 'Yeah,' I managed, wrapping my cold hands round my mug. 'I guess it's important for her business.'

'Absolutely.' Dad glanced up as the waitress appeared with a huge plate of cholesterol for him. He glanced at me. 'I ordered you fruit salad. I know you like fruit.'

The steel band round my head tightened another few notches and I felt like screaming. Why was everyone trying to force food down me? 'Fruit salad?' The waitress put it down in front of me. I breathed in, trying to gather courage. Fruit wasn't so bad, and I needn't eat much of it.

But as she set the bowl down in front of me, I saw that cream had been poured all over it and hot panic rushed to my face. How could I possibly eat that? I stared at it, then looked out of the window, felt like running away. 'Got to go to the ladies.' I hurried off, leaving Dad tucking in to his plateful while I rushed into the toilets and slammed the door behind me.

I sat on the loo and bent over, hugging myself. I couldn't go back out there. But I had to. Dad would be wondering what on earth was happening. He'd come and find me. Ask why I wasn't tucking into bloody fruit salad with cream of all things. Shit and shit and shit. What was I going to do? We had another fifteen minutes before Kayla arrived, and I wasn't sure if she'd make things better or worse.

Slowly I straightened, got up and did some squats to try and steady my nerves. I looked at myself in the mirror: fat face, bulging cheeks, hair that looked straighter and thinner than it used to. I took a deep breath and let it out slowly, preparing to do battle.

Then my phone pinged. It was a text from Nick. *Walk sometime after Xmas?*

I gave a sigh of relief. This felt like a godsend. I could escape and meet Nick. *That would be great. Will text when we're back from my gran's. See you soon!*

In reply I got a thumbs up and instantly felt my stress

levels go down. I took some more deep breaths, and when I got back to the table, Dad was busy wiping his plate with bread and butter. WTF? He looked sheepish but grinned and said, 'Hope you don't mind, but I wanted to finish before Kayla got here.'

'No problem,' I said, glad I didn't have to watch him eat. 'Oh look, here she is.' I pointed outside. Through the window, we could see her striding down the street, talking on her phone.

'Phew.' Dad got up quickly and took his plate to the counter before hurrying back. He waved as Kayla came in; she was still on her phone but waved back and made her way to our table, where I heard the end of a conversation about yoga before she ended the call.

She leaned forward and gave me a kiss on each cheek; who does that? Then turned to Dad. 'You had some brunch, babe?'

Dad nodded, looking like a schoolboy who'd been caught eating sweets, but Kayla didn't appear to notice. She didn't know him that well, then.

'I'll have the small vegan breakfast and a chai latte with oat milk, please,' she said to the waitress, then she sat down and smiled. 'Hi, Jess, sorry about that, got caught up with a client. You know how it is.'

How could I? I was still at school for God's sake.

'Everything good?' She didn't wait for an answer but carried on. 'I spent ages trying to decide what to get you for Christmas, but I think I've got just the right thing.' She smiled.

'Thanks,' I said uncertainly. 'Mum said I wasn't to worry about getting a present for you cos we can't afford it.' I glared at Dad.

'No. Quite right,' he said. 'But we can still give you something.'

'Something special, you know?' Kayla looked all hopeful.

I hated it when expectations were raised. Now I was going to have to pretend I loved it. My stomach churned uneasily while Kayla pulled out a bag that contained several of those patterned present bags. She handed it over with a glance at Dad, and sat back while her chai latte arrived.

I peered inside, pulled out the contents of the first bag. A bottle of some vile-looking green juice.

'That contains all your vitamins and minerals; stops you getting tired,' Kayla said.

'Thanks.' I put it to one side. At least Emma and I could laugh over it later. Next came a card, which I opened cautiously. This contained a voucher to a spa near Penzance.

'It's just opened and belongs to a client of mine,' Kayla said. 'You can have a massage, a swim and lunch in their vegan restaurant.'

So it was a freebie? I didn't like the idea of anyone seeing me naked, let alone touching me. And as for eating anywhere, forget it. 'Thanks,' I said. I'd give it to Anna or Mum.

'Very thoughtful,' said Dad, smiling proudly.

'I thought we could go together.' Kayla beamed. 'Have a girls' day out.'

No way... I forced a smile. 'I'll save it till after my exams,' I said, though they weren't until after Easter.

'The last one's from me,' said Dad and I turned to him with some relief. Surely he would have come up with something I might actually enjoy? He pushed another envelope over the table. Slowly I opened it. A card in his writing, from him and Kayla. Another voucher but this time for a photography shop in Truro. Dad and I had been there and they sold everything you could think of. It was ace.

'Thanks, Dad. That's amazing.' I leaned forward and kissed his cheek, which was warm, smooth to the touch and smelt reassuringly of his old aftershave. 'Thanks, Kayla,' I added, as she looked a bit left out.

'I thought we could have a day out in Truro after Christmas. Have some lunch, go to the museum, get some equipment from the shop.'

'Yeah,' I said. At last, a day out with Dad. I could skip lunch.

'And Kayla can come along too,' Dad said. 'If she has time.'

Kayla smiled, then perhaps thought better of it, for she said, 'You two have your day together. Jess and I can have our spa day another time.' She smiled when her food arrived and checked her watch. 'We should leave in twenty minutes, babe. Don't want to be late.'

Considering she was always going on about being relaxed and chilled, especially during meals, I nearly laughed, but she cleared her plate in record time, then looked over at my fruit salad that loomed, untouched, in its bowl. 'Better eat that, Jess. Fruit's good for energy, you know?'

I didn't like her tone, nor did I intend to eat any of it. Especially not when she spoke to me like that. 'I didn't realise we were having brunch,' I said. 'I had a bacon sarnie at home.'

Kayla frowned. 'You have to eat something, sweetie,' she said. 'Your dad's been looking forward to this all week.'

I nearly said, so what? But managed to stop myself. 'I'm not hungry.'

'Have some of the spirulina,' Kayla said in a wheedling tone that got my back up. 'It's ever so good for you.'

'No thanks.' I put the presents on the floor and glared at her.

'I went to a lot of trouble to get that,' she said, and for some reason her little girl voice really annoyed me.

'Well don't bother,' I snapped.

'Jess! Apologise at once!'

I looked at Dad and then Kayla, whose face had gone blotchy through her foundation. She looked mad; so did he. And suddenly the wave crashed, and everything from the last few months came and knocked me over. 'I didn't want to come here,' I cried and my voice sounded all wobbly and pathetic. 'I didn't want brunch and I didn't want any presents. I just want things to be back to how they were.'

Dad didn't seem to realise how much shit he'd created by going off with Kayla. And why did she go after a bloke who was much too old for her and already had a partner and teenage daughter? It was her fault as well.

'I can't turn the clock back,' Dad said. 'I met Kayla and we fell in love. I'm not apologising for that. Now will you please eat your fruit salad and we can go.' He glared at me. 'We're not going until you've eaten it. All of it.'

That was it. I stood up and grabbed my rucksack. 'I am *not* eating it,' I said. 'I didn't ask for it and I don't want it.' I shoved the table forwards, the bottle of green stuff wobbled and fell over, crashing onto the floor with satisfying splinters of glass and what looked like sick flooding everywhere.

Kayla wailed, Dad shouted, and I ran like hell out of the café, down the street to the bus stop. I was shaking all over and felt hot, salty tears dripping down my face into my mouth. Why was everything going so wrong? Why did it all feel out of control?

S L Rosewarne

I grabbed my phone, sent Nick a text asking if he was free. He always made me feel better. He texted straight back. *Sorry, busy with Dad today. But ring any time you like. And see you after Xmas, OK?*

And while I knew I wouldn't ring, that message was so cool, it was as if he was on my side. I wasn't on my own. That made me feel warm all over.

Chapter Twenty-Eight

Christmas Eve

Laura

That night, staying with Merryn, Jess went to bed early while Laura and Merryn sat in the living room with a glass of wine each, staring at the woodburner. Two comfortable armchairs faced the stove, while an old sofa, covered in patchwork blankets, was positioned on the other side of the room. A comfortable atmosphere, with the relaxing smell of woodsmoke and the quiet fizz and crackle of the fire.

Laura felt herself unwinding for the first time in what felt like years. 'The flames are wonderful, aren't they?' she said. 'They're always flickering and dying, changing shape and colours; look, that one was green and then blue.' She wondered if Merryn had had a chat with Jess, but knew better than to ask. She'd tell her when she was ready.

Sure enough, as her mother sipped her Merlot thoughtfully, she said, 'Once we got busy making some pots, it was like seeing the old Jess. She had a quarter of a sandwich for lunch, which I suppose was something.'

'And she didn't throw it up?'

'Not to my knowledge.' Merryn put her glass of wine onto the table next to her. 'She's really excited about this photography trip. And she said several times how much she liked a boy called Ryan.'

'Really? She never tells me.'

'Yes, but I'm not her mother. You never told me when you were her age.'

'I suppose not. What did you say?'

'I said that if she was trying to make an impression, she should feel good about herself. Be confident, and that boys should like her for who she was, instead of trying to be someone she wasn't.'

'Good for you. What did she say to that?'

Merryn stretched her long legs in front of her. 'That she didn't feel very sure of herself, so I said the best thing was to concentrate on doing something she loves, that she's good at.'

'Like starving herself?'

Merryn shrugged. 'Like photography. We spent a long time looking at what she'd done and I told her how talented she is, gave her some tips on composition.'

'That's great. She badly needs to gain confidence.'

Merryn sipped her wine. 'I was wondering if Jess might come and stay with me more often. Give you both a break. And I always love having her.'

'That would be wonderful, thanks, Mum. When would suit you?'

'Any time as long as I'm not in Cardiff.'

'Of course. When are you going?'

'Not quite sure yet. Michael said he'd take me, and we thought we'd turn it into a holiday. I've never been before.'

'How did you meet?'

'Online. Got to be careful about who you meet these days, of course, but he seems genuine enough. He's generous, too.'

Laura stared at her. 'Good for you, Mum. Internet dating; I wouldn't know where to start.'

Her mother winked. 'Open the app and swipe until you find someone you like the look of.' She got up, reached for her glass. 'I'm only sixty-five, you know. About time I got back in the saddle.'

Chapter Twenty-Nine

Jess

Gran's so easy to talk to. She asked about school and boyfriends and I told her about Nick and Emma being my friends, and a bit about Ryan. She looked at me and said, 'Does he make you laugh, darling?'

And I realised he doesn't. He's really fit and when he looks at me with those piercing blue eyes I can't think straight (is that how Mum felt about Dad, I wonder?) but I get nervous around him. He's had loads of girlfriends, and had lots of sex, so why does he bother with me? I didn't ask Gran that, but it was like she knew, cos she said, 'He's very lucky to have a clever, talented girlfriend like you, Jess.' And I felt myself get really hot and had to stare at my feet. Mostly cos Gran never says things just to be nice, so she must really mean it. And that's difficult for me to get my head around, cos I don't feel clever or talented, or anything other than shit, really.

And then Gran looked at me and said, 'It will be all right, darling. I promise.'

And I wasn't sure whether she meant anorexia, or Ryan, or school, or what. But just her saying that gave me hope. Even if she is wrong.

Emma and I message all the time and I'm looking forward to a walk with Nick, and Gran said these are the sort of friends we all need. Mum says we can stay for as long as we want but I want to get back and I've got my date with Ryan though I'm really nervous about that.

Diary of Jessica Kate Hocking

30 December 2023

Dear Dad,

Despite being with Gran, who I love to bits, I'm starting to feel what's the point about everything? We all have to die at some point, and it would make more sense for me to go first. There, I've said it. I've made such a mess of my life and all I do is fuck up.

You might be sad if I went, but you and Mum and Gran are so much stronger and wiser than me. You'd get over it. But I couldn't bear it if anything happened to any of you. I wish I believed in another life, cos then I'd have no qualms. But I don't buy that. It's too slick. And where do all those people go? Doesn't heaven get full? Where's the overflow?

This thing inside me is growing bigger by the day, like cancer spreading through me. It's taking all my energy, all my missing-you energy and turning it against me.

I thought that losing weight was my best friend, was the greatest thing I could do. But I have a horrible feeling it's not my friend at all.

Yet I can't stop it. But I can't tell anyone, not even Emma or Nick. Certainly not Ryan. They'd think I was nuts.

None of the social feeds say anything about this. It's all about how great it is to lose weight. But I can't think straight and I don't know what to do and I can't sleep and I can't tell anyone cos they wouldn't believe me, and I'm really, really frightened.

Best love, Jess xxx

10 January 2024

Dear Dad,

Sometimes, when I'm really exhausted from missing you, missing my old friends, missing Mum (we don't talk like we used to), our old house, and old life, and the old me, I don't have enough energy to feel anything. And that's kind of a relief. What spare time I do have I revise, but I can't concentrate.

I went over to Em's in the holidays and had a few walks with Nick, who loves Eddie. Nick's quiet but funny and he's just so easy to be with. He doesn't care what he looks like and he has a really old phone which is just for texting and calls – he's not into socials at all. And when the others at school call him names, he just ignores them, so they stop. I wish I was like that.

Gran suggested I do a project on Eddie using the pictures of him since he was a puppy. I made a start, but my brain won't work properly. The other day Mum found some photos of me when Eddie was little and I was a toddler. Then suddenly he was a grown-up dog and I was only three. I was grinning even though I was FAT FAT FAT.

Didn't see Ryan cos he's off school with some bug. So he said. Perhaps he doesn't want to see me. It was almost a relief, but I haven't got the energy to be disappointed. Nick doesn't ever mention Ryan but I get the feeling he doesn't like him much, and that bothers me.

Emma's seeing Tessa Strong on the quiet. They had their first kiss a few nights ago and she's all starry-eyed about it. Tessa's in the year below so we don't see her at lessons but E and T keep meeting up at break and I don't want to get in the way. I'd like to get to know T better but she's v sporty so she's often at the gym or doing hockey or athletics. Does Emma wonder about Tessa the same way I wonder about Ryan? Emma's so kind to me – I wish I could stay with her rather than go home. But I worry that our friendship will change now she's with Tessa.

Some days I wake up feeling really fat and bloated and beastly. Those days are terrible because I know nothing's going to make it better. Those are the days when I just want to disappear.

Chapter Thirty

21 January 2024

Jess

'I'm so nervous when I'm with Ryan, my stomach goes all sort of liquid,' I said to Emma. 'Is that how you feel with Tess?' I worried about asking; I'd never talked about this sort of thing before. Ryan and I had only met twice this year. I guess they were dates, cos he kissed me after, both times. I felt him hard against me and that made me nervous cos I don't know if I'm ready for sex.

Emma grinned. 'I don't feel nervous, more really excited. I love kissing her. Is Ryan a good kisser?'

I nodded. 'People say about your knees going weak and I thought that was a stupid cliché. But my legs really do go all wobbly.' Often they go shaky cos I haven't eaten much but that's different. 'I've never wanted to have sex with any of the other boys I've met, but I think maybe I would with Ryan. One day.'

'Everyone else has sex. They all say it's no big deal.' Emma looked at me with her big green eyes. 'I think it should be a big deal though. I mean, what's the point if it doesn't mean anything?'

I nodded. 'That's how I feel, but I guess you don't know till you do it.' I sighed. 'They all seem to want this perfect body. You know, flat stomach and big bum. But I'm not perfect.'

Emma looked at me. 'No one has a perfect body, Jess. That's boys just being really immature and crap.' She leaned forward. 'If you don't feel ready to have sex with Ryan, don't.'

I let out a big breath of relief. 'Thanks,' I said.

'So what did you do with him the other day?'

'We went ten pin bowling with some friends of his and I wasn't very good, but he just laughed and showed me how to do it then they all had cheesy chips.' Ryan gave me one of his, which I spat out in the toilet afterwards. 'It was nice to do something with other people, like I used to do in Newlyn. And we're going to go next week as well. So it seems he really does like me.'

'Of course he does,' said Emma gently. 'You don't need to doubt yourself, Jess. No one else does.'

And she gave me such a lovely smile that I hugged her. I couldn't speak, but that was the nicest thing anyone's said for such a long time.

And then that evening it was Photography Club so I thought I'd ask Mr T about something I'd seen online.

'Do you know Jack Retallack, sir?' I said.

Mr T smiled. 'Of course I do! One of the best photographers of his time. Certainly one of the best Cornish talents. Why?'

'I saw that he's died and some of his work's coming up at a local auction soon.'

'That will be interesting,' he said. 'You like his work?'

I nodded. 'Yeah, and they had some of his prints online, and one of them is of my dad.' I wouldn't normally talk that much to a teacher, but Mr T's different. 'He's a young boy picking mussels on the beach. I mean, only me and Mum and Dad know it's him, but that picture became really famous with his work, and I can't stop thinking about it.'

'If it's that important, you should go to the auction; try and buy it.'

I hadn't considered that, but when I told Emma later, she thinks it's a sign. And the more I think about it, the more I really really want that print. The guide price is £300 but it could go for more, as there are lots of Retallack geeks out there.

'Wouldn't your dad get it for you?'

I shrugged. 'I'm not in his best books at the moment.'

'You can ask, though, can't you? Go on, message him now.'

So I did and held my breath, waiting. I showed her the reply: *Sorry, can't afford that right now.*

'Can't he or is that an excuse?'

I shrugged. 'It's obvious that he doesn't want to pay for it, but that's only made me more determined.'

Emma smiled. 'Good for you!'

'I can't ask Mum. There's the Paris trip to pay for and she's skint. And Gran has already been really generous so I can't ask her.' I frowned. 'I wish I was sixteen then I could work legally.'

'Not long now! But I'll get thinking. Between the two of us I'm sure we'll come up with something,' she said.

I nodded, though it all seems rather unlikely.

I haven't told her, but I've been getting really dizzy and my hair's coming out in handfuls. I'm feeling really crap and frightened and very alone.

I haven't seen much of Nick recently as he does different classes. I miss him. Thank God for Emma.

Chapter Thirty-One

Laura

Laura had phoned Rachel Lomax, the therapist recommended by Ben, and heard a recorded message to say that the counsellor was away for two weeks over the festive period but would be in touch on her return. But she hadn't rung back, so Laura decided to ring her again. After another hour spent online looking at eating disorder forums, local therapists and reading up on anorexia, always a dispiriting task, she heard Jess come in.

'Hello, darling. How was photography?'

'It was good. We're studying Cartier Bresson and some other French photographers who formed Magnum Photography. It's really cool.' Jess leaned back against the worktop, texting fast, as ever. She stopped and looked at Laura, twisting her hair round a knobbly finger.

Whenever Laura looked at her nowadays she felt nauseous. The bones on her daughter's hands and face – the only part of her not covered in bundles of clothes – seemed to become more prominent every day.

Laura had overheard Jess talking to Emma about Ryan when she was round the other night. She seemed in a better mood, so perhaps now was a good time to say something. 'Did you say you were seeing someone, love?' Trying to sound ever so casual. 'It's just, you know, if you wanted to invite them back…'

Jess turned away quickly. 'No thanks, Mum.'

What was that supposed to mean? Yes she was or no she didn't want to invite them back? 'I don't want to interfere, darling.'

'Then don't.'

'It's just that if you're going to have sex you need…'

Jess flushed a pale pink. 'It's none of your business.'

'…contraception. I can make an appointment for you with the doctor…'

'Mum!'

'…and I don't need to go in with you.'

'Mum, really!' Jess spun around and stomped upstairs.

Laura breathed out. Well, it needed saying. But did Jess's reaction mean they were having sex or not? Perhaps they were just kissing and cuddling. Laura got up and started chopping vegetables as she pondered the conversation.

Mind you, if Jess's periods had stopped, at least she couldn't get pregnant. But it was the idea of her fifteen-year-old daughter, so naive and vulnerable, possibly having sex that filled her with dread. Jess hadn't ever had a serious boyfriend before. She'd only have sex because she was desperate to be loved. And then her heart would be broken. Again. What could Laura do?

She looked down as her phone pinged with a message from Anna. *Have you heard about What if it all works out? xxx*

Laura frowned. *What's that?*

It's about trying to eliminate all the what ifs… We concentrate so much on what might go wrong that we don't think enough about what if it all works out? Take a look at the video. XXX

Laura smiled. *You're amazing. Thanks so much for always being there and cheering me up. xxx*

She sighed, filled with a sense of deep gratitude at the people she had in her life. Anna, Merryn and Ben. Fabulous support just when she really needed it.

Chapter Thirty-Two

Jess

Today Emma's sixteen. She had a family meal after school, then she's having a party on Saturday night. She invited me and Tessa to both. I said no to the tea, but I'll go over later.

Emma never fusses over me like most people do. The other day Jazzer said I looked like a sick scarecrow and what the fuck did Ryan see in me and Emma said, 'Better a scarecrow than a fat slob like you. Jess is way cleverer than you'll ever be.'

I felt like crying when she said that, but in a good way. I love how she sticks up for me, like I do for her.

I'd like to ask Nick if he thinks Ryan likes me but he goes all quiet whenever Ryan's name is mentioned. I get the feeling that he thinks less of me for seeing Ryan, and I don't like that. But I don't know what to do about it.

I guess Ryan and I are still dating. We play pool with his friends every Thursday at the Helston club after school: we walk there and get the bus home, and we usually do something on Saturday nights; he's coming to Emma's party. I still feel nervy with him. Plus he's started going on about having sex and there's all this talk about strangulation and choking during sex, which sounds terrifying. I mean, sex is a big deal for me anyway but why would anyone want to do that? I know I'm nearly sixteen but I've changed my mind: I don't want to have sex with Ryan. But I can't say that.

Also, I know he's slept with loads of other girls – well, several, certainly – and I'm terrified that if he sees me with no clothes on, he'll hate me. Perhaps I could keep my clothes on?

We've got the Paris trip soon and I'm really looking forward to that, though I hope I'm going to be OK. I'm so tired and dizzy. I can't get warm and now, cos I don't want sex, I wonder if I'm frigid as well? Or gender fluid? People talk about gender identity a lot at school and I don't know who or what I am. It's really confusing.

If I refuse to have sex with Ryan, will he dump me? Everyone else says they have sex and it would prove that he likes me. Though Emma and Tess both said don't be stupid and don't do it. I wish I could ask Nick cos he's like a brother but I don't think he'd like it.

I've finished my project on Eddie and after class, Mr Thompson asked me to stay behind and we looked at what I'd done, and he said that I was very talented. I had a huge grin. I felt alive and special, and like how I used to be. The old me, the one that got lost.

On my way home, that feeling disappeared when I realised I'd got tea ahead of me and I'm so frightened of eating anything. I really miss the person I used to be. But she's gone now and I think it's too late for her to ever come back.

I really don't know what to do. I sort of feel I need help but who do I go to? They'd only make me get fat.

And I still don't know how I'm going to get that Retallack print. I did some cleaning for Anna but she hasn't got any more at the moment. And on top of all that we've got more mocks coming up soon. That terrifies me, cos I know I'm hopeless at exams anyway and I can't think straight at the moment.

Diary of Jessica Kate Hocking

5 March 2024

Dear Dad,

Not too long till our Paris trip – after mocks – and part of me's really looking forward to it cos Paris must be such an amazing place to take pictures. Having studied Cartier Bresson's work, I can imagine walking through Montmartre waiting for his 'decisive moment'. I love the idea of waiting for a picture to happen, and what better place than Paris?

The other part of me is really scared, cos I'm scared of everything right now. I lie in bed curled up in a tight ball to try and get warm. This thing inside me has taken over. Most of the time I just want to give up but I can't even do that.

Mum mentioned about this therapist who helped someone Ben knows. But the idea of someone poking inside my head is terrifying. And therapists only make you eat and I won't do that. I couldn't bear to get FAT.

I haven't had periods for months now but I so don't miss them, nor do I miss having boobs. What are they for anyway? Except for feeding babies and I couldn't bear to get pregnant and fat so I will never have kids.

Half of me wants to say yes to sex with Ryan cos at least it shows that someone wants me, but on the other hand, he must be nuts. Why would anyone want to look at my disgusting body?

Talking of which, there are so many TikTok videos with tips on how to lose even more weight and ignore hunger pangs and stuff. At least these people know what it's like: we speak the same language. But there's nothing about how terrifying the whole process is. How out of control it makes you feel, or what to do when you're so frightened but you can't stop.

I wish I could see the way out of this but I'm stuck on this horrible treadmill and I'm too frightened to stay on and too scared to get off.

Shit. Shit. Shit.

At least I'm going to Gran's this weekend which means having a break from the horrible cottage and Mum, who's always nagging me.

Chapter Thirty-Three

Laura

Laura arrived at the station on Sunday twenty minutes before Jess's train was due to arrive. While it had been a relief to have some time to herself, without having to worry about Jess, she found that by Saturday morning she was too restless to keep still so she decided to paint the cottage. Dear Anna had rung, insisted she'd love a painting party, and the two of them had got stuck in, with good results. Now she felt physically tired, but had a sense of achievement, and was dying to show Jess.

She'd also had a brainwave about getting Jess to see the therapist but had felt it would come better from Merryn. However, she hadn't texted to say if it had worked, so Laura feared the worst.

Laura had always loved stations; they were great for people watching, and she'd read a piece about trying to look for the good things when out and about. Today this was easy. An elderly stooped man and his wife, tenderly holding hands. A harassed-looking young mum with a wailing toddler who suddenly stopped crying and gave Laura a beaming smile; a balding middle-aged man who talked lovingly to his three-legged dog. Who were they and where were they going? She and Jess would have invented their life histories within minutes.

Jess's train arrived and as she came through the barrier, Laura was shocked. Was Jess actually thinner than on Friday? Laura scooped up her daughter and held her so tight, Jess struggled.

'Mum, what's the matter? I can't breathe.'

'Just glad to see you.' Laura inhaled the familiar apple smell of Jess's hair and let her go. 'So, how was the weekend?'

'OK.' Jess's stock answer to everything.

'Anna and I had a painting party. We got the kitchen done and the bathroom, and started on my bedroom. Had a meal and some wine on Saturday night. Took Eddie for a few walks.' She smiled. 'How was Gran?'

Jess bent down to pat Eddie who grinned up at her with his usual besotted expression. 'She's cool. We went to some galleries in Wadebridge, did some shopping.' She paused and the silence grew. 'Gran said she'd buy that print for me. The one in the auction.'

Ah – had Laura's idea worked? 'Really? That's kind of her.'

Jess looked down, kicked a stone with the toe of her boot. 'As long as I see…' Her voice disappeared in a gulf of tears. Laura gathered her daughter in her arms and let her cry.

'There, there,' she said, patting her back.

Jess pulled back. 'The deal was that she'd only get it if I go and see this therapist. The one that you told me about.'

Laura's hopes rocketed upwards. Hooray! Her idea *had* worked! But much better that it came from Merryn. 'I think that's a very good idea,' Laura said carefully.

Jess looked up, her face screwed up and blotchy. 'I'm really scared, Mum.'

Laura held her bony fingers as gently and firmly as she could. 'You are the bravest girl I know,' she said. 'And you know what? The scariest bit is making the decision. After that it gets easier.'

'I hope so. I feel really stuck.' Jess wiped her nose on her sleeve. 'It's got really horrible now and I don't know what to do.'

Laura's euphoria shattered. The earlier heartbreak of losing her own father, of Ben leaving, then Chris, was nothing compared to this admission from her daughter. She could hear all her pain and fear and confusion and wished, more than anything, that she could stop this awful thing that had taken control of Jess. She took a deep breath, tried to steady her voice. 'Well, this lady helped a friend of Ben's, and she's fine now.'

'Really?' Hope wavered in Jess's voice.

'Absolutely fine,' said Laura firmly. 'I do wish I could solve this for you, darling. But I can't, and you really need some outside help now. I'll ring this woman tomorrow and see when we can get an appointment. And apart from that, you just say and I will help however I can.'

'Thanks, Mum.' Jess looked up and gave a watery smile.

As they walked down the road from the station a large truck thundered by and drowned out any hope of conversation. 'Come on, let's get back before it rains,' Laura said, and they hurried on. When they arrived at the cottage, she opened the door so Jess could go in first.

'Hey, Mum!' Jess stared around her at the newly painted

yellow kitchen. 'It looks much bigger and brighter, doesn't it? Cool.'

'Glad you like it. I've done the bathroom, too. Wouldn't dare do your room!'

Jess plodded upstairs to check, leaving Laura alone with her thoughts. At least there was a glimmer of promise now. The only trouble was, would this therapist be able to see Jess? If so, how long would they have to wait? How much would she charge? Chris had better bloody pay for it.

Diary of Jessica Kate Hocking

18 March 2024

Dad,

Mr Thompson says photography is not just about light but seeing the things other people don't see. That's what Jack Retallack was so good at and is why I so want this print. Gran's bribed me. She said she'd get it for me if I agreed to see this therapist person.

I opened my mouth to say NO cos the idea of seeing any shrink fills me with terror. What do they do? Ask questions and trick you into replying? Peer inside your head? Invade your privacy? I couldn't trust anyone like that. They'd want to make you eat and get fat and no one's going to make me do that. EVER.

But then I remembered Mr Thompson saying that he believed in me. And that sort of made me feel braver. I know you agree that my photography is really important, and I'd love to become a professional one day (if I survive that long), and cos the print's of you, it feels really significant. And it's being auctioned by Mum's friend Ben.

So, I had to say yes.

I could see from the gleam in Gran's eyes that she was surprised cos she thought she'd won. But that was OK. She's so much easier to talk to than Mum; I hate seeing her face when she thinks I'm not looking. Like it's her fault. Like she can't bear to look at me. I must look a real freak.

I've started feeling like a hamster chained to a wheel and it's exhausting and sucks the life out of me. I need to escape and I'm frightened cos I know it's destroying me. And Mum. And Gran.

Is there really a way out of this, Dad? What do you think? I couldn't ask you this in real life. But could this woman really help?

Love you loads XXXX

Chapter Thirty-Four

Laura

On Monday morning, a gentle breeze ruffled the surface of the water and tiny wavelets left traces of lace on the fine sand as Laura and Eddie walked to work. Leaving the outskirts of the village, she noticed mallards swimming on the mud-brown river, the wonderful rich emerald greens and turquoise of their plumage brightening the morning.

She spotted a jay disappearing into the trees on the far shore, and two magpies cackled at her. That's two for joy, she thought hopefully. The spring sun made a watery appearance, casting fleeting jewels of light on the water. A calming start to another day with not enough sleep.

Laura was on her own in the gallery, planning the next exhibition, so before she started on her to-do list, she left a message with the GP receptionist asking them to ring back about a referral to Rachel Lomax for Jess.

She also rang Ben about his viewing that night.

'All going well, though there's quite a lot to do,' he said.

'There are a lot of people coming, so we've decided to break with tradition and auction the first fifty lots this evening. I hope that'll drum up more interest in the rest of the sale.' He paused. 'You can tell Jess her print is lot 39.'

'I will, thanks,' Laura said and her stomach fluttered in anticipation. 'She's so excited. Best of luck, Ben.'

'Thanks,' he said. 'I'm part really excited and part terrified. A lot hangs on this.'

By lunchtime there was no news from the therapist or the GP, so Laura took her cheese and pickle sandwich and sat in the park where tentative sunlight lifted her spirits.

She texted Jess saying the print would be auctioned tonight at around 6.30, and got an instant reply.

Can't wait! C U there at 6. XXX

Laura smiled as she read it, imagining Jess's excitement, then started when her phone rang. She saw a withheld number and her heart thudded painfully fast.

'Is that Laura Hocking? My name is Rachel Lomax,' said the voice. 'I had a phone call from your daughter's GP this morning. I'm a therapist who specialises in eating disorders and I understand you'd like to make an appointment for your daughter.'

'Oh, yes!' Laura breathed. 'Yes please.'

'Can you tell me a little about her?'

Laura could hardly believe she was actually talking to this woman. 'Yes, Jess is fifteen and she's been having trouble eating for a while.' Despite stating the facts, Laura felt a surge of relief, of joy – could this woman be their saviour?

'I can see Jess for an assessment, but you'll need to take that to your GP and if they decide that therapy is the right treatment, they'll refer her. But I must warn you, I have a twelve-month waiting list for NHS clients.'

'Twelve *months?*' Laura said, horrified.

'But I do take private patients, and I have a cancellation next Monday at 5pm.'

'Yes, please,' Laura said quickly. 'I mean, providing we can get the referral, of course.' She cleared her throat. 'How much do you charge?'

Rachel named her fee and Laura swallowed hard. Chris had said he'd pay. This appointment was more important than anything. 'OK, thank you.'

A few minutes later she rang off, having established that the address wasn't far from the bus stop on the outskirts of Truro. At last, she'd made some progress; she just needed to follow up the referral. Then, before she could change her mind, she rang Chris, listened to the phone ring then click onto voicemail.

'It's Laura,' she said hurriedly. 'We both know that Jess needs help, and a therapist who's been recommended for treating anorexia has just rung to say she can see Jess next week. There aren't any NHS appointments for another twelve months, so Jess will have to see her privately, which will be £55 per session. I know it's a lot, but this is Jess's only chance.'

She rang off and hoped to God that Chris would stick to his word.

Six o'clock that evening found Laura walking to Ben's premises. Bright light spilled out onto the pavements that were slippery with rain, and Laura could hear muffled chatter coming out of the open door. She paused, feeling like a child on her way to a birthday party, unsure if she'd know anyone there. She took a deep breath, stood up straighter, put her shoulders back and walked in, wondering if Jess had arrived.

Once in, Laura was hit by the warmth emanating from overheated bodies and red wine. A discordant smell of various perfumes and aftershave caught her as she looked around. Jake and a girl of around his age were standing in front of a table laden with bidding paddles, like table tennis bats, and next to them a small, rotund man was handing out red and white wine or soft drinks.

Laura made her way through the throng of bodies and stood before Jake. 'Hello,' she said. 'Can I get a bidding paddle for later on?'

'Sure,' said Jake and he handed one over, making a note of the number. There wasn't time to talk as a woman behind Laura wanted a paddle as well, so Laura turned to get a glass of wine. 'Very good turnout,' she said to the man.

'Ben's really pleased.' The man beamed. 'Mind you, I think he invited most of Cornwall. What would you like to drink?'

'Red wine, please,' said Laura and she accepted what looked like a huge glass. 'That's…'

'A VIP glass,' said the man and winked.

Laura laughed and did a double take as a young man pointed his camera at her.

'Do you mind? We're taking pictures for the auction website,' he said.

'OK.' It was a good idea; she would ask Jess to take pictures for the gallery's next private view for their social media pages.

Laura looked around and made her way over to a gallery owner she knew. She spoke with several artists who

lived nearby, a man who owned a framing shop she wanted
to do a deal with, and several people who'd called into the
gallery on spec.

Ben was busy talking, fetching and carrying, so she kept
out of his way, not wanting to intrude on his special night.

The main auction area consisted of two large rooms
with interconnecting partitions that had been pulled back.
Furniture for sale was at the front of the room, paintings
hung on the walls, while china and smaller items of
furniture were displayed in cases at the back of the room.

At one point Laura saw Jess over the other side of the
room. She was going to wave but there were too many
people, then she realised that Jess was with a tall, blond boy:
Ryan? He had striking blue eyes that seemed to dart here
and there, rather straggly long hair, a tall body that looked
as if it hadn't finished growing yet. However, he was
attentive to Jess, Laura noted, whispering in her ear,
pointing things out to her. Perhaps he was OK after all.

'What do you think?' said a voice in her left ear and Jess
whipped around to see Ben standing there.

'Great party,' said Laura, feeling flushed from the wine,
which was making her head swim a little. 'I like the way
you've laid out the chinaware among the dressers and tables.
It shows everything off really well. Congratulations!'

'Thank you. It took some doing,' Ben said, smiling. 'But
I'm pleased with the attendance. Let's hope the prices
match their enthusiasm.' He glanced across the room,
where Jess saw them and gave a half nod. 'Did you get hold
of the therapist?'

'Yes,' replied Laura. 'She's got a cancellation next
Monday, and I spoke to Jess's GP this afternoon and she's
referred her straight away. I'm so grateful, Ben.'

'That's such good news, I couldn't be happier.'

Laura smiled back and looked round the bustling room. 'I thought auctions were usually in the daytime?'

'They are, but as that's when a lot of people are at work, I thought I'd combine the launch and viewing with selling the first fifty lots so that people who are new to auctions can see how exciting they can be. I'm hoping this will encourage more people to bid online as well as coming to the sales on Tuesday and Wednesday.'

'Good idea.' She raised her bidding paddle and smiled. 'I've got my paddle.'

Ben looked at his watch. 'Excuse me, I must check everything's OK, then we can start.'

Laura watched Ben cross the room, confer with a colleague, then take up his place on a podium at the far end of the connecting room. He tapped on the podium with his gavel to get everyone's attention, and waited till the talking stopped.

'Welcome everyone, to the launch and viewing of my new auction house.' Cheers erupted from the guests, so he waited until the noise died down before continuing. 'It's lovely to see so many of you here tonight. We'll start the sale in a minute, but just to remind potential buyers that catalogues are at the back of the room, on that table over there, and you will also need a paddle to register your bid.' He paused while everyone turned round to see if anyone was late. 'Now, if everyone's ready, we can start. Lot number 1, a collection of Clarice Cliff ceramics...'

Laura watched Ben perform, flanked by two helpers who tapped away at laptops as items were sold. The process was being videoed by a young woman with tattoos and pink hair; she showed the prices being logged and which paddle number had bought them. She pointed the lens at Ben who was scribbling notes on a sheet that was later passed to his helpers. Across the room, Laura noted Jess moving around with her camera. Had Ben asked her to take pictures, too?

As she checked her catalogue, looking for lot 39, her stomach fluttered with nerves. While she'd attended lots of auctions, she'd never bid for anything, least of all anything as important as this was to Jess. According to the catalogue, the guide price for the print was £300–400, and Merryn had said she'd go up to £400. It seemed a lot of money for a print, but would that be enough?

Laura bit her lip and tried to concentrate. Ben was like an actor, testing his audience, building the tension, bringing it down. Adding humour to get a satisfying ripple of laughter around the room. He's good, she thought in surprise. Really good.

Laura cast around the room looking for Jess, hoping she wasn't going to miss her big moment. She kept checking the catalogue, seeing the lot numbers tick by, up to 20, then 25, and noticed her hands shaking while she started feeling queasy. Oh, why had she agreed to bid for something so vital? What if she was outbid?

Suddenly she saw Jess over on the far side of the room. She was whispering to Ryan, if that was him, and she looked up at him and gave that shy smile that Laura loved so much. Don't you dare hurt her, she thought. As she looked back, Laura gave a hesitant wave, unsure if Jess wanted to join her for the bidding.

At that moment Jess saw Laura. She turned back to Ryan and whispered in his ear. He nodded, then watched as Jess made her way through the crowds to Laura's side.

'OK?' she whispered.

Laura nodded; mouth dry. She desperately needed to pee, but they were on lot 30 – if she went now, she might miss lot 39.

'I'm nervous,' whispered Jess. 'Are you?'

'Yes,' croaked Laura. She'd have to cross her legs and hope for the best. She decided not to voice her other fears. Jess must have this print, no matter what.

And suddenly the moment arrived. 'Lot number 39,' announced Ben. 'A print by the late Jack Retallack, one of our best known Cornish photographers. He lived in Hayle and sadly died last summer. This print of Newlyn became the image that was synonymous with Retallack's work: Cornwall, the sea, everyday people going about their everyday lives, but with the tiny details that made Retallack's work so memorable. Now, as a starting price, what am I bid?'

The bidding was slow to start with, and Laura put her paddle up several times, her heart thudding so loudly she grew quite frightened, but she outbid two other people up to £150. She was getting the hang of it. She could do it! Then, as she started to relax, another paddle was raised at the back of the room. Looking round, it belonged to a tall, elegantly dressed woman in an expensive-looking navy coat and brown knee-length boots.

The bidding increased, up and up, until it reached £300. Laura tried not to look at Jess, whose face was one of white disbelief, then gradual horror. £350, and still the other woman continued. Laura went up to £380 knowing she couldn't go much higher, but the navy coat carried on bidding. Could she go up anymore? Laura had to sit down, her legs were shaking so much. She could scarcely breathe, yet still the other woman carried on.

'I can't go any higher than four hundred,' Laura whispered and Jess nodded miserably. Her face was blotchy and she looked as if she were about to break down.

'And now we have a phone bidder,' Ben announced. An

assistant was waving to Ben while talking on the phone. The phone bidder upped the price, in competition with the bidder in the room, and as the price continued to escalate, Laura's hopes plummeted.

The bidding finally stopped at £550, way above what Merryn could afford. Disappointment flooded through Laura like cold concrete. Jess's face crumpled and she hurried out of the room. Laura was desperate to follow, but she knew Jess would want to be by herself. And anyway, what could she say? Laura stood, motionless. This was totally out of her control. Shit, she thought, with sudden realisation. How do I get her to the therapist now?

Chapter Thirty-Five

Laura

Laura felt all hope drain from her. The dreams of Jess beginning to recover vanished in an instant. In a few months, her organs would start shutting down and she would face a horrible self-inflicted death. All because somebody else took what should have been Jess's.

Fury built inside Laura. How could anyone do that? It was so unfair: they had no idea how much this meant to Jess. She sighed. There must be other prints online, though probably not featuring Chris. Perhaps Ben could talk to the buyer, persuade him to sell given the circumstances.

She glanced up, realising that Ben was racing through the last lots. His gavel came down with one final crash and that was it for the day. There was a splattering of applause, which grew steadily louder to hoots and more clapping. The photographer and videographer were there, getting it all. Ben was getting down now, smiling, laughing, greeting the punters like the professional he was. Despite her profound disappointment, Laura realised he'd done very well.

She glanced around to see if she could see Jess; she was over by the wine table, a hunched figure, her back to the room. Ryan stood beside her looking awkward, not touching her. How dare he? Poor Jess needed a big hug, to be taken care of. Dammit! She felt another surge of anger. Why couldn't things work out, just for once? Meanwhile, she must go and see Jess, see Ben and beg, plead...

'Laura?'

She looked round to see Ben standing in front of her. 'Well done, Ben, that was brilliant. Now, if you'll excuse me, I need to get to Jess.' She turned to go, felt a hand on her arm.

'Laura, I need a quick word about the print.'

'Yes, Jess is really upset, she'll probably want to go home...'

'She doesn't need to be upset. She's got it.'

Laura whipped round. 'What do you mean?'

Ben smiled. 'Sorry about that but I had to have a fallback position in case someone tried to outbid you.'

Laura frowned. 'I don't understand...'

Ben leaned forward, indicating with a jerk of his head that she should follow him to a less crowded spot outside in the corridor. Once there, he said, 'Sorry, but I had a feeling that might happen and I didn't want to worry you beforehand.' He paused. 'I realised how much the print meant to Jess, so I had an agreement with a friend that he would step in and bid for me if it got to more than your mother could afford.'

Laura stared at him. 'Wow.'

'It's quite common in this business. If you really want something, you get a friend to bid on your behalf.'

Laura's head felt muzzy. 'So that phone bidder was a friend of yours?'

Ben gave a sheepish grin. 'Yes. I had to stop the woman in the navy coat getting it.'

'But that means we owe you over £200.'

'No. The guy owes me a favour.'

'Two hundred quid's worth?'

'Favours don't always equate to money, you know. This guy owes me big time.'

'Well, I'd still like to repay you. But thank you very, very much.' Laura felt bubbles of joy rise up inside her. Jess would be so happy – *and* she would have to see the therapist. Oh, thank God! She flung her arms around Ben in relief, joy and excitement. Then realised, suddenly, that she'd better untangle herself – this was his first auction, for heaven's sake. She only hoped this wasn't being recorded.

'My pleasure.'

Laura looked at the smile spreading over his face. 'I still don't understand how you're so blasé about losing £200 but I trust you know what you're doing.'

'Sometimes a few tricks of the trade are needed, that's all. Ah, Jess!'

Laura turned to see a red-eyed Jess walking towards them. Poor girl, she looked as if she'd lost everything. Ryan was behind her staring at his phone as if for redemption.

'Good news!' Laura cried hurriedly. 'The print's all yours!' She longed to hug Jess, but didn't dare, especially in front of the boyfriend.

Jess frowned, clearly puzzled, but even that looked as if it took too much effort. Slowly she looked from Laura to Ben, then back to Laura. Laura saw a ray of hope in her eyes and suddenly she was like the old Jess: excited, laughing, eyes sparkling. Watching Jess's face change was like watching magic take place.

'Really?' she breathed.

Laura nodded. 'You have Ben to thank for it, but yes, it's yours.'

Jess looked back at Ryan, then Ben. 'Thank you!' she cried and burst into tears. 'You don't know how much this means to me. Apparently Dad was fishing on the rocks round the corner from Newlyn. Jack Retallack took the picture and then used "Outline of a Fisherman" as his trademark and signature. You can see it's Dad if you look closely enough!'

Laura fished out a tissue and handed it to Jess.

'Dad couldn't see why I wanted it so much, but...' Jess's voice trailed away and she flushed. 'You're sure? It's really mine?'

'Yup. All yours.' Ben's smile was infectious.

'Wow!' Jess glanced at Ryan, who wouldn't meet anyone's eyes, but Jess seemed oblivious. She reached up and gave Ben a tentative hug. 'Oh, thank you so much... I thought... but that's amazing!' She gave Laura a hug as well. 'Oh, I can't believe it, I'm so happy!' She beamed and looked over at the podium next door, as if the print was there. 'When do I get it?' she said breathlessly.

'We have to sort the paperwork tomorrow. Come by on your way home from school,' Ben said. 'You can pick it up then and show me the pictures you took tonight.'

'Certainly will.' Jess twirled round to Ryan. 'Isn't that brilliant?' she said.

'Yeah.' He nodded, not looking at Ben or Laura. 'Come on, let's go.'

'See you, Mum,' said Jess. 'We're going to a friend's,' and she almost floated out of the room.

. . .

When Laura got home that night – Jess had promised not to be late – she glanced down at her phone and noticed three missed calls from Chris. Quickly she dialled and heard his gruff, 'Hello?'

'Hi, Chris, sorry I missed you. You got my message?'

'Yes. £55 an hour! Who is this woman? How come she charges so much?'

'I told you. It's the going rate,' Laura replied. 'Some of these specialists charge £75 an hour.'

'Well, is she good enough? How come she's not charging that much?'

Chris clearly wasn't thinking straight. 'She's come highly recommended, by a friend whose daughter was very ill indeed, and she helped the daughter a lot.' Laura decided it was best not to mention that Ben was involved in the recommending.

'But £55… How many sessions will she need?'

'I have no idea. Why don't you come with us and you can ask her yourself?'

'Yes. I mean, no. When is it?'

'Next Monday at 6pm. In Truro.'

'I've got a meeting at 4.30 so I'll try to make it. Can you text me the address?'

'Of course. But Chris, you'll pay for it?'

'I'll have to,' he said. 'You won't, and we need to save our daughter.' And with that he put down the phone.

You bastard, thought Laura. You fucking bastard. But as long as you pay, that's the main thing.

Diary of Jessica Kate Hocking

10 March 2024

Dad,

You're an idiot not to rate this print; it sold for a fortune. Also, it's the only picture I've got of you when you were young. Anyway, I'm so excited and I'm picking it up from Ben, the guy who helped save Eddie, who's really cool. I feel like I've got the real you back again; you're glancing round, looking at me and you're partly in the sea and partly on land so you're in an in between place. Like I am now.

When I thought someone else had bought the print I was SO disappointed, I had a good cry in the toilets. I try not to feel sorry for myself but I thought this is the first thing that could have gone right in bloody ages and is that too much to ask for? Evidently, yes. Then I went to find Ryan but he just said 'let's watch the footie'.

Ben was amazing; he said he'd give me £40 for the pictures I took at the auction, which will go towards my Paris fund, so I'm going to do some editing and I hope he'll be pleased. My first paid gig!

The shit part is, I have to see this therapist next Monday. I keep telling myself that it'll be worth it, and when the print's hanging up in my room I hope it will be. But every night that goes by is one night nearer to seeing this woman and I'm so scared.

Gran said it's the start of getting better, which made it sound slightly less scary, but I'm still shitting myself. What will this woman say? What will she do? Ask what I eat? There are so many questions I want to ask, like why does my stomach hurt so much? It really aches. And my hair is coming out in clumps. I can't sleep cos all I can think about is food and yet I mustn't eat, that's giving in. If I did have sex with Ryan at least I wouldn't get pregnant cos of not having periods. But I don't want to have sex with him and I'm worried he will have a go in Paris. But I'm not going to do it while I still look like I do. All these worries tumbling round in my head, not making any sense. And on top of that we've got exams…

We have to write an essay on Does the Camera Lie? and all I can think of is how much I lie: about my weight, what I eat, what I think, that I throw up, what exercise I do. And how exhausted I am. And so shit scared.

And now I have to survive until Monday after school.
HOW?????
Love you, Dad. Wish you were here.

Chapter Thirty-Six

Laura

Laura felt almost euphoric waking the following morning. Jess's delighted face was the best thing she'd seen for such a long time. As she lay in bed, listening to the seagulls arguing outside, Laura thought of Ben's extraordinarily generous gesture. He must be owed a huge favour, for he'd said he was short on money. What a kind friend he was. Mind you, she would have to pay him back. Though how?

Laura got up and showered, hoping for some inspiration. She made tea and toast, shouted at Jess to get ready for school, and still had no ideas. She'd rung Merryn last night to tell her the good news, but all her mother said was 'hmm. How generous'. As if she'd almost expected Ben to behave like that. It was most curious.

Having finally seen Jess off to school, Laura and Eddie set off for work. It had rained overnight and the ground was wet beneath her feet, reminding her that her boots had started leaking. But a patch of blue sky appeared, 'big enough to make a pair of sailor's trousers' as her grandmother used to say, which augured well, Laura hoped. The air felt fresh and spring-like. Another sign of hope?

She was walking towards the gallery when her phone pinged. It was a text from Anna.

Had a text from Jess. Need to talk. Can we meet for a drink after work? 6pm in the usual? XXX

Laura felt her stomach clench. What was it? I'm her mother, why didn't she ask me? But Jess had given up asking Laura anything. Quickly she replied, *Sure. See you there. XXX*

That evening the pub was empty save a few locals propping up the bar, and Anna who was sitting by the fire, two glasses of red wine in front of her. Laura gave Anna a hug and when she was sitting down, Anna handed Laura her phone so she could read Jess's text.

Hi Anna. I'm worried cos I'm going to see therapist next Monday and I don't know what she's going to say. Will she want to weigh me and ask about what I eat and stuff? I thought you might know. Love Jess XXXX

Laura handed the phone back, wishing she was able to comfort Jess. But she was as much in the dark as her daughter. 'Poor lamb,' she said. 'Have you replied?'

'Not yet. I thought I'd talk to you first. I don't want to put her off. That was a brilliant idea to get Jess to see the therapist. I'm looking forward to seeing the print.'

'Yes, it's good. Weird seeing Chris as a boy, though.' Laura smiled faintly. 'But now we're on a countdown till Monday.'

Anna reached over, squeezed Laura's hand. The touch was bonding, reassuring, even if her fingers were cold. 'I'll give her a ring later and try to reassure her. I mean, I know what we'd ask from a medical point of view, but I'm not a therapist. I would have thought she'd concentrate more on why Jess might have developed anorexia rather than what she eats. And it's not difficult to work out why, is it?'

'No. I mean, she's been so brave but you can see it's a losing battle and she's so thin now I'm really frightened.' Laura paused. 'I still think I should have stopped Jess becoming ill. But logically I know that's impossible.' She paused. 'I was reading online that organs could fail in some cases. Is that true?'

Anna looked down. 'It can happen if people fall below a certain weight.'

'How come?'

Anna hesitated. 'When you lose weight, at first you lose fat, but once that's gone, you start losing muscle; not just from your limbs but from the muscles that pump your heart and make your lungs work. Malnutrition means the body doesn't have the vitamins and minerals it needs that are important for providing energy to keep the major organs like the brain, lungs, heart, liver and kidneys going, and also for keeping blood pressure levels right. As starvation continues, the immune system starts to fail so it's much harder to combat infections. There's also the risk of having extremely low blood sugar or heart rhythm disturbance. Potassium levels can drop, and as potassium is a heart stabiliser, that can be dangerous.'

Laura stared at her. 'Oh my God.'

'But that's only in extreme cases.'

Laura sipped her wine. 'I'm even more glad she's seeing this woman on Monday.'

'What's she called?'

'Rachel Lomax.'

'Oh yes, I've heard of her. She has a good success rate. We're hoping she'll do some sessions at the new unit.'

Laura exhaled. 'That's good.'

'You'll let me know how she gets on?'

'Of course I will. I feel this is Jess's last chance. Her only chance.' Laura bit her lip. 'She's suffered so much already, and I have to make sure this works.'

'That's not up to you,' Anna said gently. 'It's up to Jess.'

'Yes, but I'm her mother and I can't bear to see her fading away like this. I have to make her see that life is worth living.'

Anna leaned over. 'That's for Jess to sort out with Rachel Lomax. You've done all you can for Jess. You're the best mother I know. I couldn't cope with an anorexic daughter. I'd lose my temper, panic, say all the wrong things…'

'That's what I do all the time and I kick myself,' Laura said. 'I just want Jess to have the best chance. She has to realise how talented and special she is, how much we all love her. That she has a future.' She paused. 'If this therapy doesn't work, she won't survive, Anna. And I couldn't bear that.' Tears stung her eyes as she thought of Jess becoming even worse, until she finally just gave up. 'I won't let that happen.'

'No one could do more than you have, Laura,' Anna repeated. 'And Rachel sounds the best person for Jess. So I'm with you, every step of the way. And ring, any time.' She smiled. 'I can supply valium, alcohol, coke – you name it, I can get the drugs!'

'Coke?' Laura smiled.

'No, actually, I made that bit up. But a bottle of wine, always.'

Laura gave her a hug. 'Thanks, Anna. You're the best friend, and you're going to be amazing in this new role.'

'Well, I hope so. I mean, growing up's so hard, isn't it? And there seem to be additional pressures nowadays. But I love caring for people. Talking to them when they're scared. Talking's so important, as a nurse. Thinking of the little things that make them feel better about themselves; you know, washing their hair, or wheeling them outdoors into the sun. Arranging a Zoom call with their relatives if they can't come and visit. Doing their make-up, or nails. All those little things can make such a difference.'

Laura sighed. 'I tell you, if ever I'm in hospital I want you to look after me. All the time. You've really found your calling, haven't you?'

'You have too. I was having a look at the online shop at the gallery, and I can see why it's such a success. You've done a brilliant job.'

'Thanks.' Laura smiled. 'I did a free course in expanding your business, so I thought I'd get the gallery shop up and running, and it's doing well. I can learn from that and help Mum with her business, too.'

'That's a great idea,' Anna said. 'Well done, you. And it could lead to other kinds of work?'

'Yes, maybe. It's all knowledge, which helps.'

Anna smiled. 'How's Jess's friend Emma?'

'She's fine. Jess, Emma and her girlfriend, Tess, seem to have formed a sort of teen trio.' Laura smiled. 'I was worried Emma might drop Jess when she got a girlfriend but they seem very supportive, which is great.'

'I'm so glad she's made friends at last,' Anna said. 'Emma sounds a brilliant friend and that's so important, isn't it? I mean look at us. Friends since the age of five!'

Diary of Jessica Kate Hocking

15 March 2024

OMG, Dad,

The appointment is after school tomorrow and I can't sleep, so I thought I'd write to you.

No one understands. I don't WANT to do this: I CAN'T STOP.

I'm so terrified I can't stop shaking. My life is such a mess and yet I'm so scared of changing. I can't, I just CAN'T put on weight, that would kill me. But I couldn't possibly tell anyone about the messy thoughts in my head; they'd think I was mad.

When I first agreed to see this woman – Rachel – it almost felt like a relief. But that lasted about two seconds, and now I keep hoping something awful will happen so we can't go.

I started off feeling that losing weight was the only way to control my life, but now I feel like it's controlling me. A tiny part of me thinks that perhaps life CAN get better again, and I won't be stuck in this cycle forever. Perhaps seeing this Rachel could be an end to this treadmill that I'm stuck on. But how can that ever happen? How can I let it? What will she say? So many questions roaring round my head all day and all night.

The other day, in the street, I heard someone say 'how could she do this to herself?' And a neighbour said 'don't you know what you're doing to your poor mother?' Like I don't hate myself enough.

What they don't realise is that I don't have a choice.

Chapter Thirty-Seven

Laura

By the time Jess and Laura arrived at the therapist's office, Laura's legs were trembling so much she was relieved to sit down, while Jess's face was ashen with fear.

The waiting room was unremarkable: magnolia walls, copies of sailing and women's magazines lying in neat piles on a coffee table. The chairs were padded, which was a mercy considering Jess had no padding whatsoever on her bottom, and there were the usual innocuous prints of Cornish seascapes.

When the door opened, a small woman with shoulder length auburn hair came in. Her bob swung shinily like in a shampoo commercial and she wore black jeans and a green jumper. 'Jessica Hocking? And Laura?'

Laura nodded and was relieved when the woman smiled. 'Come with me.' They got to their feet and followed this neat woman down a corridor into a small room that contained a desk, three comfortable chairs and some large abstract paintings on the walls. A sash window looked out over a courtyard, and a box of man-size tissues took pride of place on the desk, along with a laptop.

'I'm Rachel,' said the woman with a smile; her large mouth was accentuated by pink lipstick and her dark brown eyes assessed Laura and Jess carefully. 'I had a phone call from Jessica's father earlier,' she addressed Laura. 'He's not able to come to the session today but we did have a long chat and I think he understands the importance of Jess getting help.'

Laura glanced at Jess, who was still white with terror. She'd obviously been hoping that Chris would turn up. So he'd let her down again. Still, for now, as long as he paid... 'Good,' she said warily. 'And he's covering the fee?'

Rachel nodded. 'He's paid for the first three sessions,' she said, and then outlined what would happen today, before saying to Laura, 'Would you mind if I spoke with Jessica on her own, first? Then we can talk afterwards.'

Jess looks like Eddie, begging me not to go out without him, Laura thought. Still, this was an order, and Laura wasn't in any position to refuse. Why not talk to me first, she wondered as she got up, walked back to the waiting room. Staring at the speckled rust and pink painting on a blue background, Laura realised that if Rachel had asked to see Laura on her own, Jess would probably have run off. Laura only hoped Jess wasn't too petrified to talk to this woman with the painted mouth.

Laura's stomach twisted and lurched. I daren't hope for much, she thought, but at least help is here, if Jess'll accept it. Laura got up, paced round the room, trying to work off the shakes in her legs. Sitting down again, she bit a loose bit of skin by her thumbnail. It bled and stung, which took her mind off what was going on down the corridor.

Time ticked on. Ten minutes became twenty, then thirty. Did this mean that Jess was talking? Or that she wasn't? Laura was dying to go to the loo but didn't want to miss Rachel if she came back in. She flicked through a magazine, taking nothing in, and finally Rachel reappeared and asked Laura to join them. She hurried down the corridor wondering how Jess was. Angry? Weepy? Sullen? What had they talked about?

As she entered the room, Laura checked her daughter's face. Blotchy, which meant she'd been crying. Well, that was a good thing, wasn't it? Jess wouldn't look at her and Laura felt guilty, hated herself for bringing her here. But what option did she have?

Rachel sat down, consulting the folder on her desk. It looked like she'd been making copious notes, but of course the writing was upside down, so Laura couldn't read anything. 'Jessica has been very brave in talking to me, and I understand how hard it is for both of you,' Rachel said, smiling at Laura. 'As a mother, this must be so difficult. What I propose is a series of sessions with Jessica, and with you sometimes, to help Jessica cope with her fears about gaining weight. We will also talk about what you both need to do to ensure she can become healthy again, and stay healthy.'

Laura nodded, holding her breath. Their future lay in this woman's hands. 'The long-term effects of under-eating can have a very detrimental effect on the body, so we will talk about that, but mostly we need to understand what is causing Jessica's anorexia, and to find coping mechanisms for her, so she can learn how to manage difficult times, not just now but in the future. Does that sound OK?'

Laura nodded again. 'That sounds just like what Jess needs.' She glanced over at Jess, who was staring fixedly at the wooden floor. 'What do you think, Jess? Is that OK with you?'

Jess looked up slowly. She bit her lip and a tinge of pink came to her pallid cheeks. She was trying very hard not to cry, Laura realised, as her eyes brimmed. She fumbled in her jacket pocket for a tissue, but Rachel got there first, handed over the box of hankies. 'I know it's a lot to think about,' she said gently, 'and of course it seems frightening. But look on it as a journey. You said you like sailing?'

Jess nodded. Blew her nose. 'I went a few times with school.'

Rachel smiled. 'Well, this will be like a sailing trip. Some days you will have the wind with you, and it will be a real adventure, finding out about yourself. But other times might be a bit bumpy and you'll have to reef in – did you do that?'

Jess nodded. 'Yes, when the wind gets up. You have to make the sail smaller.'

'Exactly. And sometimes you have to make the decision not to go out, if the weather's too bad. Then you stay at home and make sure the boat is safe, do any repairs. Your body is the boat: you have to look after it, or you won't be able to sail.'

Jess nodded briefly.

'It might sound daunting, but exploring who you are can be very liberating. It gives you strength and power. Finding what you're good at, what you want to do in life, and how to do it can be the best thing we ever learn.'

'I like photography,' muttered Jess. 'That's my best subject.'

'In that case, you're ahead,' Rachel said with that open smile. 'Learning about yourself can be hard work. Like sailing, you have to focus, think about where you're going but also what's best for the boat – or your body. It won't be easy, Jess, but the rewards will make it all worthwhile. Not everyone can do it, but I think you have the necessary courage and strength – in fact, I'm sure you have.'

Laura tried to swallow but unshed tears stuck in her throat. Maybe there really was a way out of this awful mess. She was going to say something, then realised she'd just been jolted into positivity by a highly skilled motivational speaker. She glanced at Jess. She was giving tiny, hesitant nods. Her shoulders were hunched but she was making eye contact with Rachel. Wouldn't it be amazing if this feel-good message actually got through to Jess? Would she actually stick with it?

Jess looked at her. 'I've got to go to the loo,' she whispered. Laura nodded as Jess disappeared from the room. Would she make a run for it?

Rachel smiled. 'I think she'll be OK,' she said. 'I don't think she'll leave without you.'

Laura gave a watery smile. 'I hope not.' Her head was spinning with everything Rachel had said. 'So what happens now?'

'Well, because Jessica's weight is very low, I would normally advise inpatient treatment. Have you heard about the new mental health clinic for teenagers in Truro? They do have a few beds for eating disorders, but there's a waiting list. Otherwise it means waiting for a bed at the units at Exeter or Bristol.'

'But Exeter and Bristol are hundreds of miles away,' faltered Laura. 'And I don't have a car.' The prospect of train journeys to visit Jess was horrifying, it would take hours to get there, hours to get back and she could only go at weekends. And where would she stay? It was unthinkable.

Rachel nodded. 'I do sympathise. I'm afraid there isn't nearly enough provision for mental health care, and anorexia is way down the line. But Jess felt she didn't want to go down that route yet, so I said I'd give you both a diet plan for her to follow, so she can go to school and live normally, while trying to put on weight at home.'

While part of Laura was relieved at the idea of Jess staying at home, she thought of the endless fights over meals. 'I don't see how she's going to do that. Meals are such a nightmare for us both. She's so cunning and devious over food.'

'Most anorexics are, unfortunately.' Rachel gave a mother-to-mother smile. 'I don't honestly think Jessica will be able to put on weight. Not for want of trying, but because if she could have done it on her own, she would have done so by now. But at the moment that's the option she's chosen and I'd rather she came back to me asking for help rather than be told what to do. We have discussed a clinic and she felt she'd rather try it this way first.'

'OK.' Laura almost felt dizzy with all the information swirling around her head.

'Are you all right? How do you feel?'

Laura bit her lip. 'Overwhelmed. Frightened.' She looked up. 'I keep wondering what I could have done to stop this.'

'Nothing,' Rachel said firmly. 'In Jess's case, it seems that her father leaving was a trigger for her to want to take control, but very often it can be a chance remark that is taken the wrong way. Most people wouldn't react as Jess has, but for her that was the anorexic trigger.'

I don't know if that's supposed to be encouraging, Laura thought. 'What are her chances of recovery, do you think?'

'Well, we've caught it relatively early, and from what she said, she has a lot of support, which is very important. Often it can be about gaining confidence, self-esteem. But quite often recovery happens for no apparent reason.' She smiled. 'Which, in my profession is both a profound relief and incredibly frustrating. There are no set answers.'

Laura nodded, though her head was spinning.

'I'm aware there's a lot to take in,' Rachel continued. 'But basically, Ms Hocking, Jessica needs to be able to see a future. A reason for continuing. That's how I hope to help.'

Laura blinked, felt tears burning her eyes. She was about to speak when the door opened and Jess reappeared. She'd been crying, Laura could see, but held her chin up which was promising.

'Well, here are the diet plans. Jessica. I'd like you to follow these.' Rachel passed them over. 'There are different ideas for meals, nothing too fancy, but to give you an idea of what your body's been missing all this time. You need calcium, iron, lots of vitamins – all sorts.' Rachel held out a small blue book with a black spiral. 'I'd like you to write a diary – would you be able to do that?'

Jess took the book and turned it over in her hands. 'I have a journal. Gran gave it to me.'

'So you've got a writing habit already? Well done. In this one, I'd like you to record anything you want about how you feel, what problems you have, so you can tell me when we meet next week.'

Jess nodded and put the book in her rucksack.

'So when do you next see Jess?'

'Same time next week if that's OK?'

Laura thought about work. 'Would it be possible to make it a little bit later, so I don't have to leave work early?'

'I could do six, but I'm afraid that's the latest I can manage.'

'Perfect.' Laura exhaled, unaware that she'd been holding her breath.

'Now, if you'll excuse me, my next patient is waiting.'

Laura and Jess got up, shook the outstretched hand while Rachel smiled. 'I look forward to working with you, Jessica. I'll see you next Monday but in the meantime, here's my number.' She handed out business cards to them both. 'Any troubles, write in your diary but if it's urgent, give me a ring.'

Laura and Jess took the cards and made their way out of the room, down along the corridor and out into the street. Laura held out her hand, felt Jess's cold bony fingers wrap around hers. 'How do you feel, darling?'

Jess leaned into her. 'I'm so scared,' she said.

'I know, but you've done brilliantly.'

Jess turned so they could have a long, proper mother-daughter hug. A furious, deep love for her daughter flooded through Laura, giving her hope and strength. Whatever happened, they would get through this, she vowed. She'd make sure they would.

Diary of Jessica Kate Hocking

17 March 2024

Dad,

At last I saw Rachel, the therapist. Counsellor. Whatever.

She's quite stylish, wears tight jeans, has small boobs: she'd look better if she lost weight. Wonder if she's on a diet. Bet she's never made herself sick. She must be about Mum's age, with big brown eyes, shiny brown hair, a round face and dimples. No make-up except bright pink lipstick.

She told Mum to go out (nicely) and then she weighed me. I'd thought she would, so did my usual pre-weighing routine: drank lots of water (Dad, you have no idea). Phone in my back jeans pocket, a lead weight from the kitchen and as much heavy stuff as I could fit in my hoodie pockets.

That's always worked at the doctor's, but this time Rachel asked me to take my hoodie off, then said 'And your phone, please, Jessica,' and held her hand out and I felt furious and stupid and panicky all at the same time. Thank God Mum wasn't there; she would have freaked out. You would have gone ballistic, Dad.

I knew how much I weighed, of course, though scales varied. I'd lost a bit more, which was good.

Got dressed again and Rachel said 'You've been having a really rough time, Jess, haven't you? But I'm here to help. I promise that if we work together, things will get much much better.'

She didn't rush me and wasn't judgemental and that was such a relief. And the idea that she might be able to help is amazing. But what does 'working together' mean? It's just a trap to get me to eat and get FAT FAT FAT.

Normally I'd never cry in front of a stranger, but she kept asking questions and suddenly it all came out and I told her that I really couldn't bear it any longer and I wasn't able to get out of this on my own. And Rachel just smiled and said admitting that was the first and most important step.

And then I panicked and thought what the hell did I say that for? I wished I'd kept quiet cos she talked about inpatient treatment and that freaked me out. I've been feeling so weird recently, like everything's going wrong in my head as well as my body.

Rachel then said if I don't get help, my organs will start shutting down. I'd already looked online and asked Anna and she said yes that's right. Heart, lungs, liver, etc. It's all over socials, too. I would need a breathing tube, ultimately. My periods stopped months ago. I have a layer of hair over my arms. My bones are already too brittle, apparently, which means if I fall over I'm likely to break something, if not now then in the future.

But I don't have a future.

If it's more of this then I don't want it. But what's the alternative?

If I don't do as she says, I'll die.

But would that be so bad? We all get to die in the end. Why the fuss?

Rachel says there is a way out, but I have to really want to get better. To believe I can. But that seems impossible. I haven't got the strength to fight this any longer. It's like a greedy monster that's sucked the life out of me.

I felt like saying, I just want to lose a few more pounds, and it was like she could read my mind, cos she said 'You will never be thin enough for the anorexia, Jessica. Not until you're dead.' And that really shocked and frightened but almost excited me.

But she says we can fight it together. I liked how she said 'together'. Ever since you left, Dad, I felt I've been battling everything on my own. Rachel says she will help me every step of the way but I must *help myself. She said I should really go into a clinic now but I can try and put on weight at home if I like. So of course I said yes − anything rather than a clinic.*

So she's given me two weeks to try putting on weight at home. Diet sheets and all that stuff.

Part of me thinks it would be such a relief to let go. To give up this terrible responsibility. To let someone else make decisions. I have a feeling Nick would say go for it and he's usually right. I have to do something. I feel under so much pressure about exams; (everyone's panicking), having sex with R, doing all my exercises, social media posts and then worrying about food all the time is just too much. So I guess I have to give it a go.

Either that or I surrender. And go under. No more fighting.

All my love, Jess xxx

Chapter Thirty-Eight

Laura

A few mornings later, Laura woke, listening to the patter of rain outside, a can clattering down the street in the wind. She remembered lying in bed with Chris, hearing the foghorn in the distance; a sound she'd always liked. The distant other-worldly noise boomed reassuringly through the night air and in between was a rich stillness, so thick you could almost feel it. Chris hated the sound, but it made Laura feel safe and secure. This morning had a similar quality to it; as if it was taking a deep breath, preparing itself for the day ahead.

Since the meeting with Rachel, Jess had been her usual antagonistic self, arguing over food and bursting into tears of rage. Laura sighed, pushed the duvet aside and headed for the shower, needing time before facing the breakfast battle. 'Remember, what if it all works out?' she muttered to herself in the shower.

When she got downstairs, Jess was already in the

kitchen, busy at the cooker. 'I thought I'd make us porridge, Mum,' said Jess. 'OK?'

As she turned round and pushed her hair out of her eyes, a foul smell hit Laura in the face. What on earth? Jess didn't seem to notice, so Laura scanned the kitchen for a stinky cloth or putrid food. Nothing. Taking a step closer to Jess, she was about to ask if Jess could smell something off. Then she realised it was her daughter's breath.

'Sure. Lovely. Thanks.' How long had Jess's breath been like this and what had caused it? Laura made a note to check. She made tea, wondering what had brought on the porridge: was this prior to seeing Rachel? So she could say she'd made breakfast? 'A bit of milk would be nice, love. Tastes horrible with water.' And had more calories, of course.

Reluctantly Jess got milk from the fridge, poured a tiny amount into the porridge and stirred. 'There, it's ready,' she announced, pouring a huge ladleful into a bowl that she pushed towards Laura. She measured a teaspoon of porridge into the second bowl and sat down.

Laura opened her mouth to protest, then, with an effort, shut it again. She fetched a packet of mixed nuts, raisins and seeds that Jess had decreed were vital and scattered a layer onto her porridge. Jess took the packet and added one nut, two raisins and four seeds.

Laura started to eat, then stopped. Jess was laboriously stirring the blob of porridge and its grains of garnish. Just. Eat. It. She quickly thought of a diversion. 'The woman from the framing shop's coming in today. Shall I ask her to take a look at your print of Dad and see what she suggests?'

Jess nodded. 'OK. But can you bring it back? I'm doing some shots of the silhouette, and I want to make a bigger piece out of them.'

'Sounds good.'

'Maybe she can do the new frame when I'm in Paris.' Silence. She looked at her mother. 'What?'

Laura dug some pumpkin seeds out from her lake of porridge. 'About Paris, Jess…'

Jess tensed, like an animal sensing danger. 'What?'

'Finish your breakfast first.'

'What about Paris?' Jess pulled herself upright.

'Eat first, we'll discuss this afterwards.'

'What's going on, Mum?'

'The school rang. Miss Beaumont says they're worried about you. They'd like you to be a bit… better before you go to Paris.'

Jess's face crumpled. 'But I've been wanting to go to Paris for months. It's the only thing that's keeping me going.'

Laura flinched. While Jess was dishonest over many things, there was no doubt she was telling the truth here. 'I know, love. But you can't blame the teachers for being worried. What happened if you collapsed?'

'I won't.' Jess's eyes flashed and for a second she looked like the feisty girl she had been.

'But they don't know that. We don't want you getting ill and having to be flown back.'

'I won't get ill.'

Laura took a deep breath. 'Will you eat when you're out there? And I mean eat, Jess, don't lie to me.'

Jess squeezed her eyes shut. 'I'll eat,' she whispered.

'Promise?'

'Promise.'

'Let me see your hands. No crossed fingers.'

Jess opened her eyes, laid two skeletal hands on the

table. 'Don't make everything so difficult, Mum,' she said wearily. 'It's bad enough as it is.'

'You're supposed to be trying to put on weight before you see Rachel again.'

Jess stared at the table, tracing round a wooden knot with her finger. 'I want to try,' she said slowly. 'But I can't stand the feeling of food in my stomach.'

Laura took a deep breath, got up, turned to stand at the sink. In the street a young boy was running past, school blazer flapping like wings while his mother followed him, holding hands with a smaller boy. They looked so happy, so carefree. So normal.

Whereas the sheer enormity of what Jess had said was so stark, she couldn't think what to say. Laura turned round. 'I know it's really difficult, darling, but you have to try. Or you won't be able to go to Paris.'

Jess glared at her porridge, raised a teaspoon to her mouth and swallowed, gagging. It was agonising to watch. 'There. Done. OK?' She pushed her bowl forwards and got up. 'Don't pressurise me, Mum. You don't know what it's like. If I can't go to Paris I might as well die.'

Laura felt as if she'd been slapped. 'No, I don't know what it's like, but I do know that you'll die if you don't eat.'

Jess looked up at her, mouth open, eyes wide.

Having started, Laura couldn't stop. 'Don't you understand that this is your last chance, Jess? If you don't eat, it won't be me in charge anymore. You'll end up in hospital. You could even be sectioned. Then God knows what'll happen.'

Tears streamed down Jess's face. She turned and ran out of the room as if she was being pursued.

Laura sat at the kitchen table, shaking. Why had she said that? And yet what was she supposed to say to try and get through to her? She sighed, reached for her phone and typed 'bad breath anorexia'.

'Regardless of the reason for **fasting**, missing out on meals can lead to **halitosis**. Without regular meals or fluids, the mouth slows its production of saliva. Without this bacteria-fighting moisture in the mouth, the tongue and palate can start breeding billions of extra bacteria,' Laura read. Should she tell Jess? It might be an incentive for her to eat something, though she had a feeling it was too late for that.

She stopped herself from looking at the other websites as she walked to work. She knew the data by heart now. 'Anorexia has the highest death rate of any mental health condition, with up to 20% of patients dying from the illness.' She'd made the mistake of googling it months ago. 'Anorexia recovery' was another one to miss, as well.

When she got to the gallery, Laura rang the school. Miss Beaumont listened to Laura outlining the morning's drama and promised to have a quiet word.

Laura sat on a bench eating her sandwich, wishing she'd made a change from the habitual cheese and tomato. The cheap cheese left a metallic taste in her mouth and the tomatoes had made the bread soggy. Sometimes she thought longingly of the days when she could afford to buy a sandwich that someone else had made. With exotic ingredients like coronation chicken, or crab, as a real treat.

When her phone rang she started, saw it was Chris. She'd already told him about the first session with Rachel, so what did he want? 'Hi, Chris, are you OK?'

'Yes. Just wanted to talk to you about this therapist. I talked to her the other day and I gather Jess has another appointment this afternoon. How many sessions is she going to need? I can't afford to pay for more than three. I could probably pay half.'

Laura was so furious and exhausted, she wanted to scream. 'For fuck's sake, Chris. This is our daughter. She's in this state because of YOU. I told you, she'll die if she doesn't get treatment. Is that what you want? Another fucking disaster on your hands, but this time you'll be responsible for the death of your daughter.'

She could almost feel the shock reverberating down the phone. As there was no reply, she said, 'You can ring me when you've managed to find a few hundred quid to keep your daughter alive. Knock it off the cost of decorating a room in your new house.' And she terminated the call.

Laura sat back. Why the hell had she done that? Antagonise the one person who could – and should – pay for Jess's counselling. Oh well, she'd put the cost on her one remaining credit card if necessary. She'd make sure Jess got the sessions somehow.

She looked round, noticing signs of spring all around her. Bluebells were poking their blue spikes tentatively through the earth, the sun was a degree or two warmer, and in a nearby bush, a group of sparrows argued loudly. She leaned back, absorbing the gentle warmth of the sunshine.

'Laura?'

She jerked up, recognising the voice. 'Ben!' She squinted at him, standing above her. 'How are you?'

'Fine, thanks.' He smiled at her. 'I've just been unloading pieces from my van. I called in at the gallery and Andrew said you'd gone out.'

'Would you like to sit down?'

'No thanks, I'm going to get some lunch then I've got to get back to work.'

'Actually, I'd better be heading back too. I said I'd get Andrew a sandwich so I'll walk in your direction if that's OK.'

'Sure.' Ben waited until she got up and they walked off towards the sandwich shop. 'So how's Jess? Do you think Rachel might be able to help?'

'I very much hope so. Jess liked her and said she thought she could trust her, which as you know is so important. But she's been a nightmare since we got home. And now the school's worried she won't be well enough to go on the Paris trip.'

'How long are they going for?'

'Only four days. But it's long enough for her to be ill.'

'Have you asked Rachel her opinion?'

'No. That's a good idea. Thanks, Ben.' She sighed. 'I think it would do Jess good to go, but I don't blame the staff for their concern. I said she could go if she promised to eat, but I don't suppose she will.'

Ben was silent for so long that Laura wondered if he'd heard. 'I was just remembering my sister-in-law. It must be incredibly difficult for Jess,' he said thoughtfully. 'Mind you, it's impossible for everyone concerned, particularly you.'

'It is.' Laura was grateful for his consideration. 'Anyway, how are things with you? Sounds like you're having a grand time – I've been watching your travels on Instagram.'

Ben laughed. 'Most of it's fakery, trying to generate interest in the business.'

'But all those lovely things you found…'

'Well, I did find some, but not that many. Some I just borrowed for social media. I'm trying to sort out a cash-flow problem. I've got to look for another loan.'

'I'm so sorry…'

'I'm not asking for help,' he snapped.

Maybe it was the abrupt way he spoke, combined with this morning's argument, but suddenly Laura felt like she was on a massive wave which was about to break. 'Sorry.' She gulped and tried to swallow her tears as she turned away. 'I just feel really confused about everything and I can't sleep and...'

'Hey.' Ben pulled her towards him and put his arms around her. 'Here, come on,' he said, and it was such a relief to be held and comforted that Laura relaxed and wept into his coat. It smelt of wood polish and musty furniture and was strangely consoling. After several minutes, she pulled back and fumbled for a tissue.

'I'm really sorry, Ben. I've been so worried about Jess. And bills, and Chris... you know.'

'You don't need to apologise. You must still miss him.'

Laura didn't, but she did feel better for a cry. She drew back and gave a watery smile. 'Can I cook you supper as a thank you? For everything.'

'There's no need.'

'Oh.' Laura winced. 'What's the matter with my cooking?'

He grinned. 'I don't know. I've not tried it for a while. And I'd love to come for a meal. But I've got Jake from tomorrow.'

'Bring him too.' Instantly Laura felt cheered. 'It'll be a treat to cook for people who actually want to eat.'

Ben smiled at her. 'Thank you. We'll enjoy that. When?'

'Saturday at six thirty? Jess will be in Paris by then. All being well. I'll let you know if she can't go.'

'Perfect.' Ben's smile widened and it seemed he was assessing her. 'We'll see you then.' And he turned, waved and walked away down the street.

Laura watched him go with a sense of unexpected calm.

She felt relieved at having such a good friend, but also a slight pang that he'd gone.

Her footsteps quickened as she walked to get Andrew's sandwich, feeling quite excited about Saturday. Now, what could she make from the reduced-sticker food section in the supermarket?

Chapter Thirty-Nine

Laura

Later that afternoon, while Jess saw Rachel on her own, Laura sat in the waiting room, her stomach turning cartwheels as she wondered what they were talking about. Alongside Laura's nervousness jostled the profound relief that an expert was now involved. Someone who could – please – save Jess.

'Ms Hocking?' Rachel appeared in the doorway. Her hair was clipped back from her face which emphasised large eyes and a round face. The bright pink lipstick was still in place, contrasting boldly with her grey shirt dress.

Laura followed her down the corridor, heart thudding loudly, hope and fear colliding with every footstep: after all, Jess's life depended on this woman. Inside the consulting room, Jess was sitting on a chair opposite Rachel's desk. Her eyes were pink and blotchy, but she gave Laura a wan smile.

'Jess has been working really hard today, Ms Hocking.'

'Please, call me Laura.' She sat down awkwardly, unsure how to respond.

'We've been discussing Jess having a short spell as an inpatient.'

Laura felt as if she'd been punched; she couldn't breathe. 'Inpatient?' she whispered, her mouth dry.

'Jess feels it's far too hard to try and put on weight at home. So she'd like some help.'

Laura tried to swallow and looked at her daughter, whose eyes were brimming with tears. Laura tried to banish the image of Jess in a Victorian hospital, chained to a bed, that sprang to mind. 'Right,' she whispered.

'I will ring your GP and the Children and Adolescent Mental Health Service and recommend that Jess gets treatment as soon as possible. They will let us know when a bed becomes available.'

'I thought there weren't any mental health services for children in Cornwall?'

'No, but a lot of independent services are being used by the NHS these days.' Rachel smiled encouragingly. 'It's highly unlikely that a bed will come up very soon, but Jess has told me how much she wants to go on this Paris trip, so as long as she promises to eat as much as she can, I think it would do her a lot of good,' Rachel continued. 'I'm happy to talk to her teachers if that helps and explain the situation. After all, it is only for a few days.'

Laura didn't really register the news about Paris, she was still trying to process the fact that Jess would be going into hospital. Anything else was more than she could take in right now. But as she glanced at Jess, she saw her face: terror mixed with relief. A stay of execution. 'That's great.' She tried to smile. 'Jess has been looking forward to Paris for so long.'

Rachel looked at Jess. 'As long as you promise to stick to your diet sheet. Every day…'

Jess nodded fervently. 'Of course.'

She was so convincing that Laura almost believed her. Except that she knew she wouldn't eat much, and she suspected that Rachel knew, too. But it was probably better for Jess to be away for a few days than sitting around at home. 'As long as you're sure she's well enough to go,' she said.

'I feel it's a matter of risk versus benefit,' Rachel said. 'Yes, Jess is very unwell. But this trip is imminent and it's not for long. So if that helps her emotionally and educationally, as well as furthering her talent as a photographer, that seems a lot of benefit for the risks involved. Do you agree?'

Laura nodded. 'Yes, now you've put it like that, I do.'

'Good. As I said, I'm happy to talk to her teachers, as long as Jess will come and see me as soon as she gets back. If either of you has any problems in the meantime, you have my number.'

'That's very kind, thank you,' Laura said, glancing at Jess, who looked as if she'd got a get- out-of-jail-free card.

'That's settled then.' Rachel looked quite calm, as if the Paris trip and hospitalisation were minor everyday occurrences.

'That's great,' Jess said, smiling a real smile for once. She looked at Rachel. 'And I promise to eat properly. I won't let you down.'

Rachel smiled. 'This isn't about letting me down, Jess. It's about learning to look after yourself.' She looked at Laura. 'Are you all right? Do you have any more questions?'

Laura felt as if she'd been knocked over by a truck. 'I'll need to work out transport,' she said, thinking aloud. 'You know, if we need to travel for Jess to get to hospital.' Her head was spinning, but Jess was staring at the carpet so she couldn't see her expression. 'What about the Sowenna Unit at Bodmin?'

'There's a long waiting list and they don't have many beds, I'm afraid,' Rachel said. 'It's possible that a bed will come up there, but unlikely.'

Laura nodded. Jumbled thoughts fell over themselves in her head. She wanted someone to vacuum them out, to make her head a quiet, ordered place where she could formulate constructive thoughts. She looked at Jess. It was agonising to see her daughter's vulnerability. She so wished she could do more to help, to make this horrible illness go away. Despite agreeing with Rachel, Jess didn't look well enough to do anything, let alone go to Paris.

'Please don't hesitate to ring,' repeated Rachel. She was looking at Laura with sympathy, as if she knew how Laura felt. 'There's a lot to take in.'

'Thanks.' Laura stood up, legs shaking. She shook Rachel's hand, turned to Jess and gave what she hoped was a reassuring smile. Jess smiled back, looking, for a moment, like the confident girl she had once been. It was good to know that hidden underneath those poor bones was still the essence of her daughter. I can do this, Laura told herself. She took a deep breath, let it out slowly and walked towards the door with Jess. I have to do this. I have to be strong for Jess.

Chapter Forty

26 March 2024

Jess

She's clever, Rachel, and I kind of admire her for that. Somehow she makes me tell her the truth. Today she said 'Could you describe yourself, Jess?'

Well, I know that trick. I know exactly what I look like. I weigh myself every morning. I hide the scales in the back of the wardrobe in my room. Mum doesn't know about them. She'd ban them.

Anyway, I look at myself in the bathroom mirror, which is spotted with age and has a chunk of glass missing from the top left-hand corner. But I can still see myself, and it's weird cos the body I see looks thin; I can count my ribs and all my bones stick out, but I feel fat.

So I said 'Fat stomach, legs like sturdy telegraph poles, big knees.'

She didn't contradict me like most people do, but said 'What about your feet?'

'I have big feet with long toes, like a man.'

'What about your face?'

That's more difficult to describe. 'Big nose. Square jaw, round cheeks.'

I thought no one would want to kiss me, but Ryan does. Though of course I didn't tell her that. He's still on at me about having sex but I've said no. He's losing patience, though. I'm worried that when he sees me naked, he won't want to have sex cos of the way I look. So I don't know what to do.

The other day he said 'Don't you ever eat anything? A bloke could cut themselves on you. I like something to hold on to, you know. You're even thinner than Fran and she was scrawny enough.' And I thought, does that mean he's sick of me? I couldn't bear it if he was. But I can't eat just to please him.

I don't know what he sees in me, though. When I asked him, he'd had some vodka so he was in a good mood and he said, 'Because you're different and you're a challenge.' I wasn't sure how to take that.

Anyway, Rachel said 'And your eyes? Your hair? What are they like?'

'My eyes are green flecked with brown. And my hair used to be long and thick but it's been coming out in clumps for ages now.'

Rachel said 'Why is that?' She smiled so I knew she wasn't being mean, that she's on my side. Sort of. But she had me there.

I had to say 'Well, maybe I'm not eating the right food for my hair to grow.'

So she asked about my nails.

My nails are a disaster: broken off and cracked, bitten and split. I held them out.

'And your teeth?'

I shrugged. Another disaster area. 'I've had toothache for the last six months, on and off.' I didn't mean to tell her that, it sort of slipped out.

The dentist took out three teeth cos I've had abscesses that wouldn't heal cos I've got gum disease. He said this was because I'd been 'neglecting my diet'. That I should be 'a healthy weight'. Like the other fat people in his surgery? No thanks, buddy. Not for me. Ever. He then asked to see Mum and went off to talk to her in another room. I s'pose he said the same thing to her cos she was all white and worried-looking after.

Anyway, quite often when I tell Rachel something she doesn't reply but sort of listens with the whole of her body, like she accepts what I say but doesn't judge me and I almost feel safe with her. I mean, I don't trust anyone, but I get the feeling she likes me, or at least cares about me. Weirder still, she seems to understand what's going on in my head.

So I said 'My teeth are crap too,' and when I started talking, more came out, without her even asking. I even told her what it was like trying to eat. 'Like trying to climb Everest in bare feet. I can't do it.'

She nodded, like encouraging me to go on. So I did. 'Food has become such a massive thing for me. Like at school last week, I was watching them in the canteen, thinking how can they just sit there and eat turkey curry with rice and not think about the million calories in each plateful?'

'How would you feel if you ate that curry, Jess?'

I shuddered. 'It'd fester in my stomach and grow and grow and make me so fat. Not just curry but any food. It's evil and dangerous and disgusting and terrifies the hell out of me. It's like every bit of food is at war with me, and it's winning.'

I stopped, but again she just nodded and said 'Carry on.'

And suddenly it was really good to tell someone how I felt. 'I'm too scared to eat anything now, and while I hate being around food, there's a weird fascination in watching other people eat.' I paused, but she didn't seem bothered. 'The smell of that curry tortured me. I imagined having just a bite and my mouth filled with saliva and in a way I long to be able to eat but I can't. I can't. I won't, won't get fat.'

Rachel just nodded, and we talked some more and the way she put it, going to a clinic would be a relief. I panicked, but to be honest it would be so good to hand over responsibility. I can't do this anymore. I can't fight it. I'm not strong enough.

But then I thought, exams... 'What about my GCSEs?'

'I understand you're halfway through. When do you finish?'

I told her and she nodded. 'There are no beds available right now,' she said. 'So that means you can finish your exams, and then... why don't you go to Paris as long as you promise to eat what's on your diet sheet?'

I stared at her, wondering if there was a catch, but I could feel a smile spreading across my face, cos going to Paris would be amazing.

Then she said 'You know you will *have* to eat while you're there, or you'll collapse, and believe me you don't want to end up in a Parisian hospital.'

That scared me a bit. I don't know how I'll manage but I must. It's only for four days, and I so desperately want to go. 'I'll be taking pictures,' I said, 'and that's how I feel safe.'

And she said 'Tell me more.'

So I said 'I feel inside my camera there is hope.' I've never told *anyone* that before.

Rachel smiled and said 'Yes, but that hope comes from you, Jess.'

Until she said that, I thought she knew what she was talking about. That I could trust her. But it's just the same cheery shit they all talk.

Chapter Forty-One

Jess

Exams were even worse than I thought they'd be. I found revising *so* hard it was like my brain had slowed right down and I couldn't remember stupid stuff that I knew really well. But I'd look at the exam paper and, like, for English we had to read a passage and then comment on how the writer uses language to describe a person's appearance. Mention the writer's language features and techniques.

Well, that's easy, I thought, but when I read the passage again, I just couldn't *think* and nothing made sense. What were language techniques? Or features? What did they mean? I couldn't ask anyone, and everyone else was scribbling away and I felt so useless I just wanted to cry. I mean, I used to be good at English at my last school. Now I don't understand anything.

Maths, chemistry and physics were as bad as I thought they'd be. Gross. I even went to bed the night before each one with a pile of textbooks under my pillow cos there was a podcast saying how you can absorb information overnight if you do that. Like, how? But even so, I thought anything was worth a go, I was that desperate.

It didn't work – I couldn't answer any of the questions. But after a while I just tried to pretend it didn't matter, and I made things up so at least I was writing something instead of staring at my blank exam paper.

Photography was OK – that was the only one. Over the year we had to do research and contextual investigations, experimentation, recording of ideas and presenting a final piece. Because we'd been working on it every week, we didn't have to sit and spew out loads of crap, so I chose to write about the Box Brownie and although I knew I could have done better, I don't think it was too bad.

I saw Nick after the exam and I'm so glad he's going to Paris, too. It's so cool to have a male friend who you can just be yourself with. He doesn't like exams, either, though I think he'll probably be fine.

Em and Tess don't mind exams. They're much cleverer than me, I know, and they revised at home every night like I should have done, but instead I had to post online about what I'd eaten (or rather, not eaten) and how many steps I'd done, how many floors I'd climbed, that sort of thing. When I saw the likes on my Instagram that made me feel better, but not for long. These people might think like me, but I've begun to wonder, who *wants* to think like me? I'm sick of it. But I can't unthink the way I think right now.

And even that doesn't make sense.

I know I've failed all my exams and I don't want to think about how disappointed Mum and Dad will be. Disappointment is somehow worse than anger or shouting – I could take that cos I could shout back. But it's the resigned expression they get when I've let them down that I know will make me feel even worse than I do at the moment. And that takes some doing.

The only thing that's keeping me going is the Paris trip. I'm part scared and part really excited, and I don't know how I'll manage or how to make myself eat, but the fact that we'll be taking pictures makes me feel safe. And I've been looking forward to this for *so* long, I couldn't bear for anything to happen to stop me going.

Chapter Forty-Two

Laura

Jess begged Laura incessantly, so having got Rachel's endorsement for the Paris trip, Laura went into school to see Miss Beaumont and the photography tutor. The school was understandably nervous about Jess going on the trip, but Laura pleaded Jess's case (*"please*, Mum"), and to her delight, Mr Thompson said he'd keep a special eye on Jess, and apparently Emma and Tess and Nick said they would, too. So the trip was on.

Laura helped Jess pack but, as she came into her bedroom with her washbag, Laura could smell her daughter's breath. Surely the kids at school could, too? Laura didn't want others to tease her. But what to say?

For the first time in months, despite her agonising thinness, Jess looked more cheerful. 'Don't worry about me, Mum.' She glanced at her mother. 'What's up?'

Laura took a deep breath. 'Well, darling, you might

want to get some mouthwash or something. Your breath's a bit... smelly. It's due to not eating.'

Tears sprang into Jess's eyes and her face crumpled while Laura cursed herself.

'I've got some, Jess,' she said. 'I hope you don't mind me saying, but I didn't want anyone else to... to... She drew Jess to her and held her tight.

'Thanks, Mum,' said Jess, her voice muffled against Laura's jumper. 'I'm OK now.' She pulled back so Laura gave her the mouthwash and Jess headed for the bathroom. When she returned she shoved the mouthwash in her case angrily. 'OK, done now.'

'And don't forget to go to the Musee d'Orsay. You'll love it there. And...'

'Mum, leave it.' Jess gave her a brief kiss on the cheek. 'Come on, we'd better go. Don't want to be late.' Her mood seemed to have recovered, thankfully.

Half an hour later, Laura and Jess arrived at the school and Laura scanned the teenagers heaving bags, chattering and laughing as they boarded the coach. Jess was with Emma and Tessa, more animated than she was at home, but then everyone was excited. Jess looked at least half the size of her slimmest friends, and Laura once again wondered if this trip was a good idea. But what was the alternative?

She waved until the bus disappeared from view, chatted to a few other mothers then started walking home. They'd had a stay of execution over hospital and she only hoped Jess would enjoy the trip, that nothing would go wrong while she was there.

Laura wondered if Ryan was on the bus. Would he sit with Jess? If they were going out, what did that mean? Had they had sex? If so, had they used protection? It was difficult to believe anyone would want a girlfriend as thin as Jess, but

Ryan had been around for several months so he must have feelings for her. 'Don't you dare hurt my daughter,' Laura repeated like a mantra, shoving her hands in her pockets.

The weather was warmer and she was glad to see more outside activity. In the park, dog walkers had churned up much of the ground, but a few battered-looking primroses showed their faces, and Laura noticed the first violets poking their heads up.

Around the harbour, a small boy rowed his dinghy, oars dripping deftly in and out of the water, while the first of the day-tripper boats headed up the river to Truro with a long low hoot of its horn that echoed round the harbour. Another dog walker enjoyed the sand freshly washed by the tide, and a fresh breeze encouraged surfers to try out the mounting waves. Soon the pier would be full of visitors, stopping to take pictures of the church tower on their phones, dripping ice creams and pasty crumbs, while gulls edged ever closer, fixing them with cruel, determined eyes.

On the way home, she walked round the supermarket, picking up a large pack of minced beef with a reduced sticker. Ben and Jake needed protein so she'd make spaghetti bolognese. Not very inventive but filling and nutritious. As she queued to check out, she looked at the people in front of her and realised that two down was Kayla. She hadn't seen Laura and was busy talking on her phone.

Laura glanced at her basket, always interested to see what other people were going to eat. Something organic and wholesome, no doubt. But Kayla's shopping consisted of a large pizza and a tub of full-fat ice cream. Oh, and a big bag of Kettle crisps.

Laura's mouth twitched. Well, who knew? As she loaded her yellow sticker purchases onto the belt, she heard Kayla saying, 'No, Chris is out tonight so I'm going to do a workout, a stir fry, have an early night.'

Stir fry my foot, thought Laura, grinning. What a hypocrite! I can't wait to tell Anna about this. She was tempted to tell Jess, but felt that would confuse matters too much.

Kayla hurried off, still talking, and Laura thought of the meal she would cook on Saturday. The prospect of a relaxed evening with people who enjoyed eating was incredibly cheering. An entire meal that wouldn't be an exhausting war, with the table as battleground.

Even so, Laura missed Jess already and wondered how she was feeling. Looking at the tracker on her phone, she saw the school bus was on the way to the ferry. But would Jess eat? Worrying about Jess was second nature, but recently it had ratcheted to mountainous levels. As Laura carried the shopping home, she reflected guiltily that over the next few days, life would be quieter but so much less stressful without her daughter. She'd splashed out on a bottle of wine, might have a glass while she was cooking the meal. Have a shower, think about what to wear.

And when she got home, there was Eddie's little face at the door, welcoming her back.

Chapter Forty-Three

Laura

At six on Saturday evening Laura pulled on clean jeans and her favourite red jumper. As she applied mascara, the doorbell rang and she jumped, smudging her nose and eyes. Swearing, she grabbed her flannel, scrubbed at her face and ran downstairs.

Jake and Ben stood on the doorstep, Jake carrying a bunch of red and yellow tulips, Ben with a bottle of red wine. 'Jake was worried about being late.'

'Lovely to see you.' Laura said, conscious of the black splodges around her eyes. 'Please come in.' She showed them into the kitchen, produced wine glasses and a tumbler for Jake. 'Now, Jake, I've got water or orange juice.'

'Water's fine, thanks.'

'Right,' Laura said, intent on fixing her smudged mascara. 'I've got to nip upstairs…'

'I'll do the drinks,' said Ben. 'You do whatever.'

Laura shot upstairs to try to repair the damage. In the

mirror she could see one eye untouched by mascara, the other one looked like a black eye. Grimacing, she scrubbed it clean and started again.

When she hurried downstairs a few minutes later, she found Ben and Jake looking at Jess's Eddie project, leaning against the sofa. Ben handed her a glass of wine. 'You look well,' he said, with a glimmer of a smile. 'Though I rather liked the panda effect.'

Ben had broken the tension and she relaxed. 'The doorbell interrupted my usual four-hour make-up session,' she said, grinning.

'Have you got something to put these in?' Jake said, handing her the tulips. He pointed to the photographs. 'These pictures are so cool. Look at the dog's eyes.'

'Jess is very talented,' said Ben. 'Like you. I was looking at the online gallery shop you set up; it's excellent. Easy to navigate, and you've made everything look really appealing.'

'Thank you.' Laura blushed. 'It was my first go at setting up something online.' She opened a cupboard in the kitchen, found a vase and busied herself arranging the tulips.

'So are these pictures going on the wall?' Jake said.

Laura nodded. 'When I get time. It's on my to-do list.'

'But it won't take long. All you have to do is bang some nails in the wall.'

'Jake!'

'What? Is that rude? I don't mean to be…'

'No, it's not rude.' Laura smiled. 'It's one of those five-minute jobs that I haven't got round to.'

Ben put down his drink. 'Why don't I do it? Get it out of the way for you.'

'No, honestly. I hang pictures at work every day.'

Ben grinned. 'Hammer and nails?'

Laura smiled gratefully. 'Thanks. I promised Jess I'd hang it by the time she gets back.' She foraged in the kitchen for her tool kit and handed over hammer and nails.

'She must love Eddie very much,' Jake said, watching Ben hang the pictures.

'She does. We both do.'

'So, would you ever think about having another dog?'

She shook her head. 'No, it's too expensive and we don't have room.'

'What about looking after one?'

'Jake!'

'What? Is that rude?'

Ben groaned. 'No, Jake. Not yet.'

'Can I, Dad? Please?'

'Oh all right.' Ben turned to Laura. 'I'm really sorry. The idea was to ask when we'd relaxed a bit, but Jake likes to charge straight in there, as you might have noticed.'

Laura smiled. 'OK, Jake, what is it?'

'It's a favour.' He paused, his dark eyes, so like Ben's, growing huge. 'A big favour.'

'Wow.' Laura smiled at the earnest expression on Jake's face. 'What is it?'

Jake leaned forward. 'Well, Dad has this client, and he's got to go into hospital next week.'

'Right.' Laura waited.

'And he's got a dog,' Jake continued. 'He's ever so nice and he's called Pedro and he's a rescue dog and he's six.' He beamed. 'I wanted to look after him but Mum doesn't like dogs, and Dad says we can't have him on the boat 'cos Pedro isn't used to boats and he might fall off the gangplank.'

Laura nodded. She could see where this was going.

'I'd better explain,' Ben interjected. 'Pedro is a six-year-old staffie cross, very sweet-natured and well trained. My client, Jim, has to have heart surgery next week and the dog sitter who was booked has just strained her shoulder and can't have him, so poor Jim's thinking of cancelling his op.'

'Oh, poor man. So you want me to look after the dog?'

'Well, I know you're very busy, and I can see this place isn't exactly roomy for two dogs, but you were the first person we thought of. And he'd pay you.'

Laura sipped her wine and, as if Eddie heard the conversation, he got out of his bed and padded over to her, laying his chin on her knee. 'Well, Eddie usually loves other dogs. He's getting on a bit now, so maybe a younger dog would cheer him up.' The money would be useful, certainly, and it wouldn't be for long if the guy was having surgery.

She looked from Jake's beaming face to Ben's concerned one. She didn't want to let anyone down. And she did owe Ben for Jess's print. And if she'd be paid… 'I'd have to take Pedro to work with me and Eddie, so he'd have to be able to stay in his bed while I'm at the gallery.'

'I don't think that would be a problem. He spends most of the day with Jim so he's not used to fifteen-mile walks or anything. And he's very sociable.'

'Well, I'd have to see how he and Eddie get on, but in principle, yes.'

'I knew you'd say yes!' Jake gave her a high five.

'I'll double check but Jim mentioned £25 a day, if that would be OK,' said Ben. 'He's got an account with the vet so you wouldn't need to worry about that, and he's got all his food at home plus extra money for expenses.'

Laura calculated rapidly. That was about £200 a week, which would make a huge difference. And Jess loved dogs… Her spirits lifted significantly and she could feel a big smile spreading across her face. Maybe things really would work out? 'That sounds fine,' she said. 'Just fix up a time to meet Pedro and we'll go from there.'

'That's fantastic news,' Ben said. 'If you don't mind, I'll ring Jim now because he's so worried.'

'Not at all. I'll put the pasta on and we can eat soon.' She turned to Jake. 'You hungry?'

He nodded. 'Yes. What is it?'

'Spag bol.'

'Great! Can I have cheese with it? Mum won't let me have cheese and it makes all the difference.'

'Of course you can. Here, you can grate it.'

Laura fetched a bowl, cheese and a grater and left Jake to it while she boiled water for the spaghetti. His intense concentration was touching, as was his slight chubbiness, which was a relief after Jess's agonising thinness. She sipped her wine as Ben came back into the room.

'He said would it be possible to bring Pedro round in about an hour?'

Laura nodded. 'Fine.'

'Brilliant. I'll text him now.' Ben reached for his wine and sat down. 'Jim came back to Cornwall to look after his mother, but she died so he employed me to clear her house and sell what's valuable. We were chatting the other day and he was looking so worried, I asked what was the matter and he said, "I don't suppose you know anyone who'd look after my dog."' Ben smiled. 'So I thought of you.'

'Well, I'm glad you did.' Laura added the pasta to the boiling water. 'I'm looking forward to meeting them both.'

'He's cool.' Jake finished grating the cheese, ate a furtive mouthful and looked at the bowl. 'Is that enough?'

'I think so, yes.'

Ben leaned forward. 'Are you sure you can manage? I

don't want you taking on too much, especially with Jess not being well.'

'It might help her,' Laura said. 'Anyway, she'll be going into hospital when there's a bed. So it'll be company for me and Eddie.' A lump gathered in her throat at the idea of Jess's ordeal ahead.

'I'm so sorry, Laura,' Ben said. 'But that's progress, isn't it? She really needs help.'

Laura nodded, unable to speak, her face hot with unshed tears. Hurriedly she tasted the bolognese sauce: it was rich and meaty, robust enough for three hungry stomachs.

'Have you seen Anna recently?'

Laura nodded, grateful for the change of conversation. 'Yes. She used to work at one of the big London hospitals then came home a few years ago when her Dad got poorly. He died last year but she stayed so it's lovely to have her around. She's Jess's godmother, and they get on really well. She's helped so much.'

'Does she have children?'

'No, she's been a bit unlucky in love.'

Ben raised his eyebrows. 'I know the feeling.'

Laura flushed and looked down, prodded the spaghetti. 'OK, we're ready. Do you want to sit down?'

Ben looked up as Jake came to the table. 'Washed your hands?'

'Of course, Dad.' Jake sat down, sniffed appreciatively. 'This looks fab. Can I start?'

'You certainly can.' Laura smiled watching them both tuck in with relish. 'I can't tell you how nice it is to sit down with people who actually enjoy food.' Although she couldn't escape the irony of having a boy who needed to lose weight, while Jess was the polar opposite.

There was silence while they ate, then Jake looked up and grinned, a tomatoey ring round his mouth. 'This is fab. I really like food but I put on too much weight when Mum and Dad split up.'

'Jake!'

Laura glanced from him to Ben, to see how he'd take it.

'What? It's a common reaction. We either overeat,' he wound a thick coil of spaghetti into his spoon, 'or we don't eat at all. At least I'm not starving myself to death.'

Ben's fork froze in mid-air. Laura was too shocked to speak. The silence stretched.

Jake sucked on a strand of spaghetti. 'Now what? You're not even saying, 'Jake!''

Ben looked down, then up. 'Laura's daughter Jess has a problem with food.'

Jake reached for the garlic bread. 'Is she anorexic?'

'Yes.' Ben added, 'She's not very well at all.'

'Will she have to go to hospital?'

Once again, Laura's eyes stung with tears. 'Yes, she will, Jake.'

Ben added quickly, 'But not for long, I'm sure. What made you ask?'

'They talk about it at school,' Jake said matter of factly. 'I don't know which is worse, to be really thin or—'

'Jake!'

'Sorry,' he said. 'I was just trying to…'

'It's OK,' said Laura faintly.

The silence wasn't as heavy as last time, then Ben said, 'This is delicious.'

'I'm glad you like it,' Laura said, relieved that the conversation had been diverted. After they all finished, Jake got his phone out.

'You can have your phone when we've washed up,' said Ben. 'Come on, Jake.'

'No, you're guests,' protested Laura.

'Jake,' Ben said, and they stood up and began to clear the table. 'You relax, Laura. It was a lovely meal, thanks so much. A real treat to be cooked for.'

Laura sat back, watching the two of them at the sink: Ben washed while Jake criticised the cleanliness of the plates and dried up. It was clear from the banter that this was an established routine. When they finished, Jake grabbed his phone. 'Can I go next door now?'

Ben looked at Laura who nodded. 'Of course. Thanks for doing the washing up.'

Jake retreated next door while Ben and Laura sat in the kitchen. It was almost as if the clock had whizzed back twenty-five years but suddenly she felt awkward and couldn't think what to say.

'Jake did put on a lot of weight,' Ben said. 'He gets called names at school.'

'I'm so sorry. But he'll shoot up soon. The weight will fall off him.'

He smiled, but the worry was clear in the lines round his eyes. 'I'm sorry he was so crass.'

'Not at all. He was just asking questions that needed answers.' She peered at the wine label. 'This is really nice. What is it?'

'Argentinian Malbec. One of my favourites. What do you think?'

Laura hesitated. What to say in front of someone who knew so much about wine? 'It's lovely. Very smooth... strong... tasty.' She shrugged and gave an apologetic smile. 'Well, you know the technical terms.'

Ben smiled. 'Smooth, strong and tasty is an excellent

description. 'What do you drink when you're out with Anna?'

'Red. Or white. Or cider, occasionally.'

He threw back his head and laughed. It was such an infectious sound. It took years off him, and Laura caught a glimpse of the teenager he'd once been. She poured more wine for them both. 'So what's happening at work?'

'I've got several more house clearances coming up and I'm putting together stuff for another sale. How about you? Do you enjoy the gallery?'

'I do.' Laura sipped her wine. 'I've been there nearly two years now. But the manager is temporary so I don't know how secure my position is.' She glanced at him. 'I really need that job, and I'm not qualified to do anything else.'

Ben frowned, looking thoughtful. 'Well, let me know what happens, won't you?'

'I will, thanks.' Laura sat back. Behind her the clock ticked and she could hear the chatter of the television next door: simple, homely sounds. She smiled. 'Jess's Eddie project looks great on the wall. Thanks so much for sorting that out.'

'She has a very good eye.' He grinned, glancing at her phone. 'Have they arrived in Paris yet?'

Laura picked up her phone. 'Yes! I hope she's OK. She's only fifteen and she's never been on a trip like this before. I keep wondering whether to text her, but I've held off so far.'

Ben sipped his wine thoughtfully. 'The staff will keep a close eye on her. It's good that she's still got outside interests; that's really important.'

'Yes, particularly as she's not doing well at school, other than photography. She said her head feels a real mess.'

'Poor Jess. So when does she go into hospital?'

Laura shuddered at the thought. 'Whenever they have a bed. It could be months, could be weeks, who knows?'

'Well, don't forget there's pet therapy in the form of Pedro.' His phone pinged. 'Oh, Jim's outside. Shall I open the door?'

'Thanks.' Laura got up, curious to see what Jim – and Pedro – were like.

Ben opened the door. 'Jim! Good to see you. This is Laura.' He stepped aside to reveal a slight man of medium height with glasses and a dark beard. Beside him was a stocky, brindled dog with bandy legs and a slightly woeful expression.

'Hello, Jim,' said Laura. 'Do come in. So this is Pedro?' She crouched down to say hello just as Eddie heaved himself out of bed and joined her.

'He had a rough start,' Jim said, coming in. 'When I rescued him, he'd been used as a bait dog on the streets.'

'Oh, poor boy.' Laura held her breath as the two dogs circled each other, sniffing each other's butts. That appeared to be satisfactory, for they curved back for more sniffs, and Eddie retreated to his bed, where he farted and sank back to sleep.

'Sorry,' said Laura, giving a rueful smile. 'But I think that means Pedro has the seal of approval.'

Jake appeared. 'Hi, Jim. I told Laura what a lovely dog Pedro is. I think he'd be happy here. It's not too tidy.'

'Jake!' cried Ben. 'That's really rude.'

'What? It's not meant to be. You know how Mum's always plumping up cushions and you've got to be careful? Well, it's not like that here.'

Laura grinned. 'I'll take that as a compliment.'

'Sorry,' said Ben, grimacing.

'Not a problem.' Laura turned to Jim. 'Glass of wine? Cup of tea?'

Jim shook his head. 'No, thanks. I just wanted to see what you think of my Pedro.'

Laura swallowed hard, touched by the love in the man's voice. 'Well, it's not me that counts, it's Eddie, and he thinks Pedro's OK.' She glanced at Pedro who gazed back, as if assessing her. Was this a good idea, when the cottage was so cramped?

But Jim was in need and so was Pedro. Laura knelt down, stroked Pedro's head and looked into his eyes. One was green, one was brown with green spots, and Pedro panted happily, nudging her with his nose. She stroked his ears and under his chin and he smiled.

Laura laughed. She scratched his back and Pedro groaned in delight and leaned heavily against her, opening his eyes as if to say, 'go on!'

'What do you think, Laura?' asked Jake. 'Do you like him?'

Laura smiled. 'Pedro's lovely. I'd be delighted to look after him.'

A hesitant smile lit up Jim's face. 'Oh, I'm glad,' he said. 'I've been so worried.'

'Can I take him to work?'

'Whatever's easiest. Ben said you work in a gallery.'

'Yes. He'll get a good walk there and back. And I can take them both out at lunchtime.'

Jim grinned. 'He'll be in seventh heaven.'

Laura returned the smile. 'That's fine then.'

'If you let me have your bank account details, I can pay you in advance, if that's OK.'

Laura blinked. He *was* organised. 'Thanks.'

Ben bent down to pat Pedro. 'I can bring Pedro's stuff round tomorrow, if that suits you, Laura.'

'Thanks, Ben.' Jim smiled. 'Much obliged.'

Laura nodded. 'Fine with me. What time?'

'Two pm?'

'That's perfect. Pedro can have his first walk in the afternoon with me and Eddie and spend the rest of the day getting used to us.'

Jim got up. 'I can't thank you enough – both of you.'

Laura smiled. It was easy to like this diffident, quiet man who clearly adored his dog. 'It will be my pleasure,' she said. 'I look forward to seeing you tomorrow.' She knelt to Pedro. 'And you, mate, how about having a little holiday here?' Pedro nudged her with his nose and Laura grinned. 'He's gorgeous. I'll make sure he's as happy as he possibly can be.'

Jim's eyes filled with tears. 'Thank you,' he croaked. 'I must go now. Don't see me out.' And he and Pedro hurried out of the door.

Ben turned to Jake. 'Come on, Jake, we'd better be making tracks, too.' He turned to Laura. 'Thank you so much for a lovely meal and also for helping Jim out. We'll see you tomorrow at 2pm.' He kissed her briefly on the cheek and ushered Jake to the front door.

'Thanks,' said Laura, savouring Ben's salty outdoors boat smell.

'Bye!' said Jake. 'I think you and Eddie will be very good for Pedro. He needs a bit of fun.'

Laura laughed. 'Thanks, Jake.'

She stood on the doorstep and waved as they disappeared down the street, Jake chattering busily. It reminded her of Jess at that age, always asking questions. Bringing friends home, filling the house with noise and squabbling and laughter. Chris, pretending he didn't mind the noise and disorder, then losing patience. Loud shouts and Jess laughing at him. How she missed that time. Although, of course, she didn't miss Chris.

Chapter Forty-Four

Jess

Paris was amazing. In fact, it was even better than I imagined, or would have been if I hadn't felt so crap all the time. And, of course, I had to try and eat which was dire.

But we had a good day at the Louvre, despite the *Mona Lisa* being such a disappointment.

'Bit of a let down,' said Nick. 'I knew she was small, but she's tiny!'

'Why do people get so excited about her?' Emma said. 'Let's go to another room.'

So we did and I walked round with my mouth open. 'To think that people painted so much stuff and it was so *good*,' I whispered, thinking no one would hear.

But Nick did. 'I know,' he said, meeting my eyes with a smile.

Anyway, after our meal we were back in the girls' hotel when Ryan came over. Boys were allowed in until ten and this was nine thirty.

'Why don't you come back to my room?' he said. 'I know you're not supposed to,' he added, seeing my face, 'but if you go up the fire escape, my room's just along the corridor. No one will see you.' He kissed me and my knees went all wobbly. 'Come on, Jessie. I've hardly seen you since we've been here. I've got a present for you.' He looked down. 'I've never bought anyone a present before.'

When he said that I felt all warm inside. I mean, I knew he wanted to have sex, but he did look so adorable, not like the Ryan he can be. So I said 'OK.'

When I got there, he kissed me again and I felt really… you know. And he gave me this gift-wrapped present. It was wrapped in tissue paper and inside was this really beautifully carved wooden box.

'It's for putting stuff in,' he said.

I turned it over and lifted the lid and it felt warm and smooth and I thought, I don't know what I'll put it in, but I'll treasure it forever. 'It's amazing,' I said and he kissed me some more, and I could feel him getting big and I started to panic.

'Come on, Jess,' he said. 'I know you want it as much as I do.'

I felt like crying and wriggled out of his arms. 'I don't,' I whispered.

He stared at me and the lovely look in his eyes had gone and he looked cold and angry. 'You fucking prick tease,' he spat. And he came towards me and I ran to the door, pulled it open and ran down the corridor. I didn't think about the fire escape, I just ran till I reached the stairs and ran down them and out of the front door and ran across the street and into our hotel and I was panting and shaking, and all the time I was listening to see if he was behind me, but I couldn't hear him, and when I got into the reception area, there was a big sofa and my legs sort of crumpled and I fell onto it in a heap.

The woman behind the desk said something in French, which I think was 'are you OK?' So I said 'Oui, merci,' and I sat there trying to stop shaking, but was too weak to move. I realised I'd left his present in his room and I wondered if he'd give it to me later, or if he'd keep it. And then I started crying and I couldn't stop, and the lady behind the desk was lovely and she got Emma and Tess cos we were sharing a room, and so I told them and they were furious.

'Pricktease, my arse,' said Tess. 'What a fucking wanker.'

And Emma joined in, with the worst names they could think of, till I started feeling better and even smiled a bit.

I didn't sleep much that night and the next morning, Ryan completely ignored me, which was a relief. I didn't tell Nick cos I felt really bad about it. But the next evening Ryan openly went off with Katy Simmons, and I saw she was carrying my box and that really hurt.

'Just shows what a bastard he is,' said Tess. 'Don't think about it, Jess. You're well shot of him.'

'But what's he been saying to everyone?' I said. 'His mates are probably all laughing at me.'

'No they're not,' said Emma. 'And anyway, if anyone asks, just say he had a tiny prick.'

It was so unexpected, I laughed. And then Emma laughed and Tess, and we couldn't stop and I laughed till my tummy hurt.

The last evening, we'd all been out together and I ended up walking back to the hotel next to Nick. I thought how easy I felt with him: I could just be myself and it didn't matter if we talked or not, but with Ryan I felt I had to say something, and try and be someone I wasn't.

Then Nick said, 'Are you OK?'

'Yeah,' I said, wondering whether he'd heard about last night. I felt so crap and looked down at my feet. He'd hate me now.

'I'm glad you're not seeing Ryan anymore,' he said. 'He's a shit.'

I was so surprised I could hardly speak. Nick never said that sort of thing about anyone. 'I didn't realise you hated him,' I said.

'He just wipes the floor with girls,' Nick said. He looked down at the pavement. 'I heard what you said to Emma and Tess. I'm really glad you didn't have sex with him.'

I could feel myself going bright red, but he didn't seem to judge me, or hate me at all. It sounded like he really cared. 'Me too,' I said, and I felt so relieved, because what Nick thought about me really mattered.

Nick nudged me and pulled a face, and he looked so ridiculous my mouth twitched and I began to laugh. Nick laughed too and when we both calmed down, he said, 'I've found a way up onto the roof. Want to come?'

I was dead tired, but I felt a flicker of excitement, something I hadn't felt in so long. 'OK,' I said.

I followed him along a corridor, through a door, up some narrow stairs and there was a fire door. Nick pushed the handle down, opened the door and stepped out onto a little ledge from where I could see the lights of Paris twinkling below us.

'Wow,' I said. 'This is better than anything I could ever imagine. How did you find it?'

Nick looked at me and grinned. 'Just, like, exploring.' He held out his hand to help me onto the ledge.

There was a wall in front of us so I didn't feel like we were going to fall off or anything, and anyway I felt safe with Nick. The ledge looked a bit uncomfortable cos my bum's a bit bony, but Nick took off his jacket.

'Here, we'll sit on this,' he said, spreading it on the ground.

We did, and it was cosy sitting there, side by side, watching Paris open up below us. Cars hooted, blasts of music blared out, taxis rumbled by, the Eiffel Tower glistened in the distance, and I drank it all in, the Frenchness of it, knowing I'd never forget this moment.

'Thanks,' I said to Nick. 'It's the best ending to the trip I could possibly imagine.'

He shrugged and said, 'Glad you like it.'

I waited, sensing he wanted to say more. But he didn't. He sat next to me, so I could feel the warmth of his leg against mine. He didn't kiss me or anything, just sat close beside me, as my friend.

Chapter Forty-Five

Laura

Ben and Jake dropped Pedro off the following afternoon, together with his bed, flea and worm tablets, feeding bowls, toys and a large sack of dried food, plus a few tins. Tucked in with the food was a note from Jim.

> *Thank you so much, Laura. I can rest assured knowing that my dear Pedro will be happy and well looked after in my absence. He is very nervous of kites and fireworks, but apart from that he is a dear, good dog and such excellent company. For a treat, he likes a cube of cheese before bed.*
>
> *I'm sorry I haven't been able to pay the money direct into your account, but here is something towards the first week.*
>
> *With my best wishes and again many thanks,*
> *Jim Boyd.*

Inside the envelope was £300. Laura stared in amazement. 'That's so generous,' she breathed. She could go shopping now *and* pay the electricity bill. 'Could you give me his number so I can thank him?'

Ben got his phone out. 'Sorry, I should have given that to you sooner. Though if there's an emergency, probably better to ring me. No need to worry Jim.'

As Laura walked Eddie and Pedro to collect Jess from the bus, dusk was approaching, but there was a warmth to the air that she hadn't noticed before. The first bluebells were pushing out of the ground like asparagus tips, while primroses grew in lemony scented clumps, a cheerful announcement that spring was on its way. A fresh tang lingered in the air from a recent shower, and now the evenings were getting longer, Laura felt as if nature was turning a corner.

Pedro seemed remarkably at ease, trotting beside her, while Eddie chased the cat on the corner, tried to scoff the sandwich crusts that someone had left underneath a seat, and nearly rolled in fox poo on the edge of the park. Pedro seemed unconcerned, content to sniff here and there. The two dogs ignored each other, which was very restful.

Laura joined other parents at the school gates and tried to spot Jess as the students began to get off the bus. She was one of the last off, accompanied by Emma and Tess and a boy with curly dark hair. Jess hadn't noticed her mother, so Laura was able to observe her with her friends: they all seemed cheerful, though there was no sign of Ryan.

Laura watched the other pupils disperse and waved as Jess grew nearer, watched Jess's face light up when she saw her mother, then the two dogs.

'It's great to see you, Mum,' she said, giving her a hug,

then dropped down to stroke the dogs. 'And you, darling Ed. And who's *this*?'

Laura grinned. 'This is Pedro. His owner is going into hospital tomorrow so he's paying us to look after him for a few weeks.'

'Really? Wow.' Jess stroked his head softly. 'Isn't he lovely?' she said. 'He's ever so gentle.' Eddie gave her a head butt. 'Not like Eddie!' She stroked Pedro's back, slowly working her way down to his haunches, while he closed his eyes in bliss. 'He's so funny!' she said. 'How did you find him?'

'Pedro's owner is a friend of Ben's and he's had to go to hospital so Ben asked if we'd help.'

'Cool.' Jess got up. 'Can I take him?'

Laura handed over the lead. 'He's all yours. He only came round this afternoon, so it's all a bit new to him poor thing. I've put his bed in the kitchen for the moment but I thought he might like to sleep with you tonight. Though Ed will have to approve the sleeping arrangements.'

'Thanks, Mum.'

'So, how was the trip?'

Jess looked down. 'OK,' she said. 'I'm certainly not going out with *him* anymore.'

'His loss,' said Laura lightly. Who was the boy with dark curly hair? She'd better not ask or Jess would clam up. 'What did you think of Paris?'

'It was really tiring walking around all day. We went to loads of galleries and there was so much to take in. But on the last day we could choose where to go, so I went back to the Musee d'Orsay. I love it there.' She sighed. 'It's weird that it used to be an old railway station. I mean, it still sort of looks like one, but if you close your eyes you can imagine all the old steam trains arriving; all that noise and bustle, and people coming and going. Those long dresses and top hats and frock coats and stuff.' She smiled. 'They've got a fabulous photography section there. Lots of it is from 1839 to 1863; did you know that's considered to be the golden age of French and English photography?'

'I didn't know that, no.' Laura paused. 'Do you think this visit will make a difference to your photography?'

'It's given me a lot to think about,' Jess said. 'I wish I'd been there earlier.'

A black cat darted in front of them and dived underneath a car. Were black cats good luck or bad? 'What do you mean?'

'Well, I think I would have got more out of it if I'd been feeling better.'

This was as near as Jess had ever got to admitting she wasn't well. Was this progress? 'Was it too much for you, love?'

'Oh no,' Jess said hurriedly. 'Well, it was all really strange. You know, strange place, strange food, strange language. And then, well, Ryan and I aren't going out anymore.' Her voice was flat.

From her voice, she obviously didn't want to talk about it. But had Jess ended it or him? What had happened? 'Oh well. Plenty more boyfriends to be had.' Laura cringed. How crass.

'Yeah, maybe.' Jess kicked a pebble viciously.

'Maybe now wasn't the best time to go to Paris, but you can always go back.' Laura wanted to say 'When you're better' but that felt like tempting fate.

They turned the corner into their street, and Jess yawned. 'Can't wait to go to bed. I couldn't sleep much in Paris. I'm shattered, Mum.'

Laura risked giving her a quick hug. 'I am too. Come

on, let's give Pedro and Eddie their evening treats, and I'm going to have a hot drink before bed.'

'I'm going to crash, Mum,' Jess said firmly. In other words, she wasn't going to have anything. Laura suppressed a sigh. While she'd missed Jess so much, part of her almost hoped that a hospital bed would come up soon. Having had a respite from tearful, fraught mealtimes, Laura didn't know how much longer she could live on a knife edge, watching her daughter deteriorate even further.

Chapter Forty-Six

13 April 2024

Laura

Jess insisted that Laura come with her to meet Chris the following Saturday.

'I don't mind, darling, but why?'

Jess looked at her feet. 'I'd just like you there. If that's OK.'

'Of course it is.' Laura suspected it was because Chris was liable to say something tactless: he had no idea what to say to his daughter. She could feel tension stretching across her head in a tight band.

'Thanks, Mum.'

They met at a café on the harbour. Chris had been told that Laura would be present, but largely ignored her. Remembering Kayla's calorific basket the other week, Laura wondered if Chris had any idea what his girlfriend was up to. It was ironic that she ate junk food in secret while his daughter ate nothing at all.

'So how was Paris, Jess?'

'It was so inspirational to, like, immerse myself in the photography,' Jess said earnestly, showing a rare spark of herself. 'And all those amazing paintings.' She sighed and took a sip of her peppermint tea. 'But it also made me feel, like, sad.'

'Why?' Chris's brow furrowed.

'Well, how could I ever get to be even a tiny bit as good as those guys?'

'When you start feeling better, that will make all the difference,' Chris said, earning a look that suggested his daughter thought he was really stupid.

'Mr Thompson wants to submit some of my images for the end-of-term exhibition but I don't think they're that good,' Jess said.

'Your grades for photography are excellent,' Laura said. Even if the rest of her subjects were terrible. 'I'm glad he realises your talent.' She glared at Chris – what was the matter with him?

'What were the restaurants like in Paris?' Chris said jovially.

Laura stared at him in amazement. Had he no idea? Ben would never have asked such a crass question.

Jess shrugged. 'Shit,' she said shortly. 'Meals took forever and everyone liked to sit around for ages, just talking. It freaked me out.'

'But that's what people do, darling,' Chris said.

Not your daughter, thought Laura. Did Chris not understand what was the matter with Jess? How ill she was. What a nightmare meals were? 'I'm so glad Em and Tess were on this trip,' she said cheerfully. 'They're good friends, aren't they?'

'Yeah.' Jess looked at Laura and smiled. 'Pedro is so cute!' She turned to her father. 'He looks older than Eddie but actually he's younger and he's very gentle and he and Ed just ignore each other which is so funny.' Seeing her father's blank look she explained, 'He's come to stay while his owner is in hospital.'

'Oh.' Chris gave a half-hearted smile. 'Good.'

Why did I never realise he doesn't like dogs, Laura thought? Never a good sign. 'Where did they sleep last night?'

Jess smiled. 'Pedro slept beside my bed and Ed slept on top of it, just to establish who's top dog.'

'Good!' She didn't sound too down, though Laura knew she'd found it even harder to eat since she got home. She knew Jess didn't want to go into hospital, but at least it seemed she'd finally realised she couldn't cope on her own.

When Jess went off to the loo, Chris turned to Laura and she saw the grief and worry etched onto his face. 'What do we do?' he croaked. 'She looks as if she might collapse, she's so thin, so weak.'

Laura acknowledged the 'we' though in fact he had done nothing. 'I know. As I told you, we're waiting for a hospital bed,' she said. 'The sooner the better. I honestly don't know how long either of us can cope with this.'

'She's just fading away and I feel so useless,' he said, looking down at his hands. Then he looked up. 'I'm sorry I complained about paying for counselling. I'll do anything to help.'

At last! 'Good,' Laura said. 'She may not need it if she's in hospital. However, I'm guessing she'll need more help when she comes out.'

Chris nodded, looking defeated. 'OK,' he said. 'I

understand that part of this… most of this is my fault.' He took a deep breath. 'I'm so sorry.'

Laura looked up at him and nodded. Words didn't seem appropriate.

He looked down at the table. 'There's something else,' he said.

Chris seemed shrunken, fallen in on himself. Oh God, what now? Was he ill? Was Kayla ill? Or – oh no, not pregnant. 'What is it?' Laura's voice came out like a cracked record.

He glanced around as if to check no one was listening. 'It's Kayla,' he whispered.

Oh no, so she *was* pregnant. 'What about her?'

'She's… She's been smoking. Vaping. Whatever you call it.'

Laura stared at him. 'Oh,' was all she could manage. 'Well, that's not a crime, is it?' She was so relieved, she nearly laughed.

'Well, no, but she's always going on about being so healthy.'

Laura tried to straighten her mouth, which kept twitching into a smile. Chris had evidently no idea what junk food his precious girlfriend was eating.

'It's not just that.'

Laura waited. Perhaps he had seen the pizza and ice-cream cartons.

'She's been eating McDonald's. And pizzas. Behind my back.'

Laura choked down a laugh. 'So it'd be OK if she ate them with you?'

Chris looked pained. 'I don't care what she eats, but she's not being truthful.'

'Nor is Jess when it comes to food.'

Chris looked as if Laura had slapped him. 'But what do I *do*?'

'Talk to her.'

'I can't do that!'

'Why not? She's your girlfriend.'

Chris looked down, drained the rest of his coffee. 'I was hoping you might have a word with her.'

'Me?' Laura laughed incredulously. 'Why me?'

'You're so good with people. You always know what to say.'

Laura stared at him in amazement. To her relief, she saw Jess returning from the toilets. She stood up. 'We've got to go now. *You* need to talk to Kayla, Chris. Ask her why she's eating in secret.' She held out Jess's rucksack for her. 'And ask her which is her favourite ice cream.'

'Do you know where Andrew is?' said Deb a few days later, hanging up her coat.

Laura looked up. 'His office is empty but I haven't heard anything from him. I hope he's OK.' She glanced at the office phone as it rang. 'Perhaps that's him. Hello?'

'Laura? It's John Martin here, owner of the gallery.'

'Hello. I don't think we've met…'

'No, not yet. I had a call from Andrew yesterday to say his father's very ill, lives in Cyprus, apparently, so he's going to fly out to be with him.' He paused. 'I get the feeling he won't be back.'

'Poor Andrew. I'm so sorry. Do give him our best wishes.' She cleared her throat. 'Andrew was out a lot anyway, so we're quite used to running the gallery without him.'

'OK, fine, if you wouldn't mind, until I see what I can

do about a replacement. I'll ring you as soon as I have more news. Thank you, Laura.'

Laura put down the phone and relayed the latest to Deb, who shrugged. 'As you said, he didn't contribute much anyway. You run the place, Laura.'

Laura looked up and smiled, feeling as if a beam of sunshine had just lit up her desk. 'Thanks, Deb. That means a lot.'

The current exhibition was due to end, so Laura went round, taking down and packing the paintings. They were full of vibrant primary colours, as if each brought a blast of summer optimism along with the bright reds, blues and greens, mingled with sun yellow and nasturtium orange.

That afternoon, after Deb had gone home, she was making a cup of coffee when her phone rang; a withheld number.

'Hello, Laura? It's Rachel Lomax, Jess's counsellor.'

Laura's heart started thudding. 'Hello, Rachel. Is there a problem? We're seeing you tomorrow, I think?'

'Yes. I wanted to give you advance notice; a bed has come up in Truro, at the Pascoe Centre for Adolescent Mental Health. It's available as from Friday and I thought you'd want to make arrangements as soon as possible. We can talk about everything in detail tomorrow.'

Everything started swimming before Laura's eyes. While she knew this would happen sometime, having it confirmed was another thing altogether. She started shaking, first her hands, then her knees, and couldn't bring herself to speak.

'Laura? Please try not to worry too much. It's the best thing for Jess. In fact, the only thing. Did you want to ask anything now?'

'No,' she whispered, her teeth chattering. 'Thank you for letting me know.'

'At least if she's in Truro, you'll be able to see her more easily.'

'Yes, sorry, I must…' Laura was trembling so much she had to finish the call. She was filled with a gut-gnawing terror that she knew she must hide from Jess. Right now she yearned for a big strong hug, for someone to tell her it would be all right. But that wasn't going to happen.

She hurried to the toilet, put her head in her hands and wept, great heaving sobs that made Eddie whine until she let him in. He sat heavily on her feet, groaning quietly.

After a while her tears stopped, leaving her drained but cleansed. She blew her nose, patted Eddie and went to check on Pedro, feeling slightly calmer. Hospital is what Jess needs, she told herself. It's what we both need. And somehow we will get through this.

She sent a quick text to Chris, her Mum and Ben. *Jess got a bed in Truro as from Friday. Oh God! XX*

Then she typed one to Anna.

Jess got bed in Truro as from Friday so have gone into total brain spin. She doesn't know yet, don't know who will be more terrified, me or her. XXX

The following evening, Laura sat in the kitchen, stunned, after the session with Rachel. Hospital was not just an idea on the horizon but something real, looming and unconquerable, like climbing Everest.

Jess looked so emaciated and fragile that Laura was amazed she could walk. Looking at her daughter made her feel sick; it was all she could do not to call for an ambulance immediately.

The doorbell rang and Laura got up as the door opened

and Anna came in, carrying a bottle of wine. 'Where is she?'

'Upstairs. In bed.'

'Can I see her?'

'Sure. Though I can't guarantee you'll get much response.'

They went upstairs and Laura knocked on Jess's door. 'Jess? Anna's here. Can she come in?'

Hearing a muffled response, Laura pushed open the door and Anna approached the small mound under the duvet. 'Jess,' she said, and her goddaughter's skinny arms emerged from the bedding to receive a hug that went on forever.

'Well,' Anna said. 'Progress.'

'Really?' mumbled Jess. 'It feels like a death sentence.'

'No. This is a reprieve,' Anna said gently but firmly.

'What'll happen?'

Anna cleared her throat. 'Well, you'll have counselling regularly, and occupational and art therapy. Later on, you can go into town for meals, plan shopping and stuff, do normal things.' She looked at Jess's shrunken face poking out from the duvet. 'I know it seems really scary right now, but it'll be so much better when you get there.'

'I hope so.' Tears brimmed from her reddened eyes. 'I'm really scared. But it's also kind of a relief.'

'Mmm?'

'Well, it'll be scary being away from home, but everything's such bloody hard work. I can't deal with food at all. In hospital, they'll control it. That'll be a relief. Sort of.'

Anna nodded, while Laura marvelled at how honest Jess was. She'd never say that to me, thought Laura. But then, I am her mother.

'Any questions, just text me, OK? There's a teacher at

the unit to sort out school work, though I know you've finished your exams, so it depends how long you'll be there.'

How long would it be? How would Jess cope being away from home, without Eddie, without her mother, without Emma? And also, thought Laura, how will I cope without her?

'You look tired, love,' said Anna. 'We'll leave you to it.' She gave Jess another hug and they made their way downstairs.

'Thanks, Anna. It's so good to see you. And thanks so much for the wine.' Laura poured glasses for them both. They clinked silently and sat back.

'So how are you feeling?'

'Exhausted, bewildered, bloody terrified.' Laura took a swig of wine. 'Rachel said they're closely watched all the time. To make sure they don't harm themselves or exercise or throw up.'

'Yes, but that's necessary,' said Anna. 'She needs someone to keep an eye on her. She can't have visitors at first, and she won't be able to use her phone at first either.'

'God knows how she'll cope with that.' Everything seemed insurmountable. 'I hope she'll be OK.' She sighed. 'I know – what if it all works out? I'm banking everything on this. Otherwise…'

'I know. But Jess is brave and strong and determined. Like you.'

'I really appreciate you being here,' said Laura. 'I don't know what I'd do without you.'

'Don't be silly.' Anna smiled. 'You do the same for me. Now, how about I take you and Jess in? I've got to be at work so it's no trouble. Save you getting the bus – she'll need a case and stuff.'

Laura's eyes filled with tears. 'Thanks again,' she

muttered. 'I've been worried about that, but going with you would make a huge difference.' In amongst all this fear and angst and unhappiness, she was so grateful she had such good friends and support.

Anna smiled and raised her eyebrows. 'And remember…'

Laura smiled back. 'What if it all works out?!'

Chapter Forty-Seven

Laura

By the time they got to the Pascoe Centre for Adolescent Mental Health on Friday, despite getting a lift from Anna, Jess was so exhausted she could hardly walk, looked so frail and so ill that Laura was just relieved she would be looked after. Laura felt quite sick looking at her daughter: she stooped like an old woman in a concave body.

They were shown to a bedroom, where a nurse with kind green eyes showed Jess to her bed, and gently told Laura that she should leave now.

Laura tried desperately hard to be cheerful, to stop the tears from welling up. It was all she could do not to grab Jess and yank her out of this cream-walled place that smelt faintly of disinfectant. To take her home. But that was no good either. Her last backward glance made her shudder. Jess seemed to have collapsed in on herself, her body hardly making a dent on the single bed.

'She'll be well looked after, Ms Hocking,' said the young doctor. 'Try not to worry too much. This really is the best place for her.'

Anna hadn't come in with her. 'I'm sorry to leave you here, but I've got a meeting in a minute and I'm not supposed to get involved with patients I know. Are you sure you'll be all right?'

Laura nodded. 'To be honest, Anna, I need to be by myself for a bit. But thanks so much.'

She hugged her friend and made her way to the bus stop, oblivious to what was going on around her. Now Laura sat on the bus, her head leaning against the cold window. Outside a persistent drizzle spattered the windows; people pulled up hoods, reached for umbrellas, dodged puddles. Inside the bus she felt apart from it all, in limbo without Jess. Or the dogs for that matter; they were at home for the morning.

A ping alerted her to an incoming text and she grabbed it, wondering if it was Jess. Surely she had to give up her phone? But it was from Ben, whom she'd been updating regularly.

I *can imagine how you both feel. Ring if you want, any time. Love to Jess, tell her I can bring you in when she's allowed visitors or needs anything. B XX PS Let me know how you get on.*

Laura smiled, gathering strength and courage from his messages. She hadn't rung him back: her head was too full of Jess, and she worried that when she spoke to Ben, he'd be busy, and she didn't want to dispel the glow she was getting from his messages.

The joyful welcome from Eddie and Pedro, who acted as though she'd been away for weeks instead of hours, raised Laura's spirits. Standing in the kitchen, stroking the dogs, she listened to the morning sounds. Bursts of music came from next door, with typical DJ banter. On the other side, intermittent hammering continued. Outside seagulls squawked loudly; it was their mating season.

But inside, the cottage felt empty in a way she'd never experienced before. She could almost see a pall of sadness drifting down the stairs from Jess's bedroom, into the kitchen where the remains of uneaten breakfast lingered on the worktops. Two mugs. One plate with a half-eaten piece of toast. Laura couldn't coax anything else down, and Jess hadn't even bothered trying.

Laura went upstairs, stood in Jess's bedroom. She missed her so much she felt hollow. Opening the heavy old wardrobe, she saw Jess's favourite denim jacket. She held it to her nose, trying to capture the smell that was so much her precious daughter. There it was: rose-scented soap mixed with the slightly chemical smell that came from the photography lab.

Laura glanced down as her phone rang. 'Hello, Mum. How are things?'

'Just ringing to see how it went.'

Hearing her mother's voice, Laura could feel tears welling up. 'She looked so ill and small and pale and...' She gulped, her words coming out in a rush. 'She's really dehydrated so she's going to have to go on a drip, and she's probably going to need antidepressants as well.'

'Oh, darling. I'm so sorry, I could have come with you. When would you like me to come down? I could be there tomorrow.'

'That's really kind, but Anna's coming to stay for a few nights. Perhaps next week?' Laura put the jacket back, shut the wardrobe door firmly.

'Of course. I'll bring food and wine.'

'That would be great, thanks, Mum.'

'Just say what I can do to help.' As ever, her mother's efficient mind was whirling into action. 'But tell me more about this place.'

Laura blew her nose. 'The idea is to get her weight up first, because people can't function when their weight's too low. So that's the priority, but they also have lots of therapy and they need to learn a different attitude towards food, how to eat again properly, how to buy food and eat a balanced diet and stuff.' She sighed. 'You know how long she takes to eat a few mouthfuls; her stomach's shrunk, apparently, so it's going to take her a while to learn to eat meals again.'

'Yes, but she was always a quick eater as a child. I'm sure that'll come back.'

'I hope so. She's got to unlearn all these bad habits, which will be difficult.' Laura sank onto Jess's bed, swung her legs round and curled up on it.

'I heard on Radio Four the other day that it takes six weeks to break old habits and learn new ones.'

'Really? Well, that's good news. Perhaps she won't be there for too long after all. I do worry about her being with other anorexics though, in case she picks up more bad habits. There's some terrifying stuff online. She needs to realise how unwell she is, not be in competition with others. At the moment she thinks she's fat.'

There was a slight pause. 'And will you have therapy with Jess?'

'Yes, family therapy's important too, apparently.' Laura stared at the ceiling, where a crack was creeping in from the window. 'I'm sure a lot is because Chris buggered off so suddenly, but I hope I haven't made matters worse.'

'How could you possibly have done that?' said her

mother. 'Life's been so hard for you both recently. You know, talking to a counsellor might help you, too.'

'Maybe,' said Laura slowly. The thought of telling someone how she felt was tempting but she couldn't imagine trusting anyone that much. 'I miss her already, Mum.'

'Of course you do, but she won't be there for any longer than necessary. There must be a lot of competition for beds,' said her mother briskly.

'You're right. I desperately hope this works. Though I know there's a high risk of relapsing.' Laura's voice broke, her face flushed and she could feel hot angry tears burning salt tracks down her cheeks.

'Oh, darling, I wish I was there. Listen, what are you doing today?'

Laura sobbed and hiccuped, blew her nose. 'I'm going to take the dogs to work, then Anna's coming round this evening when she finishes work.' She gulped. 'It'll be really nice to see you, Mum.'

'Well, let me know which day you want me to come, and I'll stay as long as you want.'

'Thanks so much, Mum. I mean, I'll be at work in the daytime, obviously but…'

'That's all right. There are a few galleries I want to see about possible exhibitions. I can do that while you're at work.'

Laura smiled, felt a rush of warmth sweep over her. 'That'd be brilliant. I'll really look forward to it.'

'Now, make sure you eat something. And have a glass of wine later, that'll help.'

Laura smiled; her mother's answer to most things was a glass of wine. 'I will, Mum.' Her stomach rumbled, reminding her it was a long time since she'd eaten.

Laura ended the call and rested her head against the

coolness of Jess's pillow to try and ease her throbbing head. She was so tired she could hardly think, but knowing that the dogs were here, that Anna and Ben were on call, and her Mum was coming all made her feel safer, protected. As if there was hope after all. That the world wasn't falling apart round her.

Chapter Forty-Eight

6 May 2024

Jess

Watching Mum leave was beyond crap.

Anna dropped us off and we met the guy in charge. He was old, probably Mum's age, but had a nice smile and asked was I clear why I was here for inpatient treatment?

I said, 'Yes, because I can't get better at home.'

He nodded and said, 'Many people find that being an inpatient makes life a little bit easier because we have a routine and a structure, so there's no stress about having to do anything yourself.'

Which sort of made sense. I guess he meant food. All we have to do is eat it. But then I thought, well all I have to do is put on weight then I can go home and lose it again.

I was shown to my room, which I share with another girl, and Mum was asked to leave. It was awful. Her face started crumpling, which meant she was going to cry and I couldn't bear it. Watching her walk down that corridor, I felt as if she'd abandoned me, though I knew she didn't want to go.

I nearly ran after her, but the nurse – Marian - said, 'OK, Jess, this is where you put your stuff,' and showed me the locker next to the bed. 'I just have to check you haven't got anything you shouldn't have.'

'Like what?'

'Laxatives, razors, knives, lead weights. You wouldn't believe what some people try and smuggle in.' She smiled and took away my case.

The girl I'm sharing with came in then. 'Hi, I'm Ros,' she said. 'How old are you?'

'Nearly sixteen,' I said.

She's not as thin as me but has been anorexic for two years, she said. 'I tried to get better through outpatient treatment but it didn't work.' She's got spots, long black hair that needs washing and speaks so softly it's difficult to hear her. 'I'm seventeen and if I can't do my exams, my parents will kill me. They want me to go to university.'

'Where to?'

'Cambridge. To study engineering.' She bit her lip so hard it bled. 'I can't fail my exams, my parents would kill me.'

I sat on the bed, not knowing what to say. Thank God Mum doesn't put that kind of pressure on me.

This afternoon I saw a dietician who asked me loads of questions about whether I was veggie, what we eat at home, what my favourite meals were as a child, all that sort of stuff. I was weighed again, and then she said we'd put together a meal plan which will be reviewed weekly. 'The focus is to get you to a medically stable place, and make sure you gain weight so you feel strong and healthy,' she said.

I felt like saying I don't need to be strong and healthy.

And then I realised that I can't concentrate at all now. All I can think about is food or the lack of it. It haunts me all the time, like when you hear a tune you hate but end up singing it all day. That's anorexia. Except that it never, ever goes away.

When I came back to my room, Ros was there so I asked her what we did all day.

She said, 'You'll have to have snacks in between meals, but not till your stomach's got used to eating again. We have individual therapy and your parents will be asked to come in for family therapy once a week. We also have a tutor to help with our school work so we don't fall too far behind.'

'What about photography?' I said.

Ros shrugged. 'I dunno. You'll have to ask the tutor about that. Homework has to be done in free time, and we have to be in bed by nine every night and they wake us up at six every morning. It's a really strict timetable and staff watch us all the time – day and night. We're never on our own.'

My head was buzzing with all this.

'Once you put on a certain amount of weight you get rewards,' Ros continued. 'Then you'll get your phone back, though you can ring your parents once a day till then.'

'It's so weird not having my phone,' I said, a chill creeping through me. How would I survive without my Instagram and TikTok feeds? Without texting Em to tell her how I am and ask what she's been up to? What about Nick? And Eddie and Pedro? I felt as if one of my arms had been chopped off.

'How long have you been here?' I asked Ros.

'Three weeks and two days,' she replied. 'The first week

is weird, trying to get used to it, but it gets a bit better after that. They try and help you see why you became anorexic in the first place and give you "coping strategies" so you won't do it again.' She shrugged. 'You have to get used to the jargon here: "Coping Strategies" is used a lot, so is "Weight Gain" and "Targets".'

All of those terms made me feel sick. I think Ros saw cos she leaned forward. 'But the most important thing is that you have to want to get better,' she said. 'You have to decide what you want to change about yourself.'

That hadn't occurred to me. I'm not sure I want to get better. However much I hate anorexia, it's my safety net. Or my prison.

'You have to cooperate,' she added. 'And to do that, you need a reason to go on. To live. Otherwise it won't work.'

My heart sank when she said that because I don't have a reason to go on. I mean, I have Mum, and Gran, and Emma, and Nick, and now Eddie and Pedro (I wonder if they could be our therapy dogs?) and of course photography. But are any of those enough reasons to go on?

Chapter Forty-Nine

Laura

The following morning, Laura awoke at five, imagining a terrified Jess. Overwhelmed. Feeling lost. Abandoned. It was torture not being able to message her, but the staff had been firm. Jess could ring once a day, but other than that she would not have access to her phone for the time being.

So Laura had to wait. She looked at the leaflet the clinic had given her, impressed by their goals. Turning the page, she read, "We aim to help patients work out why they feel the need to control their lives in such a destructive manner. We help them take responsibility for choosing food, and eating it in different environments. We discuss personal goals. Later on, we take residents shopping, with staff, and eat snacks outside the clinic. The aim is for residents to reach and maintain a healthy weight within an agreed range. We look at how to prevent relapsing, learn how to live a more normal life, and return to school."

Laura thought again – as she often had in darker

moments – about the mantra *what if it all works out?* It often felt like a mockery, but it also provided a sliver of hope. She would pretend Jess was going on a macabre all-in holiday. She could imagine the commercial, of people lying on sun loungers, or reading in an armchair. "As much food as you can eat!" Another image of a girl talking earnestly to a woman in a white coat. "Discuss your food with a dietician!" (Lots of exclamation marks.) "Lots of activities!" – a group of people doing pottery, perhaps. "Be weighed every day (no images for that one) and meet like-minded people!" No images of skeletal young women. "Lifestyle choices!" What would that cover? A trip to the corner shop if they were good?

Still, she smiled, and sent a message to Anna entitled, *Advertising copy for Pascoe Centre*, knowing she would enjoy it.

Laura felt this bloom of hope fade as she thought of how ill Jess was, what a horribly long journey she had ahead of her. 'But we all have to start somewhere,' the doctor had said yesterday. 'This is the first and most important step. And remember, when Jess does come home, recovery is an ongoing process – it doesn't happen overnight.'

'Do people often relapse?' Laura said.

'Some do,' he said carefully. 'But for now we will concentrate on getting Jess better.'

Laura wasn't sure whether that was a warning or intended to console her. She checked her phone and found a text from Ben.

Hope you and Anna slept OK. If I can help just shout. Got Jake here this weekend so we're going to build a den tomorrow! B XX

Laura smiled. Just knowing that he was around gave her a warm feeling, like a hug. *Thanks, Ben. Anna still asleep she was shattered last night, will be in touch. Hope you and Jake have a good time! L XX*

Laura went downstairs to make a mug of tea and feed the dogs their breakfast. As she waited for the kettle to boil, her thoughts turned back to that evening with Ben and Jake. How warm and homely the house had felt with them there. The cottage had never felt like home before – there was too much unhappiness embedded in the walls.

That afternoon, Laura stood at the cashpoint gazing at the screen. How come she was so overdrawn? Then she realised what must have happened. Her credit card was paid monthly by direct debit from her current account. Now she was way over her overdraft limit.

Frantically she pressed various buttons, praying that the machine would deliver some notes. It didn't, and she felt her breath quicken as if all the angst of the past months was bubbling up inside her, ready to explode. If she could have used her credit card at the cashpoint she would, but she couldn't remember the PIN and hadn't written it down anywhere.

Anna appeared beside her. 'Laura, what is it?'

Laura felt her face grow hot with shame and the rapid swell of oncoming tears.

'Cashpoint not working?'

Laura shook her head, unable to speak, as tears trickled down her cheeks. Angrily she swiped them away, pointed to the dismal figures on the screen. What the hell would she do now? She needed to buy food for herself and Anna.

Anna took in the grim news on the screen. 'Listen, I was going to pay for groceries anyway as I'm eating and drinking you out of house and home. Now, take your card out before the machine swallows it.'

Laura pocketed her card and wondered what to do.

'Right…' Anna inserted her card, waited while the cashpoint obediently delivered fresh notes, which she handed over to Laura. 'There we go. I won't take no for an answer.'

Laura stared at the notes thrust into her hand. 'I can't take all this, Anna.'

'Yes you can. I shall be really upset if you don't.' She turned and led the way into the store. 'And I'm paying for the shopping, no quibbling. Come on, I'm starving, even if you aren't. I really fancy bangers and mash.'

Diary of Jessica Kate Hocking

11 May 2024

Hi Dad,

This is all your fault and I really hate you sometimes.

We had bloody bangers and mash last night, which were dry and stuck in my throat and now they're lying in my stomach like great fat slugs and I feel bloated and revolting. I can almost see the fat creeping onto my thighs, my stomach, everywhere. I had what they called a very small portion but it was massive. Greasy bangers; sticky, dry mashed potato, tepid, congealed gravy and peas. And the smell: stale cabbage and gravy that'd been sitting on a hot plate for hours. God I hate this place. But I'm planning my escape. At least if I put on weight quickly, I can get out quickly and then lose it all. That thought keeps me going.

Not having my phone really freaked me out at first. How would I survive without chatting to Em and Mum? What would I do if I wasn't looking at TikTok or Instagram all night (which I have been). But after a few days it was almost a relief not to have to watch all those videos about people exercising frantically, not to post endless stuff about calories and weight loss. I feel freer. I can ring Mum once a day

343

and that's it. Otherwise friends have to ring and leave messages with the office.

Everything is tightly regimented, much worse than school. We have breakfast at 8.30 then the others have a snack at 10.30 then lunch at 12.30, a snack at 3.30 and tea at 6 then another snack at 8pm. And all the time there are people watching us. They watch us before a meal, while we're eating and afterwards, to make sure we don't throw up, take laxatives or use razor blades or anything to self-harm. They even come to the toilet with us if they think we're going to stick our fingers down our throats. It gives me the creeps but at least I don't have to have snacks yet. There are three anorexics, out of ten beds, and we all have different meal plans as we all have different calorie needs, apparently.

We have to eat in the dining room, and eating in front of other people really freaks me out. I feel as if they're all watching me and it's even harder to swallow.

My meals aren't as huge as I'd feared but Ros said they get bigger, which scares the hell out of me. I already feel like a lumbering old cow, weighed down by all this food. My stomach is distended and aches. I lie there at night feeling pregnant and I hate myself even more.

But if you refuse to eat, or your weight's so low your stomach can't absorb food, you have to be fed through a tube. That's what they used to do to the suffragettes and many of them ended up with punctured lungs and stomachs, so I'd rather shovel it down my own throat than have someone do that to me.

Mostly the food is like we have at home – macaroni cheese, chicken casserole and stuff. The only sweet I like here is Angel Delight cos it's easy to get down and it sort of feels innocuous. Ros said you can choose snacks from yogurt, fruit, chocolate bars and cereal bars so that's not as bad as I thought.

I have to have blood tests every day for the first week to see what nutrition I'm missing out on, and they also check for osteoporosis. We're weighed every day but they watch us beforehand to make sure we don't drink lots of water, and we have to be weighed in our underwear to make sure we haven't hidden anything in our clothes to weigh us down. They think of everything here, it's gross.

Sometimes I think of anorexia as my twin. She's much cleverer, quicker and crueller than me. She's always one step ahead. Some days I used to think I could get better on my own. But the next day, she'd trip me up when I least expected it. She had all these rules: I couldn't eat certain foods, I had to do so many press-ups before I could go to school. So many star jumps every evening. All that stuff to make sure I got through the day. It was exhausting.

She's subdued at the moment, so I wonder what she's plotting. I'm scared of her, but I'm kind of in awe of her too. She's so clever, so powerful. I wonder what she'd be capable of if she were to use all this energy constructively.

I had a session with the tutor today, and he asked what I wanted to do at uni, what my plans were for the future, that sort of thing. Of course I want to be a photographer, but I didn't want to say that cos I'm not good enough, though perhaps if I work really hard, I might get a lucky break.

Then I remembered something I'd seen on one of those anorexia websites. It said, having an eating disorder is a full-time job. It doesn't leave room for anything else. Bit like you, Dad. Your job didn't leave much time for us, did it? Mind you, you still found time for another girlfriend.

So my twin has stolen my future from me. And that makes me so angry and sad and frightened all at once. How can I fight her when she's so determined?

Chapter Fifty

Laura

The following week, Anna drove Laura to the clinic to see Jess. She'd made good progress, apparently, so she was allowed a quick visit.

The weather had been consistently gloomy: a steady drizzle persisted and umbrellas battled with a rising wind, so Laura was grateful not to have to fight buses. As they drove along the coast road, Laura tried to empty her mind, watched the waves crashing against the pier, a vast plume of white water rearing up like a wild horse, then smashing down magnificently against the walls. It was breathtaking to watch, although she was glad not to be caught in it.

Her phone rang and she saw it was Mr Martin, the owner of the gallery. 'Sorry not to get back to you earlier, Laura, but I've been in London. I wanted to see how things are now that Andrew has gone?'

'They're fine, Mr Martin. I've hung the new exhibition

and sent out the invites for the private view. We've got plenty of people coming.' There was silence. Laura's gut twisted. Should she have kept quiet? Not offered to help?

'It's going to be a few days before I can get over there, so can you close the gallery for a few days?'

'Yes of course,' she said, spirits sinking. Why did he want to close it? 'I'm happy to leave my contact number on the door if you like.'

'That would be most helpful. Many thanks, Laura. I'll ring as soon as I can get down.'

'OK, thank you, Mr Martin.' As the call disconnected, her spirits dissolved into a puddle.

'Are you OK?'

Laura stared unseeingly out of the window. 'That was the owner of the gallery. Wants me to shut it for a few days, till he can get down to sort things out.' She sighed. 'Bloody hell, Anna. I'm scared shitless about not having any money. I've got to find another job, fast.'

'Well, he hasn't sacked you, has he?'

'No, but…'

'Why on earth would he? You've been keeping the place going since you've been there.'

Laura frowned. 'It doesn't feel like that.'

'If he's said close the gallery for a few days, why not make the most of the time off?' Anna continued. 'Your Mum's coming, so enjoy some time with her.'

Laura considered. 'You're right. But I'll need to put word out about work on social media. I don't think I can sign on, because I'm not technically unemployed yet but…'

'Listen, stop worrying and write this week off, OK? We have Jess to think of. I'll have to go as there's an emergency admission I have to see to, but I'll join you later.'

Laura rubbed her eyes, which ached from lack of sleep, and nodded. As they reached the clinic, the two women looked at each other. Laura's stomach was swilling with nervous exhaustion. 'You're right, Anna. Thanks so much.'

Jess was sitting in a living room with a large TV at one end. A group of girls were sitting at a table with nurses working on what looked like art projects. Jess looked up and came over for a hug. She looked the same, thought Laura, or had her face filled out a tiny bit? She stopped thinking as Jess's arms came round her and Laura held her as tight as she could. She closed her eyes, breathing in the familiar apple smell of Jess's shampoo, underlaid with a foreign clinical smell. As she drew back, she noticed her breath wasn't as bad so perhaps food was helping.

'Let's go over here where it's a bit quieter,' Jess said, leading her to a room down the corridor with several armchairs and another TV.

'So, how's it going?' Laura stared at Jess, feeling as if she belonged to someone else now.

Jess shrugged. 'It's weird. We're watched all the time. There's no privacy.' She glared at her mother as if it were her fault.

Which it is, Laura thought dismally.

'How many other…' Laura was going to say 'anorexics' but changed at the last minute, '…people like you?'

Jess looked down. 'Two other anorexics, Mum. But we're getting some new inpatients tomorrow.' Already she sounded knowledgeable about this foreign world of hers.

'How are you managing?'

Jess made a face. 'OK. I've been having what they call small meals, which are huge, then, as you know, I'll start snacks as well later.' She spoke bravely but her voice wobbled and fear shone from her eyes.

Laura glanced at her, terrified of saying the wrong thing. Would there ever be a day when she was free of this demon?

'We've all got different target weights depending on our height and build and stuff,' said Jess, looking up as a nurse came along. 'They build up your weight gradually.'

'Ah there you are, Jess. Time for another blood test, if you don't mind.' The young dark-haired nurse inserted a needle, took a phial of blood and pressed the spot with a small piece of cotton wool. 'Press on that for me, there's a good girl.'

'What's that for?' Laura's voice sounded high-pitched, weird, even to her. What were they *doing?*

'We're tracking what nutrition Jess has been missing out on, so we know what food to give her,' said the nurse. 'She's doing really well. Aren't you, my bird?' She patted Jess's shoulder and disappeared, rubber-soled shoes squeaking on the parquet floor.

Laura sagged with relief. 'Gran's coming to stay in a few days.'

Jess shrugged again. 'Don't know if I'll be allowed visitors. Think this was a one-off.'

Laura decided to take this up with the staff. 'What about schoolwork? Photography?'

'They're going to organise something,' said Jess gloomily. 'And we have art therapy.' She rolled her eyes, making it quite clear what she thought of that.

Another nurse appeared. 'Sorry to interrupt, Jess, but supper's in a few minutes.'

Jess's face crumpled and Laura wished she could protect her, take her away. But she's here to get better, Laura told herself, when all she wanted to do was bawl her eyes out.

'I'd better go. They don't like you being late for meals.'

Jess got up, gave Laura a desultory hug and walked away, a fragile figure held together by anger and fear. Laura watched her go, feeling as if her daughter was walking out of her life. She turned around and walked back to the main entrance where she saw Anna approaching.

'According to all the staff reports, she's doing really well,' Anna said.

Laura gulped. 'Good.'

'She's in the right place and she's tougher than you think.' Anna paused. 'We really care about everyone in here, Laura. There have to be rules, or no one would ever get better.'

'I know.' The smell of cooking wafted down the corridor and they heard voices gathering down the hall. Laura reached for Anna's hand and squeezed it tight, as they had at school. 'Thanks,' she whispered as they got up and walked out of the building, back to the car.

Driving home, they sat in silence, Laura too crushed to speak.

'She's bound to be at sixes and sevens to start off with,' said Anna, negotiating a roundabout with speed. 'She's scared, she's angry, it's all so new. You can't blame her. The others are all the same. Not that that helps you, I know.'

'It just feels terrible leaving her there when she's obviously unhappy.' Laura's voice was as wobbly as she felt.

'She wasn't exactly over the moon when she was at home.' Anna's tone was soft to belie her words.

'No, you're right,' sighed Laura. 'It's just... I get that anorexia's a form of control. But it's so destructive, so devastating. So addictive. And it doesn't just hurt Jess, but everyone who loves her.'

Anna slowed down as they reached a thirty mile an hour

limit. 'It's rather like abusive men,' she said, stopping at traffic lights. 'Those men seem as addicted to their particular form of control as Jess is to anorexia. The difference is,' she changed up a gear as the lights turned green, 'Jess is getting help. Which means she will get better.'

5th May 2024
From: jessicah567@gmail.com
To: CJHocking@gmail.com

Hi Dad,

I'm emailing to let you know you can't come on Saturday. But I don't want to see you anyway.

You left a message asking me what goes on here.

The type of therapy is called CBTE which means Cognitive Behavioural Therapy Enhanced. The therapist gave me a leaflet, which you could read online if you could be bothered. It explains that lots of mental health problems, including anorexia, are a result of too much negative thinking, and when we get stuck into these thought patterns, we think we can never get over our problems. CBTE challenges this negativity so that we can alter our behaviour, but each person here has a personalised treatment plan as we've all got different problems.

At least, that's the gist of it but there's so much to take in. They help us look at our thoughts about food and body image and try and work out why it happened in the first place and get us thinking more positive thoughts. However much I hate this cycle I've got into, I'm terrified of giving it up. My habits make me feel safe. They're part of me, and I feel really vulnerable without them. You wouldn't get this, but that's how it is.

On the other hand, it's almost a relief not having to do all those press ups and star jumps and running miles, to say nothing of counting calories all the time. You didn't know about all that but it was exhausting. I've been so tired lately that it's been almost impossible.

It's also really weird having a meal and a) having to eat it all

353

and b) having someone sit with me before, during and after. 'We know all the tricks,' this nurse said. 'Vomiting, laxatives, hiding food – so don't bother trying.' I expect you're horrified, but yes I've done all of that.

She didn't say it in a threatening way, but even so I was frightened. It's us against them.

And just cos I'm here doesn't mean that the voices in my head go away. They're still telling me not to get fat, not to eat, not to put on weight, to try and outwit them. Every minute of every day.

I'm furious. I know you don't like swearing, Dad. People at school do, but I never saw the point. Now I do. I am so fucking angry I could scream. I don't want to eat this sodding food that is going to make me horribly FAT.

Every morning I see the scales go up and my spirits sink. But I have no choice. At least I can use my phone for an hour a day now so I don't feel quite so isolated. But I am so bloody ANGRY right now I don't know what to do with myself.

I hate you for leaving us in such a mess. Moving house, school, leaving my friends and everything. This is all your fault.

I hate Mum for sending me here (I know I agreed, but that was only under sufferance) and I hate myself for being so pathetic, such a bloody failure that I can't cope with my own fucking life.

I couldn't keep a boyfriend. What fifteen-year-old turns down SEX for God's sake? You didn't know about that did you? I'll never get a boyfriend again but I just don't fancy girls. Perhaps I'm frigid? Or trans. Or something. And I know I've failed all of my exams, and I'll never be good enough to be a professional photographer – what was I thinking?

I wish I'd never agreed to come in here. I don't know what to DO with all these emotions. At least when I wasn't eating, I didn't feel these thoughts so much. According to the leaflet, "starvation suppresses feelings". Well that's fine by me.

I don't want to see Mum. I don't want to see Gran. I don't want to see you. I don't want to see anyone. I don't even want to see Emma. I wish everyone would fuck off and leave me alone. And that includes you, Dad.

Chapter Fifty-One

Laura

That evening, while Laura grilled pork chops, Anna was in charge of the mashed potatoes and had opened a bottle of Shiraz.

'Cheers,' she said, long slender fingers clinking her glass against Laura's. 'I've been thinking.'

Laura looked up. 'Sounds ominous. What's the outcome?'

'How about you and your mum going away? You've got a few days off work, so now would be a good time.'

'I know, but where would I go? I'm skint.'

Anna turned the heat off under the spuds and drained them in the sink. 'You and Merryn could stay in Dad's cottage; it's empty for a week as of Friday.'

'Oh, Anna, that's really kind. We'd both love it.' Laura smiled. 'A few days away would be great. Thanks so much.' A ping came from Laura's phone as she read a message and looked up. 'It's from Jess. She doesn't want visitors after all.'

'Well that's OK. She probably wants some head space.' Anna looked round. 'Where's the masher?'

Laura fetched it from one of the kitchen drawers. 'She sounds really pissed off.' She showed Anna the text: *Don't want visitors, want to be on my own. Don't come and don't bring Gran or Anna. Don't want to see Dad either but I emailed him. Jess.*

'Not even a kiss,' said Laura, tears stinging her eyes. 'What's the matter? She's never been like this before.'

'Of course she has.' Anna nudged her. 'She's been having wobbles ever since she became a teenager. This is normal, Laura. Just because she's not at home doesn't mean she's going to turn into a saint overnight. That would be really worrying.' She started mashing the spuds viciously. 'I think it's a good sign. Anger is always healthy.'

'Really?'

'Of course. Anorexics normally suppress anger. This means she's facing up to her feelings. She's fighting to get through this. Same as you, Laura. You're fighting.'

Laura turned a chop that was about to burn. 'I don't feel it. I feel drained.'

'Of course, you've been running round looking after other people for far too long; either your Mum, Jess, or the dogs. You haven't had any time for yourself.' Anna topped up their glasses. 'Look, take it easy for a few days. Have some nice wallowing baths, with candles. Long walks with Eddie and Pedro. Eat whatever you want, when you want. Enjoy it.'

Laura blew her nose, trying to dismiss the tears that lurked too near the surface. 'You're right.' She gulped. 'And it will be good to have time with Mum.'

Anna peered into the pan. 'I'll make the gravy. By the way, how's Ben?'

Laura pulled out a packet of gravy granules from the

cupboard. 'He's been great actually. I told you, he gave me Rachel's contact details and he managed to get Jess the print that she was hell bent on having.' She paused. 'He's changed a lot since we were at school.'

Anna laughed. 'So I should hope! I'm really glad for you though. How nice to have such a good male friend – all the fun and no complications.'

'Exactly.' Laura flashed a smile to indicate that the topic was finished. 'Now, can you hurry up with that gravy? I'm starving.'

Laura's mother had only been in the house for half an hour and already she'd organised everything, which was a relief. Suddenly, Laura felt she'd been hit by a ten-ton truck. Sleep beckoned with needy arms, whispering in her ear. Laura struggled to listen to what her mother was saying.

'We just need to get a few things for tonight,' Merryn said. Her turquoise dungarees radiated energy and purpose. Her exotic silver earrings dangled dangerously.

Laura felt washed out as she trailed round the local supermarket with her mother, remembering, years ago, when she'd done exactly this as a reluctant teenager.

Merryn consulted her list as she strode in between shoppers, grabbed yellow sticker bargains as well as tinned tomatoes and coconut milk. Then she nudged her daughter. 'Oh look. Isn't that Ben?'

Laura looked up; sure enough, Ben and Jake were standing at the end of the aisle, perusing beefburgers. Almost as if he knew Laura was there, Jake looked up and waved. Laura smiled back, while Jake ran down the aisle and stopped in front of Laura and her mother.

'Hello, Laura.' He turned to Merryn. 'Do you

remember me? From Christmas time when Eddie got lost? I'm Jake.' His black curls bounced enthusiastically.

'How could I possibly forget?' answered Merryn with a smile.

Jake turned to Laura. 'How's Pedro? And Eddie?' he asked. 'Can we take them for a walk soon?'

Laura smiled. 'Of course. How about this weekend?'

Merryn held out her hand, shook Ben's hand. 'Hello, Ben and Jake. Lovely to see you both again. I'm staying with Laura for a few days.' She turned to her daughter. 'Why don't we invite them for a meal, darling?' Without waiting for an answer, she addressed Ben and Jake. 'How about supper tomorrow night?'

Jake bounced on his feet. 'Cool! Yes please.' He paused and looked up at his father. 'That's OK, isn't it, Dad?'

Ben ruffled his son's hair. 'Yes, that would be lovely. Thank you very much.' He looked at Laura. 'It'll be good to catch up.'

Laura smiled, liking the idea of two other people absorbing her mother's energies. But she suddenly felt dizzy and nauseous. 'Sorry. I just need to... get some fresh air,' she said and flashed a quick smile at them all. 'See you at the car, Mum.'

Dashing outside, Laura breathed in lungfuls of air and started to feel better. Noticing a bench round the corner, she collapsed onto it. She closed her eyes, listening to a blackbird singing its sweet song. As she sat, she became aware of voices nearby, a smell of smoke mixed with a slight sweetness and she opened her eyes.

Further down the side of the supermarket was obviously the smoking area for employees. They were smoking and chatting, laughing as some lit up, others stubbed their cigarettes out, hurried back to work. Several of them had vapes; that must be the sweet smell, and one of them looked vaguely familiar. Laura frowned. Was it… could it be…? There was only one way to find out.

Satisfied that the dizziness had passed, Laura got up. As she did so, one of the vapers said goodbye, turned and walked towards Laura.

Laura smiled. 'Hello, Kayla. Fancy meeting you here.'

Kayla's face was a study of horror, quickly replaced by a set smile. 'Hello, Laura. I was just having a chat with some of my… clients. They come to my yoga classes.' She paused. 'One of them was telling me all about goat yoga. It's incredibly beneficial, apparently.'

'*Goat* yoga?'

Kayla nodded. 'Yes, you do yoga with baby goats. They clamber all over you and it's ever so cool. So relaxing.' Her smile wavered slightly.

'Oh. Right…'

Kayla sighed. 'Don't tell Chris, will you?'

Laura almost laughed. 'About the goats?'

'No! About me vaping. It's… He doesn't know.'

Laura looked at her. It was like dealing with another teenager. 'Are you sure?'

'You've told him!'

Laura sighed. 'No, Kayla, I haven't told him. But he does know. He mentioned it a while ago. I thought he was going to talk to you about it.'

'No. He hasn't.' She turned away.

'You should talk to him,' Laura said, wondering why she was giving Kayla advice on relationships. 'He knows about your junk food.'

Kayla's face fell. 'He does?'

'He mentioned it last time I saw him. He was very concerned.' Laura almost felt sorry for Kayla, given the distress written across her face. 'Listen, Kayla, what you eat is entirely up to you. But don't be hypocritical about it. Talk to Chris. Be honest.'

Kayla's mouth opened and shut, like a goldfish. Then she took a deep breath. 'Don't you dare breath a WORD,' she said, and hurried off.

Laura watched her go, wondering what on earth Chris had let himself in for. Good luck to him, she thought, as she spotted her mother leaving the supermarket and waved. And Kayla hadn't once asked how Jess was. That said it all.

Chapter Fifty-Two

18 May 2024

Jess

I'm feeling so pissed off, I don't know what to do with myself. What's the meaning of it all? Why should I bother? What future do I have? If it's more of this, I don't want it. But I don't want to talk to anyone. They wouldn't understand, and I need distance from people.

I put on another kilo but I'm trying not to think about it too much. I do of course. There's not much else to do here other than think about weight charts and targets and stuff. But weirdly, however much I hate it here, I feel safe for the first time in ages. I have no responsibilities. It's like being in limbo; nothing here feels real so it doesn't matter so much. All I have to do is eat.

Having said that, thanks to my deadly twin, the inside of my head feels like tangled barbed wire and I have no idea where the end (or the beginning) is. Who cares anyway? I see a further succession of failures lining up ahead of me, and I really can't deal with that.

A new girl arrived, looking like she was on death row. I know the feeling. She wasn't as thin as I had been, but looked very ill. She was crying, really upset, and followed by Marian, the nice nurse.

'This is Shelly,' said Marian, looking at me. 'Jess, would you mind sitting with Shelly a minute while we sort some paperwork out? I'll be back in a minute.'

'OK,' I said, wondering what the hell to say. If I told Shelly what it was like here, she'd freak out. Then I noticed a badge of a cat on her sweatshirt. 'You like cats?' I said. Stupid, but I had to say something.

She nodded and blew her nose. 'Yeah. We've got five.'

'Five?'

She managed a watery grin. 'Yeah, five. My dad's, like, crazy about cats, he's always bringing them home.'

'What about your mum?' I patted the duvet on top of what would be her bed. 'Want to sit down?'

She sat, placing her suitcase down by her feet as if it contained something really precious. 'My mum died when I was six. Dad brought me up.'

'Oh.' There were loads of questions I could have asked but felt that was straying onto dangerous ground. Animals were safer. 'We've not got cats, but we've got a dog – well, sort of two dogs.'

She looked at me with huge brown eyes brimming with tears. 'I've always wanted a dog. But Dad said we can't have one while I'm at school and he's at work. Maybe later.'

'Mum takes Eddie to work.'

'What about the other dog? You said you sort of had two.'

I nodded. 'This friend of a friend going into hospital and needed someone to look after his dog, so we're looking after Pedro till he's better.'

'That's kind.' Shelly looked down at her lap, at her bony fingers picking at the duvet cover. 'Kindness matters, doesn't it? There's not enough kindness in this world.'

I nodded, a bit taken aback. She was younger than me – thirteen at a guess. 'No, there isn't,' I said. 'That's why it's important to be kind when we can.'

'Hi, you two!'

We both looked up to see Marian standing in the doorway. 'Sorry about that. I'm back now. Thanks so much for looking after Shelly, Jess. I'd better check her in now.'

I slid off the bed. 'No problem.'

Marian came back later for a chat. She actually seems to like me. I mean, for who I am, not as a patient. Or 'resident' as we're called.

'You did a great job with Shelly,' she said. 'Poor girl, she was so upset and you calmed her down in a few minutes. That's a real gift.'

I could feel myself going red. I wasn't used to compliments.

'Ever thought of being a nurse, or a counsellor? You'd be ace.'

'No,' I said. It seemed so long since anyone thought I might be good at anything and it made me feel really warm inside.

'Where's home for you, Jess?'

I told her, and she said she came from a farm in Ireland and couldn't wait to see her family again. 'Over here, I live on the outskirts of Truro with my boyfriend and cycle in usually but sometimes Kevin gives me a lift.' She grinned. 'I know, awful name, isn't it? I call him Kev but that's not much better.' And she gave this lovely gurgle of a laugh that was really infectious so I giggled too.

How long had it been since I laughed? For a moment, I felt almost like the old me. And I wondered, maybe one day Marian could be a proper friend.

After lunch I had another message from Nick. He'd texted every day, but I felt awkward about him seeing me in this place. It felt like failure. But he'd rung the office and left a message to say he'd call in tomorrow after school if that was OK.

I was allowed visitors now, and although I'd said I didn't want to see anyone, suddenly I really wanted to see him. Visiting hours weren't in the afternoon, but Marian said that would be fine.

She came back after lunch and we were talking about hobbies; she and Kev are into cycling and walking, and she showed me a picture of him and his dog, a really cute black and white terrier called Moll.

I showed her pictures of Eddie and Pedro on my Instagram feed (we're allowed our phones for two hours a day now) and she said she liked how I use black and white when most people use colour.

'I just love that one of the two dogs looking out of the window,' she said, and I don't think she was making it up.

'A friend of mine's just been made editor of a new Cornish magazine,' she went on. 'She's looking for contributors; do you mind if I show her your Instagram feed?'

'Course not,' I said, though I couldn't think why she'd be interested.

All this made me realise how much I miss my old

friends. And that it really matters what others think of me. I always assume they'll see my worst faults as those are the parts of me I know best.

But Marian said, 'Everyone here says how much they like you, Jess. We'll be really sorry to see you go.'

And that made me feel amazing.

We had moussaka tonight. Thick lumps of meat with claggy white sauce and greasy aubergines with slimy sliced potatoes and after we had Angel Delight (butterscotch flavour), which at least took the taste away. God I hate food. At least if I hate it, I won't ever get fat.

This therapy stuff makes you question everything. I wonder, how can I separate anorexia from myself? It's become so much a part of me, like ivy throttling a tree. Once you start attacking the ivy, you could strangle the tree too unless you're really careful.

Chapter Fifty-Three

Laura

Laura looked around her kitchen table, magically transformed by her mother and Anna to seat five. Merryn wore an emerald-green blouse and large silver earrings that caught the light when she moved her head. She looked serene and beautiful as she sipped her wine, silver hair tied into a careless topknot, her cheekbones like Cate Blanchett's.

The red and yellow roses in the centre of the table provided a colourful cheer, and as Laura sat back, she caught a waft of the moussaka recently removed from the oven – lamb spiced with oregano and cinnamon, the rich smell of baked cheese.

Sitting next to Laura, Anna wore her favourite blue and green earrings that matched her blue shirt. She was talking to Jake about school, while Eddie sat staring alternately at Anna and Jake, giving them his baleful 'I'm starving' look. Pedro eyed them hopefully from his basket.

Laura's head was spinning slowly with exhaustion, but at this moment with gratitude at her closest friends and family, gathered around to support her. It was time to say thank you, she decided and clinked her glass.

'I'd like to say a toast to Mum for this amazing moussaka, and to you all for helping me so much,' she said. 'Life hasn't been easy, but it's good to know that I've got such amazing support and that there's hope ahead.' She grimaced. 'Sorry, this sounds like a bad wedding speech.'

Everyone laughed and raised their glasses and then Ben cleared his throat. 'I hope you don't mind me stepping in here, but I'm so glad Jess has got help and let's hope this is the beginning of her recovery.' He looked down at Jake. 'And to say that Jake and I are here to help, if we can.'

Laura felt her eyes misting over as Anna called, 'Cheers to that!'

Ben continued, 'Jake and I are delighted to be here, but we'd better not stay too long as Jake hasn't done his homework yet.' Groans from Jake made everyone laugh.

Anna got up. 'And I'm so glad that Merryn and Laura have decided to have a long weekend in Dad's cottage from Friday.'

'On condition that we do the cleaning,' said Laura. 'I insist.'

Anna smiled. 'Well, if you must. But there's no need, honestly.'

'I can't wait. I don't know Fowey well and I do love exploring,' said Merryn. 'We can take the dogs on some new walks and I can check out the galleries.'

'I thought we were going to walk Eddie and Pedro this weekend,' said Jake's clear voice.

'Another time, mate,' said Ben hurriedly.

'Why not come over to Fowey on Saturday?' said Laura.

'Come for lunch then we can all go for a walk.' She couldn't really think straight, but it seemed a way of saying thank you for all that Ben had done for them.

'Are you sure?' Ben said. 'We don't want to barge in on your holiday.'

'We'd be delighted,' said Merryn before Laura could speak. 'Laura really needs a break and friends are always welcome.'

Laura nodded. 'Absolutely. Especially as I'll need to start job hunting when we get back.'

'Have you actually been given notice?' asked Ben.

Laura shook her head. 'No, but if he's shutting the gallery for the week, he's got to have a plan, and I have a horrible feeling it won't include me.'

'Well, you don't need to panic yet,' said Anna. 'Why not wait till next week?'

'I can't. I've got bills to pay. An overdraft. I have to have a job,' said Laura, tears brimming up again. Why was everything making her cry?

'Listen, darling.' Merryn wiped Laura's tears gently. 'Will you please stop worrying? My last exhibition did much better than I expected, so I'm giving you an advance on what you'll get when I die.'

'Mum!'

'It was meant for a rainy day and if this isn't rainy, I don't know what is.'

Laura gulped. 'Thanks, Mum. But I…'

Ben topped up her glass. 'I should give in gracefully, Laura,' he said, dark eyes creasing as he smiled. 'She'll make your life hell if you don't!'

Laura looked at him through a blur of tears and wasn't sure whether she was happy or sad. Crying with exhaustion or excitement. Her head was too full of these precious people around her, who really seemed to care. While poor Jess was still not speaking, miserable in the clinic.

So much had happened recently, Laura felt she was trying to hold everything together until they could get away. What would happen then, she dreaded to think.

Chapter Fifty-Four

23 May 2024

Jess

I so miss talking to Dad. I felt he was not just my Dad, but my best friend. Someone I looked up to and trusted. No way would I trust him now.

Anyway, I had a counselling session this morning with Angela. She's not at all like Rachel, who is quiet and thoughtful; this woman is loud and has a big smile, which got on my nerves at first. Everything about her is big: big boobs, big bum, dyed red hair in a big top knot, and she wears lots of make-up. She's taller than me, which makes me feel even more insignificant.

But she's good at getting me to talk; I let something slip about my twin and immediately she said, 'What's she called? And has she always been around?'

I thought, then said, 'Well, she's called Madeleine and I don't remember her being there till Dad left.'

'Tell me about her.'

I thought. 'She's posh and confident and clever. Everything I'm not. Her friends and her parents call her Maddy, which sounds all sweet and cosy but she's not at all. She's the bully who thinks up horrible nicknames. She has several for me; the most complimentary is Scarecrow.'

Angela nodded. 'And what does she look like?'

'She's my height, five foot eight, and slim with wavy blonde hair, perfect complexion, nice boobs, has a good-looking boyfriend, always has good grades, and is on the hockey team. She's perfect.'

'Except that she's not,' Angela said.

'What do you mean?'

Angela said, 'Well, no one's perfect. And if she was, she wouldn't be a bully. So why is she behaving like that?'

I had to think about that. 'Maybe Maddy didn't get enough love and attention when she was young and that's why she's desperate for it now,' I said, cautiously. It sounded a bit woo woo to me, but in here they like that stuff. 'She's actually very insecure. Like me.'

Angela said, 'Could you make friends with Maddy?'

I said, 'No way! Why would I?'

Angela said, 'It's never a good idea to stereotype people. Everyone has a reason for the way they behave – as you should know. You could miss out on some really interesting friends.'

And the way she said it – not quite telling me off, but like I was being a bit stupid – made me think, well perhaps she's got a point. And then I thought, well if I have to live with Maddy, then I suppose I'd better think of something. 'I don't know what we've got in common,' I said.

Angela smiled and said, 'You might be surprised,' as if she knows something I don't.

Then I remembered, when we were in Paris I took a

whole load of shots of someone who looks a bit like her. I told Angela and she said could she see and when I showed her, she went all quiet and I thought oh what have I done?

Then she said, 'These pictures are very strange and unsettling, Jess.'

And I thought oh no.

But she said, 'That's a good thing. I think you have real talent.' She smiled and I decided I quite liked Angela after that.

And then that evening, Emma and T came to visit with Nick! I'd actually said not to visit but Em either didn't get the message or ignored it. Either way I was so glad to see them.

I was so nervous at first cos I knew I looked crap. I'd washed my hair but it had gone all fluffy and I was wearing my really old jeans and scaggy top, and I could have died with embarrassment. But Nick didn't seem to notice what I was wearing (he was still in his school gear) and Emma just chatted on as normal but it was so good to see her, we had the biggest hug and she said how much she'd missed me, which made me cry. We went to the far TV room to get away from everyone else.

Nick told me what they were doing in Photography Club and said it wasn't the same without me, and I felt kind of warm all over. Even if it isn't true, it's a really cool thing to say.

And best of all, he made me think about taking pictures again.

I feel like my life has been out of focus for so long and recently I'd even lost interest in photography and Dad's camera, and for a moment I had a glimpse of getting it back. And that was amazing.

So I went to bed thinking that today has been the best

day for ages. I still don't want to be here, and I hate food and no way will I ever get fat, but I had a glimmer of what life might – one day – be like. And it felt really scary but exciting.

Chapter Fifty-Five

Laura

By the time they arrived at Anna's cottage on Friday night, Laura was having trouble staying awake. By Saturday, she realised how important it was to have a change of scene. Already recent events were fading into a dreamy mist. She concentrated on living purely for the moment, could think no further than this weekend.

When Ben and Jake arrived for lunch the next day bearing a bunch of flowers and a bottle of wine, Laura felt drugged she was so tired. After lunch Laura, Ben and the dogs set off for a walk along the river, winding inland to a nearby village where Jake was promised an ice cream. He seemed happy to run ahead with Eddie and Pedro, circling back every now and then to check on his father and Laura.

'I'm so glad you've been able to get away,' Ben said.

'Thanks.' Laura yawned again. 'Sorry, I suppose it's when you stop that things hit you, isn't it?'

'Absolutely.' Ben picked up a stick, threw it for Eddie.

They walked on in a silence that Laura didn't want to break. It was companionable, easy, punctuated by Jake's calls to observe a different plant or tree or one of the dogs.

Laura started to feel apart from everyone else. Nothing mattered. She'd almost become someone else; all her cares and worries were floating away.

Then her phone rang. All she could hear was crying. 'Jess? What is it?'

'It's awful here, I hate it,' she sobbed. 'Oh, Mum, I don't know what to do.'

'What's happened, darling?' I hope she's OK. But thank God she's talking to me again, Laura thought.

'They've decided on my target weight. And it means I'm going to have to be here for weeks and weeks, and it turns out Ros has been in and out of hospital for years, and I really don't want that, and...'

'Now listen, Jess.' Laura tried to steady her voice. This reminded her of when Jess was a toddler, winding herself up. 'Your target weight might seem heavy at the moment but it really isn't, darling. That's still underweight for someone of your height.' Was that the right thing to say? She held her breath.

'Is it?' came a watery voice.

'Goodness, Jess, most people would love to get down to that weight, you goose! And listen, the very fact that you've understood what Ros has gone through and know the pitfalls, means that you will beat this. I can guess how hard it is, but it took a while to get to how you're feeling now – you're not going to snap back to how you used to be overnight, are you?'

'No.' Jess hiccuped. 'No, I guess not. Sorry, Mum.' She sniffed down the phone. 'Thanks.' Eddie barked, as if he'd heard her voice. 'So, what are you doing?'

'Oh, taking the dogs for a walk with Ben and Jake.'

'OK, Say hi to them. I'd better go now. Speak later, Mum.'

Laura said goodbye and stared at her phone. That delicious sense of relaxation and well-being had vanished on the breeze and another wave of exhaustion swept over her. Was Jess ever going to get better?

'Jess?' Ben stopped walking to look at her.

Laura nodded, trying to suppress the tears that welled up like a huge dam about to burst. Ben held out his arms and she went to him. It was such a relief to feel his strong arms around her, to let go, that she wept loudly and without restraint, feeling safe and secure.

Finally, reluctantly, she pulled away and realised his jumper was damp. 'Sorry about that.' She patted it ineffectually with a clean tissue.

'Don't worry about it.' Ben cleared his throat. 'Shall we walk on? Or do you want to go back?'

'Oh no.' Laura flushed. 'I'm sorry, all I seem to have done recently is cry,' she said, as they wound down the narrow path to the river. The trees were huge and dark above them, like stern silent soldiers guarding their way, the waft of pine indicating their presence. 'Is everything OK at work?' she ventured. 'And with Jake?'

'Yes, Jake's fine, as you can see.' They both looked ahead to where Jake and Pedro were standing at the bottom of a tall tree, Pedro thwarted in his attempt to chase a squirrel. 'And work's going well. That auction brought in a lot of customers and it's been really busy, which is great. I can afford to take on someone else part time; I certainly need it.'

Ben sounded slightly on edge, Laura thought. Why had she blubbed all over him and ruined their easy companionship? She cursed herself. 'Sorry about just now,' she said, staring at her feet, encased in old wellies streaked with mud.

'It's fine. Don't mention it.'

Laura cast around for other things to say but her mind froze. A magpie cackled ahead and quickly she looked for another, for good luck. She wished she'd said yes, she did want to go back. Her eyes itched and a headache was massaging the front of her head with iron fingers.

'You know, Laura, you were wasted working for Andrew. Why don't you apply to other galleries as manager? You've got the experience.'

Laura stopped and stared at him. 'Me? I don't think so. They'll want someone qualified.'

'I bet Andrew wasn't qualified,' Ben replied. 'And you've got the practical experience now, that's what counts.'

'Maybe…' Laura turned, started to walk on slowly. Her mind was too full; she had to move, to shake it all down. But as they walked on, Ben's words began to filter through. If she could apply for other jobs, as gallery manager… that was a proper job. She could earn more money; they could afford to rent somewhere a bit bigger (nicer) with a garden for Eddie. She could even, maybe, one day afford a deposit to buy somewhere. This would open up all kinds of avenues. They could start living rather than bumping along, day to day, bill to bill…

She glanced at Ben. 'Are you sure?' She held her breath, waiting for his answer.

He stopped and looked at her. 'Of course I'm sure.'

She could feel the smile spreading across her face, loosening her tight jaw. 'In that case, I'd better rewrite my CV.'

Chapter Fifty-Six

26 May 2024

Jess

Had a bit of a meltdown cos they finally decided on my target weight. I'll be OBESE.

Marian came by later and noticed my blotchy eyes. She sat down on my bed. 'Is this about your target weight?' she said.

I nodded.

'Well,' she said, in that lovely lilting Irish voice, 'I'm five foot five and weigh about fifty-five kilos and I'm not overweight. Am I?'

I shook my head. Actually I'd quite like to look like her.

'But as you're three inches taller than me, you need a few more kilos.'

It made sense when she said it, but after she'd gone I freaked out again. Luckily I'm nowhere near that heavy yet, but it's still scary.

I realised that for the past few years, every day has been like walking a tightrope. Maddy instigated so many rules and regulations, it was exhausting. But if I didn't follow them, I felt my world would fall apart. My only reward was to see that I'd lost more weight. Maddy would whoop and smile, and I was so relieved that I hadn't let her down.

I can understand drug addiction in a way, except that I don't like losing control. I see now that anorexia starts off being about taking control, but ends up being totally out of control. But I totally understand anything that gives you that high. That feeling of intense power, of being superhuman. It's better than anything.

Except that you come down. And the downs are like drowning. In concrete.

4 June 2024

I had a horrible few days feeling really fat and miserable. I looked up 'out of control' and it said, "take as one's right or possession, or take without authority". That's what Maddy's done and if I want to get better, I need to reclaim ownership of myself. Of my head. But how can I ever change the way I think? It's hardwired now.

I was so glad to see Emma. She came after school and sat on my bed and said, in a whisper, 'I told Mum.'

I wasn't really concentrating so I said, 'What about?' She glared at me. 'Oh, you mean about Tess?'

She nodded. 'I swore Dad to secrecy, but having got all nervous about telling Mum, she just said, "I know, darling. What shall we have for tea?"'

And we so laughed about that.

Nick has come every evening, often bringing something to do with photography. 'Thought you might like this,' he said yesterday, handing over a book on Eric Newby. 'I know you can see stuff online but it's not the same as studying the pictures in a book.'

I took it and flicked through. 'These pictures are amazing,' I said. 'All about his travels.'

Nick smiled. 'He went a bit further than Paris. You could too, one day.'

The thought of travelling anywhere abroad was so unlikely that I didn't know what to say. How would I get there? What would I eat? It would be impossible.

'I'd like to go travelling,' Nick said. 'Go to Sri Lanka. Indonesia. See a bit of the world.'

I stared at him in astonishment. And felt a growing envy. I'd really miss him.

'It wouldn't be for a while,' he added. 'I've got to save up a lot of money first. But... you could come too. If you felt like it.'

The world tilted. The impossible sloped in the opposite direction and almost, for a fleeting moment, became possible.

'No worries,' Nick said. 'I'm happy going on my own.'

'NO,' I found myself saying. 'I'd love to go. But I haven't got any money so I'd have to save too.'

We looked at each other and I thought, oh no, he's changed his mind. Who'd want to go with me, anyway? But he smiled and said, 'Great. We have a plan.' And he turned a few pages and said, 'Look at the way he's shot that guy. The light on his face.' Like planning to go travelling was an everyday thing. And as we sat there, looking at the pictures, I thought how easy he was to be with, not at all like Ryan.

When I first met Nick I thought he was a bit weird. He's about five foot ten and gangly, bit scruffy, doesn't care what he looks like. His dark curly hair does what it wants, even when he brushes it, and his school uniform is too big. He's got quite a big nose and looks serious, and sometimes he's teased at school. But he doesn't seem to notice the teasing – or he ignores it – so they stop.

He's actually really clever and he's got these big green eyes that take everything in and he listens and he seems to understand. I like that. He's also got a wicked sense of humour, though he keeps that well hidden. For some reason he seems to like me. And I like him more and more. Which is kind of scary. But so cool.

I had another session with Angela. She said, 'Have you thought about how you'd make friends with Maddy?' She smiled. 'Or Madeleine, depending what mood she's in.'

'She's definitely been Madeleine over the past few days, throwing a real wobbly,' I said.

'Was she shouting or crying?'

'Both.'

'Why?' she said. 'What caused her wobbly?'

I had to think about that. 'I think it's cos she's scared.'

Angela's face brightened, like I'd said something really clever. 'Why is she scared?'

'Because she can't do what she wants,' I said. That wasn't quite right, so I added, 'Cos she's out of control. And that's really scary for her.'

Angela nodded and then she said, 'What is she good at? Apart from schoolwork and games. What are her hobbies, her interests?'

I shrugged.

Angela said, 'Perhaps she's jealous because you're the talented one.'

'Me?'

And she grinned. 'Yes, you,' she said.

And I could feel my face go red and I couldn't say anything.

Angela sat back and said, 'If Maddy was upset, what would you do?'

I had to think about that. 'Well, I'd suggest we hang out. Go and see a film maybe.'

'And what would you talk about?'

'I dunno,' I said. 'I'd ask her why she was upset, I guess.'

'How would you feel after you'd talked, do you think?'

'I suppose I'd feel good.'

'Why is that?'

And I said, 'Because it's nice to make other people feel better.' I told her about Shelly. Then it dawned on me that apart from her, I hadn't tried to make anyone feel better for a very long time.

Angela nodded and said, 'Yes, anorexia makes you very selfish.'

That really hurt and I said, 'It's not like I want to be selfish, it's that I've been taken over by anorexia. By Maddy. I don't upset people on purpose, you know.'

Angela nodded but didn't say anything. And that really got to me. I hate the idea of being selfish. And though I don't like to admit it, she might be right. All I've thought about recently is me, my weight, how to avoid eating. I haven't really considered how Mum must feel. Or Em. Or how Nick feels coming to visit me here.

And I felt really small. I think Angela knew because she smiled and said, 'That's the trouble with depression. It does make you very introverted, so you don't have the energy to think about other people. And you forget how good life is with those that you love and care about.'

That's really stayed with me. I don't want to be that selfish person. Then I realised that Mum and I haven't been close since Dad left, and I really miss that. And I don't want to be selfish with Nick or Em or Mum or Gran or anyone I love. Even Dad.

13 June 2024

I'm nearly sixteen…!

I saw Angela again today. She's going to see me and Mum together next week. She said, 'How are you and Maddy getting on?'

I shrugged. 'We're on speaking terms, which is better than last week.'

Angela looked at me. 'And how does she feel about your boyfriend?'

I could feel myself going beetroot and looked down at my feet. 'What boyfriend?'

'That thoughtful young man who comes to see you every evening.'

I still couldn't look at her. I went all hot and said, 'He's not my boyfriend.'

And she laughed and said, 'I'd work on that if I were you.' But in a jokey way.

But that got me thinking about Nick. 'I don't think he sees me as a girlfriend,' I said. 'He's just being kind.'

Angela smiled and said, 'No man is ever that kind, Jess.'

And I was going to be pissed at her for interfering, but I said, 'Well, Maddy's always had boyfriends and I haven't had much luck, so I think it's my turn. Don't you?'

And she laughed and said, 'Absolutely!'

Marian was here again today. I do miss her when she's not on duty. I'd really like to be friends, if things were different. (Nurses aren't allowed to be friends with patients.)

Anyway, she said, 'I've shown your Instagram account to my editor friend and they're looking for freelance contributors. She really likes some of your shots while you were out running with Eddie, and they'd like to use some, so can you get in touch with her? I've got her email address.'

'Use some?' I said, stupidly.

'Publish them,' she said, ever so matter-of-factly. 'I forgot to ask what they pay, so make sure you ask her.'

'I'd do this for nothing.' I grinned, nearly bursting with excitement.

Marian grinned back and said, 'That's not the point. You should be paid. So ask. OK?'

I was so thrilled I couldn't think straight. I texted Em straight away and she sent back a message with so many emoticons I could hardly make sense of it. I texted Mum, too, and she's so pleased. I can't wait for Nick to come later so I can tell him all about it.

Who'd have thought it?

Then I had a message from Nick saying he's coming at seven tonight. And for the first time in I can't remember how long, I'm thinking how amazing it is to have something to look forward to. To work towards. People to share it with.

And I realised that I hadn't thought about food or my weight with all this going on. I mean, it was still there in the background but it was like the soundtrack rather than the main event.

I sat and thought, then I took a deep breath, crossed my fingers and rang Dad.

'Jess? Are you OK?' He sounded worried.

'I'm fine, Dad.' I could hear the excitement in my voice, bubbling over. 'I've got some good news.' And I told him.

But he didn't say anything and all my excitement lost its

fizz and started slithering away. He was disappointed. I wished I hadn't told him. Why had I bothered?

But just as I was about to burst into tears, he said, in a choked voice, 'That's amazing news, Jessie. I'm so, so proud of you.'

I couldn't believe it.

Even better, he added, 'I always knew you'd be a photographer one day, but I didn't think it'd be this soon!'

I did burst into tears then. But they were happy ones.

And when he said 'So when can I come and see you?' I said 'Saturday?'

And he said, 'See you then, darling. I'm so proud of you.' And blew me a kiss down the phone like he always did.

Chapter Fifty-Seven

Laura

Laura sat at the kitchen table with her mother, drinking soup and eating French bread. A raft of sunlight shone lazily through the window, making the small room bright and cosy. The soup smelt of sun-ripened tomatoes and basil – a rich, fragrant, earthy smell – and the bread was warm and crunchy, fresh from the oven. Eddie and Pedro hovered between them, noses twitching, tails wagging in hopeful slow motion.

Merryn wore a bright-red jumper with baggy yellow trousers and green lace-up boots. Anyone else might have looked like a clown, but Merryn managed to look artistic. Natural. Herself. Better than me, Laura thought, looking down at her worn jeans, her faded green jumper. No make-up, though she had washed her hair.

Laura's phone rang as she finished her soup. She glanced over, saw it was the owner of the gallery and felt a cold clutch of fear. Standing up, Laura hurried out of the kitchen into the living room. She had to be on her own in case it was bad news.

'Laura? John Martin here. How are you?'

'I'm fine, thank you, Mr Martin.' Laura swallowed hard. This would be the time to pray, had she been religious.

'Is this a convenient time to call?'

'Yes, fine thanks.' Get on with it, she thought.

'I wanted to talk to you about the position of gallery manager recently vacated by Andrew Moreton.'

'Yes?' Laura's voice came out in a croak, hardly the authoritative tone she wanted.

'I understand from Andrew and your colleague Deborah Carey that you have been doing a lot of that work anyway.'

What had Deb said? 'Well, I've always organised the private views and I've hung the new exhibition,' Laura said, heart beating fast. Was she in trouble? 'I hope that's OK.'

John Martin chuckled. 'It's more than OK. I wouldn't have hired Andrew if I'd known how capable you are, but at least this way you've proved yourself.'

Proved herself? What was he talking about? 'Sorry?'

'I'd like to offer you the post of gallery manager, Laura.'

Laura looked out of the window. The sky was clear blue apart from one discoloured cloud like a bruise, smeared against the background. 'Me? Manager?'

'I mean, if you'd like some time to think about it…'

'No!' Laura cleared her throat, a bubble of joy rising up inside her. 'Yes! I mean, thank you.'

'I'm sorry I wasn't in a position to offer you the job last week, but I had a few HR matters to look into first. There will of course be a pay rise, backdated as of last month if that helps?'

'Well, yes, I…' Laughter bubbled up. Sheer unexpected

joy fizzing inside her. 'Thank you, Mr Martin. I would be delighted to accept.'

'Thank goodness for that. I thought you were going to say no!' He laughed, named her new salary and added, 'Is that all right?'

It was nearly double her current salary. 'Yes... that's great,' she mumbled. Was she dreaming? 'Thank you.' Her head felt light, as if she were floating.

'It's me that should be thanking you,' he said. 'Listen, I will be in the gallery end of next week. Perhaps we could discuss the way forward. Some new ideas, maybe?'

Laura could feel a smile spreading over her face. 'Absolutely.'

'Excellent. I'll be in touch nearer the time. And Laura – congratulations.'

He rang off and Laura stared at the phone, then let out a loud whoop, rushed next door to see her mother, who had clearly been listening. Merryn beamed and opened her arms for a long hug. She smelt of face cream, of cooking and a faint hint of tobacco, and Laura relaxed into the safeness of her embrace.

'So you've got a new job?'

Laura pulled back and nodded, grinning like an idiot. 'Not just a new job, Mum. I've got a fat pay rise!'

'That's fantastic, darling. But no less than you deserve.'

'Oh, Mum, I can't believe it. Me, gallery manager!'

'You've been doing that job long enough, about time you got paid for it.' She beamed at her daughter. 'I'm so proud; you've really earned it.'

That afternoon, Laura rang the clinic to arrange the next

family counselling session. Her mouth was dry: counselling sessions always made her feel as if she was under trial.

'And how is Jess today?' she asked, having confirmed the appointment.

'The first few weeks are often difficult,' said the nurse. 'Then they get into the routine and life gets a bit easier. Sometimes they need some head space.'

'Right.'

'Jess has a long way to go, but we're hoping that she's over the initial hump.' The man paused. 'And of course, her boyfriend and her best friend have been in every day. That seems to have made a big difference.'

'Boyfriend?' Laura's fury rose sharply. That bloody Ryan... On the other hand, surely he wouldn't do anything as decent as visit Jess in hospital? 'Jess's boyfriend,' she said. 'Is he tall with long blond hair, blue eyes?'

The nurse laughed. 'No, that must be another one. This is Nick. Quite tall, dark and quiet. He seems very fond of Jess.' He paused. 'And I would guess the feeling's mutual.'

'Right,' said Laura, thinking hard. Was that the boy she'd seen getting off the Paris bus? 'Thank you for that. I'll see you next Thursday.' And she ended the call.

She hesitated, then sent Ben a text. *Drink in the pub sometime? XX*

Ten minutes later she got a reply: *I'm over your way later this afternoon. Could meet at about six in the Safe Harbour? B XX*

Laura smiled, her spirits lifting still further. *Got a new job*, she wrote. *Drinks on me XX*

Relishing the light evenings, Laura, Eddie and Pedro walked the long way to the pub, along the coastal path, looking down on a sea that was myriad shades of indigo, turquoise and the palest opaque green. A slight breeze ruffled the surface of the water and a yacht was tacking across the bay, heeled right over, reminding Laura of the times she and Ben had been sailing, many years ago. She could almost feel the tug of the sheets in her hand, feel the wind blowing in her eyes, her hair. The exhilaration of feeling really and truly alive. When did I last feel that, she wondered?

And yet, as she walked towards the pub, her pulse quickened and her senses felt heightened. The air was warm on her face and smelt of salt and tangy gorse blossom. A robin sang clearly from a nearby tree. It was as if life was coming back into focus after not being able to see for ages.

Ben was already at the pub when she got there, wearing jeans and a paint-spattered sweatshirt. He had shadows under his eyes, though he smiled when he saw her and his eyes brightened. Laura hurried forwards, kissed his cheek: that same smell of salt, fresh air and furniture polish, no doubt he was cleaning up some items to be auctioned.

'So, what's the new job then?' he said, handing her a glass of red wine. 'Are you moving away?'

'No!' Laura smiled. The pub felt safe and cosy with its yeasty aroma of freshly brewed beer. She felt warmed, as if she was suddenly bathed in sunshine after months of cold and rain. So what if it rained again tomorrow? She would enjoy this while it lasted. 'John Martin rang and,' she raised her glass, savouring the moment, 'you're now looking at the new manager of the Dorian Gallery!'

Ben's face split into a huge grin. 'That is such good news,' he said. 'Oh, Laura, I'm so pleased for you.'

'So thank you for your faith in me.' She echoed his grin.

'When do you start?'

'Next week. And I thought, I'd love to start making clothes again. I could maybe sell them along with the pots and jewellery. Though I'm not sure about that.' She smiled at his slightly bemused expression. 'I don't suppose you know about my dressmaking?'

'No. I'm impressed. That sounds a great idea.'

'I used to have a small business in Newlyn, making stuff from other people's leftover fabric.' Laura sighed happily. 'But I'd have to make smaller things to sell in the gallery. Maybe little purses. Make-up bags?'

'Phone covers? iPad covers?'

'Oh, yes!' Laura smiled. 'I can't wait to get going.'

'So does this new job involve more money?'

Laura nodded. 'Almost double what I'm earning now!'

'That's fantastic. I'm really proud of you.' Ben clinked their glasses. 'Wow. That's the sort of news you need, isn't it?'

Laura nodded. 'It means I can pay you what I owe for Jess's print. And we could rent somewhere a bit bigger with a garden, or even buy somewhere if I could get a mortgage.' She grinned. 'I'd forgotten the difference that financial freedom makes.'

Ben smiled and sipped his beer. 'And what news on Jess?'

At the next table a young couple were arguing. The girl's ponytail swished angrily as she shook her head. 'No!' she cried. 'You don't under*stand*.' She reminded Laura of herself, years ago, with Ben, and hoped the young couple would work things out better than they had.

'Jess is doing OK,' Laura said. 'She has a boyfriend, apparently.'

'I met him.'

'No, not Rubbish Ryan. This is another one. Nick.' Laura looked up.

'What's Jess said about him?'

'Nothing. I spoke to the clinic earlier and the nurse

mentioned that Jess's best friend and her boyfriend have been in every day, and both seemed to be doing her a lot of good.'

Ben looked at her, smiling. 'Well, that's the best news of all, isn't it?'

'Absolutely,' Laura said. 'As you know, Jess's health has been the biggest worry for so long now. I just thought that she might have...'

'Told you?'

Laura nodded.

Ben laughed. 'She's a teenager, Laura. When we were that age there were lots of things you didn't tell your mother.'

Laura opened her mouth to protest, then realised he was right. She smiled. 'Mmm. Like the midnight feast we had on the clifftop.'

'When we first started going out, actually. It was months before you told your mum about us.'

Laura nodded. 'Point taken. I suppose I have to let go more.'

'Easier said than done. I've got all that to look forward to with Jake.'

Laura sipped her wine, watching him. Aware of his problems, when he'd been so good at supporting her. 'I wanted to say thanks, Ben. You've helped so much with Jess. We wouldn't be where we are now without Rachel's intervention and that was down to you.'

Ben shrugged. 'Oh, it was nothing.' He looked up and there was a flicker of something that Laura couldn't quite decipher. 'I'm trying to make up for being such a shit all those years ago.'

Laura clinked his glass. 'That's all forgotten. We were young, we made mistakes; it's all part of growing up. But friends make all the difference, don't they? And if we're good mates, then nothing can go wrong, can it?'

Another flicker crossed Ben's face. 'No, Laura. So here's to good friends.' He clinked his glass against hers and smiled. 'And now, I must go and collect Jake.'

'Oh, I was hoping to buy you a meal.' Laura was suddenly aware of how much she wanted him to stay.

'Sorry. I have to pick him up from a friend's at seven.'

'Oh. Well, maybe another time?'

Ben finished his pint and stood up. 'Another time would be great. I look forward to it.' He bent over, kissed Laura's cheek and jangled his keys. 'Can I give you a lift?'

'No. I've got these two so I'll walk back. But thanks.'

'OK. Must go. See you soon.'

Laura watched him hurry out of the pub. She looked down at the dogs who were sitting beside her looking hopeful. Collecting them, she put on her coat and walked slowly back, glad of the warmer and lighter evenings. Laura waited while Eddie and Pedro sniffed long and hard at a lamp post with obviously myriad messages.

She felt as if she was coming out of a long dark tunnel with light at the end of it. A new job, well, new pay, which would make all the difference, Jess was, please God, turning a corner, and she liked the sound of this Nick fellow.

She heard a toot and looked up to see Ben waving out of his car window as he drove off. Who would have thought he'd turn out to be such a great, reliable friend? She smiled and waved back, already wondering when he might be free for a pub supper. Or she could cook supper at home…

When her phone rang, she jumped. 'Chris? What's up?'

'Oh, Laura, I don't know what to do.' He was almost wailing, which was unheard of.

'What's the matter? Are you OK?'

'It's Kayla.'

'What about her?' Was she pregnant?

'She's… she's left me.'

'Oh.' Laura's smile vanished as a dozen scenarios flashed through her mind. 'I'm sorry to hear that.'

'I don't know what to do,' said a choked voice.

'What did she say?'

'She just left a note in the kitchen. She says I'm clipping her wings and she needs to be free.'

Oh yeah, thought Laura. More like, the money's not what she thought it was.

'Can I come and stay with you?'

'NO!' Laura had come to a halt: both dogs had found another vitally interesting lamp post to sniff and would not be moved. 'Chris, you walked out on us. Kayla was the love of your life, remember? You uprooted our lives, to say nothing of nearly destroying your daughter's. You can't just move back. There's no room, anyway.'

'But…'

'Sorry, Chris, but no.' How dare he even ask, after all he'd put them through?

'Can I at least come round?'

He sounded like a wheedling little boy, she thought. 'No!' she repeated. 'I've got to go now.' Laura was going to suggest ringing tomorrow but stopped herself just in time. He was old enough to sort out his own messes.

Chapter Fifty-Eight

Six months later

Laura glanced at her watch, grabbed her phone and keys and opened the living-room door. Two dark heads were bent over a laptop, the screen showing black-and-white images of Paris.

'I'm going to the estate agent's to get the keys for the new place,' she said. 'Are you OK to walk Eddie?'

Nick looked up and nodded, gave his shy smile. 'Of course,' he said. 'We're just finishing this then we'll take him out. But we'll have a snack before we go.'

Jess nudged him. Thin still, but nowhere near as skeletal as she had been. 'Don't worry, Mum. I've got my conscience here. Not allowed out without my snacks.' She groaned but the look she gave Nick was fond, flirty, full of fun.

'Great. I'll be back later. Thought we might go to the pub for supper?' She held her breath; Jess still found eating in front of strangers difficult. 'Or we can have something in, whichever's easiest.'

She caught the look between Nick and Jess. The quiet

way he squeezed her hand. Jess looked at her mother. 'Can we decide later?'

'Course we can. Just an idea,' Laura said breezily. One step at a time, she told herself. One step at a time. 'Bye! See you later.'

She hurried out of the door, down the familiar path and looked back at the cottage that had been home throughout possibly the worst time of her life. Certainly the worst time of Jess's life. It would be wonderful to move away from all that – not too far away, but nearer school, nearer the gallery, and to somewhere with a small garden and a sea view (if you stood at the end of the path and cricked your neck).

Laura called it at the estate agent, promising to return the key by the end of the day. 'I just want to measure up,' she said, though they had very little furniture. Humming, she walked swiftly towards the house that was to be home for the next chapter of their lives.

At the top of the hill she stopped in front of a small terraced house, put the key in the lock and turned it, pushed open the door. The house smelt cold and a bit damp but that was to be expected as it hadn't been lived in for a while. She wandered from room to room, taking in the feel of the place. She hesitated, then pulled out her phone. Her fingers hovered over the familiar number. Then she dialled, held her breath. Was he there?

'Hi,' he said and she could hear the smile in his voice. 'What's it like?'

'Needs some heat pushed through it, but it'll be fine. Better than fine,' she added. 'Do you... do you want to come and have a look?'

Ben chuckled. 'Good timing. I'm on the way back from Penzance. See you there in ten minutes. I've got a housewarming present.'

'Great,' she said, smiling. 'See you soon.' Humming, she continued to explore the house, opening and shutting cupboards, trying to decide where she'd put her bed, a sofa, armchairs. A while later, hearing the doorbell, she ran down the stairs and flung open the door.

'Chris!' she said. 'What are doing here?'

He looked sheepish. 'I rang Jess who told me where you were. Thought you might like some company.' He smiled; a hopeful, expectant face, clearly expecting she'd give in.

Then Ben appeared behind Chris, holding a toolbox. 'Thought I'd fix that upstairs door you mentioned.' He paused and looked from Chris to Laura and back again. 'Everything all right?'

'A slight spanner in the works,' Laura said. 'But Chris was just going. Weren't you, Chris?' She turned to Ben. 'Do come in.'

Chris's face fell. 'But I...' His voice trailed away as he took in Ben and his toolbox. He looked at Laura, his hopeful expression fading.

'Bye,' Laura said, smiling a little as she led the way in, leaving Chris standing outside.

Karma, she thought. Karma.

Author's Note

There is a nationwide scarcity of help for teenagers with anorexia, so it would be unlikely to be able to see a therapist so quickly. Due to NHS shortages, much counselling now takes place online, though help can be gained from school nurses or CAMHS according to the school/area. At the time of writing, in Cornwall there is a two-year waiting list for help from CAMHS, and there is no current inpatient facility for teenagers with mental health problems, let alone anorexia, in Truro although Sowenna (https://sowenna.cornwallft.nhs.uk) provides inpatient treatment for 13-18 year olds. Invictus Trust (https://invictustrust.co.uk/about-the-invictus-trust/) in Cornwall is a small family-run charity that helps raise awareness of adolescent mental health in Cornwall and provides support. BEAT is a nationwide charity helping those with eating disorders (https://www.beateatingdisorders.org.uk). Another useful website is www.endeatingdisorders.org.

I have tried to adhere to the BEAT media guidelines

that are so vital to try and prevent any triggers that might prompt an eating disorder.

When Jess sees Rachel for the first time, a therapist probably wouldn't have weighed Jess, but I wanted to show how devious anorexics can be when it comes to being weighed, also that Rachel was smart enough to see through this behaviour.

I suffered from anorexia for many years, as a teenager and in my twenties, and spent many months in and out of Canny Ryall Ward at All Saints Hospital, Elephant and Castle (which no longer exists). I was shown great kindness but it must have been very frustrating for the staff, to say nothing of my parents and friends, when for many years I continued to lose weight as soon as I left hospital. Anorexia is such a complex illness, but I wanted to give hope to those who are suffering or caring for someone with an eating disorder that it is possible to make a full recovery.

While in Jess's case, it's clear that her father leaving was a huge trigger for her anorexia, in many cases a trauma may not be the cause. It could be a chance comment overheard that provides a trigger. Sometimes, we don't know: I wasn't even aware I'd lost weight until a friend at school remarked that I'd got very thin. At the other end of the scale (pardon the pun), it's not always evident why some people recover. In my case I gradually gained confidence until I was able to cast off many of anorexia's chains, but that was a gradual process and one that I wasn't aware of at the time.

Acknowledgements

Thanks to Kerry Barrett, not only my editor extraordinaire but who understands about eating disorders. Abbie Rutherford for her fabulous proofreading, typesetting and all the essential stuff to make *Hunger* into a proper book. Ken Dawson who designed a fantastic cover. Rosanna Ley for all her help at the Finca in 2000 and for that workshop that inspired the importance of Jess's camera. Rebecca Collett, Rafaella Jackson, Tilly Redhead and Rona Swain for their essential advice on what it's like to be teenagers in 2024. My wonderful Tuesday Writing Group for being such a great support: you lot keep me sane. Everyone involved in the Curtis Brown Creative Advanced Editing and Pitching Course, which helped take editing to a new level.

To my readers: Roz Watkins and Jane McParkes. And to Malc and the late Twig. Thanks for being you.

My other books, including *The Rescue* and the award-winning *Lainy's Tale* are available on Amazon as well as from my website www.suekittow.com.

Please follow me on social media for news of book four (working title *Someone Else's Story*), for pictures from my walks with Lainy, and what a writer's life is like in Cornwall.

Substack: Walking – and writing – with Sue. @ suekittow.
Facebook: https://www.facebook.com/suekittow2016/

Instagram: walks_cornish_author
Twitter X: @floweringpot